Praise for *What Disappears*

"In *What Disappears*, Barbara Quick spreads before the reader a banquet of secrets, jealousy, betrayal, genius, high fashion, loss, tragedy and poignant regrets peppered with fascinating historical details and cameo appearances by some of the most famous ballerinas, writers, and artists of the nineteenth and twentieth centuries. A cinematic novel, which cuts between Russia and Paris, past and future, fear and desire, *What Disappears* has a rich plot filled with enough reversals, revelations, and unexpected twists to keep readers turning its pages long into the night."

–Mary Mackey, *New York Times* bestselling author of *A Grand Passion*

"Gorgeously written and daring in scope of drama from the poverty and pogroms of Russia to the fraught, exquisite world of divine fashion and the Ballets Russes of Paris 1909, *What Disappears* follows the poignant story of identical twins separated at nine months in a world that is changing rapidly. One sister clings to her difficult life as a dancer; the other who has lost both her great loves, struggles on with her three daughters. Between breathtaking scenes of betrayal, danger and perfect love found and lost, little is as we expect it as the twins reunite in Paris. One sister is the quiet steadfast heart of this story and the other its restless discontent. Some dreams shatter, and other come true in a way you never could have expected. *What Disappears* is a book you will find hard to put down and impossible to forget."

–Stephanie Cowell, author of *Claude & Camille: a novel of Monet and Marrying Mozart*, American Book Award recipient

"*What Disappears* is a tour de force. With a dancer's grace, agility and subtlety, Barbara Quick creates indelible scenes that unfold as her characters, both famous and fictional, discover the fragility of their deepest core values. I couldn't turn the pages fast enough to keep up with my own racing mind! How do we use the artistic self to cover or costume or hide? In this author's hands, twin-hood becomes a metaphor for the conflict between a stage persona and an offstage one. I shivered with recognition at her portrayal of the male ego, presumption, oblivion and rational thought being clouded by carnal or artistic desires. Any dancer or athlete will resonate with these characters' use of physical work to staunch or avoid the excruciating reality of emotional pain. The historic figures in the book—Diaghilev, Nijinsky, Pavlova, Karsavina, and titans of the fashion world—become ever more real through the way Quick illustrates the turmoil and self-doubt of the artistic mind, regardless of the artist's fame. Quick reveals symbolism threaded through these characters' lives that sheds light on our own in the way only great literature can do. Are we all performing our way through life, "running from whatever demons we carry around inside us… straight into the arms of death"? By the end of this masterful work, we can indeed understand that when our inner and outer selves reconcile, what disappears is in fact what remains."

–Gavin Larsen, author of *Being a Ballerina: The Power and Perfection of a Dancing Life*

"Barbara Quick is at the height of her powers in her newest novel, an epic narrative of the ballet world, European history and high fashion. Her characters are so real—so vital—they seem to say, "Come toward us and see what's inside!" And we do, following them with fascination one by one. The plot crosses back and forth across continents and time to braid an intergenerational story with unflagging momentum and gripping emotional appeal. Like her 2007 novel *Vivaldi's Virgins*, *What Disappears* sings with musical complexity and vivid sensuality."

–Grace Cavalieri, Maryland Poet Laureate

WHAT DISAPPEARS

Barbara Quick

Regal House Publishing

Published by
Regal House Publishing, LLC
Raleigh, NC 27587
All rights reserved

ISBN -13 (paperback): 9781646030750
ISBN -13 (epub): 9781646031009
Library of Congress Control Number: 2021943788

Interior layout by Lafayette & Greene
Cover design © by C. B. Royal
Cover image by Christian Mueller/Shutterstock

Regal House Publishing, LLC
https://regalhousepublishing.com

Printed in the United States of America

for Grace Cavalieri

"[Y]ou must lose things,
feel the future dissolve in a moment
like salt in a weakened broth.
What you held in your hand,
what you counted and carefully saved,
all this must go..."

—from *Kindness* by Naomi Shihab Nye

PART I

PARIS

1909

Backstage is where the magic meets the real world. Ballerinas in toe shoes and white tulle waft like blossoms detached by the wind, swirling past the gears and pulleys of stagecraft, seeming to float rather than scurry up metal stairs, past outsized props and sets and stagehands who pause in their work to watch them, always in love with one or another of the dancers. The smell of scent, cigarettes and chalk, and someone's coq au vin in a metal pail.

Behind a door marked by a star, Anna Pavlova looks into the mirror and then, sighing, closes her eyes. *Breathe!* she tells herself. She can't afford to lose another maid—not now. And her seamstress has never let her down before.

She has high expectations for her pas de deux with that young savage, Nijinsky. She's never seen another boy with such strength and elevation, combined with a sort of madness that makes him disappear into whatever role he's playing.

She'd been nervous about that huge sapphire ring he wore to their run-through that morning; he'd made a point of showing it off, telling her it had been a gift from Sergei himself. Sure enough, while Nijinsky held and turned her in a backbend high above his head—while she danced midair—the ring snagged the fabric of her costume and ripped it open all along the left side of the bodice. A disaster, with only an hour left before their call.

"Zlata, you cow!" the sylph-like dancer screams out her dressing room door. "Where is Sonya?"

Zlata returns, red-faced and puffing, holding by the arm one of the extra ballerinas who was just arriving to get into costume.

❧

Jeannette Dupres couldn't understand anything the Russian maid was saying as she pulled her, rather rudely, out of the large dressing room where all the rats change their clothes, apply their makeup, and help arrange each other's hair. The only words she recognized were "Anna Pavlova"—but these two words were enough to compel her obedience.

Sharing the rehearsal stage, however briefly, with Russia's greatest dancers has been one of the best experiences of Jeannette's lifetime, despite the chaos of those rehearsals and everyone's terrified conviction that they haven't rehearsed anywhere near long enough—and only once so far with the orchestra.

This is the stroke of luck Jeannette has been waiting for, suffering for—the chance to dance in a company of true artists, in real ballets, not the glorified music hall productions of the Paris Opera. Artists who have exhibited at the Salon are working elbow to elbow with tradesmen backstage, constructing the flats, creating and revising the brightly colored backdrops, each one a painting one might see in the most avant-garde gallery of Paris. The din of construction only stops when the stage crew takes their two-hour break for the midday meal. No such luxury for the dancers, who are kept on by the choreographer, who has been shouting himself hoarse for two weeks, trying to be heard above the pounding of hammers, the rasp of saws, and the arguments and instructions lofted back and forth across the stage, over the dancers' heads, as often as not drowning out the rehearsal piano and causing them to lose their place and have to start over again.

Posters for the Ballets Russes, featuring a drawing of Anna Pavlova, are on display all over Paris. Journalists and critics are vying with each other to find superlatives worthy of the artistic revolution promised by Sergei Diaghilev and his company.

It thrills Jeannette to know that she is part of this—a small part, but a crucial one nonetheless. Every dancer matters. Every dancer was chosen with care. And now her dream of having her own talent recognized by the greatest among them is about to come true. Why else would Anna Pavlova have summoned her?

Rapping at the star's dressing room door, the maid pushes it open when a woman's fluty voice calls out, "*Entrez!*"

Though still dressed in her street clothes, Jeannette makes her most graceful balletic bow before her idol. Pavlova's only response is to grab Jeannette by the shoulders and shout in her face, "Where's my costume, Sonya?"

Before Jeannette has time to register anything but a sense of insult, a breathless voice calls out behind her, "Forgive me, Anna Matveyevna!"

৯৯

Sonya Danilov, Pavlova's seamstress, squeezes herself into the doorway. The damaged costume is draped over her outstretched hands, a channel of straight pins curving down the delicate fabric of the bodice like a surgical scar. Sonya's little daughter—a pretty child, with honey-colored curls and a bright red ribbon in her hair—peeks out from her mother's skirt into the dressing room.

Apologizing again, Sonya explains in Russian, "My concierge is usually happy to have my youngest stay with her—but her husband fell off a ladder today…" She sees Pavlova's maid cross herself, forehead to apron, then right shoulder to left, in the Russian style.

Both Pavlova and her maid are staring wide-eyed at the two women standing side by side in the doorway.

With one movement, Sonya and Jeannette turn their gaze away from Pavlova, toward one another. They are pressed so closely together that their identical noses nearly touch. Each of them screams at the same moment with the same sound.

Sonya faints.

৯৯

Sergei Diaghilev, impresario of the Ballets Russes—massive in his frock coat and top hat—bounds into the dressing room, past Jeannette. "Come, my dears," he says, clapping his hands as if shooing chickens. "It's less than half an hour till the first bell.

Please, *mes enfants,* allow Madame Pavlova to prepare." Noticing Sonya crumpled on the floor, he says, "Good lord, there are women dying here!" He puts a handkerchief to his nose and mouth.

Dropping to her knees, the child presses her mother's limp hand to her cheek.

Sonya blinks her eyes open. And then her gaze finds Jeannette. "I knew it, I knew it!" she says in lightly accented French, laughing and crying all at once. "You live!"

Jeannette looks as if she's about to be sick. All the color has drained from her cheeks. She bolts out the door, pushing an astonished Diaghilev aside.

"Oh, wait—Zaneta!" Sonya gets tripped up in her skirt as she struggles to her feet.

"Who was that?" Diaghilev asks, using his handkerchief to scrub at the place where the woman touched his coat.

One hand pressed to her heart, Sonya exhales a couple of times in quick succession before finding her voice again. "That, dear sir," she gasps, "is my long-lost twin!"

KISHINEV

1880

Nadia Luria held her squirming newborn baby girl on her chest, amazed that such a miniscule creature could have made her swell up so, bigger than she'd been with Lev, Faya, or Daniel. She was so much tinier and more delicate than any of them, with long-fingered, graceful hands, damp tendrils of hair, bright blue eyes, pink cheeks, and a lusty cry. She looked perfect, and yet something felt wrong—something beyond the ominous sounds coming from the shop, through the bedroom door. A discomfort from deep inside Nadia's body.

Her breathing quickened. Sweat broke out on Nadia's forehead while the midwife cut the cord and tended to the baby.

Whatever it was felt like a mistake, as if time had run backwards and Nadia was starting to go through labor again.

The midwife mopped at the blood between the mother's thighs. Gently pressing on her belly, she bent down to take a closer look.

Raised male voices could be heard from the next room, punctuated by the ringing sound of objects crashing to the floor. Nadia prayed it wasn't the pair of Sabbath candlesticks her grandmother had carried with her all the way from Poland and God knows where before that. Her limbs shook as if with fever.

"Listen to me, Nadia," said the midwife. "There's a second baby. You have to push it out!"

A second baby?

The sounds from the next room were growing louder and more frightening. Nadia felt a stab of pain in her belly, just as if one of those Cossacks out there had stabbed her with a knife.

"Misha!" she wailed.

The midwife spoke into Nadia's ear. "Push, little rabbit!"

Nadia tried to push—but the pressure only got worse. She was drenched in sweat, her mind racing. What had God been thinking, giving her twins? She heard a loud crash that could only be one of their sewing machines hitting the wooden floor.

How would she manage alone, with five children now, if something happened to her husband?

"Push, Nadia!"

Nadia bore down with every ounce of strength she could find in her body, beyond anything that seemed right or safe or tolerable. She heard her own screams filling the room. It felt as if a flaming knife were cutting her open, as if she were a lamb being slaughtered. She could feel blood flowing out from between her thighs, too much blood. Was she dying?

"Push!"

Nadia made a final grunting effort, her eyes rolling back in her head, the room suddenly silent. And then the pressure was gone. Sound rushed back to her ears again. She tried to look over her belly to see this second baby, but she was too weak.

There was no new baby cry, announcing its presence in the world. Was it a boy? Another girl?

Had she given birth to a corpse?

She heard the little bell above the door of their shop, followed by the sound of muted male voices, the whinny of horses outside, the crack of a whip, sleigh bells—and then silence, punctuated by the crackling of the fire in the stove.

The room flickered with shadows cast by the candlelight. Nadia's voice was barely above a whisper. "Why have you turned away from me?" she said to the midwife, adding faintly. "*Oy gevalt,* what will become of us?"

Where were her babies? Where was Misha?

Exhausted beyond all endurance, Nadia was overpowered by the need to sleep.

❧

Working quickly, the midwife rubbed both infants with a warm, damp cloth—both the one born healthy and the one she'd pulled out by the feet, her skin blue, no sign of life in her.

She swaddled the two babies together in a single blanket of fine-spun wool, which she placed near the stove. And then she turned to the mother, mopping up the pool of blood, assuring herself that the hemorrhaging had stopped. She listened at Nadia's chest—then held a mirror beneath her nostrils.

Nadia's breathing was faint—but, still, she breathed.

Rolling Nadia's inert body first to one side then the other, the midwife put fresh sheets on the bed and tucked her in beneath the goose-down quilt. And then she carried the candelabra to the little nest by the stove where she'd placed the babies.

Murmuring a prayer, she folded a corner of the blanket down.

Both babies were as pink as geraniums now. One had her skinny little arm flung over the other's torso. They were pressed close together, face to face, looking like one newborn lying beside a mirror.

"*Elohim gadol!*" the midwife bellowed, feeling as pleased with herself as she was with the Lord of All Creation. She nestled the infants, one at a time, into their mother's arms.

Nadia opened her eyes to the sight of her two tiny but perfect-looking baby girls, their little hands still reaching out for one another, touching one another, as they must have done during the past nine months inside her. Inhaling the new-baby smell of their little heads, she caressed them, murmuring their praises, while the midwife told her how the second one nearly died.

"Blue, completely blue! Roused to life again by her sister's warmth, she was. Such a life-giving hug I've never seen before, in all my years of catching babies!"

With tears in her eyes, Nadia whispered a prayer of thanks. And then she remembered the men in the next room and the terrible sounds—and the final sound of the little bell above the door. "And my husband?"

The midwife shook her head. "It seems they've taken him away, Nadia. But you mustn't give up hope."

Hope! What hope was there, when a Jew was arrested by agents of the tsar's secret police?

The silence was filled by the small new sounds of the babies' voices, their sighs and squeaks, their pretty little mouths opening and closing, innocent of any knowledge or sorrow.

"What will you call them, these perfect little girls?"

Nadia and Misha had already picked out the name Sonya, if the baby was a girl, in honor of Misha's late mother.

The midwife, whose father was a rabbi, suggested the name Zaneta for the second girl. "It means *God's gift* in Hebrew."

"Zaneta!" Nadia sighed. "A good name."

Would these babies never know their father? Nadia held them close, recalling every nightmarish rumor she'd ever heard about the prison camps in Siberia, and all those poor souls who died on the journey.

"You saved your sister," she whispered to little Sonya, who was the bigger of the two, although, in every other way, they looked identical. Stroking Zaneta's forehead with one finger, she said, "You mustn't ever forget! You have this gift of life because of her."

॰॰

Using all her savings, Nadia hired a lawyer to try to secure the release of her husband. So far, all the lawyer had managed to find out was that Misha was accused of making a suit of clothes for a man connected in some way to *Narodnaya volya*, the underground group of hotheads who'd made an attempt on the life of the tsar.

Other women from the Jewish community helped, when they could, with advice, comfort, and food, as Nadia's situation became more and more dire. It was impossible to take on new work, or even to collect for work she'd already completed, with two newborns and a five-year-old at home, and no one to help her. It was weeks after the birth of the twins before she was even able to walk properly. She sent her eldest boy, Lev—who was big for his age, light-haired and blue-eyed—out to work as an apprentice in the stable yards, even though he was only ten years old. Through the rabbi's efforts, eight-year-old Faya was taken in by a wealthy family on an estate in the countryside, to help with the housework in exchange for room and board.

Nadia couldn't sleep for worrying whenever her youngest son, Daniel, went to bed hungry. She'd been able to nurse the twins for a scant six weeks before her milk ran dry. They were living on boiled buckwheat groats and tea, and whatever charity was offered by their neighbors.

An emissary of the ladies' aid committee, delivering soup one day, urged Nadia to take her infants to the Jewish orphanage for girls, just until she was able to set her life to rights again. "They won't remember anything about it when they're older—and the matron there is very kind, very good. Your babies won't have you, for a short time. But at least they will have enough food."

Nadia could barely restrain herself from telling the woman to get out of her house. The very idea of it—an orphanage! No child of hers would ever be taken to live in such a place, not while she had breath in her body.

She accepted the soup with chilly thanks, hastening to tell her benefactor, "We're expecting word, any day now, about my husband's release."

It was a lie. But what else could she say?

No letters—not a single message—had yet arrived from Misha. The newspapers were full of reports about the government's efforts to find all the members of *Narodnaya volya*. All who were found were executed. At least, the lawyer wrote to Nadia, her husband was—as far as they knew—still alive.

ço

Nadia's eyes in the mirror looked desperate and hollow. A few small new commissions came her way—through the ladies' aid committee, she suspected. How was it that she had become the recipient of charity, she who had often been the object of other women's envy?

The rabbi brought it to her attention that Daniel had distinguished himself in his age group, learning to read and write short passages in Hebrew. Even before Misha's arrest, little

Daniel amazed and amused them by reading out loud, while seated on his father's lap, from the *Russian Bulletin*. Such a gifted child, the rabbi told Nadia, came with a special burden of responsibility.

She tried to think about what Misha would want her to do.

Alone in the shop, unable to afford to hire help—trying to tend the twins and also be attentive to Daniel—she was falling behind with her work, rather than getting ahead, sleeping late after sleepless nights.

Why had she and Misha ever moved away from the shtetl, so far away from their families, having only one another to depend on? Why had she insisted on marrying someone she loved?

Nadia woke in a panic every morning and, often, several times during the night. She was hungry—her children were hungry. And their situation was only getting worse.

And then one morning she woke knowing what she needed to do. She almost couldn't believe she was going to do it—but she had to. There was no other choice.

It would be a temporary measure, she told herself, while she labored to earn enough to put some money by and keep herself and her little prodigy alive.

EN ROUTE FROM FRANCE, AND IN KISHINEV

1880

There were rumors of war on the limpid April day in 1881, when Monsieur and Madame Dupres of Nantes boarded their train at the Gare de Paris-Est—although word of it didn't reach them until the train stopped in Hanover. When he saw the headlines, Monsieur Dupres proposed, as gently as he could, that they turn around and go home again, to wait until the political situation was less uncertain. His wife told him that he was welcome to return home, if that was what he wanted to do. She would make the journey by herself, if need be.

Madame Dupres was thirty-eight and had not yet managed to bring a child to term, despite three pregnancies. Three times, she'd endured the agonies of giving birth to a tiny corpse. In the midst of the *crise de nerfs* she suffered following her last miscarriage, she conceived the idea of adopting a Jewish baby girl from the place where her grandmother had been born—Kishinev, a place that, to her, seemed as remote and unreal as something from a fairytale.

One of their suitcases was filled with baby clothes and blankets of the finest quality, acquired by Madame Dupres with such joyous anticipation over the years, then tucked away. Finally, they would be used. The baby would be hers because she would come from the city where Madame Dupres's grandmother had spent her childhood before marrying out of her faith and moving to France.

The idea was completely mad. It was only because Monsieur Dupres feared his wife would kill herself otherwise that he made the necessary inquiries, procured the necessary papers, and agreed to undertake the journey to Russia.

He loved his wife very much, despite her tainted relative. Her grandmother was long dead, after all. None of Monsieur Dupres's colleagues at the Bureau de Change knew about his wife's ancestry. Most of his family were also ignorant of this unfortunate connection except for his eldest sister, who promised she'd never tell. The child would, of course, be raised a Catholic. Madame Dupres was determined never to let her daughter know she was adopted.

کہ

The journey of Monsieur and Madame Dupres was long but uneventful. They were both exhausted when they arrived in Kishinev, after dark, and managed to find a place to stay. Early the next morning, they found someone to take them to the orphanage, which turned out to be a modest two-story house at the edge of town.

Monsieur Dupres, nervous about getting stranded there, told the driver to wait. A neat young woman answered the door, looking at them with some amazement as Monsieur Dupres told her who they were and why they had come. The matron was away, she explained without letting them in. "I am her assistant," she added, dropping a little curtsey. She spoke decent French.

"But we were expected," said Madame Dupres.

"If you could come back tomorrow, please, matron will be returning then, although possibly very late." They heard children's voices, one of them raised in anger, and then the sound of another child crying. "I hope you will excuse me—" Starting to close the door, she added, "Day after tomorrow is even better."

Madame Dupres clutched at her husband's arm. "Show her!" she told him.

He braced the door with one of his fine leather boots and took a letter out of his coat pocket, handing it to the girl.

She struggled to read it, moving her lips as she parsed the

words. Then she looked up at them, chagrined. "I myself am not authorized to approve adoptions."

"It has already been approved, mademoiselle," said Monsieur Dupres, "as you have just seen for yourself." He plucked the letter out of her hand, tucking it away again.

"What's your name, dear?" Madame Dupres asked as she and her husband pushed their way inside.

"Golda, madame."

There was a smell—a smell of poverty, although the place seemed clean enough. They heard the aggrieved child's voice again. Two curly-haired little girls ran by, giggling. Monsieur Dupres held a handkerchief up to his nose.

Golda looked embarrassed. "You are—forgive me for inquiring!" Continuing in a low voice, she asked, "You are Jewish?"

Monsieur remained silent, despite his promise to his wife. To his surprise, she spoke then in another language, a language he'd never heard her speak before, in all their eighteen years of marriage.

Golda nodded, apparently satisfied with what had been said. Madame Dupres resisted the urge to cross herself, although, silently, she repeated a fervent prayer of thanks to the Virgin for the love her grandmother had shown her, and the few words of Yiddish she'd taught her as a child.

"If I am understanding correctly, you have come for a baby girl. But the youngest orphans in our care now are not babies anymore."

A cascade of silvery, distinctly babyish laughter reached their ears from the floor above them. Madame Dupres reacted to the sound like a hunting dog that scents its prey.

Following her gaze, Golda said, "Oh, that is just Sonya and Zaneta, always making jokes together. Special case. I can show you youngest orphans, in dayroom now. Very nice girls! I cannot authorize, but you can look. This way, please."

But before she could stop them, Madame Dupres, surprisingly fleet in her high heels, had launched herself upstairs. Her husband had to take the stairs two at a time to keep up with her.

Golda scurried after them, calling out, "Madame! Monsieur! Not that way, please!"

Passing two empty dormitories on the hallway, they entered a third, smaller room, where all the bassinettes were empty, save one. Madame took her husband's hand, leading him straight to the bassinette that held Sonya and Zaneta.

Entranced, Madame looked down at the babies, perfect baby girls, perhaps nine months old.

One slept, or pretended to sleep, while the other looked up with large blue eyes at the two strange faces hovering above her. Her delicate brows knitted and her tiny chin began to quiver. But then her gaze lit on the brooch Madame Dupres wore on her lapel. It shimmered with a setting of dark pink rubies and very small diamonds. Very small. Very shiny in the slanting light that came in through the window.

The baby's face broke into a smile as she reached out, with one dimpled hand, toward the magenta-tinged sparkles of color and light.

Madame Dupres's eyes filled with tears. She reached down and gathered the baby into her arms, embracing her with all the unused genius of her frustrated maternity. "Oh, my sweet little darling—I knew I'd find you here!"

Neither Madame nor Monsieur Dupres paid any attention to Golda's objections, which segued from French to Russian as her voice became more and more agitated. "I will lose my position, you ridiculous people!" she shouted at them in Russian. "Do you have a heart in your body? Have I not used the correct word for twins? *Jumelle!*" she shouted in French. "*Les jumelles!* Zaneta is one of two. They must not be separated!"

❦

Startled by the noise, opening her eyes, Sonya registered the empty space beside her in the bassinette. She saw Zaneta high above her, held in the arms of a person who looked nothing like anyone she'd ever seen before, with feathers on her head and blood-red lips.

Sonya's little face crumpled and her chest started heaving.

She began to cry with the sound of a hinge in need of oil. Grabbing hold of the side of the bassinette, she pulled herself up onto her knees. And then she wailed with such force that Monsieur Dupres put his hands over his ears.

He looked briefly at the infant in his wife's arms. "Hello, baby," he said as if he'd just tasted something sour.

Madame Dupres was laughing now. "Oh *cheri*, we could take both of them, couldn't we?"

"Are you mad? One will be quite enough." Still wincing at the sound of the other baby's piercing cries, monsieur called out, "Let's go! The driver is waiting."

Madame Dupres glanced once over her shoulder at Sonya. And then, holding Zaneta tight, she escaped out of the infants' dormitory with her prize.

Golda hurried after them downstairs.

From a pocket deep inside his coat, Monsieur Dupres took out an envelope stuffed with cash. "A donation, mademoiselle—for the good work you do."

Blinking back her angry tears, Golda glanced down at the thick wad of banknotes—and then pushed his hand away.

"For the orphans," said Madame Dupres, not unkindly.

Monsieur Dupres put the money on the matron's desk, then sat down and helped himself to a piece of writing paper. He used his own fountain pen to write a note filled with the deceptions he and his wife had agreed upon, although, as a man of probity, it pained him to do so.

Madame knew that she had what she needed now—and this baby, her baby, would have everything she needed. The world had come round to where it was supposed to be.

PARIS

1909

Shoving past the monocled man in formal dress and his mustachioed servant, Jeannette realizes it's the impresario of the Ballets Russes himself she's just treated so rudely. She curses under her breath as she makes her way down the dimly lit corridor, past the open door of another dressing room where she glimpses a man in costume and a half-dressed ballerina, one long leg wrapped around him, his hands cradling her ass, her face buried in his neck. Why don't people bother shutting their doors?

She sees the bald pate of the regisseur approaching and ducks her head to avoid his gaze, worrying about having her pay docked again. He leaves an overwhelming scent of cigarettes in his wake, as if he himself were made of burning paper tightly wrapped around a pinky's worth of fragrant tobacco.

Jeannette's heart is beating as hard as if she'd just done a series of complicated jumps in a cross-floor exercise.

Explanations percolate inside her, words and possibilities that gleam and shimmer, threatening to surface from the murkiness of her oldest and least understood feelings and memories. Looking at that woman's face had been like looking into a mirror. Who was she?

The company's choreographer, Mikhail Fokine, hired Jeannette on the spot when she auditioned as an extra dancer for the Russian Ballet's season in Paris. Had he recognized something in her that she had failed to see in all her days of gazing into mirrors and dancing past them?

Russian. Russians. But Jeannette is French, through and through.

She starts to climb the metal stairs, then pauses halfway up, gazing down at the floor below and all the people scurrying about there, each of them busily preparing for the performance—the painters with their color-spattered smocks and brushes; the carpenters with their hammers and saws. Ballerinas in toe shoes, looking like little flocks of ducks as they make their way through the dust-filled air, trying to avoid nails, tacks, and the wandering hands of the workmen.

No answer she can think of makes any sense.

The backstage bell chimes four times: thirty minutes till she needs to be on stage. Jeannette forces herself to look away—to keep climbing, taking care not to stumble.

Her aunt's words come back to her—her sour, cold, unloving aunt, who so often spoke in a way that was full of portent and yet impossible to comprehend. *What can you expect?*—Jeannette had overheard her say to her father, more than once. *It's a question of blood.*

Jeannette had thought it was her menstrual blood that had so offended her aunt's sensibilities. It disgusted Jeannette too. For an embarrassingly long time, she thought she was the only person who bled that way, every month. She always did her best to hide it, scrubbing away any evidence, disposing of the soiled rags, using scent to cover any lingering odor left behind.

Blood. Her blood. One of her dance mates finally let her in on the secret, that all of them bled, in just the way she did. It had so often felt shameful to Jeannette, being an only child. Being without a mother who might have helped her make sense of what it meant, being a girl. Becoming a woman.

Her cousins, all from her father's side, seemed as close and happy together as a litter of puppies. They all resembled one another. None of them resembled Jeannette. Their hair was lank and straight, where hers was abundant and full. They had freckles, enviable bosoms, and sturdy limbs. They made fun of her narrow feet with their high arches and long first toe.

She used to stare at photographs of her mother, looking for the ways in which she might grow up to look like her. But she didn't really resemble her mother either, no matter how carefully she studied the photos and ransacked her memory.

How could it be that Jeannette looked so uncannily like Anna Pavlova's Russian seamstress? It was evident from the moment they'd stood face to face in the doorway, their proportions exactly the same, their skin fine textured and fair, their identical eyes deep set, their faces heart shaped, both of them with narrow, long-fingered hands.

Jeannette knew of doppelgängers in literature and even in the ballet literature: Odette and Odile in *Swan Lake*. She suddenly remembers that English painting Paul Poiret had made a great point of taking her to see, when she and he were still going about together. She'd been more impressed by Paul's nervous excitement over showing it to her than she'd been by the painting itself, which showed two identical couples in medieval dress happening upon each other in the forest. There was a look of horror in the eyes of the two girls, each a mirror image of the other.

Just as the backstage bell chimes again, an idea falls upon her with the weight and rudeness of a piece of scenery toppling over. That pretty little girl in the dressing room, with her honey-colored curls and wide-set eyes—that little girl looked like the child she and Paul might have made, if he hadn't been such a pig.

KISHINEV

1881

Following the matron's advice, Nadia refrained from visiting the orphanage, even though she thought about her babies every day and, especially, every night. She stinted herself on food at first, so that Daniel would have enough. She sewed for such long hours that her hands hurt and her head ached. At night, alone in her bed, she was plagued by guilt.

The matron's note, when it arrived, felt to Nadia like God's judgment upon her. Zaneta was gone, taken away by a prosperous-looking couple from France who came and went while the matron's new assistant was in charge.

Nadia pleaded with the driver to make his horses go faster, crazed with fear that something would happen to the other twin before she got there—cursing herself for having ever let her babies out of her sight.

The deeper meaning of this disaster was crystal clear: God had chosen to give his gift to someone more deserving. Nadia had been too weak, too gullible, too trusting. She knew she would never forgive herself.

The moment little Sonya—much grown, fussing and squirming—was brought down from upstairs and handed over to Nadia, the baby heaved a ragged sigh and fell asleep with her mother's heartbeat in her ears.

"Look at that," the matron said very softly. "She's been inconsolable since yesterday." She pulled the mother toward a chair—fearing Nadia was about to topple over—patted the mother's shoulder, and gently touched the top of the baby's head. "I asked the police commissioner for his help, to see if the pair of them could be stopped at the border." She sighed. "But when he heard your name—"

"Of course," said Nadia. She would expect nothing else from the Russian authorities. All her efforts to secure her husband's release had come to nothing. Every day, her hopes of seeing him again grew dimmer and dimmer.

She refused the money the matron tried to give her, looking her straight in the eye and saying that, before God, she would never stand accused of selling her child.

❧

When Nadia arrived home with Sonya, Daniel looked suspiciously at the baby. With her big head and abundant dark hair, she didn't at all resemble the tiny little sisters who had so mysteriously been taken away from him, nearly a year ago. "Who is this?" he asked his mother.

"This is Sonya, Daniel!" Holding back her tears, Nadia placed the baby in her brother's arms.

He held her stiffly. This infant's blue eyes were flecked with gold. She had chubby arms and thighs, whereas his little sisters had been delicate and lean, more like miniature children than babies. He sniffed the top of her head. She even smelled different.

Looking into her eyes, he whispered, "What did you do with my sisters?" The baby reached up to grab at his glasses. Daniel tickled her, and she laughed with a silvery, bell-like sound.

Could his sisters have merged into one larger child? Maybe, he thought, that's what happens with twins, especially those who are born looking exactly alike. Or perhaps this child was a changeling, like one of those he'd read about in his book of fairytales! His mother certainly seemed entranced by her, entranced and also, somehow, fearful, as if the baby might at any moment disappear.

Daniel's urge to elucidate the truth of any given situation was already in evidence, even at the age of five. When he looked at this child his mother called Sonya, he felt something he couldn't puzzle out. Something that made him love her, even though he knew he should probably fear her. The changeling in the story had similarly charmed everyone who laid eyes on her.

❧

Every night, after her children were asleep and she'd worked as long as she could by candlelight, Nadia grieved her lost baby, casting her thoughts abroad in the world, wishing she could find and comfort her. Praying that Zaneta was safe. She couldn't bear the idea that any of her children would ever learn the truth about what had happened to the youngest member of their family.

After deflecting Daniel's outlandish questions as long as she could, Nadia lied for the first time ever to her beloved son. He was remembering things incorrectly, she told him. There had briefly been two babies—identical twins. That much was right. But only one of them had survived.

She finally saved enough to bring Faya home again—poor Faya, who had been worked so hard that Nadia was loathe to give her any further chores. Like Daniel, Faya was a studious child, although her particular talent was for numbers, which she loved adding and subtracting, multiplying and dividing. Nadia decided Faya could help her with the bookkeeping, which used to be Misha's province.

Lev came home once a week, smelling of horses and leather. Cheerful and kind, generous by nature, he was well loved by everyone. Little Sonya especially adored Lev.

When word came that men from the army were visiting each Jewish household in Kishinev, snapping up all the boys over twelve years of age, Nadia sewed a set of Cossack clothes for her seventeen-year-old blond, blue-eyed son. She brought them to him at the stable yards, with enough silver sewn into the hems to buy forged papers and a passage to New York.

"Promise me you'll write!" she said, fearing that she'd never feel his arms around her again.

How hard it was to let go—and yet it was the way of the world, Nadia reminded herself. She was determined not to let her son be stolen away by the tsar's army, where Jewish boys were used as cannon fodder and harassed, if they survived, into converting.

"Leave right away," she urged him.

Lev's arms trembled, ever so slightly, as he held her. "Say goodbye for me, Mother, won't you?"

She nodded, taking a last long look into his eyes that were the blue of cornflowers. Her own maternal grandfather had such eyes, though his had been rheumy and rimmed with red. It seemed inconceivable to her that her Lev would ever be old.

"Tell Sonya I'll send for her, when I'm able."

"We'll see about that, my son. The important thing now is for you to be careful and wise—and get yourself safely to the New World."

❧

Misha was finally released from prison, nearly a decade after his arrest. It didn't take Nadia long to understand why: he arrived home weak and ill, with a cough and fever. "It's the flu," he told her in a voice she barely recognized, faint and short of breath. "So many of the others were getting it, prisoners and jailors alike. Many were dying."

People everywhere that year, in 1890, were coming down with the flu that had spread from Saint Petersburg, moving west with the railroad lines, infecting the king of Belgium, the emperor of Germany and, they said, the tsar himself. It was spreading to every corner of the world.

Nadia wore herself out, trying to nurse her husband back to health and also keep the children safe. But the flu seemed to defy all her precautions. The day after Misha's return, Nadia put Faya to bed with a fever and chills. Daniel, who normally didn't allow anything to keep him away from school, stayed home for two days with a painful headache.

Ten-year-old Sonya, untouched by the illness, helped her mother as best she could, especially after Nadia herself came down with a cough. Bundling up against the cold, Sonya ran back and forth to the pharmacy for doses of quinine, salicylate of soda, and whatever advice the beleaguered pharmacist could offer them.

Nadia proffered golden spoonfuls of her chicken soup while

she sat by Misha's bedside and Sonya hovered in the doorway. "I dreamed of your cooking, day and night," he struggled to say, "but I can't taste or smell anything now!"

Sonya saw him steal a look at her, shyly, as one would look at a stranger.

He'd never seen her before—and she'd never seen him. Nadia encouraged Sonya to stay close—to speak to her father. They had a lot of catching up to do.

Misha was too ill to speak—and Sonya had no idea what to say. She kept repeating the word *Papa* to herself, thinking how the word evoked a feeling she'd never felt before. Once, when she sat looking at his face on the pillow, he met her gaze with his deep-brown eyes—and she was startled to see how kind he was, and that it even seemed as if he loved her. She smiled, gently squeezed his hand, and said the word *Papa* out loud.

But his illness only grew worse, no matter how tenderly they cared for him. It sounded as if each breath he drew and expelled belonged to a man who was drowning.

The doctor, shaking his head, diagnosed acute pneumonia. On the seventh day after being reunited with his wife and family, Misha Luria died.

NANTES

1887-1896

Jeannette Dupres was seven years old when her adored maman contracted scarlet fever. Jeannette was sent away, for an unspecified period of time, to live with some cousins from her father's side. Arriving in a carriage two weeks later, dressed in mourning, Monsieur Dupres brought a new black dress for Jeannette to wear to her mother's funeral.

Everything good and sweet in Jeannette's life up till then was buried that year under the rich dark soil of the Pont du Cens cemetery in Nantes. Her father's eldest sibling—a dour woman who had always seemed faintly repelled by Jeannette, despite her pretty looks and winning ways—came to keep house for them. Jeannette's papa immersed himself more and more in his work at the Bureau de Change, often dining out and returning home long after Jeannette had cried herself to sleep.

Her aunt, hoping to find a way to distract the child from her grief, enrolled her in the elementary ballet class at the École de Danse Classique.

Jeannette took an immediate liking to the studio, the teachers, and the other girls there, all of them devoted to the study and practice of ballet, to the discipline of training their bodies to move in prescribed ways passed down over hundreds of years by masters of the art. She loved the special clothes required for class—white satin slippers and tights, tunics or frothy tutus—which made her feel like part of a flock of beautiful birds.

Her teacher was pretty and kind. With practiced hands, she gathered Jeannette's long hair into the requisite chignon and pinned it in place. Jeannette looked on in the mirror, her eyes wide. She loved the mirrors, which lined every wall.

First position, second position, third position—legs turned out, hands and arms shaped just so. One hand on the barre, toe pointed, leg extended—one long line. Back arched, neck long. Fifth position—shoulders back, arms overhead in a perfect oval. Head held high. Posture—she'd never thought about posture before. It was all a revelation.

Flushed and excited after her introductory class, Jeannette seemed, to both her father and aunt, like a changed girl—and she slept beautifully that night. The next day, she informed her papa that she wanted to take as many ballet classes as he would allow—every day, if possible.

She didn't tell him that the dance world—for she soon realized that's what it was—conferred on her a greater sense of belonging than anything she felt amongst her cousins or, since her mother's death, at home.

That world was not without its bitter pills. Although Jeannette had the requisite long legs and short waist just right for ballet, her turnout was poor. Even worse than that, she was told that her long first toe would make it difficult, if not impossible, for her ever to dance *en pointe*. These disabilities only made her more determined to work her way up from the lowest place in the line, to demonstrate that—although she was now motherless, and her father was cold, and her aunt was scandalized by everything about her—Jeannette would prove herself worthy, after all, of love and admiration.

Alone in her room, she read her school assignments lying flat on her back, her bottom shoved against the wall and her legs spread-eagled, using gravity to remake her body. She devised a set of exercises to increase the rotation of her hips and improve the turnout that seemed to come so naturally to many of the other girls, whose fifth positions were perfect—who could drop into splits as if they were made of rubber instead of flesh and bone. The physical pain would sometimes make her cry—and also helped her know that she was making progress. She wiped away the tears impatiently.

At night, or in idle moments at school, Jeannette fantasized about having an operation to cut off the tip of her big toe, giving her the perfect squared-off feet made for toe shoes.

When she was finally allowed to take classes *en pointe*, both of her big toes bled, leaving brown stains on the rags and cotton wool she stuffed inside her shoes. She woke up the next day with several of her toenails turned black and blue. She kept the blood a secret. The pain lent a prescient intensity to her dancing.

By the age of fourteen, Jeannette was given leading roles in all the school's recitals.

Her aunt disapproved, judging the girl's obsession with dance to be unnatural. Her papa attended the recitals, and applauded at the right times, always judiciously. Once he told Jeannette that he was proud of her hard work and dedication, adding that he hoped she would soon find a worthy goal.

Her goal was to become a professional ballerina, despite her aunt's protestations that no decent people would ever allow their son to marry such a person. The stage was the realm of the demimonde.

But only when Jeannette was dancing on stage did she feel fully alive, excited, and happy. She didn't care if this meant she was a wicked person. She didn't want what her father and aunt envisioned for her future.

She dreamed of feeling an audience in her thrall—astonishing them with her skill and artistry as a dancer. Moving them. Weaving a web of magic around them.

At home or with her extended family, Jeannette felt a helpless sense of failing again and again to measure up or fit in—or even to be seen. She knew that dance classes would soon come to an end for her, as the school only taught girls up to the age of sixteen. She was offered a place there as an assistant teacher. But what Jeannette wanted, she was quite sure, couldn't be achieved in Nantes.

In any case, her father told her, not unkindly, Jeannette was at the time in life when she would need to lay the ground for her future—to acquire the skills and charms that would allow her to take her place in respectable society, to have her own home and keep her own table. In a very few years, to start a family.

Her father's words terrified her.

The day after her sixteenth birthday, Jeannette packed a suitcase, gathered the little bit of money she had—and, choosing a time when she could leave undetected, boarded a train bound for Paris.

PARIS

1896

Jeannette stood motionless at the back of the darkened cabaret, ignoring the tray of cigarettes and sweets she was supposed to be selling, still trying to figure out whatever was behind the magic of Loïe Fuller's performance.

The diminutive American was every bit as much a conjurer as a dancer, swirling meters and meters of a moonlit silken garment around and above her head, now hiding, now revealing her form. She seemed to grow to the size of a mythical bird—a phoenix—with outstretched fiery wings, all the while turning and turning, the fabric unfurling like a sail, then folding like a rose, lit by a luminescence in otherworldly colors. The lights that revealed her came not only from above and beside the stage but also somehow from the fabric itself. It shimmered, glowed, and transformed the dancer, creating the illusion of an ever-changing storm of fairy dust raining down from the heavens.

The gentlemen with their top hats and monocles sat as if hypnotized, their aperitifs held motionless midair.

There was some element involved in the stagecraft, something physical and yet invisible, that mystified Jeannette. All the waiters and the other cigarette girls had also stopped whatever they were doing, to simply stand there and gape.

When la Loïe rose up from the bow that was a perfect mime of a dying rose—when she unfurled the fluttering silken sails of her sleeves, turned back to ecru silk again—the applause was so great, and the men stamped their boots so hard, that all the glassware on the little wooden tables rang like bells.

This was Jeannette's seventh time seeing the performance,

but it was no less thrilling than it had been the first time. Rumor had it that Madame Loïe concocted whatever it was that made the colors so magically glow with the help of a brilliant and determined young Polish woman, a chemist—some said an alchemist—who'd been spotted in the audience more than once, always in the company of her husband, Monsieur Pierre Curie.

The lights were lit again. Jeannette adjusted her décolletage, ran her tongue over her teeth, and smiled—because this was always the moment when the most generous tips were handed out. She needed to make out well today if she was to earn enough to pay the rent on her little rattrap of a room. An elderly gentleman pressed a five-franc piece into her palm. A younger man, who didn't seem very gentlemanly at all, stuffed a note into her bodice, squeezing her bottom with his other hand as he did so. And then a very clean-looking young apprentice, in apron and wooden clogs, turned to her with tears in his eyes—real tears. He ran his hands down her arms as if she were a marble statue of the Virgin. And then he leaned forward and kissed her on the mouth, chastely, his eyes half closed. He looked as if he were about to swoon. Jeannette waited a moment before pushing him away.

Looking as surprised as she, he bowed with incongruous elegance. "Forgive me, mademoiselle," he said. "I was overwhelmed by the sensations of beauty."

She couldn't help but smile. She'd been kissed out of the blue before, but never so sweetly. He was about her age, maybe a year older. Looking into his clever brown eyes, she could see something formidable and compelling about him, despite his youth and humble garb. "Who are you?" she asked.

The apprentice rose up to his full height—he was broad shouldered and barrel chested but not really very tall. His eyes seemed to sparkle with a remnant of Loïe Fuller's pixilated light. "At your service, mademoiselle!" he said, sweeping another dramatic bow. "I am Paul Poiret."

KISHINEV

1896

Alone at the table with Faya, Sonya dabbed at her lips with a napkin, glanced into the mirror, and announced that she would go to the pharmacy to pick up the medicine for their mother's cough.

Faya gave her a look that said she knew quite well why her little sister was so willing to go out into the frosty night. Half the Jewish girls in Kishinev, it seemed, had a crush on Jascha, the pharmacist's son. Faya wondered whether Sonya, with her pretty looks, had managed to win Jascha's favor. Good for her then, she thought—and good luck in finding approval from Jascha's family as a suitable match.

"I'll clean up," was all she said.

Sonya put on her new Astrakhan hat and coat and rushed out, through the shop, into the night, the little bell on the door tinkling behind her. She was too excited to mind the frigid air— and, anyway, it was a very short walk to the pharmacy, especially when she walked so quickly, practically running. Still, the cold made it hurt to breathe and brought tears to her eyes. It was a relief when she stepped into the warm, camphor-scented air of the pharmacy. She'd been certain she'd find Jascha there, at this late hour. And yet it was the pharmacist himself who stood at the counter with its décor of glass bottles in a rainbow of colors, patent medicines, and beautifully labeled jars proclaiming the merits of the nostrums and creams they contained.

The pharmacist looked down at her over his glasses. "Is your mother's cough still dry?"

Sonya nodded her head. Sometimes she thought the pharmacist liked her. And at other times she thought he seemed wary of her. Did he notice the times when his son had touched her wrist or her palm, ever so briefly, across the counter, when he took the coins she handed him?

Jascha's father turned from Sonya to call over his shoulder. "The medicine for Nadia Luria."

"I have it ready, Papa." Jascha rose up from where he'd been working at a lab bench in the back.

How Sonya loved his serious and handsome face! The dark hair that fell against his forehead. The golden gleam of his spectacles. The heat and humor of the warm brown eyes behind them. The graceful curve of his lips. She wondered what it would feel like to be kissed by him.

Jascha handed the little package, neatly wrapped in brown paper and string, to his father. Over his father's shoulder, Jascha looked at Sonya with a barely suppressed smile, filled with mischief and something else. Something that made her feel odd and a little wobbly, as if it were she, and not her mother, who was ill.

And then another customer came in, demanding the pharmacist's attention. "My son will ring you up," he said to Sonya with a look that seemed to her a bit severe.

Everyone had the greatest expectations for Jascha, who was going to graduate, she heard, at the top of his class, justifying the expense and struggle his father had in getting him admitted to the secondary school. Jascha aspired to become a doctor, even though the difficulties associated with obtaining permission to study medicine in Saint Petersburg would be far greater still, given the strict quotas for Jews.

Sonya took her gloves off, ostensibly to accept the coins—but really because she hoped Jascha would touch her naked skin. She had a sudden image of the two of them, standing beneath a wedding canopy—and, mortified, felt herself blush.

Smiling now, Jascha took a little dried flower from his pocket and slipped the stem under the string of her package. A magenta flower. Sonya, who prided herself on her originality, had told Jascha once that magenta was her favorite color. Bending close to her bowed head, he whispered, "I'll catch up with you at the corner. I won't be a moment!"

᳇

The moment stretched into many minutes, until Sonya was fairly sure she was going to freeze, despite her warm coat and hat and the scarf she'd wrapped over her face. "Just a minute more—and then I'll go," she told herself. And then, "That's it! How could he have made me wait like this, in the snow!"

And then Jascha appeared at the margins of the pale green, snow-filled light of the streetlamp under which she stood, stomping her boots, breathing out white puffs of steam.

Without a word, he unfastened two buttons of his overcoat, took both her gloved hands in his and placed them inside, snug against his chest.

"Forgive me, Sonya! My father gave me one thing and another to do before I could get away." He lowered the scarf from her face, then stroked her cheek with his fingertips. "Like silk," he murmured. Through his shirt and waistcoat—and through her thick gloves—she could feel his heart thumping. "I have news," he whispered. "But you can't tell anyone." He took off his glasses, tucking them into his pocket. "My family is emigrating—to Argentina!"

It took her a moment to take this in—to try to understand what it might mean for her. Argentina! "But why there, Jascha, of all places?"

"There is a famous medical school in Córdoba, and a large population of immigrants from all over Europe. And," he smiled, "a shortage of pharmacists!"

"But how will you manage? You don't speak—" She had to think for a moment. "You don't speak Spanish."

"It's like French, but less difficult."

"You've already begun?"

He made a wry face and then said, with the precision with which Jascha did everything, "*Ya estoy estudiando.*"

Snowflakes swirled around them as she looked into his eyes, trying to figure out what he might be thinking—and what the words might have meant. Then Jascha bent his face down close to hers, closer than the two of them had ever been before. The ice that had formed on Sonya's lashes melted in the warmth of their two faces almost touching. She could smell his anise-scented breath and sense the smoothness of his clean-shaven jaw. His arms, surprisingly strong, pulled her closer. Her back arched. Her hands inside her gloves—inside his coat—were beginning to thaw. His lips, slightly parted, touched hers, and her eyes fluttered shut as if against her will. She knew there was no music playing—but, still, it was as if she heard an orchestra. *This, then,* thought Sonya, *is a kiss!*

"I'll write to you," he said, "as soon as we're settled."

"Only then?"

"As soon as we reach Córdoba."

✺

In late spring, a letter arrived for Sonya from Argentina. Her hands were shaking as she read it. *It's March and yet the leaves on the trees are red and orange now*, wrote Jascha, *and the air has turned chilly, although it will never get as cold as our Russian winter. The cold is one thing I won't ever regret leaving behind.*

But did he regret leaving *her* behind? Sonya's eyes raced down the page, rushing past further descriptions of weather and the landscape. And then she made herself back up and pay attention to every sentence, looking for the words she was desperate to read. *My sister is to be married to a businessman she met on the boat, my dearest girl.*

She closed her eyes for a moment, feeling a surge of hope. And then she started to read the sentence that followed, convinced it would contain a proposal of marriage. She read it a second time, noticing Jasha's perfect handwriting, realizing that what he wrote was unmistakable. *Will you come to the wedding?*

His sister's wedding? In what capacity, pray tell? As a guest? As a friend?

She read on. *Father says that we can pay for your ticket.* But what else does his father say about her? What sort of girl do they think she is, anyway?

Sonya forced herself to keep reading—not to give in to the sense of disappointment unfurling inside her. *The pharmacy he bought is much livelier than our little shop in Kishinev.* And yet they were among the more prosperous Jewish families of Kishinev. Are they millionaires now, able to pay for her ticket from halfway around the world? Do they think themselves too good, too rich and refined for the likes of Sonya, whose father sat rotting for ten years in a Russian prison only to be felled, on his release, by the flu? She, whose mother could not have managed without help from Daniel, who sends whatever he can, despite his own struggles as an apprentice lawyer in Saint Petersburg—where restrictions have grown ever tighter on the number of Jews admitted to the bar.

The wedding is to be held on the fifteenth day of November. You will leave Russia when the snows are deep and arrive in a world filled with blossoming jacaranda trees. Their blossoms are purple rather than magenta—but, still, I think you would find them beautiful. Springtime in the month of November—can you imagine? Everything here is up-side-down.

There were more words about the city where they'd settled and Jascha's progress with Spanish, which had been hastened by someone he'd met on the boat. He wrote of the medical school and the exams he'd need to pass before he enrolled.

It made Sonya want to scream with frustration. She knew Jascha loved her. He'd shown her—*my God*, she thought, the way he'd kissed her! Had his father convinced him to write like this, leaving his options open—without an offer of marriage? Did Jascha hope to win his father's blessing for the match with Sonya there, by his side?

Or had Jascha's feelings for her changed? Had he met someone else? She reread the part about the person he'd met on the boat, who'd helped him with his Spanish, wondering if that person had been attractive and young. Perhaps a Jewish girl from a much better family than Sonya's.

She had felt so certain of Jascha's love for her. Why couldn't he have written in a way that would assure their future together?

That would give her the courage to say yes to his proposal to come to him.

Sonya told herself to wait—to be patient. Perhaps that first letter was written in haste. Perhaps it was written with Jascha's father looking over his shoulder.

She waited and waited for another letter. She was unable to elicit any advice from her mother, who said that Sonya must really make the decision by herself.

Days and weeks passed—and no other letters arrived.

ೞ

Nadia finally offered the opinion that it would perhaps be dangerous—both to Sonya's person and her reputation—to undertake such a journey by herself, in response to such an uncertain proposal.

If someone else could accompany her, that would be one thing. But Nadia couldn't possibly leave the shop with Faya, who hadn't the foggiest idea how to run things—and Faya flat-out refused to go to South America. She had a terror of ocean voyages—and absolutely no desire to travel in a country that was likely to be populated by savages.

Nadia was dead set against interrupting the trajectory of Daniel's brilliant career in Saint Petersburg to send him off on such an errand.

For the ten-thousandth time in her life, Sonya reproached God for taking the one person in this world who could have been her best companion and friend. Between the two of them, if her twin sister had lived, they would have been able to figure out exactly how to respond to Jascha's proposal. Zaneta could have traveled with her to Argentina, making the journey right and proper, no matter what Jascha's intentions turned out to be. Or Zaneta could have reassured her that Kishinev was the place where Sonya was meant to stay. Where happiness awaited her.

ೞ

Kishinev was a large enough town—but in so many ways, it was like a village. Sonya saw the same people—and witnessed the same sights and sounds—every day. She didn't have to look out the window to know whose cart or carriage was rumbling past the shop. She could often identify people merely by how they made the little bell ring when they opened the shop door.

Kishinev was all she had ever known. How could she ever feel at home in a foreign place, with strangers whose native tongue wasn't Russian?

She loved the color and emotional range of Yiddish but associated the language with people from the *shtetls,* who looked askance at the idea of assimilation. Russia was her home—as much as the Jews were always seen as aliens within the Empire, forced to live under separate rules, with far fewer opportunities. With the constant fear of being blamed, once again, for whatever hardship was visited by Nature or the tsar on the Russian people.

Sonya *felt* Russian, even though she also felt, as a Russian Jew, that she was different.

The newly crowned young tsar, widely criticized for being weaker than his father, seemed to take special solace in turning the people's wrath away from him and toward the Jews instead. Crop shortages, famine, an unsolved murder, oppressive taxes, the closure of factories—the young Tsar Nicholas and his advisors found a way, every time, to promulgate the idea that if only the Jews were gone, life would be so much better in Russia. Idealistic and energetic Jewish men, who excelled in the few professions open to them, were characterized as leeches and bloodsuckers. When times were particularly bad, the government encouraged Russians to attack their Jewish neighbors, with whom—especially in Kishinev—they usually coexisted in peace.

But what was life, if not unfair? Daniel, now married and with a child on the way, was still relegated to practicing as an apprentice lawyer, even though he was regarded as one of the most distinguished legal minds in the capital. He treated his mother and sisters to fascinating descriptions of Saint

Petersburg when he and Klara came to visit—of the glorious architecture, the poets and writers in the cafes, the brilliant new plays in the theaters, and the unlimited wealth, power, and influence enjoyed by the nobility and their circle.

The Jews who lived in Saint Petersburg, all of them by special dispensation, were themselves, by and large, well off and well educated. How different her life would have been, Sonya thought, if Jascha's family hadn't emigrated to Argentina—if they'd managed to get him into medical school in the capital instead.

Daniel had acquired as a client one of the teachers at the Mariinsky Ballet School, helping her through a fraught and complicated contract negotiation—and yielding, for Daniel and his wife, occasional tickets to the Imperial Russian Ballet. His mother and Sonya asked all sorts of questions about the costumes of the dancers. They were especially riveted by gossip about the new tsar's protégé—reputedly, his mistress—Mathilde Kschessinska, who danced as the Mariinsky's *prima ballerina assoluta* and had no shame about wearing the outsize gems that Nicholas gave her, even when she was supposed to be playing the part of a dirt-poor peasant girl. She flaunted her privileged status and flirted with him openly, whether or not the tsar was sitting in the royal box with his new German bride.

Daniel made his mother and sisters laugh till tears ran down their faces, telling about how Kschessinska arranged to have a flock of chickens released on stage during the debut of a new young rival, who nonetheless won the collective heart of everyone in the audience. "Someday soon," Daniel told them, "I'll take you to the ballet. Once I'm admitted to the bar, life will change for all of us—you'll see!"

But life was changing for them, all on its own.

Nadia coughed so much, night and day, that she only rarely joined Sonya in the workshop now. Customers had taken to consulting the daughter, instead of the mother, when they wanted to order new clothes.

KISHINEV

1897

Sonya often ran into Masha—a girl she'd championed during their school days, when Masha, misshapen and lame, had been ostracized by the other children. No one but Sonya would ever share a desk with her without complaining, as if afraid that her lameness might be contagious. When their schooling was complete, Masha fell into the position of housekeeper for the priest.

"You'll never guess!" Masha said, seizing Sonya's arm outside the pharmacy. "Old Kozlov, the tailor whose family has made the uniforms for the cathedral school since the beginning of time—they found him dead this morning!"

Masha looked especially pleased to share this nugget of news with Sonya. "Slumped over his sewing machine, and his half-wit of a daughter running to the priest instead of going for the doctor!"

"Blessed be the one true Judge," murmured Sonya. Her mind was racing. Hats and coats, hundreds of them! Bolts and bolts of felt and wool that must have been bought already. Every tailor in Kishinev would be running to the priest, with samples and endorsements, hoping to win that commission.

Sonya had been marking time only in terms of how much time had passed since Jascha's letter, and how much time remained until his sister's wedding. But now she made herself think about the calendar as it pertained to Kishinev. There were only two weeks left before the start of the school term, when all the children's new uniforms would be needed.

She said nothing more, out of respect for the dead.

But Masha, her eyes sparkling, could read the question in

Sonya's eyes. "I've already recommended your shop to the Reverend Father. Go home, my old friend, and gather whatever help you'll need to get this done!"

❧

With her mother's blessing, Sonya negotiated a good price on the fabric—and found two skilled seamstresses willing to defer their wages on the promise of being paid double the going rate.

The work was hard and there were never enough hours of daylight. Sonya swore that as soon as they were paid, she would make the investment to have gas lighting installed. In the meantime, she kept so many candles burning, and the air of the workshop grew so warm, that the three of them stripped down to their chemises, as if they were working in a factory somewhere in the tropics.

After snuffing out all the candles in the shop, cleaning up and eating whatever Faya had prepared for supper, Sonya took turns with her sister, sitting at their mother's bedside until the medicine worked and Nadia fell asleep.

❧

Once the hats and coats for the parochial school were all delivered and paid for, a change was brought about for Nadia Luria and her daughters. Sonya was able to write to Daniel that he needn't send them money anymore.

Faya, happy to leave the business of the shop to Sonya, found a math tutor for herself and continued her studies. The little sister had become the stand-in for their mother, the person charged with keeping all of them safe.

It hadn't at all been what Sonya had wanted or imagined for her life—but she couldn't fail to see that this *was* her life now. All her fondest dreams had disappeared as stealthily as frost flowers on a windowpane.

She tried to remain alert, even though she was sometimes weary as she sat—sometimes late into the night—at her mother's bedside. When Nadia couldn't sleep, Sonya read to her or brushed her hair, which was so thin now, so different from the way it had been, full and glossy, before she'd become so ill.

When Nadia's eyes grew heavy, Sonya eased her down onto the pillow. If her mother clung to her, Sonya slipped under the covers and held her close, matching her breathing, breath for breath. She thought about how her mother had held her close and been there for her throughout her life, from the very start. Why was it then that Sonya felt, in some deep part of herself, unlovable and bad?

༝

The bell was tolling in the square when Sonya awoke too late to tell the hour. It was still night. Her mother's eyes were staring. Her lips were pale.

Sonya leapt out of the bed, terrified that death had come in the night, while she slept by her mother's side. But then Nadia blinked her eyes, and Sonya closed hers in a silent prayer of thanks. She dipped a clean cloth in the water jug, then moistened her mother's once rosy lips, now caked with white. When Sonya proffered a glass of water, Nadia shook her head—and then clutched at her daughter's hand.

"Something…confess to you," she murmured.

Sonya bent closer to hear her. There was no noise in the room but the shifting of the embers in the stove. Moonlight poured through the window, bathing them in its quicksilver glow.

Nadia's brow was furrowed and her lips kept pressing together then opening as if she were going to speak. Sonya tried to imagine what her mother, so brave and kind and good, might possibly want to confess.

And then she spoke, with more clarity than she had in weeks, without coughing. She held Sonya's eyes in her gaze as she said, "Both of you lived."

It was as if Nadia had saved her strength, over days and weeks, to say these words.

Sonya was fully awake now, every part of her listening.

"Zaneta *almost* died, but you saved her." Nadia's dark brown eyes grew wide. "A newborn, no bigger than a rabbit! You put your little arm around her—and brought her back to life again." Sonya required a long moment to take this in. And then a feeling of relief started flowing through her—like an elixir, soothing the hurt she'd always felt inside. The aching, vague, formless sense of it having been her fault somehow, that she alone had survived the passage into life begun by the two of them.

Letting go of her mother's hand, Sonya looked at her as if at someone she didn't know—had maybe never known. She'd never doubted her mother's truthfulness before. How could she have neglected to tell this part of Sonya's story—to give her this gift that now gave her such comfort?

"But how did she die then?" Sonya paused a moment. "How long did my twin sister live?"

A fit of coughing kept Nadia from saying more for several agonizing minutes. When she finally spoke, it was in the faintest whisper. "Daniel will tell you," she said, "after I die."

৬৹

Faya had to rush out to send a wire to Daniel, and another to Lev—and bring the message of Nadia's death to the rabbi.

"*Courage!*" Faya told her sister with a hug. "It won't be long before the people from the burial society get here." The little bell on the door tinkled as it closed behind her—and Sonya was left alone to keep watch over her mother's corpse.

Frightened, still disbelieving, she sat beside the bed.

Creases and furrows had marked Nadia's face during her last, long illness. But it was as if death had erased them. Dreading this moment for days now, for weeks, Sonya had been unprepared for the reappearance of her mother's extraordinary beauty.

First wiping away her tears, Sonya planted two kisses on Nadia's forehead, which was still warm and as smooth as marble now—one kiss for herself and another for Daniel, who had always been their mother's favorite. Who probably wouldn't be able to get there on time from Saint Petersburg within the twenty-four hours prescribed by tradition as the longest time they could wait before consigning their mother's body to her grave.

Sonya stroked a lock of hair away from Nadia's face, touched the waxen skin of her cheek, and then reached up and touched the skin of her own cheek, and felt the life inside. How was it that she was still alive? *Smooth as silk,* Jascha had said.

She was an orphan now, and her girlhood was over. The future stretched out before her like an unlit passageway.

§

Sonya and Faya had little in the way of comfort to offer one another. Their mother was what they had had in common. Who would each of them be without her gaze? What would connect them, one to the other?

Both sisters mourned, side by side and yet alone in their sorrow. It wasn't until Daniel walked in—their distinguished and accomplished brother in his beautifully tailored suit, sporting a torn black ribbon in tribute to the deceased—that Sonya felt the rekindling of curiosity inside her about her mother's last words.

"My dears!" said Daniel. "I took the first train."

They gave him tea. They reminisced about their mother's goodness and kindness, about all the ways in which she'd always been there for them.

Sonya wondered at her brother's poise in this painful situation—but then, she thought, it was part of his professional training to maintain a studied demeanor. She suddenly felt self-conscious about her tearstained cheeks and uncombed hair. Although they weren't observant, she and Faya knew enough about Jewish tradition to follow some of the rules surrounding death. They'd covered all the mirrors and sat on low benches. Sonya wondered if she looked just as awful as her sister.

"I must speak to you, Daniel!" she blurted out. Looking at Faya, she added, "Alone?"

"Faya, my dear," said Daniel. "Go rest! You look so tired."

"Even in this time of grief," said Faya, "I am dispensable. Very well then. Let the important members of this family have their say!"

Sonya tried to give Faya a kiss. But Faya pushed her away before sweeping off to their mother's bedroom, where she was choosing to sleep now.

"Well then," said Daniel, lighting a lamp. He took Sonya's hands. "Pretty Sonya! We will find a husband for you."

"A husband?" Sonya looked at her brother with disbelief. "Did you think I wanted to speak to you about a husband?"

"What else then?"

What else then! Daniel always spoke to her with a touch of irony, as if Sonya couldn't possibly know anything that Daniel didn't know already. She looked him straight in the eyes. "Mother confided something to me shortly before she died. Something that—astounded me."

She had Daniel's full attention now. He fidgeted in his chair.

Sonya spoke in a low voice, so that Faya wouldn't overhear them. "Mother told me that Zaneta didn't die on the day both of us were born. She said you knew the truth—and that you would tell me."

☙

Daniel knew as well as anyone that people said all sorts of things on their deathbeds, without consideration for the consequences to the living. He couldn't tell, just by looking at her, how much Sonya knew, or how much their mother might have divulged. Intercepting those letters from the pharmacist's son had been Nadia's own decision. Destroying them had been Daniel's. They had, between them, mother and son, agreed that it was for Sonya's own good.

Daniel kept his face neutral, giving nothing away.

What a travesty it would have been for their family to allow the prettiest and most capable daughter to leave them, to travel to a part of the world so far away from Russia—from civilization itself—that her own mother would never see her again!

He paused a moment to find the right language to use, and

the right way to say what he needed to say without saying too much.

"I was determined to tell you the truth myself, if Mother didn't."

Sonya was sorry now that she'd asked. The look on Daniel's face disturbed her. "What truth?" she said.

Her brother looked like the lawyer he was, about to present his client's case before a tribunal. "Father was arrested on the day you and Zaneta were born. By the time Mother had paid for his legal defense, there was no money left. Lev was bound as an apprentice, and Faya was sent to the countryside to work as a maid. They worked her unconscionably."

Sonya looked at him with impatience. "I know all that!"

Daniel paused long enough to let her know he was displeased at the interruption. "Out of funds, out of food, and probably half out of her mind, Mother took you and Zaneta to the Jewish orphanage at the edge of town."

Sonya could hardly believe her ears. "The orphanage?"

"It was meant to be a temporary measure, but while you were there, Zaneta was accidentally given away to a French couple who'd come to adopt a baby girl."

It took Sonya a few ragged heartbeats to find her voice. It hurt to breathe. An orphanage! Why had she and Zaneta been taken there, while Daniel stayed at home?

She also felt something stirring inside her, a memory, although it was all sensation—wordless and confused. "Didn't Mother search for her? Did you search for our sister after you were grown up?"

"Of course we made inquiries everywhere. But the couple who took her left a false name and address."

"But did you find nothing? No trace of her?"

"Nothing, Sonya. We found nothing. The world is a very large place."

"But, surely, Daniel—"

"Try to think about it logically, if you can. How could one find a girl who was brought to France as an infant, whose name was undoubtedly changed, and whose adoptive parents left no trace of their transaction?"

"But there must be some way of finding her!"

"I'm afraid there isn't."

Sonya stared into space across the chasm of time, envisioning possibilities that no one else would be capable of seeing. As if she were imbued with special powers. And then she turned her gaze on her brother, scrutinizing his face. "Do you know—did she and I, as infants, look alike? I know that some twins do and others don't."

"You were, from what Mother said, and from what I can remember, nearly indistinguishable. Of course, she and I could tell the difference."

For the first time since Daniel's arrival—for the first time since her mother's death—Sonya smiled.

Daniel knew that he would have no trouble finding a match for Sonya. She was, quite aside from her good looks, an excellent businesswoman. Despite their mother's long illness, Sonya had managed to keep the shop running, hiring more workers and winning an important new commission from the parochial school.

Daniel congratulated himself—and the blessed memory of his mother too—that they hadn't let Sonya run off to Argentina to live God knows what kind of life in the wilderness there. Well brought up, well protected, his little sister showed every promise of leading a life that was upright and good, a credit to their family. By any prospective mother-in-law's calculations, Sonya was a catch.

"I will find our Zaneta!" she said with all the optimism of someone who has yet to learn life's harshest lessons.

Taking his sister's hand in his, Daniel spoke to her as if speaking to a child. "I had a colleague in Paris hunt for her. He's very good, I can assure you." He tried to hold Sonya's gaze but she was looking off into the middle distance, her eyes shining. "The people, whoever they were, left no trail. Who knows whether they even lived in Paris? They might have come from anywhere in France—or even from one of the colonies."

Turning back to him, Sonya seemed about to burst with happiness. "But I have what no one else has, as a lure to anyone who knows her." She straightened her shoulders. "If we looked just alike as infants, we will look just alike now! I swear to you, Daniel—I will find Zaneta!"

How foolish women were, even the most competent of them, with all their romantic dreams! Daniel patted her hand. "Of course you will, Sonya. But first we must find you a husband. You, and Faya too."

KISHINEV TO SAINT PETERSBURG

1902

When Daniel was finally admitted to the bar, he and his wife Klara planned a big party, which Daniel especially urged Sonya to attend.

She could read between the lines of the letter he wrote to her. This party marked his entry into a new social stratum and a new life. He wanted Sonya to be there, but not their sister, even though he didn't say so explicitly. Far away in Kiev, at thirty-three, Faya had just given birth to her first child, a little boy. Daniel speculated that Faya wasn't likely to want to travel yet. He was similarly tepid in extending an invitation to Sonya's husband, Asher. Daniel considered him to be a wonderful fellow, and Asher had proven himself to be a worthy and reliable match for Sonya. But he was, in Daniel's estimation, a bit unpolished for the crowd of jurists and their wealthy clients he was gathering for his celebration—whereas Sonya, with her extraordinary beauty, would only enhance his status among them. His children, Daniel wrote, begged him to ask Sonya to bring her daughters with her—their cousins couldn't wait to show them Saint Petersburg.

Sonya knew she couldn't go to the capital without her husband—by all the rules of propriety she'd ever learned, it wouldn't be right. Sending her regrets to her brother and sister-in-law, thanking them for their kind invitation, she explained that she had scads of orders to fill for the Christmas season, and would be faced, as usual, with a shortage of help over the holidays.

Nonetheless, Asher found her sitting in their bedroom, one afternoon soon after she mailed her letter, staring out the window and sighing as the exiting sun stained the winter sky in shades of magenta and pale yellow.

"You want to go to your brother's *groys partey*, don't you?" Asher put his hand on his wife's shoulder. She reached across her chest to put her hand on his.

"Of course, I do. I know it's selfish of me, and wrong." She sighed again, very softly. "My life is here, with you and our girls."

Sitting down beside her, Asher turned her around to face him. "You were barely more than a girl yourself, when I met you, when I saw your beautiful face for the first time. And, *oy veh ist mir*, you were faced with this mug of mine for the first time."

Sonya loved how Asher could always make her smile. She looked with tenderness into his eyes, which seemed deeper and darker without his glasses. She touched his strong jaw and thought with a maternal sort of pang about whatever blow it was that had broken his nose before they met. For a boxer, Asher was an exceedingly gentle man, tender with Sonya and brimming over with affection for their children. Sonya knew that he would do anything to promote their happiness and protect them.

She leaned into him and he folded his arms around her.

"Do you think there's time," he whispered, "before the children wake up from their nap?"

She pushed away so that she could look into his eyes again. Perhaps the time had come, she thought, when the feelings she was meant to have as a wife would finally come to her—would flood her, as they had so long ago, under that streetlamp in the snow.

She nodded—then closed her eyes, parting her lips slightly. She wanted to hear that orchestra again—to feel her body awash in sensation. To feel ready on every inch of her skin for his touch. For his hands.

"Well, then!" He leapt up with that athletic grace he had, closed their bedroom door and unbuttoned his trousers, all in one movement before giving her a wet kiss on the mouth and then applying himself to unbuttoning her shoes. "How *do* you manage these, every day?"

Sighing again, but with a different feeling, she bent down to help him. There was a momentary frisson of the type she'd hoped for when, briefly, he held her stockinged foot in his hands. "That feels so good," she said.

"Ah, but this will feel even better!"

He lifted her into the bed and rolled over on top of her.

What she felt, she knew—she could tell—wasn't anything like what he was feeling. He groaned and sighed as if he'd just seen the face of God.

"Oy, Sonya! How did I get so lucky?"

She stroked his cheek, which needed a shave. There was something, she decided, wrong with her. Asher was a wonder of a husband, always kind and good to her. He recognized the business as hers, and allowed her to make all the major decisions pertaining to it. An excellent tailor himself, he did everything he could to contribute to their success. He didn't drink or go with other women. He was always gentle with their children.

There was something, Sonya decided, that was missing in her, or that had somehow gone wrong. She should never have allowed Jascha to kiss her! She would never know that feeling again—and it would always remain a girlish, unfulfilled longing that had nothing to do with marriage and mature love. Part of her was, and would always be, caught there, under that streetlamp, in the light-filled, falling snow.

Asher sat up, seeming as if he'd just been filled with air. "You will go—you and the girls!"

"Don't be silly, darling. It wouldn't do. And, anyway, what would I wear?"

"And this from the best dressmaker in Kishinev! What would you wear? Make something new! Something extravagantly beautiful. As beautiful as you are."

She was about to argue with him—and then stopped herself.

Why not go? Such an opportunity might not arise again. She might even be able to justify it, professionally. She thought of all the ladies she would see at the party, in all their finery. "I could make sketches of the clothes there. We might even expand our line, you know, to make our ladies more fashionable. More in keeping with trends in the capital."

"Another one of your excellent ideas, *mayn klug froy!*"

Sonya felt very grateful for Asher in that moment—there were precious few husbands, from what she'd heard from friends, who would be so generous and kind. She kissed him tenderly, looking at him with love.

She did love him. Those other feelings might well come, in time, as well as the courage to confide in Asher, even to guide his hands—to slow him down.

Looking in the mirror, pinning up her hair again, Sonya felt certain that they would be able to talk about those things that were so very private and yet so important to a husband and wife. She peeked over her shoulder to smile at him. "I should write to Daniel and Klara—send another letter, right away."

"I'll go wake the girls," said Asher. Enfolding her in his arms again, he added, "How did I ever get so lucky?"

৵

Asher helped Sonya, with Olga and a hatbox in her arms, onto the train—then hopped down and handed up Naomi. Then down and up again to carry their suitcases to their compartment and get them settled into their seats. He tucked a blanket around Naomi, who, fighting back tears, was holding tight to her favorite doll. Addressing himself to the doll, Asher admonished her to be good, eliciting a reluctant smile from his firstborn.

Both girls adored their papa. Naomi always wanted to show her drawings to Asher first, delighting in his affection and praise. And lately, whenever he read in little Olga's presence, she would crawl up into his lap and look at the pages with such focused attention that Sonya joked the baby was teaching herself to read. Once, Sonya found Olga with Asher's specs perched crookedly on her face while she stared at the front page of the newspaper. "It's not the glasses that confer the power, little one," Sonya told her. When she took the glasses away, Olga began to wail.

The whistle blew and the conductor intoned his announcement that the train was about to depart. Asher's eyes filled with tears, and both girls started crying, when he kissed all three of them goodbye.

Sonya, for her part, felt only a guilty sense of excitement.

᪥

When the train pulled into the Vitebsky station, there was Daniel waiting on the platform with Klara, their three children, and a darling old nanny in tow.

For Sonya, it seemed like a fairytale from the moment she stepped out into that palace of art nouveau décor, into a palette of colors she'd never seen. She was momentarily speechless, gazing up and around at the whimsical archways, the stained-glass paintings, and the vast cupola that rose far above their heads.

Daniel managed everything—enlisting a porter, giving instructions about their luggage, making sure they'd left nothing behind. Klara was all warmth and kindness. The nanny opened her arms to little Olga and took Naomi's hand as Daniel led the way to an elegant café, right there in the station.

Daniel procured what seemed the best table in the place, with its own chandelier. Plates of food began arriving, deep-red bowls of borscht and platters heaped with fragrant, thick hunks of rye bread.

"So many pieces of color!" said Naomi, looking with wonder at all the stained glass surrounding them.

"Oh, an artist!" said Daniel, giving Sonya a look of approval. "The architect responsible for all this magnificence is one of our boys, I want you to know." It clearly filled him with pleasure to introduce the wonders of Saint Petersburg to his sister. "Sima Minash—although you can bet he had the devil of a time getting his licensure."

Everyone talked at once. All of them laughed.

Klara had brought a heavy fur coat and hat for Sonya, and miniature versions of each for Naomi and baby Olga—relics,

Klara explained, from her own children's past, which she'd been saving for just such an occasion. After their meal, they all bundled into a carriage waiting for them on a wide and gracious avenue, next to what Daniel identified as the Vvedensky Canal, where the fat globes of the street lamps glowed in perfect orange reflections on the ice.

The cold made their winter in Kishinev seem mild by comparison. But they rode nearly as comfortably as if they'd been indoors. Sonya gazed out the carriage windows at the silvered branches of trees that lined the roads, the gigantic glittering icicles and, all around them, the parti-colored and gilded domes of what seemed an endless array of fanciful cathedrals.

Daniel's girls insisted on the zoological gardens for their first stop. Naomi and Olga were enchanted by the bears, lions, tigers, and an ancient elephant that turned a hand organ with its trunk while beating a drum and cymbals with its foot. Daniel threw copper kopeks through the bars of its enclosure, and the children squealed with delight when the elephant retrieved the coins with its trunk, passing them to its keeper.

Over the next few days, they saw palaces and parks, galleries of western and Russian paintings, and a mind-numbing display of gold and gems that served no purpose beyond attesting to their owners' wealth. There were rooms filled with jewel-encrusted tableware and jewelry made of diamonds as big as hailstones.

Sonya felt how she, her children, and even Daniel's very grand family were dwarfed, standing before Mikhailovsky Castle, below the equestrian statue of Peter the Great. The statue seemed to embody the endless, unstoppable power of the Russian tsars. In one palace, now a shrine, they saw a life-size wax figure of Tsar Alexander II, wearing the clothes he'd been wearing when he was killed, in 1881, by a bomb detonated on the streets of Saint Petersburg by *Narodnaya volya*, one year after Sonya and Zaneta were born.

As Sonya stood transfixed before the wax simulacrum, she wondered who had been tailor to this tsar. The clothes looked as if they'd been made somewhere in the West—and perhaps, she reasoned, no Russian would be trusted to hover with shears around the person of any member of the emperor's family. The statue, with its bulbous eyes and mutton-chop whiskers executed in such detail, seemed almost alive.

The message conveyed by this statue, and all the others, was that the tsar was indeed immortal, no matter how many bombs might be exploded in his path or bullets fired into his body. Kill one tsar and another one will rise up, as if by divine intervention, to step into his place.

Daniel was vocal in his belief that change was coming to Russia. But Sonya, without ever saying so, believed that her brother was, like their father had been, a hopeless dreamer.

༄

More pleasing than any of the monuments for Sonya was the chance to attend the Imperial Ballet.

Daniel had begun to serve as an occasional legal advisor to the up-and-coming ballerina, Anna Pavlova, who paid her legal fees, for the most part, with complimentary tickets. There were only ever two tickets at a time, so Klara stayed home with the children while Sonya accompanied her brother to the Mariinsky Theater, where they would see Pavlova perform in *Giselle*. "She's also one of ours," he whispered when they had settled themselves in their seats and the lights were lowered.

"Pavlova?"

"It's not generally known—and if it were, it would certainly jeopardize her career. Everyone knows she's the illegitimate daughter of a washerwoman. But what they don't know is that her father was a Jewish banker named Poliakoff."

"How much you know, Daniel!" Sonya hoped she never had a secret she needed to keep from her brother.

The houselights dimmed, the orchestra began to play, and the curtain rose. Sonya forgot about everything else, in thrall to the spell cast over her by the dancers, the sets, the costumes, the music, and something else she could only describe to herself as magic.

༄

At the party afterwards, Sonya felt more attractive than she'd ever felt in her lifetime. She saw several women with lorgnettes—and quite a few of the gentlemen—look admiringly at the dress she designed and made for the occasion.

"Let them wonder where you bought it!" Daniel whispered to her as he passed by with Klara on his arm.

Sonya didn't dance—neither she nor Daniel thought it would be proper. And she was grateful, really, because she'd never learned to dance. But it delighted her to watch the beautifully dressed couples swirling around the room in each other's arms. It was flattering to be asked to dance, several times, by gentlemen who didn't know or didn't care that she was Daniel's married sister.

Daniel's great surprise for Sonya and all his guests—and even Klara—was that Pavlova had agreed to come to the party and perform her famous solo from the third act of *La Bayadère*—"as a trade," Daniel explained in an aside to his sister, "because she spent all her savings on a three-month-long trip to Milan to study with a famous old ballet teacher at La Scala."

It was a revelation for Sonya to witness Pavlova's art at such close range, close enough to feel her own life, and time itself, obliterated by the ballerina's embodiment of the spirit of the murdered temple dancer, Nikiya.

The emotion evoked by the ballerina—wordlessly and yet without mime—seemed like nothing less than a miracle. Sonya found herself in tears at the end, and realized that she'd been transported somewhere completely outside herself. Outside of time. It was, she thought with some amusement, a feeling she knew she'd never be comfortable trying to convey to someone else, very much like the feeling she'd had from Jascha's kiss.

After Pavlova had changed out of her costume and held court for a while, surrounded by admirers, drinking champagne, Daniel brought his sister over to meet his guest of honor. Pavlova at first gave Sonya a perfunctory smile, but then looked at her with interest when Daniel mentioned that her tailoring shop, in the region where they came from, was widely known and widely lauded for the beauty and originality of her designs.

"Is that so?" Pavlova said. "Which of the Parisian couturiers do you prefer?"

"My sister hasn't been to Paris yet, Anna Matveyevna. But she's going soon."

Sonya had always believed in her brother's truthfulness. She blinked now, wondering whether this was some act of bravado—or a lawyer's machinations. She said nothing, waiting for him to say more.

But it was Pavlova who spoke first. "How very convenient!" She lowered her voice. "Kschessinska, that bitch, has eclipsed us at all the parties since she sent her dressmaker to Paris." She took both of Sonya's hands in hers. "When you go this season, you must watch the parades for me in the great fashion houses on rue de la Paix! Chez Paquin, chez Doucet. Madame Louise Chéruit... And there's another, I've heard, a newcomer who is creating a great stir at the House of Worth, scandalizing everyone."

"People in Paris have the leisure to be scandalized by clothing?" Daniel looked amused.

"Why, he practically gave apoplexy to our dear old fat Princess Bariatinsky with a coat he designed for her. She suggested that Monsieur Worth have him shot—but then all the ladies of Paris clamored for the same model. I don't recall his name. Paul something."

"How very convenient, indeed," said Daniel. "Sonya will survey all the latest designs—and confect a brilliant new dress for you on her return."

When Sonya just stood there, too surprised to say anything, Daniel touched the small of her back—and she bowed.

"I remember now: *Paul Poiret!*" said the dancer, glowing with happiness. "Oh, just wait till Kschessinska sees me at the next Winter Palace ball!"

In a bit of a panic, Sonya was about to explain that her brother was mistaken—she had no travel plans. But Pavlova had turned away from her, focusing her attention once again on Daniel. "You're worth your weight in gold, you know."

"I try to give good value."

He and Pavlova shared a look that made Sonya wonder if he might be something more than a lawyer to the ballerina.

Later, as she lay in bed, she remembered that look—and thought about how impossible it was for anyone to understand anyone else's marriage. All the nuances, complexities, and small disappointments contained in that space that could never be seen, not really, by anyone from the outside. She so liked Klara, and hoped that her brother loved her as well as he seemed to.

She thought about the casual lie he'd told to Anna Pavlova about Sonya's travel plans—and pondered whether people in Daniel's circle actually took such journeys, on the spur of the moment, as a matter of routine. Paris! In her mind, she saw it as a city entirely dedicated to haute couture, with dress and millinery shops everywhere and a populace of exquisitely attired men, women, and children.

Drifting off to sleep at last, Sonya resolved to confront her brother in the morning about that completely irresponsible promise he'd made on her behalf.

⁊

She found her brother in his library, poring over a huge book with very small print, working just as hard as if the gala of the night before hadn't ever happened.

He looked up at her. "I'm so glad you decided to come to our party! It was worth the journey, wasn't it?"

"Beyond my wildest expectations." She sat herself down in one of the room's comfortable leather chairs. "But what was that all about, that lie you told to Anna Pavlova? It's unkind of you to tease me."

"Tease you? I wasn't teasing you." Daniel took off his glasses, leaning forward on his elbows. "I know you've longed to go to Paris, ever since that day you learned the truth about Zaneta."

Sonya stared at him. "You meant what you said?"

"Of course, I did. Your husband can manage things for a few days, can't he, without you?"

"But, Daniel—" Sonya did a quick calculation. "The season there is about to start!"

Paris

1909

Taking the final steps two at a time, breathing hard by the time she reaches the doorway, Jeannette bursts into the attic dressing room with its rows of mirrors and *l'oeil de boeuf* windows, the slanting late-afternoon sunlight thick with rice powder. Every surface is littered with discarded makeup brushes, powder puffs and broken kohl pencils, pots of jewel-colored eye shadow and rouge, unattached wings, wreaths with missing flowers, and a garment rack crammed with tulle skirts that stir when she opens the door, as if filled with invisible dancers. The floor is an obstacle course of ruined tights and worn-out toe shoes, feathers and parts of costumes gone astray, and twenty or so ballerinas—some with patrons, some without—every one of them, it has seemed of late, younger than Jeannette.

One of her old colleagues from the Opera Ballet glances up at her, away from the mirror. "Still in your street clothes? You're going to get another fine."

Cold, even though the room is steaming, Jeannette feels as if she's moving underwater. She thinks again about the cousins she knew in childhood—how different all of them were from her and yet so like one another in the way they looked and even what they cared about.

The bells chime again: fifteen minutes till they need to be on stage, each dancer in place, every part of her posed, poised, and ready for the moment when the curtain rises.

Working with suddenly clumsy hands, she strips off her clothes, down to her corset—and turns her back to her friend with a wordless appeal to be unlaced. Her forest fairy costume is where she left it when the Russian maid interrupted Jeannette's preparations, filling her with such a glorious and stupid sense of hope that her life was about to change.

While she's putting on her makeup, it seems as if she's seeing two faces, one superimposed upon the other: her own, and that of the Russian seamstress. "It's mine!" she says inside herself, wishing she could make that thief of faces simply disappear. An image of the pretty little girl in Pavlova's dressing room flashes in her mind again. She wonders how it would feel to be loved by such a child. To be the center of the world for such a child.

After rouging her lips, she sucks on her index finger to imprint the excess color there instead of on her teeth—then wipes her finger off with a rag.

Jeannette takes a long hard look at herself in the mirror. She is the center of the world for no one.

She puts on her toe shoes, pointing and flexing each foot to make sure the ribbons are tight enough but not too tight, securing the knot on the outside of each ankle with a gob of spit. She knows she needs to focus—and needs to stretch before she goes downstairs again.

Snatches of music and random squeaks float up the stairway as the horn players puff and blow and the fiddlers tune and bow and do whatever they need to do before they play. And then the oboist coaxes out a single, pure A and all the musicians follow suit, adjusting and tuning until they find the same note and the sound of a single complicated instrument reaches the dressing room.

All the other chorus dancers are already warming up, using the garment racks as a makeshift barre. Several of them shriek when Vaslav Nijinsky leaps past their open doorway, his thigh muscles bulging in his white tights, the long curling hair of his wig and the chaste poet's blouse making him look like something in between a man and a woman. With his high cheekbones and Tatar eyes, he is the most exotic-looking male Jeannette has ever seen.

She would like to dance with him—to be lifted into the air

by him, as Pavlova is in their glorious pas de deux that seems like a dance between a man and a butterfly. Jeannette has never learned choreography like Fokine's, unmoored from the familiar tropes of ballet. The choreography for *les Sylphide* is doubly hard, because the chorus dancers never stop moving and every movement is interconnected. They're supposed to move like water. Like trees in the wind.

It's terrifying. So much that Jeannette could do with ease before is hard now. At twenty-nine, she already feels old. She knows that her jumps aren't as high. Her heart sometimes pounds so audibly that she dreads the places in the score when the orchestra plays pianissimo. Every night at home, after rehearsing for hours and hours, she plunges her feet, bruised and aching, into a bucketful of ice.

She spends far too much of her pay on ice. Just the night before, she was woken out of a dead sleep by a pain in her left knee so intense that it kept her awake, worrying. *Is it over? Am I through?*

She didn't have a single newspaper clipping that she might have framed and put on her wall. How often she'd fantasized about seeing the words: *A lively performance by demi-soloist Mlle. Jeannette Dupres... An expressive moment of tenderness in the pas de trois featuring...* Today she had thought, like a fool, that her moment had arrived, finally, and none too soon.

She is nearly used up now as a dancer, alone in the world, without a pension. Without a husband. She could have had a husband if she hadn't continued, with such naïveté, to believe that Paul Poiret would eventually marry her. That it was Jeannette, and Jeannette alone, he really loved.

She finishes her hasty warm-up with a *reverence*, catching a last glimpse of herself in the mirror, realizing with horror that she forgot to put on her wreath of pink silk roses. Pinning it as she scurries down the metal staircase, taking the last steps two at a time, she tries to seem invisible as she bolts past the regisseur, who is standing with his clipboard in the wings. He narrows his eyes at her and growls, "Ten francs, Dupres!"

And her rent is due!

The *Prelude* is at the second-to-last bar. All the other dancers are poised and ready in the twilight onstage when Jeannette runs on, lowering herself down as noiselessly as possible among the other members of the corps and the demi-soloist, all of them reclining at Nijinsky's feet, with Anna Pavlova posed adoringly on one side of him and Tamara Karsavina on the other.

Someone whispers something nasty-sounding in Russian. Jeannette tries to slow her breathing in the four seconds left to her before the *Nocturne* starts and the curtain rises.

Paris

1903

Paul Poiret was determined not to linger any longer than necessary in his position as junior designer at the House of Worth. Landing the job in the first place had been a coup. But now, in his second season, he found himself chafing at the bit, constrained by the institution's hidebound rules and his own lack of power. He had seamstresses at his disposal. But there'd still been no one assigned to help him accomplish those crucial and yet pedestrian tasks facing him as he oversaw the assembly of his newest creations.

And so Paul himself went to the Gare du Nord to meet the shipment of Canton crepe, organza, and Habutai silk due to arrive on the Nord-Express just hours before the showroom parade, when all the final details of his six ensembles would need to be actualized.

He told the cab driver to wait. He engaged a porter.

Cloaked in a cloud of steam, the Nord-Express arrived, by the station clock, just on schedule. Though Paul winced at the ear-splitting sound of the brakes as the great beast squealed to a stop, he was filled with the sense of excitement and pleasure he always experienced at train stations. His body was still aglow from the delicious lovemaking he'd enjoyed with Jeannette— and in less than twenty-four hours now, he would astonish Paris with dresses of an elegant simplicity that hadn't been seen since the time of the ancient Greeks.

His mannequins, all chosen for their slim figures, were indulging in their best-loved beauty regimes, so as to look their best. The seamstresses in his department were hard at work. He had every reason to hope for a triumph that would set the world of fashion ablaze. If he could save enough, and get his license by then, he would launch his own *maison du couture* in the fall.

As the steam evanesced, he waited at the place on the platform where he thought he'd have the best chance of seeing the baggage car unloaded—and making sure his specially commissioned bolts of silk weren't mistakenly or otherwise claimed by other hands.

And then he saw, staring out of one of the windows of a third-class carriage—inexplicably but unmistakably—Jeannette. Jeannette who, just hours ago, he'd dropped off at her flat. With an expression of wonder on her face, she was gazing out the window, straight past him, as if looking out at a magical landscape.

Oh, that devil of a woman! How in blazes—and why in blazes—was she on this train?

Forgetting momentarily about his bolts of silk, he hastened to the door of her car.

"Chérie," he said, removing his hat and handing her down.

She looked at him quizzically. "Pardonnez-moi, monsieur?"

And then he started laughing, overwhelmed by her cleverness. By God, he didn't think she'd had it in her to pull off such a prank.

"'Pardonnez-moi, monsieur?'" he minced, mocking her fake foreign accent. "'Monsieur,'" he repeated, laughing so hard that tears actually ran down his face, into his beard.

When she only continued staring at him wide-eyed, he stopped laughing. "Enough," he said in the same tone he used when a seamstress made the mistake of failing to follow his instructions precisely. He examined her ensemble, head to toe—it was an excellent simulation of a foreigner's idea of high fashion, very correct.

"Yes, it was funny and clever of you—and God knows how you got on this train. But I have work to do. Won't you be missed at your—whatever?"

She blinked—and then a tall and well-dressed, mustachioed man rushed toward them, pausing for just a moment to stare at something he held cupped in his hand. With an expression of relief, he looked up at Jeannette—and then, standing before her, ignoring Paul, he bowed.

With one long attentive gaze over her shoulder, full of curiosity but devoid of any sense of even knowing who he was, Jeannette turned away from Paul. She and the man—he looked like a banker or maybe a lawyer—started speaking together in another language. Was it German? It wasn't German, but it was something very like it. Paul realized that he was staring with his mouth open.

"Monsieur Poiret?" the porter said at his elbow. "The trunk has been unloaded—there."

The doors at Chez Worth would open in less than three hours. Paul absolutely didn't have time now to deal with whatever game this was that Jeannette was playing—or whatever game it was that fate was playing, if the woman actually wasn't Jeannette but someone else. Someone who looked exactly like her. The idea was strangely exciting.

"Make haste," he said to the porter. "We haven't a moment to spare."

ॐ

Sonya had trouble concentrating on what Monsieur Blum was saying to her—and was a little self-conscious that he was speaking to her in Yiddish as he apologized for being late.

So if this was Daniel's friend, René Blum, who was the bearded young Frenchman who'd greeted her with such familiarity and handed her down from the train just now? Was it possible—at this, her very first moment in Paris—that someone had just mistaken her for Zaneta?

Daniel had warned her, in a tiresome lecture, that Latin men were all unconsciously flirtatious—and that she had to take care not to encourage them in the slightest way. That unless she adopted a contemptuous mien in Paris, she was bound to be mistaken for a woman of easy virtue. But surely, she told herself, her brother had been exaggerating, out of concern for her safety.

She wasn't a child. The man had not been merely flirting with her—he'd spoken in a manner reserved for one well known and perhaps even well loved. She wasn't sure, but she thought he'd used the *tu* with her. She wished she'd worked harder at her French lessons! At the end of their brief exchange, he'd expressed exasperation. There was no mistaking it. And when she'd turned for the merest moment to greet the real Monsieur Blum, who was running toward her—looking up from a photograph he held cupped in his hand—the bearded man had disappeared into the crowd of Parisians on the platform.

Was it possible that the bearded man had mistaken her, Sonya, for a woman of easy virtue?

She burned with shame. How grateful she felt about Daniel's thoughtfulness and care in having his colleague and friend come to meet her! Kind Monsieur Blum took charge of everything, finding her luggage, whisking her off in a carriage to the small but very respectable hotel he'd arranged for her short stay in Paris. Telling her that he was at her disposal during her time there.

As he said *au revoir,* his eyes sparkled. She could tell that he, too, was flirting with her.

๑

Paul Poiret could hardly breathe for excitement as he sat looking out at all the titled ladies and their liveried servants in the packed showroom at Maison Worth.

The waiter, too handsome for his own good, passed out glasses of champagne. The various little dogs—just as well coiffed and nearly as bejeweled as their owners—trembled on the laps, and at the feet, of the crème-de-la-crème of Paris.

Paul was also trembling, although he hoped no one could tell. His entire future depended on an overwhelmingly favorable reaction to his designs today.

The elder of the two Worth brothers, Monsieur Gaston, possessed the commercial savvy to understand the value a forward-thinking designer could add to their enterprise as the newly born twentieth century struggled to its feet. But the younger brother, Jean, viewed Paul Poiret as nothing more than an upstart—a *louse,* he'd called him—who would damage their reputation as the dressmaker of choice for the crowned heads of Europe.

But that's what Gaston had, in effect, hired Paul to do—create designs for the everyday activities engaged in by the new century's women of fashion, who didn't only go to balls and soirees, but also rode the omnibus.

A buying frenzy evoked by Paul's ingenious little dress with its vertical pleats was bound to send Monsieur Jean into one of his fits of nervous dyspepsia. Paul had come within a finger's breadth of being sacked when that foul Russian princess heaped scorn on his magnificent kimono coat. But then all the beauties of Paris showed what a fool she'd been—and Monsieur Jean took to his bed for a week.

Oh, the sweetness of revenge! How Paul wished his loathsome first master, the umbrella maker who'd tortured his youth, could be here now to see his triumph!

But would he triumph? He watched as all the titled ladies peered through their lorgnettes at his dresses, whispering among themselves. If only he could hear what they said! What he would give to be a fly hovering just above one of those wrinkled décolletages! He hadn't seen a single critic yet. But the critics mattered far less than the word of any one of these grandes dames. Would they clasp him to their sagging bosoms so that all the young ambitious ones, the beautiful ones—the social climbers—would be pounding at his door every Saturday night, from here on in, begging him to concoct a new creation, especially for her, on time for the Sunday races at Longchamp?

Paul raised his eyebrows, seeing Jeannette walk in. She walked right past him.

He was sure she'd told him of a class or rehearsal that would prevent her from attending the opening today. Secretly, he'd felt relieved. He didn't like mixing business with pleasure. He didn't want to have to worry about what Jeannette might say or do.

He didn't recognize her ensemble. Was it new? She was walking strangely, a little clumsily. *Was* it Jeannette?

༄

Sleep-deprived and overwhelmed by so many new sensations, Sonya felt far from her best and brightest by the time she reached the last of the fashion houses on her list. The parade was already in progress at Chez Worth. There wasn't a single vacant chair in the rows arranged along each long side of the showroom. Her feet hurt from all the walking she'd already done in the beautiful shoes she'd bought the day before, with their steel-cut toes and three-inch heels. But faithful to her mandate from Pavlova, she was prepared to stand and suffer.

Although she worked hard at taking in each detail of each mannequin's ensemble, she found her attention wandering. She hoped they'd walk through more than once, as was done at the other houses she'd already visited that day. She had a small sketchbook hidden in her reticule, in case there were too many innovations to commit to memory—although she knew well enough that she'd be shown the door if she were caught making sketches of the designs. She limited herself to making notes in Russian with the gold-embossed pencil she'd been given at the entrance, along with a printed sheet that listed each dress by name.

She drifted off in a fantasy that Zaneta herself was on the stairway in one of the designers' ensembles. Their eyes locked. Both she and Zaneta were, momentarily, unable to move. And then Sonya, in her daydream, ran toward her twin, enfolding her in her arms, unleashing in her a heretofore unrecognized flood of feelings of relief, enlightenment, and love.

The real scene before her eyes shifted into focus again. The last mannequin swept downstairs and the parade, as she'd hoped, began again. The room was stuffy. Sonya felt unbearably thirsty and hoped refreshments would be served. Six of the dresses seemed quite different from the others, different from any dresses Sonya had ever seen before. She took notes—and then allowed her gaze to wander from the line, examining the faces and the outfits of the other women who'd come to inspect the clothes.

They all looked very grand and imposing. Some of them were well past the age of coquetry but not yet done, apparently, with fashion. There were a lot of lap dogs, and there was more than one liveried servant standing behind his lady.

One of these grandes dames received a message from her chauffeur and got up to leave, nodding first at an elaborately decked-out, bearded gentleman who lounged on a leather fauteuil at the far end of the room, near the door. Sonya slipped into the vacant chair, hoping that her relief at being able to sit down wasn't overly obvious.

She stole a look at the bearded man in his throne-like chair, which must have afforded him the best view of the scene in its entirety. With a jolt, Sonya recognized him as the man who'd handed her down from the train. Who had, against every rule of gentlemanly behavior, spoken to her, even though they hadn't been introduced. Who had—and now she blushed—perhaps insulted her with his overly familiar greeting.

Here he was again! She ducked her head, hoping he hadn't seen her. He must, she realized, be one of the brothers Worth, either Monsieur Gaston or Monsieur Jean. She had assumed they would be much older men than the man who sat lounging there, exuding the casual sense of entitlement of a young prince of the realm.

But then two older men, impeccably and conservatively dressed, entered the room—and everyone, including the bearded young man, rose to greet them with polite applause.

Sonya reasoned that the younger man must be one of the Worth's designers. Could he be the one, that Paul Poiret, who'd been singled out by Pavlova as someone whose designs for the House of Worth she especially wanted Sonya to see?

When the waiter offered Sonya a glass of champagne, she accepted gratefully. Before he walked past her, she put her empty glass on his tray and took another.

She was so terribly thirsty. It must have been the pickled

food she'd eaten at supper the night before, in a Russian cafe. Or the dust from the streets as she walked today, unable to determine where the omnibus stopped but often finding herself behind the omnibus in the wake of dust and horses.

She cautioned herself to drink slowly. Her head was already spinning. And suddenly, now, she felt so very tired—and so out of her depth. If she could just close her eyes for a moment—could just rest them for a moment from the sight of all these swirls of color, these mannequins who looked too perfect to be real. This creamy murmur of French voices and French smells. These bubbles teasing her nostrils. The sense of destiny creeping up behind her—her destiny upon her.

꙳

It was clear to Paul by the time his last mannequin made her graceful way down the stairs—it was evident from the widened eyes, licked lips, and escaped words of the grandes dames—that his dresses would be the talk of *le tout-Paris*. So much for the withering comments and dire predictions of Monsieur Jean! In six months' time, it would be Paul Poiret, with modest gestures of gratitude, receiving the accolades and applause in his own showroom.

When the parade at Maison Worth was over, the bookkeeper had the devil of a time writing down all the orders for Paul's designs. Paul was giddy with exhaustion by the time the last carriage had carried away the last devotee of fashion and he'd shooed the last mannequin, sometimes with a pat on her pretty derriere, into the dressing room to change and go home.

What a triumph for him! Every one of those titled ladies was hastening back to a grand house in the seventh arrondissement to rest and change for dinner—to stand before a mirror and imagine herself in one of Poiret's dresses. Perhaps to think about eating only soup. Yes, telling the cook that tonight, and all the nights of this week, she will eat only soup. No bread.

Paul looked over at Jeannette, collapsed on a chair in the corner, her shoes off, an empty champagne glass toppled on the carpet beside her.

And then he looked more closely. This wasn't Jeannette! Her hair was different, as was her body, for the love of God. This woman was softly rounded where Jeannette was taut and tight. How could he, with all the expertise of his gaze, have failed to notice?

And yet this stranger was so like her, with Jeannette's heart-shaped face and graceful neck, deep-set eyes, and delicately sculpted nose. Long-fingered hands that were precisely like the hands he knew and loved so well, the fingers he'd kissed a thousand times.

Careful not to wake her, he lifted the hem of her skirt enough to be able to study the slender feet encased within the sheer ivory-colored stockings. There was the distinctively long first toe, sure enough, and the ballerina's improbably high arch and slender ankle. But the toes were straight and smooth, unmarked by any of the insults and injuries suffered by Jeannette's feet during her long years of dancing in toe shoes.

Could it be that Jeannette's doppelgänger—for what else could she be?—shared her sensual proclivities? Paul could hardly breathe. Could it be that fate was rewarding his hard work and perseverance not only with this professional triumph, but with the bonus of a second, slightly different version of his *petite amie?*

Moved almost to tears, he cupped her unspoiled left foot in both his hands, first caressing the arch with his thumbs. She moaned. He had to use every bit of self-control he had, and he knew he didn't have much, to keep himself from running both hands up her leg. He didn't want to wake her—not yet. So he caressed, very gently, a little bit more, with all the expertise he'd acquired in worshipping Jeannette's body.

The lovely creature sighed a sigh that ended in another little moan.

He darted away from her just as she was waking, pretending to busy himself with the order book, giving her time to get her shoes back on and set her clothes to rights.

"Please excuse me, monsieur," she said with that wonderful accent.

His heart was thumping. "Ah, mademoiselle," he said. "I didn't realize anyone was still here."

"Madame," she corrected him. She sat with her hands folded in her lap, looking very prim and proper, very unlike Jeannette. It was adorable.

"I am Paul Poiret," he said, with a smile. "Would madame perhaps like another glass of champagne?"

She shook her head no.

Paul wondered how much French she spoke—for, of course, he realized, she was the same foreign person who'd so confused him at the Gare du Nord.

With pleasure he was hard pressed to conceal, Paul sat down in the chair next to hers. Even at that distance, he could sense the heat radiating from her body, inside her many layers of clothes. He stole a look into her eyes—Jeannette's eyes! "Who are you?" he asked in a whisper.

He could see her struggle as she labored to find the right words and string them together in the right way. She bit her lip, and then she said, "I am the long-lost twin of the person you have mistaken me for. Please, Monsieur Poiret, I beg you! Tell me her name!"

Paul turned away from her then and had a long stare out through the beveled glass of the front doors, onto what was the sudden calm of the rue de la Paix.

A single carriage rattled by.

He could not have made up a more delicious fantasy. Turning back to this magical creature—this apparition—he realized the importance of proceeding with the utmost caution. "My dear, lovely madame," he said, "I'm afraid I have no idea what you're talking about."

໖

"I must go," Sonya said, feeling herself blush.

Speaking with what she hoped sounded like the haughtiness of a well-born Parisian lady, she added, "Forgive me, monsieur, for delaying you."

"Forgive you? Why, madame, I would be delighted to be

delayed by you for hours and hours. Do you have dinner plans?"

What was the right way to respond?

Sonya hardened her face in the way Daniel had instructed her to do, looking past the designer, out at the fading daylight. "In fact, I do have plans, monsieur," she said carefully.

Her mind was racing.

What if this was her sole chance of finding out Zaneta's whereabouts—and Sonya passed it up out of fear? The very thing she'd hoped for seemed to have happened, just as she'd imagined it might. And Paul Poiret was clearly lying to her, feigning not even to recognize her from the station. There was no doubt in her mind that he'd mistaken Sonya for her twin.

"But what a shame," he said. "Could your plans, by any chance, be changed?" He took Sonya's hand, brushing it with his lips.

Sonya snatched her hand away and sat up straighter, gazing furiously outside again. *Think!* she told herself.

Without doubt, Anna Pavlova would want Sonya to curry favor with the designer, perhaps to convince him to make a dress or a cloak for the ballerina, who was so well known and so well loved.

He looked like a gentleman. But *was* he a gentleman?

And what was she? There were limits to what she'd do for a patron, even so grand a patron as Anna Pavlova. Were there limits, Sonya asked herself, to what she'd do to find her sister?

"Perhaps, monsieur," she said in a measured tone, "my plans tonight could be—re-evaluated."

୨ଚ

Paul smiled. It was, unmistakably, a Russian accent underneath her very proper schoolgirl French. Most alluring. "Let me know where you're staying—and I'll send a carriage."

"Absolutely no!" she said. She looked just like Jeannette when she got mad! It was immensely touching. "It is good for me to navigate myself in Paris," she added in a friendlier tone. "If you will tell me where to meet you..."

How delectable she was, thought Paul, in every way. And

what an amusing contrast to Jeannette, who loved nothing more than having a carriage sent for her. So alike—and yet so different. "Well then, if that's your preference, Madame— Madame—?"

"I am Sonya Danilov, Monsieur Poiret."

"*Enchanté*, Madame Danilov!" said Paul, inclining his head in a little bow. "Eight o'clock. Will that suit you?"

He presented her with the business card for a petit restaurant where he knew there was no chance of meeting Jeannette. A place he often reserved for rendezvous with other women whose company he enjoyed from time to time.

ॐ

The maître d' seated them at an intimate table set slightly apart from the others—away from the window, half hidden behind a stand of elaborately braided money trees.

They started with oysters and champagne. Sonya drank too slowly for Paul's impatient sense of what he hoped would happen. So unlike Jeannette, who loved champagne and drank it as easily as water. Sonya asked for water.

"I have a great thirst in Paris," she said.

Everything she said seemed luminous, to him, with portent and charm. "Yes, Paris does seem to have that effect upon people." His eyes stole from her face, to the base of her throat—then, caressingly, all down the length of her arms to her hands, as he slurped his share of the oysters, one by one.

Sonya raised her still-full wineglass to the success of Paul Poiret's label when he launched it, as he said he hoped to, in the fall—and began to tell him about her client, Anna Pavlova.

He took pains to appear to be listening with minute attention. He nodded and made listening noises, grateful that Madame Sonya Danilov couldn't hear what he was thinking.

Their main course arrived. Paul had recommended the *poulet rôti* with its accompaniment of tiny onions, cloves of garlic, and new potatoes basted and browned in the fat that dripped from the slowly turning chicken rubbed with rosemary, salt, and thyme. *Poulet rôti* was one of Jeannette's favorite dishes. Because

Jeannette had an intense dislike of broccoli, Paul ordered a side of broccoli for Sonya, telling her that the chef here prepared it in a special way. He was filled with the excitement of a scientist in his laboratory.

Sonya ate slowly, with evident delectation, as Paul looked on, paying scant attention to his own dinner. She left the broccoli untouched. He had to keep himself from shouting out, *Eureka!*

"You are one of a set of twins, you say?" He topped up her glass of Burgundy, poured out the rest for himself, then called the waiter over and ordered another bottle of the same wine.

"Identical twins, from what I've been told," she said, as if the fact were of little import. She was watching his face, studying him just as minutely as he was studying her.

"How overjoyed your parents must have been."

"Zaneta, my twin, was blue and cold when she was born. But the—I'm not sure what the word is for a woman who assists at births."

"Midwife," said Paul.

"The midwife—what a good word that is in French!" Sonya looked triumphant every time she managed to convey her thoughts in this language she was evidently so unused to speaking. "The midwife placed Zaneta next to me, wrapped up in a blanket by the stove. Later, when she found us—I was holding my sister close, embracing her, and she was warm again. She came back to life in my arms."

"What a moving story." Paul's eyes were wide. He thought for a moment before adding, "I can only imagine the gratitude your sister must feel."

"I am ignorant of what she feels, or even if she still lives. We were separated, you see, as infants. Our mother was unable, briefly, to support us—and placed us in... Again, it seems, I don't know the word. The place for children without parents?"

"An orphanage," said Paul in a hushed whisper. He saw her taking in the significance this had for him—and warned himself to do a better job maintaining his opacity.

"An orphanage, yes." Sonya paused, letting the word sparkle

in the air between them. "It was meant to be for a short time only. My sister, however— Am I using that word correctly?"

He nodded, eager to hear the rest of her story. "Possibly so. It is a conjunctive adverb—but that's neither here nor there. Your sister, you were saying—"

"My sister, however, was given by mistake to a French couple who had come to adopt a baby girl. They left a false name and address."

Sonya's eyes, so precisely like Jeannette's, reflected the light of the votive candle flickering on the table. Paul said, "How extraordinary!"

He tore his gaze away from her, impatient for the waiter and the wine.

"Nothing is known of them," she said. "Not their name nor where in France they came from." She looked gratified to have his gaze on her again—perhaps to feel her power over him. He saw the care with which she was striving to maintain the balance of power between them—a balance that could, at any moment, shift.

The waiter appeared with another bottle, which he uncorked. He gave the cork to Paul, who sniffed it and nodded. Sonya was watching this ritual as if she'd never witnessed it before.

With the confident and exaggerated gestures born of long practice, Paul vigorously swirled the bit of wine the waiter poured out for him in the bowl of his glass before inhaling deeply. Then, with closed eyes, he tipped his head back and tasted it. "It's good," he said, nodding again before taking charge of the bottle and dismissing the waiter. He smiled paternally at Sonya. "I'll wait till you finish what you have before I pour you some of this."

"I'm sure I won't need more," she said. And then, noticing her glass was almost empty, she drank the final sip of wine, and it seemed as if she was tasting it for the first time. She closed her eyes briefly.

Paul was imagining her face in the throes of physical ecstasy. Would it be similar to Jeannette's—or would it be completely different, given the difference in their histories and experience?

"But you ordered a second bottle of the same wine, isn't it so? I do not understand the need to repeat—" She made a timid imitation of swirling and sniffing her empty glass.

Smiling, Paul gave her a generous pour—then filled his own glass. "Two bottles, even of the same vintage—made from the same grapes at the same time—can nonetheless be subtly different, depending on the physical circumstances of their vinification and how those bottles have been stored."

"I see," she said, seeming to puzzle over the words.

"Of course," he added in a low, intimate tone, "it takes a connoisseur to recognize such differences."

Paul was inflamed in more ways than one—uncomfortably so, to the point where he considered excusing himself to take care of it. "For dessert," he said, "I would suggest the bitter-sweet chocolate *pot de crème*. They do it very well here."

ও

Sonya couldn't remember ever having eaten quite such a delicious meal, and so completely to her taste. Well, the broccoli was a misstep, but otherwise he'd chosen flawlessly. There had been times, especially during the winter months, when she'd felt capable of selling her children for some dark chocolate.

She noted, as her surroundings seemed to move subtly up and down, and the ambient sounds of the restaurant receded and then returned again, how quickly she was becoming more and more adept in French.

"You introduced yourself as madame," Poiret said to her, "and yet you're very young."

"I have two children."

"Indeed! Forgive me if my question seemed impertinent—"

"All your questions seem impertinent."

"Ah, but you'll forgive me, won't you?" He gave her a smile that was so kind and caring that she felt herself wanting to trust him. "I was only wondering," he said, "whether it was an arranged marriage."

"Yes, it was in the same year my mother died. My brother

arranged the marriage, but I agreed to it. To him." Sonya felt herself blush again.

"Arranged marriages are the tradition among certain families of the upper classes in France," said Paul, "those who wish to consolidate their wealth."

"In Russia, my family is not here—" She gestured high above her head. "But here." She lowered her hand till it lay flat on the table. "I and all my family are Jews."

"By some estimations, that is very much part of the upper classes."

"Perhaps in France, Monsieur Poiret. In Russia, the Jews are always menaced by people's hatred, especially in bad times."

"One fact does not obviate the other. Was this man your brother found for you to your liking?"

"He is the father of my children."

"But do you love him?" he asked, taking another sip of wine.

Sonya looked at him steadily, not replying. Until finally, she said, "You ask very personal questions, monsieur. Very—how do you say it?—impertinent."

"You have a gift for language, don't you? I would give anything to speak Russian as beautifully as you speak French."

Sonya placed one hand over her glass when he tried to pour out more wine for her.

Changing course, Paul announced that he would create a dress or cape especially for Mademoiselle Pavlova. A model that would be the envy of every woman of fashion in Saint Petersburg.

"You are too kind, Monsieur Poiret."

"Please call me Paul."

She looked at him with as much an expression of wounded propriety as she could dredge up at this late hour, and in her present state of tipsiness. "But how can I, monsieur? It is not as if we were old friends."

He and Zaneta were, without doubt, intimate friends. Sonya felt a pang of jealousy—a feeling she'd never expected to feel where her twin was concerned. Did Paul Poiret look at

Sonya and see a used-up married woman, devoid of sensuality? Whereas Zaneta—what was Zaneta like?

Was Zaneta in love with this Paul Poiret? He was so full of himself, so worldly and charming—so willing, it would seem, to betray her.

Resentfully, Sonya licked the last bit of chocolate off her spoon. What if she, and not Zaneta, had been the baby plucked out of the crib that day? She tried to imagine a completely different life for herself.

And then Paul reached across the table and took her hand in his. "Such lovely, long-fingered hands!"

She looked down at his hand caressing hers. His thick-fingered, strong-looking hands. Without fuss, she slid her hand out from under his and touched her hair. "I'm very tired," she said.

"Of course, madame," he said. He signaled the waiter for the check.

As Paul helped her get into her coat, he told her that he would be hard pressed to have his creation for Pavlova ready on time for Sonya's departure. He had some silk Shantung in mind. Perhaps Sonya would advise him as to the appropriateness of the color for the dancer's complexion.

"Tomorrow, of course—yes," she told him.

"But I will have to begin tonight."

The air outside was bracing. "Although my skills are modest, Monsieur Poiret, I am dressmaker enough to know that one can't see colors accurately by lamplight."

"I have special lights," he said. "An entire bank of mercury-vapor lamps. Have they not come yet to Saint Petersburg? Night work is a necessity for fashion designers here. We must be ready to respond, at all hours, to the urgent whims of the ladies."

Was there no end to his self-regard? "I leave it to your intuition, Monsieur Poiret. Without doubt, you will choose just the right colors for Anna Pavlova."

Standing in front of Sonya, with an appraising eye and the

expertise of his trade, the designer resettled her coat to make it hang just perfectly from her shoulders. "But the gift will be so much better chosen if the choice is made by both of us." In a voice that was suddenly hoarse, he added, "Together."

"Please call me a cab."

"We'll share one," he insisted.

Sonya realized that she had no idea how far they were from her hotel, or even in which direction it lay. With instructions from the concierge, she'd walked a few blocks, then taken the omnibus to the restaurant, or very near it. A kind old man, after scratching his whiskers for a moment, had pointed out the way. She'd arrived early enough to freshen up a bit beforehand. She actually didn't know if the omnibuses continued to run late at night. Was it late? Just then, as if in answer to her question, a church bell started tolling.

"Taxi!" Paul called out to a passing carriage. "Come, come," he said, handing her up as if the question were already settled.

Seating herself in the opposite corner from the couturier, as far away from him as possible, Sonya counted as the bell tolled, eleven times in all. She gazed out the window at the lights of Paris. At least he was keeping his hands to himself.

The horses' hooves clip-clopped on the cobblestones. Sonya pressed her forehead against the cold window, to keep herself awake.

When the carriage stopped, she saw that they weren't at her hotel, but just in front of Maison Worth. Did he live there? The street looked very different now than it had during the day. "Thank you so much for the delicious dinner, Monsieur Poiret," she said. "I'll come by early tomorrow to look at the fabric."

He got out of the carriage—but then extended his hand to her. "If you please, it will take but a moment to show you the fabric I have in mind. I'll tell the driver to wait."

❧

Paul Poiret's eyes were shining in the dark like those of a hungry cat.

Sonya weighed the alternatives. She could refuse his request—but then she might well miss out on the chance to win the ongoing patronage of Anna Pavlova and who knew how many of her friends and rivals in the ballet world. And then there was the issue of Sonya's chance now, perhaps her one chance, to make Poiret give up what he knew about her twin.

After all, she'd profited from her good looks, in everyday and insignificant ways, to get what she wanted throughout her life. It didn't make her a woman of easy virtue, or anything like it. She'd learned the art, through the years, of letting men appreciate what they saw in her, without behaving improperly.

Sonya answered the designer with a sideways glance at him. "I'm curious about those work lights you mentioned. What are they called again?"

"Mercury. Vapor. Lamps. Another boon brought to us by the Americans." His face broke into a genial smile. "I'll be happy to give you a demonstration. They'll need a few minutes to warm up."

She extended her hand and he helped her down from the carriage. There was something electric in his touch.

Sonya could still conjure up the feeling of Jascha's fingers when they had brushed up against her hands and wrists, so long ago, at his father's pharmacy in Kishinev. Her innocent hands. She could still, after all these years, remember how her body felt when he'd kissed her.

Poiret unlocked the large double doors of the fashion house and then led her upstairs through the darkness. At the press of a button, an array of lamps hanging down from the ceiling began to flicker. A long worktable glimmered into view as the light grew and glowed with the strength of four little suns.

All sorts of decorations hung from the edges of the table—silk ribbons and embroidered tassels, pieces of fur and fringes of leather, primitive-looking clay beads, seashells, semi-precious stones and feathers of every texture and hue—items that might be used to lend the finishing touches to one of the couturier's fanciful designs.

Serious and solemn, Paul unrolled several meters of three different bolts of patterned silk, one after the other, walking down the length of the table as he did so.

Perhaps, after all, Sonya mused as she watched him, she had no cause to feel guilty about letting herself be lured, so late at night, into the designer's lair. Pavlova would be so impressed when Sonya returned with a garment custom-made by Paul Poiret himself!

Sonya had never used such fabrics before in her own shop. She had never even seen such fabrics. She wondered where he bought them—or if he commissioned their manufacture.

"That one," she said, touching the cloth that was the color of pomegranates and sunrise streaks shot through with light, the darkest tones of which were an urgent, intimate magenta. Of course, she chose that one! She wasn't thinking about Pavlova's complexion when she chose it, although the shade would suit her well. The hue matched the dried flower Jascha had given her, the one Sonya kept enclosed within the silk pouch her mother had stitched for her so many years ago, long before Asher had come into her life. Long before Naomi and Olga were born.

Suddenly remembering her husband and her daughters—realizing she'd quite forgotten about them—Sonya put her face in her hands. "I'm afraid I'm going to be ill," she said. "I drank too much wine."

"Here, sit down!" Paul led her to a fainting couch upholstered in sapphire-colored velvet and festooned with a red pillow. He brought her a glass of water. And then, after she leaned her head back and closed her eyes, he unlaced and slipped off her boots.

He took her feet in his hands, one at a time. "I learned this from a Chinaman," he said. "A remedy for nausea."

Sonya turned her face away from him, resting her cheek against the soft nap of the velvet. She tried not to think—to shut off the stream of shaming, disapproving voices that played in her head. Concentrating on the touch of Poiret's hands on her feet, she kept her eyes closed, biting her lip to prevent herself from moaning with pleasure.

What deliciousness! *You have gone completely mad,* she told herself. A sensation of tingling warmth crept from the soles of her feet and up the inside of her legs. She pretended not to notice when he unhooked her stockings and removed them, all the while caressing and massaging her feet with an expertise that made it seem as if he knew exactly what she felt, at every point of contact between them. A little moan escaped her—and his hands, his wonderfully skillful hands, crept higher.

She bit harder on her lower lip, determined not to make another sound.

He was holding her now. Cradling her. And when his deft fingers worked their way up to that most secret place, as if arriving there by accident, she felt herself yield to him—not so much to him, but to the exquisite pleasure wrought by his touch. Rubbing, just there, where her own body, as if in defiance of her, grew moist. He rubbed her there with increasing urgency, echoed by her own fast-beating heart and ragged breathing.

And then she shuddered, and it was over. And before she could collect herself enough to push him away, he was inside her.

ာ

Paul didn't rush to move his hands up Sonya's legs but stayed focused on her feet, knowing each place that would please her most—rolling his fists in her arches, rubbing the secret little tunnel beneath her toes and in between them, stretching out the tops of her feet with both thumbs moving in opposite directions just as he'd learned to do, over the years, guided by Jeannette's delighted and helpless moans. How different were the feet of these two women who had started life as mirror images, each of the other!

His heart was beating fast and he felt a little faint, thinking about all the discoveries that awaited him, hidden in the mind and flesh of Jeannette's identical twin.

How wonderful and rich was this life of his, offering up

at every turn such rare and delightful treasures. In just a few weeks, Denise Boulet would achieve the age of eighteen and her parents would permit their marriage. How pleasant it would be, he thought, to have a little wife at home. Someone docile, sweet, slim, and unspoiled who could serve as his mannequin. Who would give him children—and was sufficiently unformed that he could make her into anyone he wished her to be.

His genius, Poiret knew, lay in honoring a woman's sensuality, whether he was designing her clothes or making love to her. What a fool Sonya's husband must be, to ignore the bud of this rare flower that slept every night beside him, just waiting to burst into blossom. How shortsighted were those men who thought only about their own gratification!

Just after he entered her, a vision appeared in his mind—a mantle of black tulle, draped over a gown of black taffeta hand-painted with a floral design. Yes, irises! He held on to this vision until the glorious moment of release.

Gently, decorously, he arranged the fabric of Sonya's skirt around her and gave her a handkerchief to dry her tears and whatever else needed drying. She wept like a virgin, although, of course, she hadn't been. He felt a pleasant sense of satisfaction that she had, despite her tears, enjoyed herself.

As soon as he'd put her into a carriage and came back inside, he began sketching out the black taffeta dress. It would be the garment that would launch his career.

Paris

1909

Pavlova turns to her maid, demanding to know where she found this doppelgänger of her seamstress.

"In the big dressing room, Anna Mateyevna!" Crossing herself again, Zlata adds, "What can it mean?"

Vassily Zuikov, Diaghilev's valet, speaks up from the hallway. "She is Jeannette Dupres, one of the coryphées for the Paris Opera. We hired her as an extra dancer for *Les Sylphides*.

"*You're* well informed," Diaghilev mutters.

"She's uncommonly pretty!" the valet mutters back at him, caressing the waxed tips of his black moustache and raising his eyebrows behind Sonya's back.

Little Baila, holding her mother's skirts around her like a curtain, waits till she has the valet's attention and then sticks her tongue out at him.

"Well, never mind," Diaghilev says. "Come, come," he adds in his public voice, clapping his hands at everyone in a bid to dispel any chaos lingering in the room.

Taking note of the tunic with its double row of straight pins, Pavlova looks with horror at Sonya. "It's not done yet?" When Sonya doesn't answer but only stands there in a daze, Pavlova shouts, "Have you gone deaf?"

Diaghilev seems to notice Sonya for the first time since she got up off the floor. He takes a closer look at her through his monocle, as if to check for signs of disease before approaching her. "There, there, *courage*, my dear," he says, leading her, with her little girl in tow, to one of four chairs ranged around a table littered with playing cards, cigarettes, and coins. "You'll be able to get this done in no time, won't you?"

Sitting, holding her daughter close, Sonya looks up at the impresario, his jet-black hair sporting a stripe of pure white, his waist cinched in and his clothing perfectly elegant and in style.

From her lower vantage point, Baila notices that one of his shoes has a little gap at the front, where the stitching attaching it to the sole has started to come undone. She wonders if his socks get wet when he walks through puddles. Because she knows this secret about the big tall man, she feels rather sorry for him. She wonders if it would be all right for her to give him some of the coins that are scattered across the little table. She wonders if anyone would notice if she picked up one or two of them for herself. She is thinking about the darling little puppy she saw for sale on the rue des Rosiers.

"Do you have a sewing basket here?" the big tall man says to her mother, speaking as if he were speaking to a child.

Baila, at the right level to notice, retrieves what she recognizes as one of her mother's sewing baskets from underneath the dancer's dressing table.

"What a lovely little girl you are," Pavlova says. "Come here, dear."

Baila watches her mother start to thread a needle. Then doing what she's seen countless ballerinas do, both in Paris and Saint Petersburg, she walks up to Pavlova and drops a little curtsey.

"Charming," says the dancer, taking a chocolate bonbon from a lacquer box and dropping it into the child's hand. "Perhaps you'll be a ballerina one day."

Baila retreats behind her mother's skirt again to savor her prize. She is a little afraid of Madame Pavlova. But she likes the big man with the stripe in his hair and the broken shoe. The chocolate is the most delicious thing she has ever tasted.

Sewing and pulling out pins as she goes, Sonya says to the impresario, "Can't someone please go after her, sir? I've been waiting for this moment for such a long time!" She uses the back of her hand to wipe away the tears that are welling up in her eyes. She wishes someone had offered *her* a chocolate.

"There is no need, madame," says Diaghilev. "Your sister will be keenly aware of the honor she's won in getting this job, dancing on the same stage with the great Pavlova."

The ballerina steals a look at herself in the mirror and raises her chin just a little, which makes her neck look even longer.

"But if she doesn't come back—" says Sonya, gazing out into the twilight of the corridor.

"She would not think of missing the dress rehearsal," Diaghilev assures her, "any more than she would think of failing to show up on payday—which isn't, by the way, till next Friday. You'll have ample opportunity to speak with her."

The dancer turns away from the mirror. "Shall we get you a ticket for one of the performances, Sonya? And one for your little girl?" Baila peeks her head out again. "Hello, darling," Pavlova says to her. "Do you speak French?" she asks her in Russian. Baila nods.

Using her best and smallest invisible stitch, Sonya is making short work of attaching the bias-cut patch she cut out, ironed, and pinned earlier in the day. Looking up, she says, "I would love to attend a performance!" When Baila tugs at her sleeve, she adds, "Both of us would."

"Excellent," Diaghilev says. "Vassily, see that it is done."

Just then, the regisseur, reeking of cigarettes, pokes his bald head in at the door. "Good evening, Madame Pavlova," he says, exhaling two serpentine trails of smoke from his nostrils as he bows. Squinting one eye, he scans the dressing room for any possible projectiles within the star's reach. "Mr. Fokine would like to respectfully request—" He puts his hand on the doorknob and says over his shoulder, "that you allow Madame Karsavina adequate time for her bow, at the end of *Cléopâtre*."

Pavlova stamps her foot and swears, first in Russian, then in French. The regisseur shuts the door behind him just in time to avoid getting beaned by one of the ballerina's toe shoes.

‹›

As soon as Sonya is finished with the repairs to Pavlova's

costume, she hurries home with Baila, barely paying attention to the child as they make their way through the welter of carriages and pedestrians—ignoring the headache that has blossomed since her collapse in Pavlova's dressing room.

Yes, she keeps telling herself—*I was right all along! She lives. She lives here!* And then, *My God, she's a dancer! How amazed Mother would have been!*

In the same instant, she realizes that she must have also been right, that day when she'd first seen Paul Poiret at the train station—when he'd first seen *her.* It's too awful to contemplate all the lies he's told her since then—and how willing she was, in the end, to believe him.

Zaneta, in the flesh. How beautiful she was! How glamorous.

Bursting through their door with Baila, Sonya sets about putting together an omelet for the children's supper. She doesn't fix anything for herself but retreats to her room with some hot water and a sponge. What to wear? She puts on her best dress, another sample that Paul had given her. She finds a very old pot of lip rouge—and sticks her head out the door to ask Naomi if she can use her paints.

"My paints, Mama?"

"Your paints, child. Hurry up, please. Some brushes too."

It's much harder work than she might have thought. But when she's done, at least by candlelight the effect is just about what Sonya hoped it would be. She finds a length of silk and, just as Paul had done when designing on a model, she wraps it turban-style around her head. She puts on the pair of gold earrings Klara lent her for Daniel's big soirée and then gave to her again, for keeps, when she left them to live in Paris.

Really, the resemblance now is astonishing. Sonya waits till the bell tower chimes eight—and then opens the door just enough to call out, "To bed now, you three!"

"But what about our story?" Olga wants to know.

"Aren't you going to kiss us goodnight?" cries Baila.

"Tonight you must kiss each other goodnight. Olga, tell your sisters a story."

"Can't we see you?" asks Naomi with a hint of mischief in her voice.

"I need to go out briefly. I'll come in and kiss you as soon as I return. But," she adds, "you had better be asleep by then."

All three girls run to the window and look out after Sonya leaves, trying to catch a glimpse of her on the street below. All they see is an elegant lady, clutching at her turban and running as fast as she can in high-heeled shoes in the direction of the Saint-Paul Metro station.

"Is that Mama?" asks Baila.

Naomi clucks her tongue instead of answering no. In just a year, she has come to sound and look exactly like a French girl. She wonders what her mother is up to. She shoots a look at Olga, warning her to say nothing.

❧

Sonya knows that Paul will be at dinner at this hour, either at home with his family or out with friends. As she hoped, Émile Rousseau, his bookkeeper and business manager, is working late and lets her inside when she rings.

"Madame Jeannette—" he begins in a less than friendly tone of voice. And then he recognizes Sonya and clears his throat. "I beg your pardon, Sonya. My mind was on my ledger books. Monsieur Poiret isn't here."

Sonya's heart is racing. "Oh, how silly of me!" She wishes he hadn't recognized her so quickly—but now she has the confirmation she needed. Paul knows about Zaneta—he knows Zaneta! He has known all along and he has kept this knowledge from Sonya.

She would like to strangle Paul Poiret, to see him die a painful death. "I came to see if—" Her voice trails off as a couple more pieces of the picture fall into place. "I came to see if I could borrow—the evening bandeau I was working on the other day. The one with the aigrette made of spun glass."

She can see Émile's mind working, trying to discern whether the name *Jeannette* had meant anything to Sonya. She wants to leave, as quickly as possible. She wishes she had never come out tonight—wishes now that she didn't know. "But perhaps I'm deluding myself to believe that I can wear such an elegant thing without appearing ridiculous! I see now, Émile, that my idea was a mistaken one."

"But, au contraire, Sonya, I can picture you precisely in that headdress. If you'll forgive my boldness in saying so, I believe it would be particularly stunning when worn with Monsieur Poiret's midnight blue evening dress; the one with the empire waist and diaphanous sleeves. I predict there will be half a dozen new orders for the dress after you've worn it." He pauses. "You are going somewhere special tonight?"

"Yes," she lies. "I've been invited to a rather grand soirée."

Sonya thinks, *Why not take the dress and never bring it back? No matter that it's one of the newest and most expensive models.* She deserves her revenge—she deserves much more than this. What Paul owes her is incalculable.

What a fool she had been, to believe his tale—to doubt the certainty of her intuition, from the very first moment he'd spoken to her at the Gare du Nord. Her certainty that he'd mistaken her for her twin.

What was it, she wonders, about powerful men that makes them feel entitled to satisfy their urges, without the slightest bit of consideration for the wreckage they leave in their wake?

Sonya can't bear now to look backward, at her own wake—to think about Baila. To think about Zaneta and Paul. To think about Asher! She tells herself she will deal with all these feelings later. Right now, she must look straight ahead.

She smiles demurely at Émile Rousseau, a man whose probity she trusts. One of those rare trustworthy men. "If you really think he would approve the idea."

"I'll just fetch the garments in question…"

"No need, Émile. I'll wrap them up myself and go home again to change. It wouldn't do to show up at a Ballets Russes event with shopping bags, would it?"

KISHINEV

1903

Sonya was called into the shop by one of the new assistants she'd hired on her return from Paris. "It's the priest's girl," said Ana.

"She's hardly a girl!"

Ana shrugged. "I can't very well say 'the priest's woman,' Sonya Morisovna. It would sound quite improper."

Sonya smiled. She liked Ana. It was gratifying to have such competent, kind, and pleasant people working for her, especially now. She was expecting Asher to arrive home that night with new rolls of velvet from Turkey. Having grown up speaking Yiddish at home, unlike Sonya, he had proved himself very useful in the matters of these international buying expeditions. Thanks to his industry and hers, their shop was becoming known as the best place to buy coats and hats in Kishinev, for all the people of means, both Christians and Jews.

It was Easter Sunday and the shop was officially closed, in accordance with the Christian laws. The rush of orders for the holiday had all been filled on time. Ana's mother had allowed her to come in nonetheless after attending church. She was there to tidy up while Sonya balanced the account books and made an inventory of what they still needed to buy for the upcoming season.

She made sure Naomi was comfortably settled with her scraps of pattern paper and the bright red box of chalk crayons sent from America by Lev and his wife for Naomi's fifth birthday. Signaling her to be careful not to wake her baby sister, Sonya tucked the covers up around little Olga's shoulders before stealing a glimpse at herself in the mirror.

She was sure now—she'd missed two periods. She would tell Asher tonight. She knew he would be overjoyed. She looked at herself and thought, "Who are you?" And then she tucked a lock of hair behind her ear and walked out through her sitting room into the shop.

Her old schoolfriend, the priest's housekeeper, appeared to be more than usually discomfited. "Please, Sonya…" She looked pointedly at Ana.

"Could you give us a moment, dear?" As Ana put on her hat and coat and stepped outside, the little bell above the door rang merrily. "Whatever is it now, Masha?"

Masha took a folded-up edition of the *Bessarbets* from her coat pocket and held the front page out for Sonya. The headline, in bold type, read *Death to the Jews!*

Sonya read without touching it. "I'm always glad to see you, Masha. But did you really think it was necessary to disturb me in my work today with this—news? That rag of a paper is always publishing such hateful screeds."

Masha, because of her twisted spine, was almost a head shorter than Sonya. Still she managed to assume a pose that made her look of equal size. "The Holy Father received a visit this morning from Tchemzenkov."

"The police chief? What of it? He probably came to make confession."

"I assure you, Sonya, it was nothing so benign." She lowered her voice. "They are planning an action against the Jews—a pogrom!"

Sonya had grown up with frightening tales of the pogrom in Kiev on another Easter Sunday, in 1891, when she was still a little girl, close on the heels of the pandemic, when so many lives had been lost, including her own father's life. Scores of men had been murdered, for no crime other than being Jews. Their wives and daughters were raped, their houses demolished, and children were torn screaming from their mothers' arms.

But that was all long ago. "Surely not, Masha! The mayor

himself is a friend to the Jews of Kishinev. His wife is one of my customers."

"I listened at the door. Tchemzenkov urged the Holy Father, in so many words, to offer dispensation to any who commit acts of revenge today against the Jews."

Revenge! For a beautifully tailored coat made from the finest imported cashmere? For a silk hat that could be worn proudly by a grand duke?

Sonya looked around the shop she and Asher had worked so hard to make into a lovely, welcoming place, filled with the tools of their trade. The gleaming, gilt-inscribed sewing machines and quilted taffeta dressmaker's dummies from Paris. The hat blocks lined up on their shelf beneath the worktable. The silver scissors of many sizes hanging neatly on their hooks, and the scrolled irons on their racks above the fire in a newly built ceramic stove. Where the finest etched tea glasses, ensconced inside their silver filigree *podstakannik*, were always at the ready near the samovar. Where customers stood before the floor-length triptych mirror while one of the kneeling assistants made measurements and Sonya wrote them down. Asher often sat cross-legged on the table in the light from the shop window, doing the hand-sewing for which he'd achieved a degree of fame in the village where he came from and had been, along with his good nature and small fame as a boxer, the source of the matchmaker's recommendation. Finished hats stood perched atop tall poles, and hundreds of spools of colored thread were on display in their glass-fronted cabinet like wildflowers on a hillside. Papier-mâché French-made hatboxes lined the upper shelves. The cutting tables were always kept meticulously clean and the stove had a fire burning in it day and night so that customers would never feel the cold.

"I'm sure you're mistaken. This is the twentieth century. The world has changed."

"You are one of the very few people in Kishinev, Sonya Morisovna, who has ever been kind to me. And I have kept from you the terrible things I have overheard people say…"

"Well then?"

"I will not allow you and your children to be slaughtered like lambs!" She pulled a ring of keys from her pocket and shook it so that the many keys rattled. "You mustn't stay here. They are planning to smash all the Jewish shops—and as many Jewish heads as they can find."

"Hush! You'll lose your post—and then what will you do?"

Masha came up close to her, so close that Sonya could smell the garlic on her breath and a faint whiff of the tobacco Masha was in the habit of stealing from the priest's study. "He's fond of you, Sonya. He told me once that the attic of the church would be a good place to hide, if your family was ever in danger."

Sonya was about to speak when a very singular sound reached their ears, above the sound of a passing cart and the distant sounds of singing or shouting—it was hard to tell which. Exploding suddenly in the air, there was the noise of breaking glass.

"Hurry, Sonyuschka—it's begun! Rouse your daughters! Take their coats and some quilts." Masha was holding her head in both hands. "No—leave the quilts. I'll bring them to you later."

It was shouting, not singing—Sonya could hear it clearly now. She flinched as if she'd just been stuck with a pin when another crash of breaking glass reached her ears. "What about Asher? He's not coming till tonight."

"Leave a message for him, somewhere—but don't, for the love of God, leave word about where you've gone. Hurry!"

Sonya's hands were shaking so badly, she could hardly hold the piece of chalk. She couldn't think what to write. Finally, she wrote, *We're safe.* She couldn't think what else to say without compromising Masha. And then she made a cross, the Russian cross, at the bottom of the note she committed to a remnant of black cloth left over from a mourning coat they were making for the baker's wife, who was newly widowed. Later she thought what an unlucky choice that had been—and even whether it meant that she herself was to blame for what happened afterward.

৯৶

With some water and food Masha smuggled to them—with their quilts and a chamber pot tucked under the eaves—Sonya and her daughters hunkered down in the attic of the church, in the smell of dust and mice, waiting until Masha came to tell them it was over.

Would it never be over? Sonya ran out of stories to tell her children. Her voice grew hoarse from singing the same bedtime songs over and over again. While her daughters slept, she hovered as close to the window as she dared, looking out at the horrors unfolding far below.

Her gratitude for this place of safety was mixed with a bitter taste of guilt, worrying about her Jewish neighbors and friends. Worrying about Asher. Praying he had also found a place to shelter.

Her nerves were so frayed that she spanked Olga when she wouldn't stop crying. Naomi, horrified, demanded to see her papa. Sonya wished for him then, wished that he were there with them—that she didn't have to face this alone with their two little ones.

Would the rioters wrest the truth from Masha—and come for them in the attic of the church? How long would they be locked up here? What if Masha failed to come again with more food and water? What of Ana and the other assistant? Would they run home to their parents? Were their parents part of the mob? Had Sonya herself, through her own guilt and dread, somehow made this happen?

She held her children close and vowed to be a better person, a better wife and mother—to be worthy of the blessings God had given her. How she wished she could turn the hands of the clock backward and undo what she had done, so thoughtlessly and recklessly, in Paris.

Dawn was just breaking on the third day when Sonya heard Masha's whistle from the stairway. She roused the children and put their coats on. Masha peeked in and whispered, "Come quickly." And then she led them down the stairs and out the little door onto the alley, urging them to hurry away as swiftly as possible.

Sonya held Olga tight and led Naomi by the hand. Looking first to the right and then the left, making sure no one saw them, she walked out onto the boulevard, telling her daughters they'd see their papa soon.

All the shops and houses owned by Jews had smashed windows. The pharmacy, where Jascha had once worked at a lab bench behind the counter, had anti-Jewish slogans painted on the jagged edges of what was left of its plate-glass windows. Her heart beating fast, Sonya walked gingerly, finding a path for herself and her children through the shards of broken glass that seemed to have brought the blue sky down to the ground.

Furniture that had never seen the light of day was strewn over the sidewalks, tipping over into the gutters. Cushions and pillows had been slashed open. The sun shone through a haze of horsehair and goose feathers. Eiderdown clung so thickly to the trees that it seemed as if the branches were coated in hoarfrost. The acrid smoke from gilded picture frames and scorched family photos mingled in the air with the ashes of beautifully printed books and scrolls. There were parti-colored broken bottles and jars under the street lamp where Jascha had kissed her, on that winter night, so long ago.

Sonya tried not to make eye contact with the policemen who were hosing blood off the sidewalks, into the gutters. How many of her friends and neighbors had been wounded? She prayed to be allowed to find Asher, whole and unharmed, waiting for them at the shop. She hoped the shop itself had withstood the mob, perhaps even, somehow, escaped their notice. The sound of weeping and wailing came from the cavernous windows, seemed to come from the skies themselves.

And then they walked past the courtyard of a building that had once been a small, Jewish-owned furniture factory. Instead of furniture, the workshop was filled now with the bodies of men, women, and children, laid out on blankets on the floor. They were only partly covered by the bed linens draped over them as makeshift shrouds. The marble-white faces that showed were contorted with looks of horror. Their heads were bruised and bloodied, their broken limbs stuck out at odd angles.

Hardly able to breathe, Sonya rushed the children past, hoping they hadn't seen what she had seen, in a glimpse: Asher. Oh, the look on his face! She held Olga tight and gave Naomi a shove, directing her gaze up to the trees. "Look at the branches, child," she said, her voice quavering. "The feathers—it looks as if it has snowed."

He was dead. Asher was dead. It couldn't be!

The windows of their shop had been reduced to bright shards on the cobblestones outside their door. The threshold was stained with blood. Sonya recoiled from it, whimpering, knowing that it was her husband's blood.

In an instant she understood that he had tried to stand up against the mob, to defend what was theirs—his fists against their crowbars and cudgels, his death a testament to the fierceness of the love he felt for her and their children, and a wish to be her hero. How foolish she'd been to think he'd be there, safe and sound, waiting for them. How horrible she'd been to abandon him in his danger, only thinking about herself and the girls. But that was always her way, wasn't it? Always thinking about herself, as she'd done in Paris.

Her guilt was intermingled with the realization that she was, at twenty-three, a widow now. A widow with two young children and another on the way. She'd been harboring the news of her pregnancy for him, the hope that she would, this time, give him a son. She had prayed it would be his son.

Never in her entire life had she felt such despair and such a sense of self-loathing. The little bell above the door was hanging at an angle, like a songbird caught in some netting and left to die.

The morning sun shone through the gaping windows, but Sonya was shivering so hard that her teeth chattered.

Everything was in ruin—the mirrors smashed, the furniture ravaged as if attacked by wolves. Every time she pressed her hands against her eyes, trying to staunch the flood of tears, she would see Asher's winsome smile and the way he'd so often looked at her, his eyes filled with gratitude and love. She hadn't deserved him. He wouldn't have loved her if he'd seen who she really was.

What would become of her and her daughters—and this baby growing inside her? Where could they turn?

Her sewing machines, dented and cudgeled, were sunken into their cabinets, separated from their treadles. Unwound spools of thread and bobbins, multicolored tangles of bias tape, and crumpled pieces of pattern paper were scattered everywhere.

Who were these people—these neighbors and merchants, these men she'd wished good-day, who'd tipped their cap to her and tousled Olga's curls? Who were these monsters who had murdered her husband and left her children without a father, destroyed their shop, leaving Sonya and her children without a home?

The glass in the frames that held their family photographs was shattered. The photographs had been ripped into pieces, along with all the leather-bound books that had filled their shelves. Asher's books!

What could cause people—the normal, everyday people of Kishinev—to suddenly turn so hateful? What had she and Asher ever done to offend them? Hadn't she always been a good neighbor and friend? Wasn't her shop always a lovely, welcoming place, where Jews and Christians alike drank glasses of tea while Sonya confected beautiful clothing and hats for them? Hadn't the mayor's wife, delighted with her new cloak, kissed Sonya's cheeks and told her that she was one of Kishinev's treasures?

She bent down and picked up a pair of Asher's glasses, crushed by someone's boot. Close to her ear, she heard Olga murmur, "Papa!"

The curtains were hanging in tatters from the broken windows. The beasts had ripped her fine linens from the beds and used her dressmaking sheers to slash the mattresses open. One pair of sheers, engraved with her name—a gift from her mother—was left on the floor, the two halves wrested apart. There were goose-down feathers everywhere.

Sonya's dresser drawers were all pulled out, dumped onto the floor, the wood crushed, their contents mostly gone.

Everything that mattered to her, save her children, had been ruined or stolen.

Reaching underneath a pile of torn-up silk and a twist of yarn with two button eyes, little Naomi found and retrieved the dried magenta flower given to Sonya, so long ago, by Jascha. "Here, Mama," she said, handing it to Sonya, who only sobbed harder.

PARIS

1909

Tamara Karsavina tried to take a philosophical stance about Anna Pavlova's ridiculously late arrival in Paris. Dancing in her idol's place, Karsavina had won accolades throughout the company for the gracious way in which she'd stepped into the always tricky role of prima ballerina. The management was pleased with her. The press was already buzzing about her. And she did the work that needed to be done, working harder than she'd ever worked before, always striving to maintain an aura of kindness and good cheer.

All of this was accomplished under the most difficult circumstances—more than the usual share of last-minute changes, involving a slew of new choreography that needed to be mastered. Rehearsing in a theater that was under construction, sometimes being exiled to a rehearsal space under the eaves that was more fit for salamanders than dancers. Eating, when the dancers were given time to eat, on packing crates backstage. And yet, throughout all of it, she loved the camaraderie of her classmates from the Mariinsky School, which helped her make light of their backbiting, their occasional ill will, and the jealousy of the other dancers who envied her success.

Now that Pavlova has arrived, she will take back what is hers, and Karsavina's triumph with the Ballets Russes will be nothing more than a glimmer in the dark sky, a star that burns brightly for a moment, only to disappear. With some trepidation, she knocks at the prima ballerina's dressing-room door, the same room that she herself so lately occupied.

A woman's voice, not Pavlova's, answers, *"Entrez!"*

Packing trunks and hatboxes are piled one atop another,

folded clothes are stacked and strewn everywhere. A slim, dark-haired woman stands with her back to the door, holding a petticoat up to the light before folding it neatly into an open trunk.

She turns and Karsavina bursts into astonished laughter. "It's you!" she says in Russian, grabbing Sonya's hands and pressing kisses on her cheeks—left, right, left.

"Tamara Platonovna!" Sonya is flattered that the dancer, so big a star now, remembers the sweet connection they made, the year before, in Saint Petersburg, when Karsavina was still a student at the Mariinsky School.

"I can't believe it's you," says the dancer. "Do you live in Paris now?"

"I do. Madame Pavlova asked me to put some things in order for her, before she leaves."

"She's leaving?" Karsavina looks giddy with relief.

Sonya holds a finger up to her lips and glances out into the hallway, quietly closing the door behind her. "It's because of you," she says, her voice almost a whisper. "She's very jealous of you. Regardless of what she says, that's the reason why she's leaving."

"After such a small number of performances?" Karsavina's face is suffused with happiness, although she's doing her best to conceal it.

Smiling fondly at the ballerina, Sonya asks, "Do you still have that dress I made for you?"

"It is my favorite. I've worn it so much, it's now in tatters. Every time someone complimented me, I have lied shamelessly, saying it was bought for me in Paris." She pauses. "Should I have said that I got it from you?"

"Absolutely not, my dear. Not for a dress with the Paul Poiret label. Won't you sit?" She lowers the lid of one of the packing cases, and they sit down, side by side. "I don't want you to think I make a practice of stealing the work of other dressmakers," says Sonya. "In fact, I've sewn that label into clothes I've made just three times—and not for profit, I can assure you. My motive was rather one of revenge."

"Did Monsieur Poiret wrong you?"

"Grievously, I'm afraid."

"You know, before we met," says Karsavina, "I concocted an elaborate story to explain your presence in that little shop window on Zagorodny Prospekt—and the perpetually sad look in your beautiful eyes."

Sonya blushes. "And what was that story?" She wonders whether the ballerina, so effusive and intuitive, might not have guessed what everyone else so far has mercifully failed to see.

"It seems so silly now. I'm ashamed to tell you—"

"But I want to hear!"

"I imagined that you had fallen in love with a Christian. And that your father cursed you and sent you away, forever to be exiled from your family as well as your religion."

Sonya takes a deep breath, straightening her shoulders. "My father died when I was only ten years old, in the flu pandemic of 1890. He was a bit of a radical, and my family was only minimally observant, which did nothing to spare us, of course, in 1903."

"Did you come from Kishinev then?"

"My husband, Asher, was murdered in the pogrom. My family's business was destroyed. I had two young children and another on the way."

Karsavina's eyes well up. "Forgive me!"

"There's nothing to forgive. I always enjoyed seeing you, in your student days, when you passed by my little shop window. After Asher died, my brother Daniel set me up in Saint Petersburg and introduced me to Pavlova."

"Will you go with her when she leaves?"

"No. I intend to find my own path, here in Paris."

Karsavina beams at her. "And have you met someone special here?"

Sonya smiles back at her but doesn't answer the question. A great deal of gossip preceded Tamara Karsavina's arrival in Paris. Apparently, Fokine, the company's handsome young, and now-married, choreographer, had for years been hopelessly in love with the beautiful ballerina. Her mother prevented their marriage, holding out for someone with better financial prospects. Karsavina was wed, not long ago, to a middle-aged banker. But there are whispers everywhere that Fokine is still in love with her.

Sonya says, not unkindly, "I've heard *you* have a husband now."

"Yes, I'm married now—and I'm doing my best to be a good wife." She does her best to smile but gives herself away with a troubled sigh.

"Can you keep a secret?" asks Sonya.

"I hope so." This perks the ballerina up again. "Of course, I can."

"I traveled to Paris, at the beginning of 1903, thanks to my brother and also Pavlova, who wanted me to look at the fashions for her. But the real reason was because I wanted to find my sister—my twin sister—who was separated from me when both of us were put in an orphanage, briefly, during our infancy, while my father was in prison and my mother wasn't able to support us on her own."

"Did you find her?"

"Just two days ago. After six years of searching, always hoping to meet her. Never succeeding. And then, coming face to face with her—right here, in this doorway!"

Karsavina claps her hands in a mime of ecstatic applause. "That's the most romantic story I've ever heard! How thrilling for the two of you, to find each other again."

"It was thrilling for me. She didn't know about me, you see. She still doesn't, really. I don't know what she thought, seeing me like that—a stranger who clearly looks just like her. She looked fairly horrified—and ran away."

"But you've arranged to see her again? You know how to find her now? Who is she?"

"I only know that she was hired as an extra dancer for the company. She has a French name. I doubt she even knows she's Russian—or that she's Jewish. Monsieur Diaghilev has arranged for me to attend the performance tonight. And he assures me that she won't leave the Ballets Russes before your run is through."

"Sergei is usually right about such things." Karsavina's eyes and smile are so bright that it seems as if stage lights are always shining on her. "Your secret is safe with me!"

Sonya sees in the young dancer a potential friend and ally in this place that's so far away from Russia, filled with people who can't be trusted. She takes the ballerina's hand in hers and looks into her eyes. "I have another secret," she tells her. "One much deeper and darker." She has an urgent desire to tell her all about Paul Poiret's unforgivable perfidy. She'd sworn to herself she'd take the secret to her grave—and yet how it presses against her heart now. What a relief it would be to have a friend to share the burden with her.

Karsavina slips her hand out of Sonya's and stands up—then busies herself with smoothing the fabric of her skirt. She's thinking about Diaghilev's secret—the one that Dr. Bodkin explained to her, that day they drove out together to Versailles. The secret that has made her feel so uncomfortable ever since. How hard it is to reconcile her love and esteem for Diaghilev with this ghastly knowledge about his sexual habits! What a blockhead she'd been, almost willfully blind throughout her years at the Mariinsky School. Those boys she'd surprised in dark corners and closets, hastily pulling up their tights or wiping their mouths. She burns with humiliation now, knowing what she's learned from Dr. Bodkin but still unable to make any sense of it. High society in Paris teems with such people, both male and female, it would seem, who lust for others of their own gender, in defiance of everything sanctioned by God. Bodkin says it's love, nonetheless—they can't help the way they are. They're still as good and kind and worthy as others—and as vulnerable, maybe more so, to feeling hurt and rejected. They are also children of God.

She forces herself to smile again—and, in the same instant, wonders whether she'd been mistaken just now. There's nothing about Sonya that reminds the ballerina of those other women, most of them wealthy, who've fallen in love with her—and whose attentions Diaghilev, irrespective of her feelings and always desperate for money for his enterprise, has begged her to encourage or, at least, not to discourage.

Sonya has no idea what it is that caused Karsavina to jump back as if burned. Nonetheless, she experiences a sense of relief that fate, or whatever it is, has kept her from so very nearly exposing her daughters, and especially Baila, to her shame. What if her words had reached Zaneta's ears, at this most crucial and delicate time? Sonya would have sabotaged what she's worked so hard—and sacrificed so much—to achieve.

What a fool she was, on the verge of blurting out her secret to someone she hardly knows! Most dancers are gossips. Why would Karsavina be any different, despite her endearing manner and innocent eyes? Friendship and trust have to be nurtured, slowly and carefully, over time—and no one but family, in the end, can really be trusted. She thinks of Daniel. Sometimes, even members of one's own family can't be trusted.

Sonya sits up straighter, looking past the dancer at the dressing-room door. She still has a lot of work to get done. The last thing she wants is for Pavlova to find her closeted here with her rival. Sonya has no need of Karsavina's friendship, now that she's finally found her sister. Zaneta will be the friend and ally that Sonya has always longed for.

Jeannette, she corrects herself. She needs to remember now to use her sister's French name, probably the only name she's ever known: Jeannette. It's pretty similar to Zaneta, a clever transliteration from Russian to French. Sonya wonders whether Jeannette will even remember the name she was given by their mother.

Karsavina, perhaps having second thoughts about whatever it was that offended her, looks contrite. She sits down again, and places her hand on Sonya's shoulder. "I'll keep an eye out for your sister, now that I know she's dancing with us." She looks with fondness into Sonya's deep-set, mournful eyes, admiring, as she'd done from the first day they'd met, her porcelain skin. "I'm certain I can help find a way to bring the two of you together again."

☙

Sonya's eldest daughters are united in their outrage that little Baila will get to go to the performance with their mother while they are to be left at home. Eleven-year-old Naomi says it's unforgivable that Baila, who cares nothing about fashion, will be there among all the ladies in their finery, at the biggest social event of the season—Baila, who couldn't describe someone's dress or hat if her life depended on it. Who would pass over a designer frock from Louise Chéruit for one of the stray kittens that ate out of garbage cans in the Marais!

Nine-year-old Olga clears her throat, then says in her perfect French, "But this would present an ideal opportunity for me, Mother, to make the acquaintance of a grande dame who might be in need of a mother's helper."

"You are *my* helper, Olga."

"Don't pretend that we don't need the money."

"Hush, my child. Remember your age, please. You sound more and more like an old woman every day."

"I'm suffocating here, in this mean apartment, with these children!"

Both Sonya and Naomi are trying as hard as they can to suppress their laughter.

Sniffing, Sonya takes Olga's face into her hands and looks into her near-sighted eyes, which so resemble Asher's. In the six years since his death, Olga has grown to resemble him in so many ways. He would have been very proud, thinks Sonya, of this bookish, brilliant, and ridiculously precocious child. "It was an accident that Baila was invited to go this time, instead of one of you. But there will be other opportunities."

"There will be only one Saison Russe," sighs Naomi.

"I'll try get some backstage passes from Madame Pavlova. You'll be able to see the costumes and sets then, up close." She's thinking about the likelihood of finding Zaneta backstage, among the other dancers. Perhaps, in a way, it will be easier if she has all three of her daughters with her. How could their aunt possibly resist them?

"Oh, will you, Mother?" cries Naomi. "You're an angel!"

Olga suddenly looks like a nine-year-old again, on the verge of tears.

Sonya hugs her. "I will watch everything very carefully to-night, my little wordsmith—and I promise to tell you every detail about all the people I've seen and heard, as soon as we get home. All the society gossip! All the outrageous things the artists do." When Olga looks up at her hopefully, Sonya adds, "You and Naomi can wait up, if you want to."

Baila tugs at her mother's skirt, her eyes wide. "Will that lady be there tonight?" she asks in a whisper.

"Who, Mother? Who is she talking about?" Both Naomi and Olga want to know.

Sonya touches the tip of Baila's nose. "She will be on the stage tonight, but looking very different than when we saw her."

Sonya assumes an expression that her children recognize and honor, one that says, *Don't speak to me now!* A faraway, fierce look that always makes them afraid that she isn't who they thought she was—and they might, at any moment, lose her altogether.

What wouldn't she give, Sonya wonders, to have Zaneta in her life—that other self, that self outside herself, who will nonetheless understand her as no one else can? What wouldn't she give, or give up, to feel as whole as she must have felt during those months that she and Zaneta existed side by side, both be-fore and after they were born, until they were so rudely ripped apart?

She has been dreading her thirtieth birthday. Now she won't have to face it alone. Although she's not even sure she believes in God, Sonya prays that Jeannette will be on stage that night, as Sergei Diaghilev promised.

PARIS

1903

Paul insisted on the blindfold, once both he and Jeannette were ensconced inside the hired carriage. She knew by now not to argue with him when he wanted to involve her in one of his romantic escapades, which were always slightly mad but lots of fun.

"I know you'll laugh at me," she said as Paul tied a teal blue silk scarf over her eyes. "But I've left my corset behind, in the dressing room. There was no one there to lace it for me—and your note was so urgent!"

"There is no need for Madame Gaches-Sarraute's instrument of torture," he assured her, "where we are going today."

Jeannette took a deep, unconstricted breath. It was a lovely feeling to be in street clothes, for once, without a corset. "But *where* are we going today, my love?" With her eyes covered, her sense of smell was suddenly keener. She thought she smelled food—and then, unmistakably, she heard the sound of a cork eased out, with expert care, from a bottle of champagne.

"Are you thirsty, after all your *battements* and *pliés?*" He placed her hand on the stem of what felt like a champagne glass.

The bubbles tickled her nose. "Both thirsty—and famished!"

She drank. Paul lifted her skirt and placed his hand on the smooth flesh of her inner thigh, just above the rolled-down top of her stocking—but no higher.

"I have wonderful news," he said. He kept his hand where it was.

They hit a rut in the road that splashed champagne all down the front of her blouse. "*Merde!*"

"Don't worry yourself. Here, let's unwrap that beautiful body of yours."

"Oh, Paul—for goodness' sake!" But she enjoyed the feeling of his hands, with their slight electric charge, as he unbuttoned her buttons and slipped the blouse off her shoulders and down the length of her arms.

Paul was whistling, something he only did when he was in the best of moods. She heard the creaky sounds of a wicker hamper being opened—and suddenly the food smells were stronger. Paté and various types of cheese, including a ripe and unmistakable *époisses,* of which, she knew, Paul was particularly fond. Fresh, sweet apples. Grapes, if she wasn't mistaken. Putting his hand over hers, he refilled her glass and then poured one for himself.

"And am I to be nude, wherever it is you're taking me?"

"Ah, no, my fairy princess! You will be arrayed in costumes that will bedeck, two weeks from now, the reigning fashion queens of Paris."

"Do I have to pose again *en plein air*? Oh, Paul, it's cold outside! I'll freeze."

"We'll make a little fire. You'll be just as warm as a new-baked croissant. And you'll be the very first to model the fall line of the soon-to-be king of fashion, Paul Poiret."

"You are incorrigibly conceited."

"I am going to launch my own label. And I think I've found a place for my *maison de couture*, on rue Auber—conveniently enough, for you and me, just behind the Opera."

So that was why he'd asked his mother for the 50,000 francs! Jeannette raised up her free hand to lift the blindfold and steal a peek at him. She wanted to see his face at the announcement of this stunning news. Paul was wildly successful in everything he did—but this, at the age of twenty-four, was truly astounding.

He grabbed her hand and filled it with a hunk of crusty bread slathered with a marvelous-smelling truffled paté.

"Oh, you know how to bribe me, don't you?" She took a bite

and chewed it with delectation, followed by another gulp of champagne. "Why so far from the rue de la Paix? How will you ever get the grandes dames to visit your shop?"

"Ah, you'll see! Eat and drink—and rest, my dear. Relax! We have a long road to travel before we reach our destination."

Jeannette felt him press something small, round, and supple against her lips—a grape, she guessed from the texture and fragrance. It burst, when she bit down on it, with a vivid sensation of taste and, somehow, a dark purple color, even though she couldn't see it. She resolved to try eating blindfolded by herself sometime. She already felt a little tipsy.

He unbuttoned her boots then, very gently, and slipped them off, along with her stockings.

She sighed with pleasure. "Oh, it's not fair!"

First kissing the high arch of her left foot, he cupped it in his hands as if it were something holy. "I brought some oil, *cherie*. My footsore darling!"

It was a lavender-scented oil. Just the smell of it—and the familiar sense of anticipation—made her happy. How she loved Paul's unconditional acceptance of her! His desire for her, whether she was dirty or clean. She moaned softly as his strong thumbs massaged her arches and stroked her metatarsals, comforting the little trough beneath her mangled toes, running his oiled fingers and thumbs up over her ankles.

She knew he found her pleasure to be arousing. It was all part of the choreography of their relationship, in its seventh year now. After thoroughly and knowledgably rubbing first one of her feet and then the other, eliciting what he judged to be the requisite complement of sighs and groans, Paul stole both hands up one of her legs, under her skirt. "I love your thighs, just there," he said. "Everywhere else along your legs, the muscles are hard and strong. But just there, on the inside—just beneath your *origine du monde*—"

Earlier that year, in the spring, he'd taken her to a party where, in the wee hours, inside the bedroom of their host, a Turk, he'd shown her Courbet's notoriously explicit painting of a woman's most private parts, revealed in a way they rarely were in real life, not least to women themselves. Far from feeling shocked, Jeannette had found the painting to be both fascinating and strangely beautiful.

"Must I keep this blindfold on?"

"I insist!" He laid her back against the cushions and pulled her culottes down, murmuring tenderly and kissing her, here and there, along the way.

"Incorrigible," she said.

Unlike other men with whom she'd found herself in close proximity, Paul always smelled good. His hair and beard were meticulously groomed. He somehow managed to smell as if he'd just emerged from a swim in a mountain lake, or from a rainy walk through the woods.

"You mustn't, Paul," she said. "If you had told me..." She whispered in his ear, "I don't have my sponge with me."

He climbed on top of her, anyway. "My little wife!" he said in a husky whisper.

Jeannette chose to hear it as a promise.

❧

When she woke, the light was magically perfect outside the carriage windows—low-slanting in a landscape of golden leaves mounded up like a molten sea surging around gray islands of rock, all of it presided over by trees with their most glorious autumn foliage on display.

Paul gave the driver some money to take himself out for a rest and a meal while Jeannette hastened to clean herself up. She was still only half-dressed when Paul, after unloading his painting things, extended his hand to her. Looking around first to make sure they were alone, she leapt barefoot out of the carriage and did a series of passé turns on the leafy ground, ending in an *arabesque allongé*.

Paul, who was setting up his easel, shouted, "*Brava!* I must paint you in that last pose."

"Only if you have fairies who can hold my leg in the air."

Jeannette rubbed at a spot on her foot where a twig had poked her. "Oh, Paul, don't you understand the slightest thing about how the body works?"

"How the body works is *your* art form, *cherie*. Mine is knowing how it looks."

He took off the rest of her clothes. And then, one costume at a time, mostly just draped over her and pinned, he posed her and painted what he saw, using his favored English horsehair brushes and gouaches.

"I hereby declare war on the corset!" he said as he put the finishing touches on one of his watercolor sketches. "No longer will the female body be entombed and distorted, divided into two badly fitted pieces by the wretched things. These designs are much better without."

She walked behind the easel to inspect his paintings, admiring how chic she looked in them—herself and yet not herself. She'd never seen any clothes like these before.

Paul stood before his drawings with his head cocked first to one side, then the other. "Yes, yes—they're brilliant. If I were designing the world, every female would have the body of a ballerina." He slung an arm around her, pulling her close. "But you are shivering—and I promised you a fire."

He gave her his own jacket to put on over the final ensemble with its sheer fabrics and flowing lines. And then, with a degree of woodcraft that never failed to surprise her, he arranged some stones and sticks and built a little fire for them. They sat there, enjoying the flames and eating the rest of the picnic Paul had brought for them. Jeannette nestled against his well-padded shoulder. She felt a little drunk, quite exhausted suddenly, and very safe.

"What a good muse you are, my dear. When I am done forming you, there will be nothing left of Jeannette Dupres, minor dancer for the Paris Opera Ballet."

Why did he always have to remind her of her own unimportance in the world—while puffing himself up so constantly? "What shall I be then?"

"Why, people will look at you and say, 'There goes Paul Poiret's mannequin!'"

The driver tramped into view, obviously cheered by his outing.

"My good fellow!" Paul called to him. "Lend us a hand here. Help me put leaves into the carriage."

"Are you mad, Paul?" Jeannette whispered as she put her clothes to rights.

"A mad genius, perhaps. Come now, my dear—we need your efforts too. The light is fading."

He was scooping up great handfuls of leaves and throwing them through the door of the carriage, along with some low-hanging tender branches still bedecked with bright yellow foliage. The driver, no doubt thinking about the big tip he was likely to get, pitched in with gusto.

Jeannette mostly stood by watching. She didn't think she wanted to be anyone's mannequin, not even Paul's. Not if it meant the obliteration of all she'd worked so hard to achieve. All she'd sacrificed to become a dancer. She knew there were countless aspiring ballerinas who would tear her eyes out for the chance to steal her place in the company. After all these years, Paul still had no idea about who she really was, apart from knowing every secret about what pleased her body. In that, he was the world's expert. Her artistic aspirations meant nothing to him.

When he handed her up into the carriage and they sat down, they were half-buried in detritus from the trees—and both of them had yellow leaves stuck in their hair. "Like a fairy king with his queen," Paul said, clearly ignorant of the hurt he'd caused. He had none of the self-consciousness of the other women-liking men Jeannette knew: Paul Poiret liked nothing more than playing dress-up.

"We're bound to get spider bites," she said. "Really, you are the most impractical person I have ever known."

"Nonsense! I am a visionary—haven't you noticed?"

Jeannette was already starting to feel a little itchy.

"What are you going to do with all these leaves?"

"Have you still failed to discern my plan?"

She hated when he spoke to her that way. The feeling of safety, comfort, and magic she'd felt earlier was nearly gone now. "There's no need to be insulting. How can I know your plan when you haven't breathed a word of it? I'm not a clairvoyant."

"They're for my display window!" he said with so much childish glee that she forgave him a little.

"Leaves in a window? You *are* mad."

"You'll see, my child. All the fashionable people of Paris are going to flock to the windows of Maison Paul Poiret to see what wonders he has created there."

She tried to imagine what he was talking about. Dressmakers displayed clothing in their windows, not leaves. They wouldn't last very long, as she knew from the walks through the park she used to take with her mother, when she would be allowed to pick out two or three of the most beautiful autumn leaves to take home with her and press between the pages of their Bible.

It was so comforting, thinking about her mother—and also so very sad. Paul pulled her closer—and raked his fingers through her hair as she drifted off to sleep, imagining that she was a little girl again, safe and whole.

PARIS

1909

Jeannette stands for a long time, in a light rain, concealed behind a topiary outside the gate of 109 rue du Faubourg St. Honoré. A beige Renault Torpedo, its protuberant headlamps gleaming with bravado, rattles up to the curb, driven by the Poirets' liveried chauffeur. The front door of the mansion opens. Paul's young wife, that celebrated gamine fashion plate, Denise Poiret, trips down the path and lets herself into the car. She is wearing emerald-green kid boots and a hat unlike any Jeannette has ever seen before.

Patiently Jeannette waits a little longer, until a wagon and workmen arrive with more furnishings for the Poirets' new home, which is being readied for yet another of Paul's increasingly famous parties.

While the gate is open, she walks up one side of the elaborate front garden, which looks like a miniature Versailles, past the sculpted hedges and flowerbeds and through the door, which has been left ajar.

Jeannette is prepared to shout at the Poirets' servant, if need be—to demand to speak with Paul. But here he is, standing just inside the entryway, directing traffic. His smoking jacket, she thinks, is quite ridiculous. He's dressed like a Chinese emperor.

"This way, madame, this way," he says to her, describing a pathway with his right hand—the hand that is the only thing about him that betrays his origins as a man of the people. She loves his hands, the thick fingers strong and clever when touching her body or making his sketches but clumsy when it came to plying a needle and thread.

When she just stands there, he tries to look at her face,

which is hidden behind the spotted veil of the frumpy little hat she borrowed for the occasion. The rest of her is well disguised beneath a plain black cloak.

"Is it you?" he says tentatively, in a low, intimate voice.

Slowly she lifts her veil. She is not wearing any makeup. She sees his confusion. She tries as hard as she can, given the circumstances, to assume an expression of goodness and innocence, tempered by weariness. She smiles without showing her teeth. She sees him panicking.

"I didn't expect you!" he says.

She will not speak—because she knows that will give her away.

"Come in, come in," he says, taking her hands, trying to pull off her gloves, trying to peer at her body beneath her cloak. "My dear heart," he says. "My dear little flea!"

Coming close to him—standing close enough to feel the soft skin of his ear against her lips—she whispers, "Say my name!" She has tried to speak with a Russian accent, easy enough to affect after spending the last two weeks with a troupe of Russian dancers.

He holds her at arm's length, smiling. "Won't you take off your cloak?"

She shakes her head slowly. Then, sighing, she makes her shoulders slump in a way no well-trained ballerina would ever do.

"Sonya!" he says, with obvious relief. "What a marvelous surprise!"

Jeannette throws her hat and her cloak onto the boldly patterned black-and-white marble floor. She wishes she'd thrown them at his face. "You knew!" she says, almost sings with the frenzy of an operatic soprano, finally making sense of what happened in Pavlova's dressing room. "And the child is yours too!" She is screaming now. "Isn't she?"

Paul holds his head in his hands. He is aware of the sudden coldness of his fingers, a faint sense of pressure at the back of his head, and, incongruously, a rush of blood to his groin. He has suffered several episodes of insomnia since first hearing the rumor of Sonya's resumption of work for Pavlova, knowing, as he did, that Jeannette was dancing as an extra with Diaghilev's troupe. He has been dreading this very scene—and yet has also been vaguely thrilled by the prospect of experiencing the denouement of this long-running episodic drama that has delighted his idle hours for the past six years. He is as thrilled as he feels at the theater when the play and the actors have taken possession of him to the obliteration of everything else.

"Does she know?" Jeannette asks him in a voice drained of feeling. "Does she know about us?"

He shakes his head no. In his fantasies, the scene always ends with an episode of spectacular lovemaking, made all the more intense by his anguish and that of whichever twin has discovered his betrayal of her.

Jeannette peels his hands away from his face, so that she can look into his eyes. "You allowed *her* to bear your child—but not me?"

Tenderly, Paul leads her over to one of the bright yellow velvet and rosewood chairs lined up against the wall—he loves those chairs. She sits, looking down at her shoes. They are stout, practical shoes of the kind she noticed the seamstress was wearing. She had to comb the flea market to find a similar pair.

He sits in the chair beside hers. He has not let go of her hands. "You are mistaken about the child," he says, looking around to make sure no one is there to hear them. "Sonya already had her children when I met her."

"Children?"

"I believe," says Paul, "she has two." He frowns, impatient with the way this sort of detail seems to elude him, whereas other things—things that really matter to him—are jealously hoarded in his memory. "Or is it three?"

"Three! Perhaps they're all yours."

"Don't be ridiculous, Jeannette. Sonya first came here in January of '03. I remember precisely, because it was the year I left Worth and launched my label."

Jeannette's eyes are wide. "The year of our excursion to Fontainebleau."

Paul makes a sympathetic face to make sure that she knows he's caught her reference. Of course! Nasty business, that pregnancy. Rather careless on his part.

"She came here looking for *you*," he says. "Well, ostensibly to scout the fashion houses for Anna Pavlova."

Jeannette snatches her hands away from him. "You never told her you knew me? How could you be so wicked, Paul?"

His sense of displeasure in himself passes quickly. He smiles and his brown eyes sparkle, like those of a naughty boy caught red-handed but nonetheless proud of the feat of mischief he's managed to pull off.

"It was too delicious," he says to the mistress he'd so recently told, as gently as he could, that it was over between them. He'd promised his wife. He catches Jeannette's hands again, then wanders up the length of her arms, which have the beautiful firmness of all the ballerinas he's ever known. And yet, of all of them, she has the silkiest skin. "Oh, my sweet," he whispers huskily. "How I've missed you!"

Again, she pushes him away.

A young woman appears in the doorway, holding a beautifully dressed three-year-old child by the hand. The little girl looks a lot like Paul—and also like the little girl Jeannette saw in Pavlova's dressing room, although not nearly as pretty. Not as pretty as the child Jeannette and Paul might have made together.

"Ah, Miss O'Reilly!" he calls out in English, and then, opening his arms wide, "Rosine, my angel!" The child leaps into his embrace, covering his face in kisses.

"*Papa, mon cher Papa!*" she says with effusive adoration.

Jeannette would have given anything for such a warm and loving relationship with her own papa. The nanny—who is so pretty that Jeannette knows it must be annoying to Paul's wife—straightens the child's dress when he sets her down. "Say 'Good morning,' Rosine!" the woman, hardly more than a girl herself, says with a charming Irish accent.

"Good morning, Rosine!" the child lisps, giving a toddler's version of a curtsey. Paul and the nanny both burst out laughing.

Jeannette, overcome with a sense of humiliation, feels herself start to sweat. "Bonjour, mademoiselle," she says to the child. Looking at the nanny, head to toe, she says icily, "Miss O'Reilly."

She can't stop thinking about that last child Paul had planted in her. Her third pregnancy, all in all. She knows she's lucky to still be alive. She knew two dancers who died from botched abortions, and one—though made an honest woman by her patron—who died in childbirth. Rumor was that the baby was sent to an orphanage.

Mothers were never happy when their sons married dancers. Paul had been about to introduce Jeannette to his mother once. But then, at the last moment, he changed his plans. Too frightened, she'd guessed. It was just about the time he asked his mother to lend him 50,000 francs.

Jeannette entertains the possibility that Paul doesn't know about the little girl she saw in the dressing room. It makes her insides ache, thinking about the tenderness with which that child had caressed her mother's hand, bringing her round again—and the joy and ardor in the eyes of the Russian seamstress as she looked up at Jeannette. How it had been like discovering a mirror that showed a version of her face much kinder than the one she saw every day.

She looks at Paul without the scrim of love she's felt for him since they were both in their teens. How stout he's grown! Was he always such a cad? She gathers up her cloak and hat. She forgets her umbrella.

"Goodbye, goodbye!" says little Rosine, happy that she will have her father to herself, at least for a few precious moments.

"Yes, thank you for coming by, madame," says Paul, all businesslike. "We will, of course, be delighted to have you as part of the cast for our soirée—won't we, my pet?"

"Oh yes, Papa!" the child chimes in.

Without even bothering to answer or say goodbye, Jeannette heads out the door. Too late, she remembers that it's raining—and realizes that she's left her umbrella behind. She doesn't want to go back inside that house or ever to see Paul Poiret again.

There's something that she *does* want—although she can't find the words yet to express what it is. Ignoring the rain, she strides toward rue de Penthièvre with her head pounding and a sense of hollowness inside her that isn't only hunger.

✥

Despite the rain, Jeannette walks all the way from the Poirets' house to the Opéra Garnier, arriving with her clothes soaked through, her stockings slipping inside the ill-fitting, ugly shoes. She knows it's too early for anyone but the stage crew to be there. But still, she reasons, they'll let her in and she'll be able to wait. She hopes the heat is on.

It would be unbearable to wait at home now.

She knows she should go home, change her clothes and rest until the pre-performance class convenes. She should eat. But she can't stand the idea of seeing her little apartment now, with its inescapable sense of belonging to someone who belongs to no one. Reflexively, she climbs the metal staircase to the dressing room, hoping the rain hasn't brought in rats—actual rats, as it sometimes did—then plunks herself down onto one of the rickety chairs.

Her clothes and hair are dripping—and she's cold. She unbuckles and shakes off the shoes, peeling off her stockings, stripping down to her poor, misshapen, much-abused bare feet. She always tries to keep them hidden out of view—the overlong first toe with its nail hideously thickened and perpetually black from the daily assault of her weight bearing down on it, through the tips of her toe shoes. Her other toenails, as often as not, missing. The bunions, bruises, and corns that make her naked feet look as if they belonged to an old woman. *En pointe,* her slender ankles and chiseled calves crisscrossed in pink silk ribbons—bathed in stage lights—fairylike. Beautiful, or so she is regularly told. She has kept her secret ugliness well hidden from the world.

The mirror shows her the only *rat* in the room—herself. How ghastly she looks, like a bedraggled puppy! She pushes a dripping hank of hair behind her ear, ashamed in a way she's rarely been before her own reflection, which seems changed somehow. Foreign.

Reaching out, she touches the image of her hand, fingertips to fingertips. There are tears in the other's eyes, the lips form a tender smile—and something starts to feel unhinged inside her.

The voice from the doorway—accented, Russian, girlish—takes her by surprise. "It's absolutely incredible, isn't it?" Tamara Karsavina is standing in the hall, looking just as beautiful as she does in her publicity photos. She radiates a positively grotesque degree of joy. "Mademoiselle Jeannette, I've been searching for you everywhere!" She floats in and sits down in the chair next to the one where Jeannette is seated, her feet tucked under her skirt. "But you are shivering! Here," she says, pulling an embroidered shawl and a pair of soft woolen stockings out of her dance bag. With a flick of her wrists, she drapes the shawl over Jeannette's shoulders and presses the socks into her hands.

Jeannette is dumbstruck. "*You*—searching for *me*?"

Tamara Karsavina is the new darling of the Saison Russe, even though it's Pavlova who's featured on the poster. Pavlova who, or so rumor has it, couldn't be bothered to show up for the first two weeks of Diaghilev's Russian Season. And maybe that was why the older ballerina was now in such a foul mood, while *le Tout Paris* went mad for Karsavina. Jeannette couldn't be more flustered if the queen of Spain had just walked in and handed her a pair of socks.

"Sonya told me what happened! How you found each other, in the doorway of Pavlova's dressing room." In response to Jeannette's look of confusion, Karsavina adds, "Sonya—Pavlova's seamstress."

Jeannette shivers again, feeling chilled in every part of her.

"Here, put on the socks. Oh, your poor feet!"

Jeannette remembers again that she forgot to eat today. She left a little bowl of stewed lentils on her counter, meaning to have them for lunch.

She actually doesn't want to hear whatever it is that Karsavina is about to tell her. The room seems to be listing, like the little boat Paul used, in the old days, to ferry the two of them down the river to his little hideaway at Meudon. How they laughed on those Mondays, when there were no classes and his shop was closed! They feasted and made love all day and night, till Tuesday dawned. She wonders, did he take Sonya there as well? Was that where the child was conceived?

Jeannette feels Karsavina's large dark eyes trying to see inside her—and braces herself when it's clear that she's decided to speak. "She is your sister, *ma belle*—your twin!"

The words are no sooner spoken than Jeannette is suffused with a guilty sense that she's always known she had a twin—that she is one of two. Rossetti's gaudy painting flashes before her eyes again—the look of shock in the eyes of those two sets of identical twins, male and female, encountering one another in the forest. Jeannette had instinctively understood the outrage emanating from the eyes of the two young women in the painting. Now she understands why—and, horribly, why Paul had particularly wanted to show it to her.

What do any of us have but the uniqueness of ourselves? Why would anyone rejoice to discover a second self—unmoored from one's own identity—taking up space that is rightfully ours in the world? A twin! But the idea is, of course, absurd. Jeannette's maman, who loved her so mightily and often said how devoutly she'd prayed and hoped for her arrival, would never in a thousand years have given birth to twins and then given one of them away.

"I have no sister!" Jeannette says in a much nastier tone than she would ever have thought possible in speaking to such an exalted personage as Tamara Karsavina. Her heartbeat is throbbing in her ears. Looking down and seeing her own bare feet, she frowns.

"Oh, do put the stockings on, please! They're very soft wool—cashmere, I believe. Don't be ashamed. What ballerina *doesn't* have hideous feet? You should see Pavlova's!"

Jeannette bends to pull the stockings on. She owned many such fine things, before she ran away from home. Before the years and years of being so terribly poor. She has a few such things still—gifts from Paul or other admirers.

"Wait here," the younger dancer says. Then, "No—it's too cold here." She takes a fistful of coins out of her little pigskin purse. "Wait at the Café de la Paix. Inside, in the grand salon. I will bring her to you."

Jeannette catches a glimpse of herself in the mirror. "I couldn't possibly meet anyone now. Another day, maybe..."

Karsavina stares at Jeannette, cocking her head, then laughs again. "You look so amazingly like her. Those are the same eyes I first saw through her little shop window on Zagorodny Prospekt, on my walks home from school. Sonya's eyes!"

Jeannette has never before had a parallel sense of being looked at, but not being seen.

Karsavina places the coins into Jeannette's hand, wrapping her fingers around them. "Promise me you won't run away. That you'll be at the Café de la Paix at one o'clock on Thursday afternoon."

Jeannette understands well enough Karsavina's power over her and every other member of the corps. One whispered word from the company's bright new star, and Jeannette would lose her job in a heartbeat. She bites her lip then says, "As you wish, mademoiselle."

"You mustn't look so glum!" Karsavina says with a laugh. "Sonya has been searching for you for years and years—and wants nothing more than to shower you with love."

Jeannette blinks her eyes once then twice before she can speak. "Can you tell me? Is it true that Pavlova's seamstress is a Jewess?"

"Of course, my dear! But then why should you have known?"

Jeannette and Paul had an ongoing, sometimes bitter

argument over the years about her stance as an anti-Dreyfusard. "Think hard, you ignorant flea!" he'd said to her more than once. But she couldn't help how she felt, could she? Jeannette had been raised to hate and fear the Jews. Had Paul known all along? Did other people know? Could that have been what her aunt meant when she spoke about Jeannette's blood—about being "one of them"?

"So pretty," rhapsodized Karsavina, "just like you. And so good and kind. She has three children—three nieces for you!" The newly minted prima ballerina is overflowing with her own romantic feelings about life. "It can only be, for all of you, a joyful reunion!"

Jeannette feels herself falling, as if she had stepped off a cliff, and a dizziness that makes her close her eyes. She remembers the change she noted in the way Paul looked at her, some years ago. How many years ago? She'd wondered then if he was noticing how much less radiant her skin was than it had been when they'd first met, when she was only sixteen, when he so often told her that her skin was as smooth as the most expensive Chinese silk. She'd wondered if he'd found someone younger, fresher, more to his liking. And why wouldn't he?

Sonya. The name is oddly, deeply familiar to her.

All at once, Jeannette knows that she's heard Paul murmur that name before, when they were both sated and half asleep. It had meant nothing to her at the time beyond the usual anguish of knowing that he had other women. So many women in the life of Paul Poiret! Models, *midinettes*, dressmakers. A fleet of terrifying saleswomen and all those exceedingly rich, imperious clients of his—although he never called *them* by their Christian names! Lovers, too, without doubt. She knew it all along but chose not to think about it. Not too often.

She'd nursed the dream, up until the very day of his wedding, that she was the only woman who really mattered to Paul. His first love from the moment of their first kiss, that day at the Folies-Bergère, just weeks before she won the audition to join the Opera Ballet.

Even after he married Denise Boulet—surprising everyone with his odd choice, this unknown, unpolished and not even very pretty nineteen-year-old dredged up from his past—he'd been convincing in the very special feelings he harbored for Jeannette. And, after all, he continued to help her in countless ways. When that bright light of his was shining on her, bathing her in lustful adoration, she simply took it in with gratitude— love. A ferocity of love she hadn't felt since her mother died and it came to seem that no one would ever really love her again—not with such hunger. That pretty little girl in Pavlova's dressing room, with her broad forehead and the impish gleam in her warm brown eyes, was so clearly Paul's. The child's look of unconditional love for Sonya exactly resembled the way Paul used to look at Jeannette. It strikes her that she's been sharing that look of Paul's—that special look, reserved only for her— all this time.

She never knew what Paul was thinking. He used to scrutinize her with the minutest attention, feeling her with his thick yet sensitive fingers, as if she were a piece of sculpture. Seeming to memorize the shape, breadth, and depth of every part of her, as if planning to re-create her in some other medium—marble or wood or stone. Was it because he'd been comparing the two of them all that while?

"It must be a lot to take in," says Karsavina, startling Jeannette out of her reverie. The ballerina kisses her three times, in the exact same way Jeannette has seen the Ballets Russes dancers kissing each other. She has been drawn to the warmth of the Russian ballerinas, which seems to go so well with their passionate approach to their art. "You won't forget, will you?"

"One o'clock on Thursday, at the Café de la Paix," Jeannette says in the dutiful voice she'd used with the nuns. A voice inside her is saying that it isn't so, it can't be possible—and another voice inside her, a much grimmer voice, answers back, "But it explains so much, don't you see?"

SAINT PETERSBURG

1903-1904

Living with Daniel and Klara, with her children surrounded by their children, it was almost possible for Sonya to imagine that her past belonged to someone else's life—not hers, that nightmare; not hers, that sense of guilt, anger, and sorrow.

The government, fearing international exposure, held its trials of the murderers and looters behind closed doors. Daniel and his colleagues in the capital rallied to win compensation for the losses suffered by the Jews of Kishinev.

They were, for a while, hopeful. But then the tsar himself launched a campaign to blame the Jews of Kishinev for what had befallen them. There was blame on both sides, he told the international press—to the horror of Jewish people everywhere. There would be no compensation forthcoming for the lost lives, the lost homes, the ruined livelihoods. The Jews had been compensated well enough, said the tsar, by the donations sent in by their sympathizers and co-religionists from around the world.

Sonya received nothing.

How had it all disappeared in just a matter of days? Her home, her husband, the family business—everything she'd so naively assumed would last forever. She felt like one of the walking dead, going through the motions of being a mother, a sister, an aunt. Her food tasted like ashes.

Daniel's family took pains to organize activities and amusements for Olga and Naomi, who day by day seemed to forget they'd ever had a father—or had ever lived anywhere but Saint Petersburg. Naomi loved playing with her big girl cousins, who petted and spoiled her. But every once in a while, she would get a stricken look in her eyes and say, "When will Papa come back to us?" Sonya would distract her by putting the child's hands on her belly to feel her baby brother kick.

Little Olga spent every unsupervised moment in her uncle's library. They all said with amusement that she was "looking" at the books. One day, at breakfast, she gave all of them a shock by reading out the headline of Daniel's newspaper. "It's not such a great surprise," he said, with a wistful look at his own children, none of whom had shown any particular genius. "I myself was also a very early reader."

Attended by her sister-in-law and a midwife, Sonya gave birth in October to a healthy baby girl. She wept because Asher's dream of a son would never come true now—and because this girl would never have a father, at least not one who could ever claim her.

The baby's name was chosen by Daniel, in honor of a long-dead great aunt on their father's side. As soon as Baila was weaned, Sonya begged Daniel to lend her enough money to buy a new sewing machine, rent a storefront, and start over again.

"I saw a place with a sign on it, on Zagorodny Prospekt," she told him before he left for work one morning. "It's very small, but the light is good."

"But we love having you here, Sonya. You and the children."

"It's just one room—and there's no apartment attached to it. We would continue to live here, until..." Her voice trailed off, as it so often did, these days.

"Of course," said Daniel, as if he knew what she was thinking but didn't say, out of delicacy.

Sonya had overheard her brother and sister-in-law discussing men they thought might suit her, when her mourning was over—all of them widowers, with children of their own.

❦

Sonya gave some of her earnings every month to Daniel, determined to pay him back as soon as possible. The rest, she put into a travel fund. She hated being in debt to her brother. She hated thinking that her daughters would come to see themselves as impoverished relatives in an otherwise prosperous family—or that she would school them, through her example, that the only path to success, for a woman, involved marriage.

She needed some way to make her shop stand out in Saint Petersburg, where all the fashionable ladies wanted to wear Parisian designs.

In 1904, she wrote a letter to Paul Poiret, whose new *maison du couture* on rue Pasquier was winning him fame as far away as the Russian capital. Sonya would be glad for the work, she told him, if he needed extra help in his atelier. She said nothing about Baila's birth—and offered no explanation about why she was now living in Saint Petersburg. She only told him that she hoped, eventually, to move with her children to Paris.

Paris

1906

The ateliers and fitting rooms in Paul Poiret's fashion house on rue Pasquier were so crowded with seamstresses and customers that Sonya was relegated to working on the stairway as she confected the hats, scarves, evening bags, and muffs to go with all the ensembles flying out the door as fast as the money was flying in.

Paul had promised Sonya, when he sent the telegram to Saint Petersburg this time, that he wouldn't keep her away from her children for more than two weeks. And yet now, after three weeks had passed, he was begging her to give him another few days. The orders, following the publication of his catalog—featuring the lavish full-color illustrations of the young artist from Angoulême, Paul Iribe—had been overwhelming.

Sonya was glad of the money she was making, and grateful for the opportunity to continue her search for Zaneta while she worked and learned about the highlights of the upcoming season. On each visit, Sonya's suspicions were confirmed anew in the way Paul looked at her, or in something he'd say. But she had yet to find anything tangible to prove that he was lying to her.

Paul's generosity as an employer allowed Sonya to travel to Paris twice a year and yet return home with her pockets full. She told Daniel and Klara about him, although not, of course, how she'd met him or anything of his deeper connections to their family.

Daniel, as a social reformer, approved of what he heard from his sister. Poiret not only complied with the recent law, which gave all employees and workers in France the right to a day of rest on Sundays, but he also retained three chefs to provide all

350 employees of Maison Paul Poiret with a delicious midday meal six times a week. Whenever Paul returned from a hunting or fishing expedition, he would parade through the showroom with whatever game he'd bagged, announcing above the squeals of half-dressed women that his workers would dine like royalty that day.

Sonya was convinced that if she persisted long enough and never gave up hope, Paul would eventually lead her to Zaneta.

During her stays in Paris, Sonya boarded with one or another of Paul's *midinettes*, who all feared him and revealed little information about where he went and who he knew. When she inquired, as discretely as she could, about the name and whereabouts of Monsieur Poiret's *petite amie*, the universal answer was always, "Which one?" When she replied, "The one who looks like me," the women shook their heads and either smiled or frowned, amazed that the Russian seamstress had the temerity to boast about her liaison with the boss. It was clear enough, to all of them, how he favored her.

Sonya told herself that her patience would eventually be rewarded. All the beautiful women of Paris—and every woman of means visiting Paris from abroad—eventually walked through the doors of Maison Paul Poiret. She would outwit or out-wait Paul. Every day she was in Paris, she woke convinced this was the day when she would meet Zaneta, face to face.

Paul was forever thinking of ways to get her alone—and she was ever vigilant about making sure he only saw her when others were around. She suspected he kept asking her to come back to Paris in hopes that, one day, she would change her mind—just as she hoped that, one day, he would change his. He certainly never left off sending longing looks her way. He didn't dare take the liberties with her that she saw him take with so many others, workers and customers alike—and she sometimes questioned the source of this bit of power she had over him.

On this latest visit, she began to wonder whether he'd broken things off with Zaneta—or else had figured out some way to ensure that she and her twin would never cross paths. He was suddenly less skittish about Sonya's presence in his workshop, even to the point of having her do her work, in plain view of all, on the stairway. Had he sent Zaneta abroad? Had he quarreled with her? Had she left him for someone else?

Sonya sat at her makeshift workstation on the landing, watching everyone who came in and listening to all that was said.

Paul had the physique and the vocal power of an opera singer, and his booming voice could be heard everywhere in his establishment. "Madame," she once heard him thunder from a fitting room where he was ensconced with no less than a personage than the Comtesse de Chevigné. "You have come to Poiret's because it is the leading house in the world. Well, I am Poiret, and I am telling you that the gown is perfectly made, it is beautiful, and it is becoming to you. If you don't like it, take it off—but I will never make another one for you!" The countess, who inspired fear in everyone else, had actually begged him, in her deep-throated, raspy voice, to forgive her. "Madame la Comtesse," he said in a more confidential tone that Sonya could nonetheless hear quite clearly. "You know the rules here—no cigarettes!"

His customers were among the most powerful women of Paris, and yet he exercised the authority of a despot over them all. Sonya overheard him say in withering tones to another grande dame, "You probably made a mistake when you ordered that gown. You are not satisfied with it. I won't have you upsetting yourself over such a trifle. I'll do it into a pretty cushion—and you can find some other couturier to clothe you for Madame Arman de Caillavet's salon this Sunday." The woman started weeping, paid for her dress, and hurried away.

Paul clearly valued Sonya's skills. But he seemed to value the novelty of her presence just as highly, registering a surprised sense of delight every time he saw her. Whenever she finished one of the accessories he dubbed *chichis*, he demanded to know, "Have you affixed the Poiret label?"

He had a terror of other people creating copies of his

designs. He barred the door to his own sister when she opened a dressmaking business not far from the rue de la Paix, convinced she wouldn't hesitate to steal his ideas. In a practice completely unknown before, he had a label designed by one of his artist friends—and had this affixed to all his creations as soon as they were made.

Perhaps because her own shop was so far away—and so little did Paul consider Saint Petersburg as a center of fashion—Sonya seemed immune to his suspicion. So cynical and so self-confident was he, that he once asked her, at the end of a long day, "Have you had any luck, my dear, finding your sister?"

Sonya looked at him for a full five seconds in silence before she answered, "Not yet, Monsieur Poiret."

"Oh, Sonya, won't you call me Paul?"

"No, Monsieur Poiret. It would not be proper."

SAINT PETERSBURG

1908

A dressmaker is not only the creator of one's wardrobe, but also the keeper of one's secrets. All the layers of artifice and protection are stripped away, till only the naked, unadorned, uncorsetted self remains, with all its imperfections on display. There can be no hint of judgment lurking in the dressmaker's eyes, which must see as a visionary sees the world, beyond what is to the realm of what can be. Every new gown or coat offers the possibility of a dream fulfilled: a new self with formidable powers to charm.

It's what Paul Poiret gave to his customers. An ensemble from his *maison de couture* conferred power on every client able and willing to pay the price—and woe betide any woman who failed to see his value.

Sonya knew how to make her customers feel at ease as readily as she knew how to finish a seam, through training with roots so deep in her childhood that both came as second nature to her. Like her mother, Sonya offered herself as a friend to her customers—a confidante. She listened sympathetically to all they said. She labored to flatter each woman's figure, both in her designs and in the words she chose in those moments when accounting for their less-than-ideal bodily attributes was unavoidable. "This color will bring out your beautiful eyes," she would say to a woman whose waistline was a distant memory. Or, "These higher hemlines, all the rage in Paris now, are so flattering to women, such as yourself, with such nice small feet."

It was a one-way intimacy—and Sonya preferred it that way. Her own secrets were unexposed and even irrelevant in the pleasant interactions she orchestrated. She tried not to think overmuch about her own secrets—to focus instead on whatever lay before her. And yet she was always filled, especially in the hours when she couldn't sleep, with a nagging sense of dread.

Life trains us to expect what it has given us already, so much so that we may fail to see a new and better pathway, even when it's there before our eyes. So harshly schooled in loss, Sonya was cautious in the way she loved her children. She knew they felt it—and that they wanted something she simply felt incapable of giving them. Of course, she wanted everything good for them. But she was ever braced for the sudden act of God or Nature—or whatever flaw it was, hidden deep within her—that might cause them to be taken away from her.

She knew there was no holding on to anyone or anything. The tsar's police had stolen her father away, consigning her family to poverty and desperation, spitting him out again a broken man, without the strength to survive. Strangers from France stole the twin who would have been Sonya's comfort and companion, not only through the trauma of their time in the orphanage, but ever after, as life dealt out blow after blow. Anti-Semitism drove her favorite brother into exile, and stole Jascha away from her, along with any illusions she had about romantic love. Her own country's hatred of the Jews had left her a widow and destroyed her home, making her into an exile as well.

Paul Poiret had given her a taste of sensual pleasure that she would pay for, she knew, for the rest of her days. That part of herself that felt guilty and filled with shame was something she tried to keep secret from everyone. How could her children love her if they saw her as she really was? Her pretty face and figure, so attractive to others, seemed a cosmic joke to her.

Out of caution for everyone who came near her, Sonya held her deepest self—her most authentic and secret self—apart.

❧

For several hours every day, Sonya sat in the window of the tiny shop Daniel rented for her on Zagorodny Prospekt. Sitting before her sewing machine, or sewing by hand, she would wait for the dancers of the Mariinsky School to walk by in the late afternoon. The very way they walked reflected their training as dancers, setting them apart. Often hand in hand or floating away from one another and then coming together again as they laughed and joked, their every movement and gesture filled Sonya with admiration and a wistful tinge of envy.

They seemed so young to her—and so carefree.

Most of Sonya's customers were older ladies, although, increasingly, she received orders for hats, coats, and gowns for their daughters and nieces. Her twice-a-year trips to Paris—and her continued work for Paul Poiret—allowed her to introduce innovations that made her clients feel fashionable, despite being unable to afford Parisian designs.

Sonya thought of herself as a canny observer who could translate details of Parisian fashion into garments that made sense for the wives and daughters of Saint Petersburg's professional class. Anna Pavlova ordered all her dresses from Paris now. But she would occasionally come to Sonya begging her to create a copy of a designer dress whose price was simply out of reach. Sonya always demurred unless the original design bore the Paul Poiret label. She knew enough about Pavlova's secrets to feel sure the dancer wouldn't dare expose Sonya's professional perfidy. Her wellspring of righteous anger toward Paul compelled her to cheat him whenever the opportunity arose, although she would never think about cheating anyone else.

The Mariinksy School students mostly ignored her where she sat in her window, watching them while she sewed. But one of the dancers—the prettiest one, she thought, with beautiful large dark eyes—always smiled at her, and she smiled back.

A lady who was in the shop consulting with Sonya, one late afternoon, caught the exchange of smiles between Sonya and the pretty ballerina. "Tamara Karsavina knows you?" she asked in a tone of disbelief.

"Only to greet me," said Sonya. "Is she a student—or part of the company?"

"I can see that you are no balletomane! Karsavina was

promoted to soloist last month—and no one can get enough of her. Mathilde Kschessinska is fit to burst with jealousy!"

The next time Tamara Karsavina walked by, Sonya smiled and bowed at her. This became a daily tradition for both of them, looked forward to by Sonya, although they never spoke.

And then, shortly after Sonya returned from one of her trips to Paris, the young ballerina walked inside the shop and blurted out, "I can't afford high fashion—but I do, so do, love to hear about it!"

"You've come to the right place then, Mademoiselle Karsavina." Sonya offered a chair to the ballerina, marveling at her beauty and grace close-up. No wonder the *prima ballerina assoluta* of the Mariinsky felt threatened by her! "I can show you some drawings of the latest Parisian styles."

The young dancer began to browse through the album, lingering over the sketch of a dress whose accessories Sonya had created during her last episode of work for Maison Paul Poiret.

"Believe me," said Sonya, "there are ways to dress as fashionably as a Parisienne, even here in Saint Petersburg—even if you don't have a great deal of money—if you know the right dressmaker."

Paris

1908

Sonya looked at Paul with disbelief that seemed to begin to waver in the intensity of his gaze. He was standing very close to her—closer than she'd let him be for a very long time.

"You believed what you wanted to believe, my precious darling." He could barely restrain himself from reaching out to touch her face. He closed his eyes momentarily, remembering the silken texture of her skin.

He wanted more, each time she was near him. He wanted to feel the sensation again of the flats of his fingers on her naked back, which was as smooth as the petals of some tropical flower. He wanted to reacquaint himself with the contours of her body as he measured them with his hands and touched all those places that he knew gave pleasure to her. And even as he had these thoughts, he wondered whether he would have been just as fascinated if there weren't that frisson of recognition, that knowledge of Jeannette's body, Jeannette's skin.

The allure of any particular woman was such a puzzle. And yet it was Poiret's business—no, it was his duty—to analyze the inner workings of that certain something that operates directly upon the senses, bypassing one's conscious mind. To recreate this allure, again and again, in ever novel forms, in the sensuous charm that is the very expression of a dress or a perfume.

What was it about Sonya, if it was indeed anything beyond the phenomenon of her endlessly intriguing resemblance to Jeannette? She was beautiful, without doubt. But she was twenty-eight now and the mother of two—or was it three? Childbirth had, nonetheless, done nothing to diminish her appeal. He always wanted her when he saw her. The more she resisted him, the more he longed to possess her again.

Denise, his marvelous wife—his muse and mannequin—was, for all her charms, merely herself. She was as unique, as inimitable, as any other one of his creations.

But both Sonya and Jeannette were, for him, like the taste of a mysterious and fascinating wine. Each sip evoking a hint of some indescribably precious, delicious memory from his deepest reaches—and a desire for more. A memory of what it felt like, as a child, to gather and crush flower petals from his grandmother's garden, imagining himself a chemist in his laboratory. Combining colors and scents with that joyous feeling of discovery—and conviction of the greatness of his destiny. He used to create fountains in that garden out of whatever he could find, coloring the water with his flower petal concoctions. Creating magic, still innocent of the putrid messes that he'd come upon weeks later, of rotted vegetable matter and foul-smelling sludge—his failures.

The flood of sensations he felt refreshed his belief in himself as someone endowed with extraordinary abilities—a mortal singled out by the gods as an artist. He created magic and the universe always rewarded him with magic in return.

Like every good-hearted father, he felt that magic power whenever his little Rosine threw her chubby arms around him and declared her love for him above all others. Denise was, he sometimes thought, a tad bit jealous of their child's preference. But, then, the child was so often with her mother, and so little with Poiret, given all his travels and all his projects and the huge success of all his ventures.

Denise, despite her relative youth, sometimes seemed to him less like a muse these days, and more like a nagging mother, always worried about what she characterized as the extravagance of his spending. She recognized his genius for bringing his work to the attention of the world—for making his creations into objects of desire for which the world would spend its gold. But, for her, it was just that: a genius for making money. His empire, over which he allowed her to rule by his side as queen, was all about amassing wealth and making their future secure. As if anyone's future could ever be made secure!

Paul didn't care at all about wealth—not really. What he wanted was another taste of that wine—another dose of the magic it conferred. The magic of endless possibility and a world that welcomed and rewarded every one of his magnificent ideas. That delicious dulling of every care, every doubt. The need to taste again—to drink more deeply. To be transported again to that timeless place of innocence and belief in his own limitless powers.

"My little bird," he said to Sonya, aware that he was acting, but also strangely moved by every word. "I can't bear to let you fly from me again—to be deprived of your presence for another six months."

❧

Sonya found herself wanting to believe him. She was stirred, rather to her own surprise, by his arguments and promises, so logically and passionately delivered.

Could she have imagined all along that he knew Zaneta? Had Paul Poiret fallen in love with Sonya, and remained in love with her, all these years? Was Zaneta—grown-up Zaneta—something that Sonya had confected from thin air, like the imaginary playmates conjured to life by lonely children?

There was no evidence. There was nothing but Sonya's headstrong sense of hope.

And here she was, alone for the first time in years—face to face—with Paul Poiret. She felt her heartbeat quickening in a way it hadn't since that furtive hour in his workshop. Was he the one who was telling the truth—and was it she who'd been deluding herself, these past five years, with a lie? Justifying what she'd done, stealing his designs, out of her conviction that he'd wronged her so sorely?

Could it really be that she'd imagined it all—that she'd merely seen what she wanted to see, out of her desire to believe that Zaneta was somewhere close by, hidden just out of reach?

It was so hard in life to recognize what was true and what was merely a reaction born of self-doubt, shame, or wishful thinking. Had her yearning been so strong that she'd seen a conspiracy where there was none? Had Paul Poiret been merely flirting with her, on that day he'd first seen her at the Gare du Nord?

"If you reflect, my little chicken, you will see the advantages of my offer. I reward a *première* at Maison Paul Poiret with 60,000 francs a year precisely to allow her to live with a certain ease—to afford her the necessary understanding of the subtleties and refinements of my designs by transforming herself as well into an artist whose medium is luxury."

Sonya couldn't help but wonder what kind of apartment she might be able to rent in Paris for that salary—and how much there'd be left over to richly feed and clothe her little girls and even afford them lessons. Studies with a painter for Naomi. Private lessons for Olga with a scholar. And, for Baila, ballet lessons with one of the many Russian emigrees now making their home in the French capitol. She could finally pay off the last of her debt to Daniel!

And Paris itself was so very appealing, with everything and everyone seeming to operate under different, looser rules about what was and wasn't permissible. Women were marching for the right to vote. Girls were allowed to pursue as much education as they wanted—they could dream of doing more than simply becoming someone's wife.

ॐ

Paul stared out one of the immaculate windows of his second-story atelier, his attention caught by the bright yellow wing-bars of a little bird he'd never seen before. It was hidden now in the lush foliage of the chestnut tree that looked so different than it had just a few weeks ago, when it was leafless and newly pollarded, as sad-looking as an amputee.

He turned to Sonya again, inching a little closer. He could smell the subtle perfume of her skin—a gorgeous smell, inimitably hers. He wished he could bottle it.

"I have been more and more impressed by your aesthetic

intuition. How, with the instincts of an artist, you always seem to know the one point where it is possible to place a spot of color in one of my ensembles. It could not satisfy there, or there." He demonstrated by touching a place at her neckline and then at her waist. And then he put his hands at a spot on her hip, at the side-seam of her skirt, at a place on her body he remembered as being particularly silky and smooth. "No, it is precisely *here* that it must be placed."

She didn't exactly yield to his touch—but it seemed to him that she registered pleasure, ever so slightly, when he touched her. She kept her expression neutral.

Poiret sighed. "It is so rare to find another who shares this need that can only be slaked by pinning on the particular detail of decoration at the precise place where it ought to be. Someone, like you, who has an inborn understanding of the secret geometry that is the key to all aesthetic satisfaction. Who knows that what is true of line and volume is also true of color and its values."

৽

Sonya also stared for a moment out the window. She wondered what her daughters were doing now, in Saint Petersburg, where the world was, no doubt, still covered in snow.

Paul was just talking, she was quite sure, because he so loved the sound of his own voice. He luxuriated in the cleverness of the phrases he used and the way he wove them together with the art and instinct for survival of a bird making its nest. She was surprised, really, that he was taking so much of his time to make his point. In a moment, she knew, he would be on to something else—and someone else. Still, it touched her that he carved out such a special place for her in his heart—and was offering her such a plum of a job.

"You were made for Paris, Sonya! This city is the center of fashion precisely because the life of the senses flowers most freely here. You and your children will flourish in France in ways you never would be able to in the snowy hinterlands of Russia, ruled by a despot, reviled as a people."

❦

Although Paul wasn't at all sure that any of this was true, he wanted it to be so—and he felt how these words resonated in his very groin, in that place where the deepest and most patriotic truths about his manhood resided.

His sense of this truth was urgent, wonderful, and strong. He felt as seized by it as when he was possessed of a new creative idea—of a vision so beautiful that the world would be forever changed by it. The world of *haut couture* would be so amazed and compelled by the genius of his vision that it would yield up everything to Poiret and crown him king.

The air felt pure and new, as if there'd been a mighty thunderstorm and a mighty rain. There was a stillness now, a clarity and freshness that would make Sonya want to feel his hands on her again. He felt capable of reading her deepest desires and intuiting exactly how to satisfy them.

PARIS

1909

The overture is long, the stage in darkness. Sonya looks down at Baila, not too distracted to notice that her youngest seems especially pretty tonight. They exchange a wide-eyed smile, both excited. The clash of the cymbals makes them start, looking away from each other toward the stage.

Sonya's eyes can't work fast enough to process all the movement of the dancers, twenty or so clouds of white tulle wafting through the altogether convincing illusion of a forest. Each fairy sports a pair of tiny wings just beneath the plunging back of the costume whose construction Sonya knows as intimately as the bodies of her children. She opens her eyes wider as she tries to pick out individual faces and features among the swiftly moving, identically costumed dancers balancing on tiptoe, rising and swaying like boughs in the wind.

Although she and Baila are seated in the last row of the orchestra section, Sonya recognizes Pavlova when she floats onstage from the wings, drifting over to her place center stage with the lightness and seeming spontaneity of a butterfly.

All the dancers of the corps de ballet look much the same—moving as if petals from a single flower buffeted by the wind, each sprite's dark or blond hair pulled back, encircled by an identical wreath of pink silk roses. They seem equally long-legged and lithe. Zaneta could be any one of them.

How did they move that way, running backwards on the very tips of their toes, as if weightless? Sonya's eyes light on the male dancer, in a poet's blouse and sporting long curling hair, dancing with Pavlova and, yes—there is Karsavina!

Both ballerinas seem equally glorious to her in the way they move, conveying volumes without uttering a single sound. They are both, in the story, in love with the poet, hungry to serve as his muse. And no wonder! He moves as if native to an atmosphere different than that breathed by other mortals—as if his veins and arteries were filled with something lighter than air. Sonya saw a helium balloon once, in Saint Petersburg, at a New Year's Eve celebration. The dancer seems kin to that magical thing. He is somehow able to hover, weightlessly, midair. She knows his name is Nijinsky—and that people think he's some kind of idiot genius. Regardless, a light seems to shine from inside him, glowing in the ghostly dimness of the stage.

Baila grips her hand. "There, Mama!" she points. "There she is! Oh, she looks so much like you!"

Someone shushes her.

Yes, Sonya thinks—that's her. Zaneta—dancing in the corps, as beautiful and skillful as any of the other ballerinas.

Sonya's other senses suddenly start working again: she hears the music—so wonderful! Chopin. His compositions were Sonya's very favorites when Klara and Sonya's nieces played the piano.

Did Zaneta have music lessons? Does she sing as well as dance? Does she charm everyone at parties with her brilliant conversation? What wealth of experience has Zaneta had that Sonya will forever lack?

She feels a twinge of envy again. Looking down, she sees that Baila is looking at her now, rather than at the dancers. Sonya bends down and kisses the top of her daughter's head—then whispers in her ear. "That is your auntie, my darling."

Not letting go of her mother's hand, Baila turns her attention back to the spectacle unfolding there on the stage, clearly enraptured.

٩୭

Sonya pulls Baila through the crowd, intent on getting backstage before Zaneta leaves the theater. Everyone wants to catch a glimpse of Nijinsky—the women crowd the hallways, pushing and shoving in their shimmering gowns and furbelows, their hats like tropical islands alive with bird wings and flowers. The scent of perfume competes with an animal smell of sweat and excitement. The men as well as the women are pushing and shoving. Sonya lifts Baila up to keep her from getting trampled—and barely manages to keep her own feet under her as the two of them are carried along up the stairs with the crowd, to the pass-door leading to the stage.

As soon as they reach the proscenium, Sonya sets Baila on the boards and pulls her through a parting in the heavy velour curtain, heading straight for the metal stairway that leads to the rats' dressing room. She's in such a hurry to climb the stairs, and the stairs are so narrow, that she lets go of Baila's hand. In the grip of anticipation and ardor—in her pounding fear that Zaneta will leave before Sonya catches up with her, maybe leave forever, never to be found again—Sonya forgets about Baila entirely.

The child, in a panic, just manages to grab hold of Sonya's skirt with one hand, while holding on to the iron railing with the other. It feels like her mother is trying to run away from her—or certainly as if her mother has ceased to care about her. The metal stairs are steep and ladder-like, with the whole of the backstage area spread out far below them between the gaps. Afraid of falling, Baila tightens her grip on the fistful of fabric.

They're both out of breath when they reach the open dressing room door.

The air of the room is warm and moist and smells of sweat. The only dancer left there is a very Russian-looking woman who sits half-dressed in one of the rickety chairs before the bank of mirrors, poring over a letter she has clearly found to be upsetting. She looks up briefly, with tear-filled eyes, when they walk in. She seems to look right through them.

The forest fairy costumes are hanging on the garment rack. There's a sullen-looking femme de ménage picking up detritus the dancers have left on the tabletops and floors. There's no sign of Zaneta.

With a murmured apology in Russian, followed by another in French, Sonya goes out onto the landing, where she can lean over and look down at the scene below.

It seems as if the entire audience has migrated backstage. Champagne corks are popping. Diaghilev is making a speech.

Sonya feels a hand on her shoulder and whips around to find herself eye to eye with Tamara Karsavina, a plain cotton robe thrown over her costume, her stage makeup looking very garish up close.

"I spoke with her!" she gushes. The ballerina searches Sonya's eyes, seeming to search for approval there—and then looks down at Baila. "Is this your little girl? She's beautiful!"

"And?" says Sonya.

Karsavina smiles. "It's all arranged."

"Tonight?"

"This Thursday, at the Café de la Paix. You'll have plenty of time to prepare. One o'clock in the grand salon."

Paris

1909

Sonya arrives at the Café de la Paix at the stroke of one o'clock, wearing her best dress and hat. She scans the terrace to make sure that Zaneta hasn't already arrived, then holds up two black-gloved fingers for the maître d'. He leads her inside to the elegant, high-ceilinged, sunlit salon. She has been to the restaurant before, both times as part of Pavlova's entourage after the ballerina won a pile of money at poker.

When the maître d' seats her at a little table near the piano, she asks him whether her sister—her twin sister—hasn't already arrived.

"I assure you, she has not, madame," he says with an appreciative smile. "I would have noticed her."

She pretends to study the menu card. Twice, she sends the waiter away, telling him that she will order when her other party arrives, repeating the word for twin sister: my *jumelle*. She loves saying it. She thinks she will never grow tired of saying it.

Finally she asks for a carafe of *l'eau mineral* and two glasses. She tells herself that it is all à propos, after all: at their very first appearance in the world, Sonya arrived promptly enough to greet her twin with open arms.

Time seems to grow slack and imprecise in the wash of sounds inside the café—the tinkle of glassware and cutlery. Snippets of conversation fading in and out of comprehension. Distant explosions of laughter as random and inexplicable as birdsong. The bittersweet melody of a concertina floating in from the street outside. The hiss of steam when the kitchen door swings open, and the soft footfalls of waiters. It is as if she were hovering above it all, disembodied, like one of the dead looking down on the living. Each breath she takes seems to occupy an eternity.

The slowness reminds her of the intervals of rest she learned to find in between the pains of childbirth. Each time, she found courage in knowing that she wouldn't have to endure the pain forever. There would be another respite, however brief, after each contraction. Each episode of agony, she told herself, was finite. She learned to enjoy these oases of rest, as if time, like dough, were subject to stretching, pressed out on a floured surface by the flats of her fingers and the heels of her hands.

It was only in giving birth that she came to understand that time is an agreement we all make with each other, for simple convenience, as we go through our daily lives. A minute in the throes of agonizing pain is nothing like the minutes we live, so profligately, every day, all of those minutes flying by—indistinguishable, unremarkable—until we come to the end of our allotment and there are no more of them.

Resting in between the pains allowed her to step outside of time. She felt the world around her growing quieter and quieter until she was alone and peaceful in a place of imagined sunlight and serenity. And in the end, she knew—if she didn't die in childbirth—her endurance would be rewarded with a beautiful new baby, the baby she'd harbored inside her for such a long time. The child she would finally have the chance to know and love and nurture. That unknown part of herself that would suddenly be manifest in the outside world as a new being: as someone else.

And then all the sounds of the café are in her ears again. Has she been waiting for minutes—or hours? What if, she thinks with panic, Jeannette has already come and gone, seen Sonya and fled? What if she collected her paycheck from Monsieur Diaghilev—or didn't—and simply left Paris?

She wouldn't, though! Of course, Sonya reassures herself, her sister will want, just as much as she does, to be reunited. How could she not, when Sonya has loved her so faithfully and ardently all these years?

And then, when she has almost given up, she sees her twin, in silhouette on the terrace, looking like part of a painting, in conversation with the maître d'.

"*Monsieur, s'il vous plaît!*" Sonya calls to the waiter, perhaps a little too loudly—but she doesn't care. "Two glasses of champagne!"

Her hands are trembling. As Jeannette walks toward her, Sonya starts laughing and crying at once. Her sister is dressed in an ensemble so similar to hers that it is as if they had consulted with one another beforehand.

Jeannette looks horrified. "Don't get up. Please!" she says when Sonya begins to rise. "I'm sorry I'm late."

"Oh, don't be sorry for anything! I am happier than I've ever been in my life."

"Surely not," Jeannette says, sitting down with what Sonya notices as conspicuous grace—far more grace than she has ever possessed. The way Jeannette moves, even off stage, marks her as a dancer.

They are both staring, one with joy and the other with what might appear to a stranger as loathing. Sonya doesn't see it, though. She is too filled with her own joyous emotions to realize that Jeannette is scrutinizing her and her clothes with intense dislike.

"So," she says, "he dressed you as well."

"I beg your pardon?" Sonya murmurs, blinking a little dazedly.

Jeannette notices the glass of champagne before her—and drinks it down, one gulp after another without pause. "*Garçon!*" she calls. "Another!"

Sonya is struck by the sudden thought that she and her twin are two completely different people—that they may, in fact, have very little in common. "I thought," she says, still smiling hopefully, "we could drink a toast to our reunion." But Jeannette has already started drinking without her. This, she tells herself, is Zaneta—all grown up. A Frenchwoman. A beautiful and graceful ballerina. Her own long-lost twin!

"But how thoughtless I've been," Sonya hastens to add. "You don't know anything yet about our story."

"I know that Paul Poiret gave you those clothes."

His is the last name Sonya wants to hear just now. She fingers the magenta taffeta of her skirt. "I could never afford to buy one of his designs," she says, with something halfway between a smile and a wince. "This was a sample—an experiment."

"And yet he made two of them." Jeannette shakes her head at Sonya. Keeps shaking it until the smile fades from Sonya's lips.

The waiter appears. "Are you ready to order, *mesdames?*" he says, looking from one to the other of them like someone watching a tennis match.

"The *plat du jour*," Jeannette says, "for each of us."

Sonya is glad to surrender the menu. She can't stop thinking about what Jeannette has just told her—and what it means about Paul's treachery. How many layers must be pulled away until she finds the full truth of what he did to her—to them? Cutting short this bitter train of thought, she falls back upon the words she'd decided to say as she cogitated, long and hard, about this moment that has finally arrived.

"I am sometimes able to remember," she says, "although the memory always seems more like a dream. There is another small person sitting close to me, shoulder to shoulder. We are laughing. And then there are voices, loud voices laughing, all around us—and we are crying. And then—"

She pauses, trying to read the effect of her words on Jeannette's face. But the face is impenetrable. It's the theater training, Sonya thinks. They learn to hide their feelings. Pavlova has told her about it. They have to, so that they can become someone else on stage. Whatever role is required of them. It's like a magic trick. It's a skill, like lining a lapel with interfacing to make it lie flat along the curves of the body.

"Does the name Zaneta mean anything to you?"

Barely perceptibly, Jeannette shakes her head no.

Sonya repeats the question in Russian.

Jeannette's posture is perfect—but she holds herself even more erect now, like a queen on a throne. "You've made a mistake," she says. "I am Jeannette Dupres, a Frenchwoman. My father works—worked," she adds softly, remembering that, of course, her father is dead now, "for the Bureau de Change in Nantes."

Sonya gazes into Zaneta's eyes. Never have a stranger's eyes seemed so familiar to her. She longs to embrace this embodiment of what was, for so long, only an idea—to enfold Jeannette in her arms and hold on tight. To burst into tears. But she knows she must resist these feelings, however much they tug at her. She knows she mustn't say or do anything that might cause Jeannette to run away.

She smiles kindly. She is careful not to take an offensive or patronizing tone when she speaks. "You started life as Zaneta, one of two twin girls born to Nadia and Morris Luria, master tailors of Kishinev."

"You've made a mistake," Jeannette repeats.

"Our father was a political activist of sorts but never a violent man. He was an idealist and something of a dreamer. He no doubt dreamed of overthrowing the tsar and bringing a new order to Russia—and of justice for the Jews. But he was arrested on the very day we were born. Taken away and imprisoned for almost ten years."

It suddenly seems impossible to communicate everything she wants to say. How can she convey the feelings of her first ten years, growing up with stories instead of a father? And then the shock of that stranger, gentle and broken, coming into her life. Looking at her with love. Who appeared only to disappear again.

"He came back to us in the year of the flu pandemic of 1890..." Sonya's voice trails off. She's overcome by the absurdity of giving all these details to Jeannette, all at once. How could she possibly take them in? "Should I stop for now? Perhaps we should eat something first."

Jeannette closes her eyes, blocking out the sight of Sonya's face. "Go on," she says, like someone bracing herself for a slap. "Get it over with."

This is not at all what Sonya had imagined. She takes a deep breath, using this opportunity to inspect her sister's face in a way she hadn't dared to before. Jeannette is wearing rouge and powder, although it has been so expertly and subtly applied as to be nearly invisible. There are very faint crow's feet at the corners of her eyes.

Sonya suddenly wishes she could look at their two faces, side by side, in a mirror. She wishes that they could stand naked, side by side, before a mirror. She decides to withhold, for now, the sad story of how their father, weakened by his years in prison, succumbed to the flu. "After Papa's arrest, Mother struggled to support us and our siblings—"

Jeannette's eyes pop open. "Siblings?"

Sonya smiles tenderly. "Lev, who lives in New York now, with his wife and children, a boy and a girl. Faya—" She doesn't want to say yet that Faya died last year. "An older sister, Faya. And Daniel—" She has already written to Daniel, although she has not yet posted the letter. "Daniel is one of a small number of Jewish lawyers in Saint Petersburg, by dint of his brilliant mind, his discipline, and persistence. Daniel was our mother's pride."

"Was?"

Sonya looks down at the soup the waiter has placed before her. It smells delicious. She takes a sip of her champagne. She can't help wondering how much this meal is going to cost them. Probably more than she spends in a week to feed herself and her children.

"Mother tried her best to take care of us—but without Papa there, working with her, it was impossible. She didn't want us to starve."

Jeannette understands this word and what it means—and what it means to go from plenty to privation. What it means to make decisions one would not ordinarily make, if things hadn't been so dire. She thinks of the men, the patrons, whose

greatest recommendations were often the meals they provided.
Even now, food is such a potent symbol for her. Dancers need
to eat. Dancers are always hungry.

"Our mother was a brave and a marvelous person. I adored
her. The orphanage," says Sonya with a look of sorrow in her
eyes, "was meant to be a temporary measure."

This isn't happening, Jeannette tells herself. *I'm dreaming. I'll
wake up soon.*

"We'd been there for less than a year when the regular
matron was away and her assistant met with a French couple
who'd come all the way to Kishinev, for a reason still unknown,
to adopt a baby girl. One baby girl." She pauses. "Perhaps, Jeannette, you can explain."

It is all, Jeannette thinks, as weird as an opium dream. She
hasn't gone to one of the dens since Paul dropped her. But
still! She pinches her thigh through the silken folds of the skirt
that is precisely like Sonya's. Is magenta also *her* favorite color?
Closing her eyes again, she expects to see Paul when she opens
them—Paul sprawled out on a *chaise longue* across the room,
smiling lasciviously at her through a fragrant haze of smoke.

But her thigh hurts where she pinched it. It will probably
leave a bruise. She's here, in the grand salon of the Café de
la Paix—and yet it's as if she were sitting at a dressing table,
before a mirror. A mirror that has softened and rounded her
and filled her face with an expression she herself has never seen
there. Maybe Paul has seen it—of course, Paul had seen that
look of love Jeannette sees now in Sonya's face. Jeannette had
loved him. For years and years, she'd loved him.

"Explain? But none of this makes any sense."

"You were adopted," Sonya says. "You were adopted by the
French couple—and taken away. It broke our mother's heart. It
left," she adds, "a huge hole in my heart." She smiles that same
radiant smile Jeannette saw in Pavlova's dressing room, when
Sonya looked up at her from the floor. "And yet, my long-lost
other self, here you are!"

Jeannette had enshrined the first eight years of her childhood as the beginning and end of all happiness, until she met Paul. Years of feeling loved and treasured, until her mother died. And then the overwhelming coldness of that loss. The grief that was only ever staunched by shutting off her thoughts and living in her body—making her body a means of transportation away from the sorrow of being her lonely, abandoned self. No one outside the dance world ever came close to understanding how the physical pain of working so hard and so constantly, always pushing herself, was the only thing that ever stood between Jeannette and despair. Paul had brought his bright light into the darkness often enough to make her feel loved or at least lovable. But the darkness was always there, waiting to swallow her. "My beloved mother died," she informs Sonya, "when I was eight years old."

"Our mother," says Sonya, as if she hadn't heard—as if she were refusing to hear her, "died when I—when you and I were eighteen. I grew up believing, up until she told me otherwise, at the very end, that I had a twin who was stillborn. That you never lived to see the light of day."

Without betraying any emotion, Jeannette has gone very pale. To think there was a mother—a second mother—who had still been alive for ten years after her own mother died! Who might have loved her. She feels cheated, yet another time, by life—by this person who had a mother until she was eighteen, and enjoyed her love. Who was part of a family that loved and accepted her. Who hadn't been abandoned, as Jeannette had been, as an undefended little girl of eight. Left alone with her monstrous aunt while her father worked and worked and hardly ever spent any time with her—who seemed to do everything he could to avoid spending time with her.

Sonya reaches across the round table, taking her sister's hand. "You're so cold!"

Jeannette tries to pull her hand away, but Sonya hangs onto it. "I only found out—from Daniel, after Mother died—about our time in the orphanage. And that you might actually still be alive, somewhere in France." She puts her other hand on top of Jeannette's, leaning toward her. She can smell scent on Jean-nette's skin. Lavender, a scent she will forever associate with Paul Poiret. "I was born first—Mother didn't even know she was carrying twins. By the time she'd pushed you out, you were blue and cold. Apparently dead."

Tears have welled up in Jeannette's eyes, much to her own amazement. She is trying to blink them away.

"Nonetheless, the midwife wrapped us up in one blanket together, and put us near the stove while she tended Mother. And when she looked at us again, both of us were pink and warm." Sonya's cheeks are flushed, Jeannette thinks, with the look of someone who is in love. "On her deathbed, Mother told me that I'd thrown my little arms around you and brought you to life again with the warmth of my body."

Jeannette has fainted before, from hunger and exhaustion. She recognizes the signs. She thinks, with horror, that she's about to vomit, right there in the Café de la Paix.

Sonya moves her chair close enough to keep Jeannette from falling—and folds her in her arms, sighing with relief at the feeling this gives her—of finally closing the circle. Of knowing that she will be whole again.

PART II

PARIS

1910

Sonya wakes to the sound of rain—more rain. Would it never stop raining? Their street has become a river. Going out to buy bread incurs the risk of drowning. The Seine has overflowed its banks, making it impossible for all but the flattest boats to pass beneath the bridges.

The boat owners are the lucky ones, able to row or pole their way from place to place around Paris. Sonya thinks about the pretty little boat Paul Poiret used once to ferry them to his cottage in Meudon. She could imagine him arriving at her doorstep, standing up in the bow, a wicker basket filled to the brim with delicious food.

She stirs herself to light the stove so that her daughters will at least have a bit of warmth when she wakes them. But why wake them at all, when she has nothing today to feed them?

Two days ago, a little dinghy tied up to the railing just beneath their balcony. Two of the baker's boys were hawking damp loaves of bread that Sonya and her neighbors were all too happy to buy, lowering baskets from their windows. They bought all there was, along with a small amount of butter and cheese.

There's no sign of the boat today, only a large fawn-colored dog, paddling madly to stay afloat in the churning black waters, its nose in the air.

Olga joins her at the window, her glasses perched crookedly on her nose, her flannel nightgown longer, thicker, and warmer than the nightgowns of most of the ten-year-old girls of Paris. Sonya tells herself that at least she keeps her children well clothed.

Olga slips her hand inside her mother's. They both watch, gasping without being aware they're doing so, as the dog, still struggling, disappears around the corner. Sonya had never noticed that their street, which seemed quite flat, sloped downhill.

"Please, Mother—let's not tell Baila about the dog. It will upset her so!"

Sonya always senses Asher in this child—his keen mind, his clear-eyed view of the world. The fierceness of his desire to keep all of them safe.

She squeezes Olga's hand—and, just then, a bit of blue sky appears, like a sign from God.

The rain lightens. Will it stop?

As they stand there, hand in hand, a piece of furniture floats into view—a tall bookshelf, half-sunk like a shipwrecked boat. With an audible roar, the waters surge—and, riveted, they see another bookshelf, just like the first one, rocking crazily back and forth as the current carries it past their building.

A few small rectangular objects glide into view from up the street on the swiftly moving river-road. And then a dense parade of books floats by, some open, some still closed, bobbing among splinters of wood on the dark river that was, a week ago, the rue des Rosiers.

Olga has begun to sob. Surely, Sonya thinks, her daughter can't possibly remember the smell and sight of the ruined and smoldering books torn from the shelves of Jewish homes and scattered, their pages fluttering in air filled with feathers and smoke, along the streets of Kishinev. Olga was only a toddler then—and she was fast asleep, her face pressed into Sonya's shoulder. Is it possible, she wonders, that Olga—precocious even as a baby—opened her eyes as they'd rushed past the ruins of everything they'd held dear? That she'd seen, although Sonya had tried so hard not to let her children see, that nightmare vision of Asher's corpse, there among the other dead—laid out, arms akimbo, faces bloodied and contorted with their final looks of horror?

Sonya wonders if it's Asher's spirit that stirs in Olga now.

Olga could withstand the sight of the poor, struggling, drowning dog, even though the sight of it was horrible. But to see these books, beautiful leather-bound, cloth-bound treasures of knowledge and words, their pages turning to pulp—their truth, their beauty, about to be lost forever—is too much for this word-loving little girl. She rips the glasses from her face, places her childish palms against the steamed-up window, and lets herself sink down, the glass squeaking against her cheek, until she's level with her mother's knees. "I can't bear it," she whimpers.

Naomi joins them at the window. "Oh dear," she says, looking out at the books floating by—and then down at her melodramatic little sister.

Disentangling herself from her children, Sonya takes her hat and cloak from the hook by the door. "I'm going out to find some food for us," she says as she buttons her cloak. They watch her climb up onto a stool in the kitchen and take down from the top shelf the stoneware crock where she keeps the housekeeping money. "No one is to leave this house—and you are to let no one in. Keep an eye on Baila. Do you understand me?"

Naomi pipes up dutifully, "Yes, Mother." Olga, still overcome with grief, says nothing.

Sonya opens the window, letting in a blast of rain and wind. "Do you understand me, Olga?" she shouts, just before the wind blows her skirt up over her head. She yanks it down, gathering the hem into a fistful of fabric before swinging one leg out over the sill. She makes a grab at her hat just in time to keep it from blowing off her head, then hurls it back through the open window. Her face and hair are already drenched, streaming with rain. She hangs on to the sash with both hands until her boots make contact with the makeshift wooden sidewalk, more than the length of her body below the sill. Sonya gets some splinters in her hand as she lowers the rest of herself down and shouts up at her daughters to shut the window behind her. Wiping the rain out of her eyes, she looks up and down what was once their street, but there's not a boat in sight.

Olga and Naomi, astonished looks on their faces, are watching their mother. Both they and she know that she can't swim. She'll surely drown if she falls. Sonya wonders if she's just done the most reckless thing she's ever done so far among the many reckless things she's done in her life. And then, already out of breath, she begins to pick her way with care along the waterlogged wooden planks, finding handholds wherever she can along the sides of the buildings.

❧

Olga continues to sit on the cold floor by the window while Naomi goes into their bedroom to comfort Baila, who is crying both for food and her mother.

It was only recently that Olga read and reread De Charmette's epic poem, "Orleanide," about Joan of Arc, who was herself of such a tender age when she rode into battle to rescue France. Olga has the sudden inspiration to follow her brave mother outside—to rescue whatever precious books she can from the flood below!

It seems an excellent idea—and she is, in any case, so tired of being stuck inside.

She writes a farewell note, using the florid penmanship she's been working long and hard to give the appearance of a grown-up's writing: *I leave you for a noble cause,* she writes. *God willing, I shall return.* Naomi will no doubt laugh at her—but she doesn't care. Hiking up her nightgown and slipping on her boots, she grabs an empty flour-sack from the pantry.

The window is easy enough to open. But she slips and falls when she tries to lower herself down from the sill, barely keeping herself from tumbling off the edge of the raised wooden walkway. Her ankle, injured, starts throbbing, and her heart is thumping in her chest. The walkway is so slippery, and there's so little in the way of railings, that she crawls rather than trying to limp and risk losing her balance again.

The pain in her ankle is far worse than she could ever have imagined. She has to go a long way and crawl quickly, getting splinters in her knees as she labors to catch up with the flotilla of books.

The rain falls harder and she starts to wonder if it hadn't been such a brilliant idea, after all. The reality of feeling so vulnerable and in such pain, in the middle of the storm, is entirely different from what she imagined. She crawls as fast as she can manage, until she gets a little ahead of the books and comes upon a ladder lashed to the sidewalk.

Her thick white flannel nightgown is torn and as blackened as if someone had washed it in ashes. She thinks about how angry her mother will be. And then an image rises before her eyes of Jeanne d'Arc similarly clothed in filthy rags as she stood, bravely, tied to a stake, watching the flames get closer and closer. Feeling their heat.

As Olga climbs down the ladder, every other step she takes is accompanied by an agonizing pain. It makes her think of Hans Christian Andersen's story of the mermaid who drank a potion to transform her tail into human legs, who traded the power of speech for the ability to dance—and yet each step she took felt like the stab of a knife in her foot. The thought of this, even more than the pain, makes Olga's eyes fill with tears.

The black waters rush and whirl around the submerged bottom rungs of the ladder. Olga wonders if it's possible to learn to swim all at once—or if she's destined, if she loses her grip, to sink beneath the waters and drown. How grief-stricken her mother will be—her mother and both her sisters too. She thinks of the fairy tale again, and how inconsolable she'd been after her mother had finished reading the story to her, revealing that the mermaid, for all her hope and sacrifice, died unrecognized by the prince.

Unlike Naomi, who had gotten over it quickly, Olga had cried for days and days.

She doesn't dare climb down to the very bottom of the ladder. Squatting, clutching the ladder with one hand—holding the burlap bag in her teeth—she leans out as far as she can reach with the other. With a perilous stretch, she manages to grab one book and drop it into the bag, which is suddenly much heavier. She plucks a second book out of the water as it floats by. The bag is too heavy now to hold in her teeth. Wincing at the smell, she pins the sodden bag to her side with her elbow, diminishing the distance she can reach out with her free hand. Shivering, she sees a smaller book approaching, one with a gold-embossed illustration of flowers on the cover. Leaning out as far as she can without letting go, she can't do anything more than touch it before it sluices by, spinning now. And then she feels her fingers slipping on the ladder rung in the same moment that she sees something dead floating toward her, a cat or a dog, bloated beyond recognition.

✨

Sonya returns home sodden and triumphant, bearing two loaves, a bottle of milk, a handful of barley, some greens, and a shinbone the butcher sold her for a wildly inflated price.

When she sees that the window is unlatched, and then finds Olga's note, she screams at Naomi until she's hoarse and both Naomi and Baila are sobbing hysterically. And then she leaves again, after taking Olga's cloak from the hook by the door. Olga, that impossible dreamer, hadn't even thought to take her cloak.

The bit of blue sky was only a false promise. It's raining again, harder, if possible, than it rained before. The raised wooden sidewalks, so hastily cobbled together, seem to have little chance of staying intact as the waters continue to rise. Sonya battles her way through this latest downpour, holding on to anything she can.

The rain makes it difficult to see beyond a few feet in front of her. The wind and cold penetrate Sonya's very bones—and yet the air is mild in comparison to the winters in Saint Petersburg. There all but the poorest people dressed for the cold in hats and furs, if they could afford them—but even the humblest would go hungry rather than forgo the necessary protection of an overcoat, even one that was bought secondhand. In the coldest winters, men were sometimes murdered for their warm clothes.

Sonya calls Olga's name so loudly and so long that she hardly has any voice left when, finally, she finds her. Filthy and bedraggled—shivering and looking genuinely scared—Olga is hanging on tight to a Gothic pillar, a dripping sack weighed down with something heavy pressed against her narrow chest. The murky waters swirl around her knees.

"Oh, you foolish girl!" is all Sonya can say, between sobs, as she embraces her child. Olga doesn't let go of her sack.

"Madame! Madame!" a passing boatman cries. "Can I help you?"

This one charges nothing for the service he renders.

Olga's skin has a bluish cast. She's so exhausted, and limping so badly, that the boatman has to carry her up to their window. He refuses the coins Sonya tries to press into his hands.

"But you are all alone," he says, taking in the plain, poor rooms and the lack of a man. "Is there some message I can deliver for you—some relative or friend who could come to your aid?" He looks at Olga. "She will need a doctor."

Sonya doesn't even know precisely where Jeannette is living now. Somewhere in the eighteenth arrondissement, if the gossip is true. Monsieur Blum is traveling. Pavlova is back in Saint Petersburg. Karsavina is in London.

Who else can she possibly turn to? Sighing, choosing her words with care, Sonya scribbles a note to Paul Poiret—and then gives the boatman the address of the great couturier's famous mansion on rue d'Antin.

PARIS

1910

A s soon as she's given Olga a hot bath, and dressed her in a clean nightgown, Sonya tucks the exhausted child into bed. Naomi and Baila keep watch by her while Sonya sets about making the soup. She thinks about her own mother as she adds each ingredient—the shinbone and onion, barley and salt—stirring and skimming and stealing looks out through the steamy windows. How she wishes she could be someone's little girl again, protected and loved. She feels her own clothing first grow cold and then eventually begin to dry.

The waters outside her window are still rising. No one has ever seen or even heard of such rains and floods, not since Noah built his ark. In some sped-up version of history, geography, and architecture, Paris has turned into another city altogether, its roads transformed into canals, the canals filled with sewage and the wreckage of people's lives.

All the buildings and monuments have turned into islands, the buildings disgorging whatever wasn't fastened to their structures. It's as if the body of Paris itself were afflicted with a flesh wound that refuses to heal.

When Olga wakes, Sonya feeds her as much soup as the child will take, which isn't much. Squeezing her mother's hands, Olga apologizes over and over again for having behaved so recklessly—and then murmurs that she only wants to sleep. Her skin, clammy and cold when she was first brought in from out of doors, is hot now. Her eyes, whenever she wakes, are dull and watery.

No one arrives to help them. Sonya wonders whether her note has even reached Paul. She thinks of the beautifully lettered sign he always kept posted on the door to the inner sanctum of his workshop: *Attention! Danger! Before knocking, ask yourself three times if it is absolutely necessary to disturb HIM.*

Like the other rich people of Paris, he no doubt fled the city weeks ago, when the rains first started. How stupid she'd been to expect Paul Poiret to help them. In the times before the flood, Sonya would have walked to the pharmacy for advice and medicine if one of them were ill. But everything has become nearly impossible now, for anyone without access to a boat or raft of some kind. They are trapped indoors, with only what they have already to sustain them—without any of the resources from the world outside they always took for granted, as a given. As a lifeline.

෨

Olga's cough and cold come on, in the middle of the night, some twelve hours after Sonya rescued her from the frigid, filthy waters.

On the second day, her coughing is accompanied by a wheeze, as if there were a small wounded animal trapped inside the prison of her ribcage. When her body isn't wracked by coughing, she sleeps—deeply, noisily, with a watery sound bubbling up from deep inside her. The last time Sonya heard such waterlogged, tortured breathing was in the days and hours before her father died.

She sits beside Olga, unwilling to let go of her hand, fighting the sense of hopelessness and grief that keeps welling up inside of her. Naomi confects a mustard plaster, following Sonya's frantic instructions. On her own, Naomi brings them sugared cups of tea, which Sonya feeds to Olga one spoonful at a time till the child vomits. She complains of pain in her chest. Waking once, a terrified look in her eyes, she whispers something about flames getting closer. About their heat.

Sonya realizes that she has no idea about the fantasies that fill her daughter's head. A better mother would have done a better job listening—understanding what Olga read, and what effect it had on her. A better, more insightful mother could have saved her child from the altogether impractical idealism that seemed to animate Olga's thoughts and actions, both of which had propelled her toward this very disaster. What kind of mother sees what she wants to see, Sonya asks herself, instead of what is? What kind of mother fails to guide and cultivate her child's genius, only wanting her to be, conveniently and comfortably, normal? Sonya understands that, once more—despite her every good intention—she's failed to do right by those who love her.

She bargains with God to take her, instead of Olga. But if Sonya dies, who will watch over her daughters? Who will shepherd them safely into adulthood?

How can she have risked her own children's lives like this, consigning them to poverty and privation, when they might have continued to live so comfortably in Saint Petersburg, with Daniel and his family, if Sonya hadn't been so stubborn and selfish?

On the third day of Olga's illness, Naomi appears beside the bed, dressed in her cloak and hat. "I will go find a doctor."

"But in this flood, my child? I won't have you risking your life as well."

"The rain has stopped somewhat." Naomi kisses her mother's forehead. "I'll be careful—I promise you."

Sonya nods. She doesn't think she's slept at all, but then she thinks perhaps she did, a bit. And then, as if only just remembering her youngest child, she asks, "Where's Baila?"

"She's sleeping now. I gave her some soup and bread."

"You're a very good girl, Naomi."

"I love you, Mama. I will return as soon as I can."

When she gets up to help lower Naomi out the window, Sonya notices that her own clothes are drenched in sweat, whether hers or Olga's, she isn't sure. She stays at the window until Naomi is swallowed up by the rainy landscape.

How hard it is to feel so helpless. Sonya envies the kangaroo, who can gather her babies back to her and keep them safe, even after they're born. She doesn't usually mind being both mother and father to her children—but she minds now. She lies down beside Olga again, folding her into her arms, holding her as close as she had before the child developed such strong ideas and sharp elbows. She drifts in and out of thinking she's in Kishinev again, holding her dying mother while snow falls outside, blanketing everything in silence. And then Sonya remembers that it's Olga she holds now, and it's Olga's labored breathing in her ears.

There has always been something otherworldly about this girl, who lives so much inside the books she reads—who seems so unconcerned about the small things that are of paramount importance to every other girl Sonya has ever known. Olga's eyes, so much like Asher's, seem to be looking past or through Sonya, into some middle distance that only she can see.

Olga's breathing becomes more and more shallow. She stops squeezing back when Sonya squeezes her hand. She makes no sign that she hears her mother's murmured words of love to her, pleading with her not to leave them.

ৎ৯

Sonya wakes with a start. There's a great banging on the door, which is still half submerged in the flood. It sounds as if the Devil himself has risen up from Hell to announce his arrival.

Baila runs to the window, looks out, and pushes it open, letting in a gust of wind and rain. "Here, messieurs!" she calls down in her surprisingly powerful voice to the boat tied up alongside the raised sidewalk outside their door. "You must climb up!"

"Who is it, child?"

"It is two gentlemen, Mama, one of them with flowers and a basket, and the other with a small black bag."

"Where is Naomi?"

"She is there, too—in the boat." A booming male voice shouts up from down below, "I have no less than Abel Desjardins with me!"

Sonya has heard of him, of course—the most famous and most expensive doctor in all of Paris. A feeling of hope surges through her. Grateful tears fill her eyes. It doesn't even occur to her that Paul will be meeting Baila—and Baila will be meeting Paul—for the very first time.

PARIS

1909

It seemed as if everyone in the Café de la Paix had fallen silent. Jeannette felt sure that everyone was staring at the two of them—dressed alike, looking just alike, and sitting as close together as a pair of lesbians. Jeannette thought she'd die of shame.

As soon as the wave of nausea passed, she pulled away from the doppelgänger who seemed determined to ruin her life, wriggling out of her suffocating embrace.

"And in the meantime," Jeannette said, composing herself, "until you found me, you thought it would be a good idea to have a child by my lover."

The words landed like a knife in Sonya's chest. Of course, her twin would be the one person to see the truth she'd been so successful in hiding from everyone else.

It took her a moment to find the words to convey her complicated feelings. "It was the only way I had to feel close to you, until I found you."

"To betray me? Is that some sort of Jewish logic? My God, you make me sick!"

Another body blow. Sonya paused, moistened her lips. Took another sip of her champagne. "I knew he was your lover because of the way he spoke to me, at the Gare du Nord, when I arrived in Paris for the first time. He mistook me for you. And then I saw him again, that same day, at Maison Worth."

"In 1903. Yes, I know—he told me."

"He told you?"

"Not then. Not until just the other day, when I came to him, dressed like you. I never want to see that man again."

"Nor do I," said Sonya. "For all these years, he kept your identity and whereabouts hidden from me, even though he knew full well that I lived in hope of finding you."

"And so you became his lover."

"He seduced me!"

Jeannette looked at her coldly. "Are you saying that he raped you?"

Sonya bowed her head, unsure what to say.

Why was there only one word for something so essentially overwhelming and confusing? Something that could happen so quickly. A gesture, a mood, that turned from one thing to something else entirely. Tenderness turning to insistence. The will of his body imposing itself on hers. His larger size and greater weight. The weight of his urgency and need. The training that all women have that becomes instinctual: to be pleasing. To be compliant. Her mind had simply shut off. Shut down, whispering, *No, this isn't happening—wait, it's happened!* And then there was no turning back.

She'd shed some tears afterward but, truth be told, he hadn't forced her. He hadn't hurt her. On the contrary, she'd enjoyed the touch of his hands and the way he seemed to know exactly how to give her pleasure.

Years after the nightmare of Asher's murder, years after Baila's birth, Sonya kept returning to Paris—ostensibly to continue her search for Zaneta. But she knew that hadn't been the sole reason. Numbed, she'd wanted to feel again—to feel herself as an attractive, sensuous woman. Yes, in a perverse sort of way, to feel closer to her twin—to know what she felt, and what it was like to be her, even if she was never allowed to know her. To experience that thing Paul Poiret had taught Sonya, which she could make happen by herself now. But it wasn't ever the same as it was when it was caused by the feeling of his hands, his mouth, his passion pressing on her. Inside her. She'd gone into another world then, each time. She'd forgotten about Zaneta and even about her own children.

Paul Poiret was a sort of magician when it came to adorning

and adoring women's bodies. How could Sonya possibly explain all this to her sister? "It was an error in judgment," she finally said, "allowing myself to become involved with him. Although I can't regret it now. I can't regret Baila, don't you see?"

"I see a self-deluded slut, worse than all the sluts I've ever known, myself included. Because at least when a dancer has sex with a man she doesn't love, she does it for reasons of survival. Whereas you—"

Jeannette paused mid-sentence, studying Sonya's face. "How could you have done that to me, knowing what you knew?"

Sonya shook her head. "You're right—it was wrong of me. Not only because of you, but also because I was married, that first time." She decided to hold nothing back. "There weren't many times, Jeannette... I was trying to understand something. But, in the end, I realized how wrong it was—how wrong I was. I don't know what I was thinking."

"I doubt you were thinking at all. Men are not the only ones who are ruled by their passions. Did he rub your feet?"

It was harder, it would seem, to hide things from Jeannette than it was to hide things from herself. "I told myself that, eventually, I would find him out," Sonya whispered, "and both you and I would get our revenge."

"And meanwhile you enjoyed the pleasures of his company and the clothes he gave you. Did he take you to Meudon?"

Sonya felt the familiar feeling of shame washing over her. The guilt she'd felt throughout her childhood, whenever she'd thought about her poor dead twin. "You had schooled him well, Jeannette, in how to please us."

"Us! There is no *us*!"

"But there is, don't you see? We are made of the same cloth, from the same pattern."

"And would to God I could tear you into shreds! You have stolen my existence—the life, the child I was supposed to have. The child he had ripped out of me."

Sonya was, for a moment, silent. "Were you pregnant by him?"

Jeannette's mouth was clenched in anger. She exhaled slowly. "Three times."

Three times. She will never forget the feeling of the blood flowing out of her, all that blood, as if she would never stop bleeding. The iron smell of it. The sense of weakness washing over her—the fear, each time, that she was dying.

The beautiful little dream she'd had, each time, of a baby— their baby. A little ballerina, all her own. A little fashion plate for Paul. A life she'd so stupidly allowed herself to dream of until he made that dream impossible—and he'd made her feel like such a fool for dreaming it.

The doctor—if he was a doctor—that last time, wiping his hands and saying there would be no more pregnancies for her, and maybe she'd be glad of it.

Jeannette pointed and flexed her foot under the table, registering a small pain in her Achilles tendon. "He promised to marry me. And then he married someone else, someone much younger, from a prosperous family. But you no doubt know the story of his life just as well as I do." She looked resentfully at Sonya. "I knew from that moment in Pavlova's dressing room, when I saw your girl, that she was his. That she should have been mine!" Jeannette sat up a little straighter. "You could give her to me, you know."

Sonya's expression changed then to one of amused disbelief. "Baila?"

"You have two others! Why should you have three children while I have none?"

Sonya would never have been able to even imagine such a question, before hearing it spoken—she could hardly credit it now. What a notion! "You don't have the slightest idea about what it means to give birth to a child, do you?" Jeannette's wounded expression told Sonya how insensitive her words had been. She licked her lips and tried again. "How could *you*, deprived of your own family, ever suggest that I give Baila away? As if she were a pair of shoes or a coat. Or a cat."

Jeannette glared at her. "You will! I'll make you do it! I'll make a dancer of her. I'll make her into a star in whose light Pavlova herself will pale by comparison. Karsavina too!"

Sonya wondered then if her sister wasn't quite right in the head. How could any sensible person make such a plan, with little to no knowledge of the individual child involved?

Baila was more physically hearty than either of her sisters, but Sonya knew as well as anyone that the Pavlovas and Karsavinas of the world were freaks of nature. Apart from her athleticism and prettiness, Baila was an altogether ordinary child. Sonya was always glad of it, feeling burdened enough by Olga's prodigious brain.

"You could help her," Sonya said. "You could even form her, if her natural inclinations tend that way—and, honestly, I think they do. I was planning on getting her ballet lessons, when I've saved enough money."

"Oh, and am I to play the maiden aunt in your household?" Jeannette was thinking about her own maiden aunt, and what a misery she had made of Jeannette's childhood after her mother died. "Ballet is a calling, not a hobby."

"She's only a child. She's not yet eight years old."

"I have no interest in being your family friend."

"How can you say that? We're sisters."

"Sisters!" Jeannette spat the word out with contempt. "Either you give the child to me—or else I will make sure that none of you ever see me again. Even if it means leaving Paris!"

"You can't be serious!" Meeting her sister's gaze, Sonya tried to fathom what could be going on in Jeannette's mind. Was she unbalanced? Or was she merely stuck in her own point of view, in the way that people in the arts tended to be? It took a single-mindedness to do what they did. Sonya considered her dressmaking to be work, rather than art. It was a way—the only way she knew—to keep bread on the table for herself and her children.

Sonya wished, in this moment, that she could stop time—because, she knew, time was running out for this long-held dream of hers. She wished she could have a long and leisurely interval of time to think about what she and Jeannette might have shared. The family meals. The larger apartment they'd find, with three bedrooms, all the rooms filled with sunlight. Walking in the Bois de Boulogne with Jeannette and the children, all of them wearing pretty dresses and wide-brimmed hats. The two of them getting dressed up together, sharing secrets, sharing makeup and accessories, readying themselves to go out to some festive occasion. To the theater! To a soirée, for surely they would, together, move into social circles Sonya could never have penetrated on her own. She imagined their laughter as they shared their observations afterward. She hadn't yet heard Jeannette laugh.

Sonya realized that she didn't have the slightest idea, really, about what life was like, and had been like, for this ballerina—this performer—who sprang from the infant who had been her identical twin.

Whatever hopes and dreams Sonya had draped around Zaneta were like garments she had designed, cut out, and stitched together without reference to anyone or anything real. It had all been a fantasy based on what she imagined Zaneta might be, tailored to what she herself had longed for, all these years. But Jeannette—this actual, flesh-and-blood person sitting beside her—wanted nothing to do with the garments of Sonya's making, which were completely unsuited to her anyway. It was clear that life had throttled Zaneta, and shrunken her heart, until she was cold and unfeeling, bitter and cruel. Jeannette wanted nothing to do with the love Sonya had nurtured and hoarded for her twin all these years—the love that had kept Sonya from loving anyone else wholeheartedly.

She'd never questioned her assumption that, of course, her twin would love her in return. What a self-deluded fool she'd been! Sonya was determined now: she wouldn't mail that carefully worded letter she'd written to Daniel, urging him to come to Paris to meet their sister. She wouldn't mail the joyous letter she'd written to their brother Lev. Zaneta was, after all, dead—and Sonya's dream of finding her long-lost twin was dead now too. Jeannette wanted nothing to do with her. Jeannette hated her.

Here she was, almost thirty. When her daughters grew up and moved away, she would be as alone as she'd always felt inside. She always knew she'd end up abandoned and alone. It was her fate.

When Jeannette took out her purse to pay the bill, Sonya stayed her hand. "No, Jeannette—I will pay."

"Don't be ridiculous! Karsavina gave me the money for this lunch. I'm not a thief."

"What are you then?" Sonya allowed herself to look into that mirror of her sister's eyes a final time before getting up to leave.

MONTE CARLO

1910

Jeannette, is it you?"

"Paul? Didn't I tell you not to call me here—not to call me ever?"

"Listen to me! She's dying. You must go to her!"

"Dying? But how is that possible? She was the picture of health when I saw her."

"The child was very ill. It was pneumonia—"

"The youngest?"

"The middle one."

Jeannette takes a deep breath, exhaling again.

"Are you there?"

"Yes." Another pause. "Who is dying? I don't understand."

"Your sister is dying. Sonya is dying."

Jeannette can only think how she wished for this—and yet the thought of it is terrible to her now. "I'm—sorry, of course. I thought you said it was the child who was ill."

"Sonya exhausted herself in caring for her. And then, she herself got ill, as soon as it was clear that the child would live."

"You don't even know the child's name, do you?" said Jeannette.

A pause. "No, I don't. Do you? She's your niece."

"She is nothing to me. Only the little one—"

"Listen to me, Jeannette! I want you to take the night train to Paris."

"There's a performance tonight. I can't afford to lose this job."

"The train leaves half an hour before midnight. For the love of God, it is a dying woman's last request."

"She means nothing to me."

"But you have meant so much to her."

"Is that my fault?"

"I will pay you. I'll do whatever is necessary. She begged me, *ma puce.*"

Jeannette can't remember ever having heard Paul cry before. Clearly, he's crying now, although he's doing his best to disguise the sound of it.

"All right. But I don't want to see her children. I don't want them to see me."

"As you wish. It can, I'm sure, be arranged."

"Wait! The little one—she can be there."

"There will also be a nurse there, in case you are hatching any plans, Jeannette."

"How little you think of me!"

"I know you."

"More's the pity."

"I'll send my car to meet your train tomorrow morning at the Gare de Lyon."

PARIS

1910

Paul arrives at the flat an hour before Jeannette is due. He brings an enormous bouquet of lilies and tuberoses and a basket of food. He instructs the nurse to see to it that the two older children are shod in boots and dressed warmly enough to spend a few hours out of doors. And then he enters the room where Sonya has been in a deep sleep, making that horrible sound she'd started making the day before—a sound like the ocean, each labored breath like a wave washing heavily up against the shore and receding again.

The sight of her is deeply disturbing to him. He doesn't understand how the doctor, who performed, it would seem, such a miracle with the child, has yet been unable to turn the course of the illness in Sonya. He thinks about his wife, so precious to him—and little Rosine, and all the other children he hopes they'll make one day. It's indescribably painful to even entertain the idea that death could come to any of those he loves so well.

Sonya is also dear to him. He has, he knows, a capacious heart. Gently, tentatively, he bends to plant a last kiss on her forehead—then crosses himself. He's so little accustomed to doing so these days. "God bless you, Sonya. Jeannette is on her way now. She'll be here soon." Sonya makes no indication that she can hear him, sleeping on, making that terrible death rattle.

All three of Sonya's daughters are sitting close together in the other room, dressed in their hats and coats. "Go in now and kiss your mother," he says to Naomi and Olga, touching each child's head. "We're going out for a ride in my little boat—and a stroll, if possible, in the Bois de Boulogne."

"And I, Monsieur Poiret? Am I not to go too?"

"Next time," he says. "For now, Baila—your name is Baila, isn't it? What a lovely name." He cocks his head, looking at her more closely. There's something familiar about the child. Something that reminds him of Rosine. His heart contracts again with love for his child.

He truly abhors death—death and illness. "For now, you'll stay here with your mother and the nurse." He wonders what Jeannette's angle is, wanting to see this child but not the others. It's imperative—it's clear that it's going to become imperative—that Jeannette take an interest in all three of them. Who else did they have? He turns to the nurse and says, "Under no circumstances is the child to leave. Do you understand me?"

The nurse, who is being paid to follow his instructions, nods her assent.

When the two older girls emerge, ashen-faced, from the bedroom, Paul hurries them downstairs. He lifts them one at a time over the flooded threshold, up onto the raised walkway, helping them down the ladder and into his boat. There he changes into a captain's hat before manning the oars.

৯০

After they've gone as far as they can in the boat, Paul ties it up and puts his bowler back on. Hailing a carriage, he instructs the driver to take them as close as possible to the Parc de Bagatelle.

What a relief for the two girls, to be outside again after being stuck for so long indoors, in and around the sickroom, locked up with all their most horrible fears.

It's thrilling to watch the sights around them. The horses, up to their knees in water, toss their heads and snort as they pick their way over ground they can't see. Their carriage is surrounded by boats and rafts of every description. Well-dressed ladies and gentlemen walk in single file along the raised sidewalks, holding on to their hats, using their umbrellas for balance. Wide-bottomed matrons are coaxed up and down ladders, their huge skirts ballooning out behind them in the wind. Scowling workmen carry furniture and supplies wrapped up in bedsheets. Medics carry people on stretchers. Everyday Parisians are going about their business, walking like high-wire artists from the circus along the narrow, rickety, makeshift walkways.

The Bois de Boulogne is more swamp than park now, with leafless trees rising up from the black waters. Their driver finds a place where the pathway is dry enough—and Paul hands the girls down, one at a time.

There are no roses blooming, of course, in February. But the pond is already filled with the gold and yellow blooms of water lilies.

Naomi is especially attentive to the sight. "It would, I think, be wonderful to paint here, *en plein air.*"

"You are—"

"Naomi, monsieur. Don't you remember? I was the one who came to fetch you last month, when my sister was so ill."

"Of course. You're the twelve-year-old—Sonya's firstborn. Your name escaped me only momentarily." He takes a better look at her. "So you have an interest in art—perhaps you hope to be an artist someday."

Olga pipes up. "Oh, she's forever painting flowers and vines and that sort of thing. Never faces. Isn't that right, Noni?"

"Yes. I like colors best. Bright colors and designs. I very much liked seeing the fabrics Mama worked with, when she was working for you, Monsieur Poiret."

"A few of Mama's friends have wanted to buy Noni's paintings."

Naomi demurs. "They're just designs. It would be lovely, though, to see them made into upholstery fabrics or wallpaper. Some people might, I suppose, want to buy them."

Paul is silent, possessed by a new idea—although he says nothing of it. After a while, he turns to Olga. "And what of you? You seem like a very intelligent sort of girl."

"Is that because I wear glasses, monsieur? People often make that assumption. But, really, a nearsighted girl is just as likely to be as stupid as a girl who sees with the acuity of an eagle."

He stops to take a better look at her. "And your ambitions are—?"

"I should like to be a writer. Not a poet or a novelist but someone who writes social commentary and theater reviews." She pauses, furrowing her brow. "Perhaps I might like to try to be a playwright one day."

"How old did you say you were? Are you a child—or simply an adult who is very small?"

"That is amusing, monsieur. On my next birthday, I will be eleven years old. I was born at the turn of the century."

He looks in turn at Naomi, who pipes up, "And I was born two years before—in the last century. It makes me sound very old, doesn't it?" When neither he nor Olga says anything more, Naomi asks, looking down at the ground, "Can you tell us, Monsieur Poiret—is our mother going to die?"

They watch a duck with a dozen or so ducklings in her wake cross the path and leap, as if falling, into the pond, all of them gliding away without a sound.

"All of us will die one day, my child. And none of us can know when that day will be."

He wonders, as soon as he has said it, about the truth of this pronouncement.

How could it ever come to pass that Paul Poiret will one day cease to be? In Paris, as in all the places in the world that matter, fashion rules supreme. He is only becoming more and more famous and successful. His is not a star that will burn brightly for a while, only to be extinguished. The gods have given him the most highly coveted gift of all: like all the greatest artists throughout history, he possesses the power to make the world see female beauty, and female allure, through his eyes.

Yes, his body—despite his amazing constitution—is mortal. He cannot deny it. But he knows in every cell of his being that no one will ever forget either his name or his art.

Poor Sonya! What will she leave behind but these children? He resolves then and there to be of use to them, if Jeannette will allow it—for surely Jeannette will rise up to her responsibility. Even if Jeannette fails in this, he will find the means to help them anyway. It's unthinkable that Sonya's three lovely girls should be left alone and undefended, without a protector.

⁓

Jeannette hardly sleeps at all on the night train from Monte Carlo, staring at her own reflection in the dark window—wondering what will happen when she reaches Sonya's apartment. Who will be there. How she'll be received. Whether Sonya will be alive or dead.

She removed her makeup, and changed out of her costume, in the little toilet compartment on the train. There wasn't anything suitable among her things to put on—nothing black.

In the backseat of the car Paul has sent for her, she thinks about the black dress her father brought to her, on that day he told her that her mother was dead, on that day when everything good and sweet in her life disappeared, in an instant, until she found ballet. Until she ran away to Paris. Until—for a while, at least—she found Paul.

Waiting for someone to open Sonya's door, Jeannette's heart is beating fast. She hopes against hope the door will open to reveal Baila, the child she has come to think of as a precious gift that was meant for her but given to someone else.

Jeannette thought all night about how uniquely well suited she is to bring comfort and healing to this little girl. By virtue of Jeannette's own loss, as well as her resemblance to Sonya, Jeannette will be able to help the child through this pain that Jeannette understands only too well. And Baila will fill that empty place inside Jeannette, the place where she's longed for someone to love her.

She knocks again, a little more forcefully. She hears voices, a scuffling of shoes. And then the door is opened—by Baila, her hair uncombed, her cheeks stained with tears.

Thrilled, Jeannette smiles down on her.

But the child's expression isn't even remotely friendly. She looks, Jeannette thinks, almost angry. Rather horrified that she's expected to let her in.

⁓

Baila has seen Jeannette only once up close, that frightening day of her mother's collapse in Madame Pavlova's dressing room. And then a second time, staring from far away at the ballerina, among the flock of other dancers on the stage, who so resembled her mother. The woman her mother had referred to—briefly, only once—as Baila's auntie.

There had been no mention of her, after that night that was at first so magic and then so horrible—after they'd tried and failed to find the woman backstage. When they'd climbed the metal stairs and Baila felt her mother let go her hand. Felt herself in danger of being altogether abandoned.

And here is that woman now, in their doorway, while Baila's mama lies in bed so ill. It can only mean that something even worse is about to happen.

෨

The nurse, a black-clad Sister of Mercy, steps out from a darkened bedroom. "Come, child," she says, leading Baila away, raising her eyes toward Jeannette and nodding at the gaping bedroom door.

Jeannette walks through, flinching when the door is closed shut behind her.

The furnishings of the room are shabbier than she expected. The beamed ceiling is low. The water-stained walls are covered in brightly colored paintings of flowers and other botanical fantasies made on sketchbook paper, affixed with thumbtacks. There's a small window, framed by pretty curtains, looking out at the waterlogged masonry of the building next door. A pair of beeswax tapers in brass candlesticks flicker on the bedside table, alongside a huge vase of tuberoses and lilies that have filled the room with their heavy perfume.

Sonya is lying on her back, her eyes closed. Her hair has been arranged on the pillow, her nightdress is tidy, her hands are clasped under her bosom.

Jeannette drops to her knees at the bedside, crosses herself, and curses Paul for making her come all this way to see a corpse—and a corpse, no less, who is like a nightmare vision of her own death. No one should have to see such a sight, she tells herself. Her eyes fill with tears. The smell of the candles and flowers is making her feel sick.

She rushes to the window and struggles, unsuccessfully, to get it open. Breathing hard, she stands there until the wave of nausea passes.

And then she hears a sound, a faint rattling, rasping sound, like an ocean wave that slaps against a shingle beach and falls and sinks away. A hissing sound. Not from outside the door, or outside the window, but from the bed. Jeannette stands still and holds her breath and sees Sonya's chest rise and fall.

Every other thought is pushed out of her head by the story Sonya told her, the story that had made Jeannette cry against her will, on that sickening day at the Café de la Paix, the last time they'd been face to face. Everyone had thought Jeannette was born dead. But then she and Sonya were put into a blanket together, and Jeannette came to life again. Sonya's touch—her warmth—had brought her twin back to life, or at least that's what Sonya believed.

Letting her cloak drop to the floor, Jeannette sits on the bed, lifts Sonya up, and wraps her arms around her back. The movements feel like a choreographic sequence in which Jeannette is partnered with someone feigning sleep. Someone like Karsavina when she danced her pas de deux with Nijinsky, in *le Spectre de la Rose*. Sonya's head lolls against Jeannette's bosom. "You see," Jeannette says out loud, "I'm here now—or you would see, if you opened your eyes."

Sonya's eyes stay closed. Her breathing is so shallow as to almost be imperceptible. She's warm, but her body is limp.

And then Jeannette remembers something else. The sensation of a heartbeat not her own but contained within the same space that holds her. Was it a memory of the womb they shared for nine wordless, sightless months of companionship? Or of that famous blanket in which they were swaddled as newborns? Or was it a memory of the crib where they slept together in a Russian orphanage?

It's a feeling of being safe. Of being one of two.

And then she remembers a sound, also wordless—a sound of laughter. Silvery childish laughter. Jeannette feels a jolt of happiness, remembering. It's like coming upon a treasure she never knew she possessed, right there among her own belongings. And then she remembers something else: a word.

She looks down at Sonya's face. And although the eyes stay closed, Jeannette wills the lips to speak. "Say my name!" she commands.

It almost seems that Sonya has smiled in response, ever so slightly. But maybe it's a trick of the candlelight.

Is she going mad? Jeannette can hear the name inside her head, spoken in a childish voice. The name wants to be said out loud, the foreign word that had meant nothing to her—a word she'd hated hearing—when Sonya first said it on that day, and every time she'd repeated it. Jeannette can hear it now, though it remains unspoken: her long-lost Russian name, shining up at her like a coin at the bottom of a wishing well.

Her name—*is* it her name?

Jeannette wonders whether she wouldn't have done the same thing, in Sonya's place. How like Sonya would Jeannette have been if her sister, rather than she, had been the one plucked out of the crib in the orphanage that day? Would Sonya have become a dancer and an anti-Semite, as Jeannette had been taught to be? What sort of person would Jeannette have been if she'd been raised a Russian Jew, in the bosom of a loving family, and then learning that her twin was alive, somewhere in France? Would Jeannette have done then exactly what Sonya had done in searching for her? It made sense that they'd both be drawn to the same man. And that the flowers on these walls were nearly all shades of magenta, Jeannette's favorite color. The color she always imagines when she pictures her own soul.

She knows that Sonya, in whatever deep sleep she sleeps, can hear Jeannette's heartbeat now—and she holds her tighter.

In the beginning, they were the same person—or not a person, but the tiny start of a person that would divide into two parts, each of them exactly the same. Wasn't it logical to conclude that each of them would have the power to resurrect the other?

Jeannette takes a deep breath and says the word out loud then, pushing Sonya's hair away from her ear, so she'll be sure to hear her. She speaks in a voice she hardly recognizes as her own, a voice dredged up from the deepest regions of her past. Their past.

"Zaneta!" says Jeannette, speaking for her twin. And then she says, speaking for herself, "Sonya!"

※

For a long time—she can't tell how long—Sonya has been trying to understand the sound that seems to be everywhere around her in the dark, a sound like the breath of the world itself. An inhalation and exhalation, but accompanied somehow by a fairylike percussion made of falling tiny flecks of gold—or sand. Yes! She understands in the same moment that her inner eyes open on a scene that she knows isn't real—not in the sense of any reality she's ever experienced before.

The moment explodes with buttery yellow light: the sea! Waves are breaking gently on a pebbled shore—and sinking, hissing as they recede.

She can smell salt spray and hear—what are those birds that look like paper airplanes, swirling and calling above her, bright white against the tender blue sky?

But she is not herself as she has always known herself— and this is not any land she has ever seen before. And there is Jascha, walking beside her, barefoot, his trousers rolled up to just below his knees. Jascha not as he was when she knew him, but much older. His still-abundant hair is the color of pewter now. His face is the same face, though a little heavier. He has a mustache. It suits him. He's smiling at something straight ahead of them on the shoreline. He's holding her hand.

Those children on the sand ahead of them—Sonya understands that they are her grandchildren. She always felt love for Jascha's progeny, even when she never guessed that his children and grandchildren would also, in an alternate route to the end of her life, be hers. It makes no sense and it fills her with joy. If this is a dream, she doesn't want to wake from it.

With difficulty—because every movement, even breathing, seems to require a superhuman strength—she looks down at her left hand, holding the fingers splayed out. Fingers that are no longer merely long and slender but also a little swollen, most of them, at the first joint. Her wedding ring, a simple gold band, is loose on her finger. She can see the veins beneath her skin, like rivers on a map. When she presses finger to thumb, the pads of both feel soft and pillowy.

The light is so bright that everything she sees seems ringed in gold.

How can it be that the moment of death is, in itself, as full and rich as a lifetime? The sense of this makes Sonya smile, but only slightly, as even the smallest movement requires such effort—and there is, she knows, barely anything left. It's all she can do to keep her inner eyes open to the swirl of time and pathways, and the multiplicity of lives, both lived and unlived. The world as she's always seen it has only been a shadow of everything that is.

Sonya feels herself slipping beneath the salty waters of a sun-warmed sea. She can't breathe—but she's not panicking. She feels a sense of peace as she drifts lower and lower, the water sluicing through her hair, the sound of bubbles in her ears.

And then another body bumps up against hers. She feels two arms embrace her, pulling her up again into the light and air.

Gasping, she opens her eyes and meets her sister's gaze.

Jeannette's entire face is suffused with a look of triumph. "And so," she says. "Now we're even!"

PARIS

1910

J eannette eases Sonya onto the pillow, drawing the blankets up over her chest.

"Yes," Sonya whispers. "We're even now." When she starts coughing, Jeannette gives her water. She stays by her side until Sonya, her face serene, drifts off to sleep. And then Jeannette calls the nurse into the room, instructing her to send for the doctor—and then to take her place at the bedside.

Jeannette finds Baila, staring out the rain-streaked window—and joins her on the banquette. "Dry your tears, child. Your mother is going to live."

Baila looks up into her aunt's face, wondering how she could have ever thought that this woman—this stranger—completely resembled her mother. Their faces, and the stories those faces tell, are so different, when one looks closely. She stares into Jeannette's eyes, thinking how untrustworthy they seem. "How do you know?" Baila says quietly.

"Sisters know these things." Jeannette can't believe she's saying this—and, in the same moment, she understands that she means it. "It must be the same for you and your sisters, isn't it? Don't they sometimes understand what no one else in the world could possibly understand?"

Baila thinks about this for a moment—then lifts one hip slightly and takes out the telegram she's hidden under her skirt. "This arrived when you were in there with Mama."

Baila has evidently read it already. It's in French, addressed to Naomi, Olga, and Baila Danilova. *I'm on my way, dearest nieces. Stop. Contact René Blum, Esq., if worst happens prior to my arrival.* This is followed by an address on rue Taitbout, in the ninth arrondissement.

Jeannette reaches out to touch Baila's beautiful honey-colored hair, which is hanging loose and looks in need of brushing—but then thinks better of it. There will, she hopes, be time and opportunity for that later.

"I think I had better go bring our good news to Maître Blum, don't you?"

Jeannette realizes that she has to move quickly, if there's to be any chance at all of getting herself, rather than anyone else, named as Baila's guardian. Who better than herself? Paul must have wired Sonya's brother on the same day he phoned Jeannette in Monte Carlo—or maybe before? Is it possible that Sonya never told her brother—their brother—about finding Jeannette? Her mind is spinning, trying to think of the best way to manage the situation. Above all, she tells herself, she must make the right first impression on the two lawyers.

Ever so lightly, she touches the child's cheek. Oh, to have such skin again! "I'm just going to change my clothes," she says, heading back into Sonya's bedroom. "I'm sure your mother won't mind if I borrow something of hers."

Coming out on tiptoe a few minutes later, dressed in black, she says loudly enough for the nurse to overhear, "Go in and sit beside your mother, my pet, and hold her hand. It will do her a world of good."

≈

Maître Blum's secretary stares at Jeannette—and then his face breaks into an infatuated smile. "It's you!" he says.

Doubly glad she's wearing Sonya's very conservative clothes now, Jeannette stands even straighter than before. "I beg your pardon, young man."

"But surely you remember me!" He lowers his voice. "I sent flowers to you twice. And you waved to me once, from the stage."

Jeannette curses every wish she's ever had to win fame as a dancer. She wonders whether she can get away with telling the secretary that he's mistaken. But then she remembers seeing him in the audience at the Opéra, in the front row. She did, she recalls with a feeling of helplessness, wave to him, on more than one occasion. She might have even thrown him a kiss. His bouquets were quite lovely, extravagant for someone working as a clerk. She can't remember his name.

"But, of course!" she says, mustering all her charm. How can she possibly make her plan work now? Such a harebrained, half-baked plan! She clears her throat, stalling for time. "I didn't recognize you, out of context. I'm surprised you recognized me."

He had sad, rather beautiful eyes. "I would recognize you anywhere."

"I beg you then," she says in a low, urgent voice. "Consign those moments, as I have, to the past—and do me the honor of meeting me today as someone previously unknown to you." She'd heard that line—or something like it—in a melodrama once, at a cabaret. She can't believe she's actually found occasion to use it.

He gazes into her eyes like a soldier facing a firing squad. "Your name, madame?" he says with perfect sangfroid. "Or is it mademoiselle?"

There is something a little heartbreaking about his willingness to forget her. "Dupres," she says. "Mademoiselle. I believe that Maître Blum and his Russian colleague will be very glad to receive me."

"I imagine so, Mademoiselle Dupres. I will announce you." He rises from the desk—a fine young man, impeccably groomed. In the fraction of a second before opening the door to the inner office, he whispers, "Your secret is safe with me."

The office has two large windows looking out over a landscaped courtyard and a fountain. Two gentlemen rise up at the sight of her. Both have graying hair and elegant clothes, and are blotting at their eyes with handkerchiefs.

One of them looks strangely familiar. "My God!" he whispers, staring at her wide-eyed. "Poiret, in his telegram, wrote that you were—"

"But this is not Sonya!" breaks in the other man, presumably

René Blum. "The resemblance! It's absolutely—astonishing!"
He's looking at Jeannette in such a way that she knows at once
he's in love with Sonya. His eyes are brimming. "So she found
you, after all."

"I can't believe it," says the other man, coming up to her and
squeezing her hands. "But it's true, it's true!" He starts crying,
then sobs out some words in Russian, followed in French by,
"Oh, my little sister! You live!"

He looks horrible when he cries. It reminds Jeannette of
the way *she* looks when she cries. She gives a cursory squeeze
to the hands that are squeezing hers, hoping this man, who is
evidently her brother, will let go.

In contemplating this meeting, and planning what she hoped
to accomplish, she'd only thought about the importance of
making the right impression. Picking the right clothes to wear
and planning the right things to say. Above all, hiding her connection to the demimonde. She hadn't thought at all about how
it would feel, being in the presence of this Russian Jewish man
who is—and now it's unmistakable as she looks at him—her
blood relation.

There's something in his looks that upsets her—an exaggerated version of her own face, and Sonya's, with a longer nose
and deeper shadows under the eyes. How odd it is, at this late
date in her life, to suddenly be faced with yet another sibling!

"How can it be," he says, "that Sonya never told me? Zaneta!"

That name again. Although Jeannette had planned to hide
her feelings, she can see that her complete lack of pleasure in
the experience, and even her lurking sense of revulsion, have
made themselves known. "And you are, of course, Daniel. Sonya's brother." Too late, she realizes she should have said, *our
brother.* Or *my brother.*

The Russian's eyes are dark with tears. "Honestly, I wouldn't
have expected you to look so much like her, after all these years
and no doubt such different lives."

What did he expect then? He knew they were identical twins,
didn't he?

"Mademoiselle Dupres," the Frenchman says, smoothing over the awkward moment with polished civility. She guesses that he is also a Jew. "Do please sit down."

Daniel is holding his face in his hands, staring at the twin stolen away from his family so long ago. "It's as if she lived again!"

Jeannette says nothing, for a moment. And then she tells them, in a quiet voice, "She lives still."

"But the telegram!" says Daniel, half choking with emotion. "Poiret told us she was breathing her last breaths."

"Why are we standing here?" shouts Blum. "Eugène!" he calls into the outer office. "Get a cab for us—on the double!"

"It's all right," Jeannette says, hoping to slow things down. "Sonya's resting now." She begins to realize, with self-recrimination, how monstrous her request will seem, under the circumstances. There's no way, within the bounds of decency, she can raise it.

"Not a moment to waste!" says Blum. "I can't understand why she didn't reach out to me!"

"Or to me!" says Daniel.

Jeannette has also wondered.

"Should we bring a doctor with us?" Blum is barely able to contain his excitement. "I know a very good man."

"The doctor is probably by her side by now. The best in Paris, I've been told."

"Thank God for that," says Daniel. "Come, René! Come—" He looks and blinks at her. "Jeannette!"

A gust of wind threatens to blow off their hats. Taking Jeannette's arm, René Blum helps her up into the cab. She wishes Eugène had hailed a bigger one. The three of them are crowded close together, knee to knee.

She stares out the window to avoid their eyes.

Did she expect them to have horns? When she thinks about it, it was her aunt, her hated aunt, who always had the most virulent, frightening things to say about the Jews. Her father was much quieter about his antipathy. Jeannette had grown up believing that it wasn't something polite people talked about. And yet it was a fact of life—they were to be feared, as a people. Feared and loathed.

Sonya seemed an exception, as were the various writers and artists Jeannette had met and come to know through Paul.

Daniel is sobbing in that particularly choking, ugly way that men have when they cry. Jeannette, who is dry-eyed, thinks once again about how emotional these Russians are. She never in her life saw any of her male relatives cry, not once. Even after her mother's death, her father didn't shed a tear—at least, not in front of her.

"I still can't understand," says Daniel, "why she didn't write to tell me that she found you."

Jeannette vows to ask Sonya, straight out, if she does indeed recover fully.

Had oh-so-respectable Sonya felt too ashamed to tell the truth about Jeannette to their brother, who is evidently a highly cultured and cultivated man? He's the very type, she knows quite well, to have a mistress who is a dancer.

What hypocrites men are! She hopes the clerk keeps his promise not to reveal that he's seen her before, on stage at the Palais Garnier.

Everything Jeannette had planned seems so ridiculous to her now. Far from having any chance of becoming Baila's guardian, she will have to find a way to navigate this maze of family relationships she's stumbled into—and all because she had to go and save Sonya's life!

~

The nurse conveys the doctor's pronouncement that Sonya is too weak to see more than one person at a time. Daniel gives himself the privilege, taking Baila's place on the chair at his sister's bedside.

Sonya opens her eyes when he takes her hand—and then she smiles that smile that has always been, to Daniel, so breathtaking in its beauty. Somehow so surprising, every time he sees her.

"I was afraid I'd never get to see you again!" he says. "Poiret's telegram—" He keeps himself from saying what he'd been about to say. Letting go her hand to wipe his eyes, he confesses, "Klara has been getting everything ready for your girls."

"Everyone, it seems," says Sonya weakly, "wants my girls." Sighing, she takes a long look into her brother's eyes. "Last year, Jeannette demanded that I give Baila to her."

Daniel is momentarily silent, taking this in—considering what it might mean. Waiting for Sonya to say more. When she meets his silence with silence, he clears his throat in a lawyerly way. "There's so much I want to ask you!"

"Ask me, then," says Sonya, gazing into his eyes. She thinks about how she has never felt very close to Daniel, perhaps because she's never felt altogether safe with him. He has always seemed, since as far back as she can remember, suspicious of her. As if he blamed her, unfairly, for something she's never been able to understand.

"How long ago did you find her?" he asks—and she feels herself again under the unforgiving light of Daniel's scrutiny.

"Just last year."

"And you never told me."

"There was nothing to tell. She didn't want anything to do with me. And then, just today, she decided she did."

Daniel was looking uncomfortable—as if on the verge of confessing something embarrassing. "I never believed, until I saw Zaneta today—"

"*Jeannette*," Sonya corrects him.

Ever so slightly, he pulls away from her. Bristles a little, at the temerity of this interruption from his baby sister. Sonya had forgotten how much Daniel cares about maintaining the fiction that he's in charge. "Do you know about the notion of *tikkun olam*?" he asks her, changing course.

"You and Lev were the only ones who ever studied Hebrew."

"It refers to the project of repairing the brokenness in the world."

"Is it your project, Daniel?"

"It's mine, yes—and I suspect it's yours too."

"I must tell Olga about it. It's just the sort of thing that excites her imagination."

She wishes it were Lev at her bedside, instead of Daniel. She always felt so happy and safe around her brother Lev, so many years gone now, and so far away. "Do please say whatever it is you were going to say, dear Daniel. I'm very tired."

Daniel sees that the time is not yet right to fix what has been broken. What he had broken, by the beliefs he'd harbored when his mother first brought Sonya home from the orphanage without Zaneta. And what he and his mother had broken, sixteen years later, destroying that stack of letters to Sonya from the pharmacist's son.

There was no sense in telling her the whole truth now, when she was so weak, and so much was still uncertain. "I only wanted to say what a relief it is, and what a mitzvah, that you pulled through."

"Our sister saved me," she says.

"As you once saved her," says Daniel.

PART III

PARIS

1911

Sonya listens hard in the darkness, deciding that Jeannette's breathing is too quiet to allow for her to be asleep. Speaking softly, she asks, "Are you awake?"

"I am now."

"I'm sorry. Never mind."

"Do you need something?" Jeannette has insisted on sleeping on a cot in Sonya's room, even though she has a lovely new bed with springs in her own room. She feels a sense of ownership vis-à-vis Sonya's seemingly miraculous recovery. Performing a miracle—or so it seems to her—has turned out to be one of the most satisfying events of her lifetime. It hasn't kept her from frequently feeling annoyed by Sonya.

"I was only wondering," says Sonya. "whether perhaps you also have a very dark place inside you, like I do. A place of hopelessness that's always there, even when you're happy—always waiting for your return."

Jeannette is silent for such a long time that Sonya assumes she's not going to answer her. It was a stupid question, anyway—just the sort of question that Jeannette has shown herself unwilling, for the most part, to entertain.

Sonya is hovering on the edge of sleep again when Jeannette speaks up from the darkness. "In the middle of the night, sometimes. Especially when I've woken up and can't manage to get myself to sleep again."

The recrimination isn't lost on Sonya. But she's used to, by now, the barbs so often contained in her sister's conversation. She sighs. "I'm always afraid of losing what I love. I wish I could be less afraid—that I could simply feel contentment in what I have, rather than always feeling afraid of losing it."

"Only idiots are simply content. But, yes—I have also always been afraid of that darkness inside me. Of feeling unworthy of being loved."

This is one of the very things Sonya has longed for—to speak like this, with such intimacy, with her sister. It means so much to her. It makes the darkness seem less dark. "Do you think," she ventures, "that it's because we're twins that we feel this way?"

Jeannette considers this. She's been spending a surprising amount of time thinking about such matters, ever since that day she and Sonya confronted one another in the Café de la Paix. "Maybe it's because your mother—our mother—" Jeannette pauses. "Maybe it's because the choice was made to send us away to an orphanage, while your brother Daniel, the worthier child, was kept at home."

"But you knew nothing of that until I told you."

"I knew, after *my* mother died, that there was something wrong with me—something shameful. And that was finally confirmed for me—you'll excuse me for saying this—when I learned of my origins."

"And do you still feel shame at being Jewish?"

"I don't know what it means to be Jewish! Is it like a new coat I've suddenly put on, a coat that I can't ever take off now, no matter if it suits me or not?"

"I've always felt quite glad when I've acquired a new coat…"

Jeannette is in entire agreement with that one—but doesn't concede the point to Sonya. The darkness is beginning to seem less impenetrable. Jeannette can just discern the outline of her sister where she lies, huddled under her duvet. And there's that fleeting sensation again in Jeannette's body, that ghost of a memory of the two of them, sharing the same small space. It's gone in an instant. "I'm the same person I've always been," says Jeannette in a bored tone of voice, "except I suddenly have a lot of new relatives."

"But that's the point, Jeannette! You are the same person you've always been—and you've always been Jewish by birth, even though the fact was kept hidden from you."

"But, honestly, I don't understand what it means. Does God love me any more, or any less, now that I've been revealed as one of those my family always reviled?"

"Hold my hand," says Sonya.

"Why?"

"Just do, please."

They stay like that, holding hands across the space between their beds, for a few moments of silence, broken finally by Sonya. "I don't myself understand exactly what it means to be Jewish." She understands, though, what it means to feel hated for being Jewish.

"Your hand is trembling," says Jeannette. "Are you sure you're all right?"

Sonya squeezes the hand that holds hers. She wishes there were a wordless way to share her memories, the good and the bad, with her sister. To convey all those feelings that are so vivid inside her—that sometimes overwhelm her. The terror that comes to her sometimes, in the middle of the night, remembering the pogrom. The memory of Asher's bruised and contorted face, where he lay, in the makeshift morgue. Her memories of riding around on Lev's shoulders when she was just a little girl. Of their father's eyes. The shop in Kishinev. The sound of the little bell on the door that tinkled every time it was opened or closed. Her mother's chicken soup. Jascha's kiss.

It's doubly hard to try to find words for all of it in French. She sighs. "Our Jewishness is something like the connection between us, I think. It's something the blood knows. Something deeper, older, and wiser than our own individual lives and all the selfish things we wish for."

"Do you think Jews are less selfish than others?"

"I wouldn't say that. I think that Jewish people come in all the types and varieties that occur in every other population. There are those who are very good and those who are less so. But there's something in the culture—I'm not sure how to describe it. An idealism, maybe. A sense of yearning. A longing for goodness. For peace. To live a good life."

"But surely people of every religion would say much the same."

"Well, no doubt. But I don't think it's all that much about religion. Because I feel Jewish even though I'm not religious."

"You've confused me completely now!"

"It's a confusing issue. But it distresses me, more than I can say, that you feel nothing but shame at our origins. I've been hoping that, on some level, you'd come to feel a sense of pride. It can't have escaped your notice, given that you move about so much in society, that an outsize proportion of the world's great artists, writers, and thinkers are Jewish!"

Silently, Jeannette concedes the point. "Nonetheless," she says, "I still have that dark and hopeless place inside me, very much like that place you describe."

Sonya squeezes Jeannette's hand again, then releases it. She doesn't think that either of them is likely to fall back asleep. Light has begun to seep in from beneath the flounced curtains that match a pinafore she made for Baila with the leftover fabric. "Does everyone, do you think, feel a sense of shame, deep inside themselves?"

"Maybe not. But maybe so. We Catholics have made a great cult of Original Sin."

Sonya dislikes the fact that Jeannette still describes herself as a Catholic. It irks her that her twin refuses to embrace their shared patrimony. It feels like a rejection of *her*. "Do you think," she ventures, "that you and I are broken in the same way, always questioning whether we're worthy of love?"

"I think we're all running from whatever demons we carry around inside us," says Jeannette, "straight into the arms of death."

ತಾ

Paul pays Jeannette and half a dozen other mannequins to go into public places wearing his latest fashion statement, the hobble skirt. After the trauma of their first such foray, the women band together to demand double the usual rate of pay: the skirts, banned by the clergy, are causing riots wherever they're modeled. Newspapers run outraged editorials every day. In the space of a month, Paul has to hire extra seamstresses to keep up with the orders, which have also begun to come in from abroad.

After the unprecedented freedoms—and scandal—afforded by Poiret's famous war on the corset, the most fashionably dressed women of Paris can now walk only with small mincing steps, their knees pinioned. The restrictions of the hobble skirt necessitate revealing a shocking expanse of leg whenever someone wearing one has to step out of a carriage or up onto a sidewalk. Jeannette accuses Paul of hating women. His standard reply to her is to protest that, on the contrary, he worships the female body.

వా

As Jeannette waits on the platform at the Gare de Lyon, an announcement blares over the loudspeakers—something about a mechanical problem, or a problem on the tracks. Only halfway through, Jeannette realizes it's the train for Monte Carlo—her train—that's been delayed. She looks up at the station clock. If she's quick about it, she calculates, there will be time enough for her to buy a jambon beurre for the journey.

She'd meant to pack some food before she left. But the atmosphere at the apartment had been too fraught. Sonya kept begging her not to go. Jeannette kept trying to convince them all that Baila should come with her. All of them, except Olga, were in tears by the time Jeannette, swearing at all of them and blaming all of them for making her late, slammed out the door with her suitcase and hatbox, determined to be on time for the pre-rehearsal meeting at the Palais du Soleil in Monte Carlo.

With the sandwich tucked into her handbag, Jeannette feels a little calmer. And then she hears another announcement, referring to the replacement train for Monte Carlo, just departing now from a platform two tracks over from where she's been sitting. There must have been a second announcement while she was buying her jambon beurre. It's like a nightmare. She's been waiting all this time at the wrong platform.

What an inauspicious start to her return engagement with the Ballets Russes!

Diaghilev's company is providing a bonanza of opportunity for the freelance ballerinas of Paris and beyond, eager to participate in any of his productions. Jeannette knows full well that she's just one of a legion of trained dancers who possess professional ambition but have lacked the luck to win the roles that would allow them to be noticed, if only briefly, by those who matter.

Stranded, having missed her train—disgusted with herself and with her life—Jeannette watches all the other people with their suitcases, their families, their lovers, and their sense of purpose, all of them hurrying past the bench where she's sitting immobilized. Her eyes well up. She feels like a fool, once again, for continuing to hope for success as a ballerina—and for some kind of redemption from that success.

There's not another train leaving for Monte Carlo for another three hours.

At the same little café where she bought the sandwich, Jeannette sits down at the bar and orders a glass of wine.

When her train, the right train, pulls up to the platform, Jeannette is the first passenger to climb aboard.

Placing her hatbox on the seat next to her, she hopes no one will ask to sit there.

When she's finally, safely settled into her seat, she allows herself to luxuriate in the sounds of travel. The guard's shrill whistle at the moment when the train is about to leave the station. The plaintive one-step rise of the steam trumpet. The leonine huffing of the engine that starts in a slow 4/4 time, becoming deeper and faster. Like a lover's urgent breathing. Becoming a steady flicker of sound. Like an *entrechat quatre,* too fast for the eye to see the individual beats of the dancer's toe shoes flickering in the air.

She folds her cloak into a pillow and leans her head against the window. It will be wonderful to be in Monte Carlo again. To see that aquamarine stripe where the sea meets the sands of the Côte d'Azur, and the royal blue of the Mediterranean beyond. What a relief it will be to fill her eyes with those colors again! Magenta flowers tumbling over terracotta walls. The wind-swept pale-blue skies and the cries of gulls when rehearsal's done as she walks on the boardwalk along the beach. Jeannette is glad to leave the grayness of Paris behind her.

It was a mad idea, anyway, thinking she'd be able to attend the rehearsals and learn the choreography while looking after the child, and on the scant pay Diaghilev's company was offering the lowest rung of dancers. René Blum had promised—or threatened—to meet her in Monte Carlo, and wine and dine her a bit, which was a pleasant prospect. Twice now, he'd sent bouquets to their apartment above the shop—ostensibly for both her and Sonya, but Jeannette could tell he was angling to go to bed with her. Sonya seemed determined not to encourage him, at least not too much. Jeannette took it as a signal that the way was clear for her. She didn't want him now—but she knew she might want him later. For now, she simply wanted to go on dancing as long as she could.

The child had actually seemed to be entertaining the idea of spending two weeks in Monaco under her aunt's supervision. Slowly, over the past months, Baila had become more and more engaged with her ballet lessons, sometimes even asking Jeannette to carry on with her beyond the two hours Sonya approved for their practice sessions every day.

It hadn't been apparent at first—but Baila was, as every real dancer has to be, extremely competitive. Every day, she was determined to do better than she had the day before. She was good at recreating the movements Jeannette showed her—and explained to her, using the language that had been most helpful to Jeannette when she was a child, just starting out. The trick was always in finding the right turn of phrase, the right comparison, that would make the movement, so abstract by itself, make perfect sense.

Jeannette had never taught before. She was pleased to find that she was good at it—or, at least, seemed good at it when it came to teaching her niece.

Baila had perfect feet for ballet, with high arches and insteps, without her mother and aunt's overly long first toe. She was more or less the same age Jeannette had been, when her aunt first took her to the École de Danse Classique in Nantes, just months after her mother's death. In Baila's case, she started lessons just after her mother *didn't* die—but Sonya's death, or the possibility of Sonya's death, was no doubt a factor in the way all of them were thinking about their lives these days.

Nothing felt stable or safe. Anything could happen—torrential rains and floods, epidemics that slaughtered thousands. Riots. Revolutions. Perhaps even a war, given all the ominous news from the Balkans. After the Great Flood of 1910, the possibility of disaster seemed to lurk around every corner. It made everyone giddy, in a way—more willing to take risks, as when Jeannette finally allowed herself to be talked into the idea of living with Sonya and her daughters. She wonders now if she hasn't done herself, and her career, irreparable harm by softening her earlier resolve—and giving in, at least in part, to what Sonya wanted.

It was pretty odd, she admits to herself, having a sister, after all these years of thinking of herself as an only child. Not only having a sister, but having an identical twin. Well, the two of them couldn't be more different, if one looked beyond the superficial similarities. And yet there were some qualities—some turns of mind—that seemed a mirror image of her worst fears and deepest pain.

It makes some sense to her that flesh and blood can be imprinted with truths that go far beyond anything describable in words. It was the truth of dance, after all—of all great art, except the work of writers.

୨ଡ଼

Stepping down from her third-class car onto the platform at the Gare de Monaco Monte-Carlo, gripping her suitcase with one hand and holding her hatbox with the other, Jeannette sees a cluster of posh-looking people meeting some passengers from first class. Here, on the same train she was on, is Tamara Karsavina, along with another woman Jeannette has never seen before. Unlike her, they are unencumbered by luggage. Jeannette watches as the two women are handed down from the train with the sort of pomp usually reserved for royalty.

Diaghilev is there in full evening dress, flanked by his mustachioed valet. None other than Vaslav Nijinsky is standing by with two huge bouquets, along with some other Russians Jeannette doesn't recognize. They are all kissing cheeks and blathering on in that language Sonya's children use whenever they want to say something they don't want Jeannette to understand. She thinks, grimly, that she'd better learn at least a little Russian if she's to have any chance of holding on to her all-too-precarious place as an on-demand extra in Diaghilev's newly formed company.

She walks as close to the group as she dares, hoping they might break into French, at some point—thinking she might even hitch a ride with them to the theater.

Karsavina catches sight of her. "Oh, it's you!" she coos, grabbing Jeannette's elbows and kissing her cheeks, right, left, right. Not letting go, she says, "I heard it all turned out well!"

"Well enough, Madame Karsavina." Still lugging her suitcase and the hatbox, Jeannette smiles in what she hopes is a winning manner. She wishes now that she'd bothered to fix her makeup on the train.

"Sergei, here's one of your new dancers for the corps, Jeannette—"

Without letting her finish the introduction, Diaghilev snaps his fingers at the valet. "Vassily! Put the lady in a cab for the Palais du Soleil, won't you?" Consulting his pocketwatch, he looks at Jeannette through his monocle and says, "You're late."

She realizes that it's hopeless to try to explain about the problem at the station in Paris. The very person she didn't want to notice has had her infraction put right before his nose.

Diaghilev turns his back on her, exerting the full force of his charm in welcoming Karsavina and her colleague, another Russian. Nijinsky had greeted both of them with a regal bow—then laughs as he embraces each of the dancers in turn. "Karsavina! Preobrajenskaya!" he says, calling both of them, in that odd way that Russians have, by their family names. The one who is not Karsavina, Jeannette notes before being led off by the valet, has a decidedly plain face and rather short legs—and looks at least ten years older than Jeannette. Maybe, she thinks—taking comfort in the fact—there's some hope for her, after all.

PARIS

1911

Olga fumes with frustration, furious at society's blindness to the truths that she can so clearly see. Everywhere, adults engage in willful stupidity. Most people, the majority of people, it seems to Olga, are incapable of recognizing the truth, even when it's right before their eyes.

After allowing Marie Curie's candidacy for membership in the Academy of Sciences, the French Institute has just rejected her in favor of a man. On what basis, Olga demands to know from every member of her family, can the Academy decide that a female scientist, no matter that she was awarded the Nobel Prize, is yet unworthy of France's highest scientific honor?

And now Jeannette has returned from Monte Carlo, and thrown their lives into chaos once again.

How can her aunt be so idiotic in the lengths she's going to in her attempt to appear well-connected and fashionable? Doesn't she know that working at a party is altogether different from attending that party as a guest?

Olga has tried again and again to explain to Jeannette, in the simplest terms, some of the rudimentary concepts of women's rights. But how can one explain such things to a woman whose work makes her nothing more than a glorified plaything for wealthy men?

When Olga asks her aunt one day, point-blank, to define the difference between herself and a prostitute, Jeannette slaps her so hard that Olga, briefly, loses consciousness. Sonya is not at home—and no one tells her what happened, all of them loath to provoke another display of Jeannette's temper and their mother's tears.

Naomi has told Olga that she understands how she

feels—and is sympathetic to her views about the need to allow the female gender—finally, once and for all—under the umbrella of human rights. But she has cautioned her repeatedly about expressing those views in ways that are bound to give offense to their elders. Theirs is a delicate situation requiring both tact and diplomacy, both of which Olga has in short supply.

Given her passionate interest in fashion and design, Naomi is just as stupidly enthusiastic as their aunt about being present at Monsieur Poiret's upcoming extravaganza, which is sure to be the most memorable event of the season, with invitations sought by le Tout-Paris.

The dancers of the Opera Ballet, including Jeannette, have been hired to perform. Jeannette already has her costume—and she's somehow wangled jobs at the party for her nieces in the cast of hundreds being assembled at the Poiret mansion to launch this latest venture of his fashion house, into the rarefied world of perfumes.

The party itself is to take the place of advertising for the scent he is calling *Nuit Persane*. The ballerinas have negotiated to receive, along with their pay, a bottle of the exquisitely packaged perfume distilled specially to evoke the memory of this latest soirée Monsieur Poiret has dubbed "The Thousand and Second Night."

All the guests and members of the cast are to dress up in costumes inspired by the Arabian tales of *One Thousand and One Nights*. Anyone arriving without a costume will be sent home or escorted to a roomful of costumes and accessories provided by Monsieur Poiret and presided over by his dressmakers. Naomi, who met several of these women during the time her mother worked at Maison Poiret, will be paid a sum of francs larger than she's ever earned for the privilege of assisting them. Even Baila has been given a little role, along with half a dozen other pretty children, who are to gambol, in Persian costumes, among the guests. Rumor has it that Isadora Duncan will appear during the revels in the garden, to dance a solo.

On their arrival, the girls are ushered in through a back

entrance, along with Jeannette, and rushed off to the costume room, where Naomi is assigned to help make adjustments with safety pins, and Baila is transformed into an alluring little Persian princess. Olga is left standing there in her street clothes. She is still in Jeannette's bad books—and wonders what sort of punishment her aunt has arranged for her this time.

Tired of waiting, she gives her name to the young woman who has been standing by the door, directing traffic. "Oh yes, here you are," she says, tapping on her clipboard with her pencil. "You're to go to the makeup station first. Strip down to your knickers, please."

Olga wishes she hadn't spoken up. Without so much as a by-your-leave, she's taken in hand by two makeup artists, who cover her, head to toe, in sepia-colored greasepaint and then dress her as a Persian boy. They have a wig for her. But her curly hair is apparently deemed good enough as is. A long silken rag is wrapped around her forehead—and a large fake-pearl earring is clipped, a bit painfully, onto her earlobe. She doesn't want to admit it, but she likes her outfit, which includes a broad silken sash and quite a convincing-looking scimitar.

"What am I supposed to be?" she says, cocking her head to one side and then another before a mirror.

"A eunuch," says the girl with the clipboard. "Let's see." She finds Olga's name again on her list. "You're to be the assistant to the seller of marmosets in the bazaar."

"Marmosets!" effuses Baila. "They're those darling tiny little monkeys we saw in the Ménagerie du Jardin des Plantes with Mama!"

Olga takes the four-foot-long banana leaf the costume mistress hands her. "What am I supposed to do with this, mademoiselle?"

"It's to help you catch monkeys—in case any of them escape."

"Oh, you're so lucky!" whispers Baila.

Olga rolls her eyes. "I'll tell you what," she says sotto voce to her little sister. "Let's slip off, when no one's looking—and switch costumes!"

Jeannette, just passing by the doorway, calls out, "Too late for that, monkey girl!"

Olga never thought she could hate anyone as much as she hates her aunt.

"Claudette!" says a fat, brown, turbaned man from the doorway. "See that she doesn't wear the glasses! They spoil the effect."

"But I can't see without them, monsieur!"

The costume mistress nudges Olga, hard, between her shoulder blades. "We can put a little leash on her, Monsieur Poiret, and the monkey seller can keep her from coming to harm."

"Capital idea!"

Olga had no idea the man was Poiret. He's wearing brown makeup, all over his skin, and a convincing-looking false nose. He looks completely different from the other times she's seen him, when he's appeared a typical, stout Parisian businessman.

She smiles wanly at him, aware of her family's debt to Maison Poiret—and slips her glasses into the sheath that holds her scimitar. For all the world like a would-be assassin, Claudette encircles Olga's neck with her outstretched thumbs and forefingers—then finds a leather collar of the right size and fits her out with a leash, lightweight and bejeweled, that fashionable women attach to their little dogs.

Olga tells herself, as she so often does, that this, too, will pass—although she can't help muttering protests as she's fitted with the collar. The whole experience makes her want to bite someone.

As soon as she and Baila are pushed out into the hall to make room for the next group needing costumes, Olga retrieves her glasses and puts them on again. Even so, it's all she can do to keep herself from tripping on the flowing fabrics of other people's costumes in the close press of bodies, or getting her bare feet trod upon by other people's curly-toed, Persian-style shoes. Baila holds her hand at first. But then she gives a squeeze and dances off when she catches sight of another little girl she knows, dressed in a costume identical to hers. Everyone already

seems drunk as they make their giggling way, bangles and bracelets tinkling, down a grand staircase into the darkness.

The long, tunnel-like foyer of the house has been decorated
with the skill of professional artists and set designers to look
like Ali Baba's cave. There is heaped-up treasure everywhere,
gleaming in the half-light. Crystal carafes and etched-glass
ewers, filled with a rainbow of poisonous-looking liqueurs, are
ranged along the length of a shining ebony table presided over
by a fleet of brown-skinned bartenders dressed in red caps,
white Punjabi pants, and belted gold tunics. The glass vessels
sit in holes and are lit from underneath, providing the room's
sole illumination.

Everyone stops for a moment at the base of the stairs to *ooh*
and *aah* and get their bearings in the low light. Olga's appetite
is awakened by strange and delicious smells of food. Sounds of
flutes and zithers, and the mournful cries of tropical birds, drift
in from the open windows to the garden.

"May I present myself, mademoiselle?" says a deep and
musical voice somewhere behind and above Olga. She turns
and cranes her head to look up at a tall, broad-shouldered man
whose skin, his own skin, is the color of black coffee and whose
identity is immediately obvious.

The unexpectedly attractive seller of monkeys seems at
home in his exotic Arabian costume, with its loose white trousers and caftan, embroidered vest, and sash. His shoulders and
his turban are piled high with a clinging, staring, disorganized
pile of white-eared, palm-sized monkeys with long ringed tails
that drape over him like the fringe of a lampshade. Cocking
their heads from side to side, and clutching at him with their
tiny little hands, they look down at Olga with interest and just
a touch of anxiety.

The man inclines his head slightly by way of a bow. "I am,
for this evening's festivities, mademoiselle, the seller of marmosets—and will be your colleague, with your permission, for the
next several hours."

He's the loveliest man Olga has ever seen, exuding the

dignified grace of a prelate and the glamour of a romantic hero, despite the scrabbling claws and perpetual motion of his cargo. Briefly, he smiles down at her with such warmth and brilliance that she thinks she might be in love.

"Do you live in Paris?" she asks him, immediately regretting her words and noticing that her voice is quavering. Couldn't she have thought of something more interesting to say?

"But where else in the world would anyone choose to live?" he answers.

He speaks the most beautiful French she has ever heard, rich and warm and precise. She straightens her shoulders and takes a deep breath. "My name is Olga. What's yours, please?"

"Gaston. *Enchanté*, Mademoiselle Olga."

She takes off her glasses and looks up at him myopically to offer the looped end of her leash.

"*Chère mademoiselle*," he says in a stern voice. "I am sure this is as unnecessary as it is undignified for both of us." He lowers himself down on one knee, like a suitor about to propose marriage—and, with gentle fingers, unbuckles Olga's collar. She has never felt so undone by the touch of anyone's hands. She realizes, with a sense of surprise, that she can't recall being touched by any man, other than the doctor who treated her sprained ankle and felt her neck and forehead during the course of her pneumonia, the year before.

Righting himself without spilling a single monkey, Gaston pitches the collar and leash away, out through an open window, into the darkness.

"Ouch! What the hell?" an invisible male voice yells from outside the window. The orchestra, instrument by instrument, crashes to a stop.

For the first time all evening, Olga laughs. The music starts again, and she puts her glasses back on. She feels that she could happily walk by this man's side forever, leash or no leash.

Gaston smiles down at her—and then, with a wink, assumes a serious, exotic sort of Persian expression. "Marmosets! Beautiful marmosets!" he sings to the crowd.

"Marmosets! Adorable marmosets!" Olga warbles.

Before they've moved very far away from the base of the stairs, several costumed guests, all of them women—many with a lot of skin exposed—come closer to inspect the marmosets and the man. They make the sort of noises Baila makes whenever she's in the presence of a large-eyed, round-faced animal that excites her maternal instincts.

A few of the women don't even bother pretending to look at the monkeys but focus all their attention on Gaston. "How much?" a silk-robed beauty asks him, batting kohl-rimmed eyes above her veil.

Olga is gratified to see Gaston act with cool indifference as he quickly makes one sale and then two more, never showing any of the women the warmth he showed to her.

"It's awfully close in here," he says in an aside to Olga. "What do you say to making our way outside?" It's thrilling to hear him speak to her just as if she were an adult.

They pick their way through the crowd of guests and waiters, out into the gardens, where sculpted bushes and flowering potted plants are all decorated with tiny lights, and the pathways have been covered in plush Oriental rugs.

"Marmosets! Marmosets!" Gaston calls out, echoed by Olga, "They make marvelous pets!"

They stroll past pink ibis, flamingoes, and a screaming white peacock wandering over the lawn. Parrots and macaws fly in tiny bursts of color past their heads, making the marmosets whimper in fear. Bigger monkeys stare out from the trees, attached to their perches by thin silver chains. The balmy air is filled with a tantalizing smell of curries, although whatever cooking is going on is hidden. Carved wooden tables throughout the garden are loaded with every kind of exotic delicacy, which Olga would have felt much better about sampling if the monkeys weren't constantly clambering down onto her head, into her arms, and then jumping back onto Gaston again.

Several different orchestras are playing softly, also hidden behind the shrubberies, the music growing louder and then fading away again as Olga and Gaston follow the maze of path-ways. Here and there they come upon throngs of braziers with blue smoking incense, tended by bare-breasted black-skinned girls. "Really, it's too much," Gaston says, reaching down to turn Olga's wide-eyed gaze away as he and she pass by.

A waiter comes up to them, proffering a tray of delicacies. "Messieurs?" he says, squinting at Olga. "Uh, mademoiselle?"

"Oh no, no, no, no, no! Get away from us, please!" says Gaston.

But it's too late. A waterfall of marmosets comes tumbling down onto the tray, upsetting it—and sending the waiter to the ground in the middle of a great pile of spilled food and crockery. Scooping up as many of the marmosets as they can, vying with each other in the courtliness of their apologies to the waiter as they help him to his feet, Olga and Gaston escape further away into the garden. They pass by guests reclining in the shadows on carpets and cushions, some of them in pos-es that Olga has only seen depicted in books she's browsed through in the bookstalls along the Seine. Gaston takes her by the hand, leading her into the Persian bazaar that has been constructed, seemingly by miraculous means, in the courtyard of Poiret's mansion.

Olga knows they are at the very center of Paris—and yet it is as if they were in another world. There are butchers and what look like the skinned bodies of goats and lambs hanging by their feet. Intricate alleyways snake in between soothsay-ers hawking amulets next to potters at their wheels, cobblers pounding on boot lasts, and tailors who come out from behind their shop stalls to accost people with their measuring tapes and shears. Wonderful smells of dates, figs, and cardamom waft up from the clay ovens of the sweetmeat vendors.

In the middle of it all, there's a raised stage and a slave mer-chant who calls out, as Gaston and Olga walk by, "Look at these two fine fellows! How much for these?"

"We're not for sale!" Olga hollers at him, brandishing her scimitar.

There's a burst then of gold, silver, and blue fireworks that light up Gaston's delighted eyes—and illuminate a line of tulle-clad ballerinas on the roof of the mansion.

"Imagine!" he whispers. "Actual dancers from the Paris Opera Ballet—here, among us!"

"It's really not all that wonderful, take it from me," says Olga.

There's another burst of fireworks. The ballerinas look like ghosts now through the haze of pale gray smoke.

"Marmosets! Lovely, lovely marmosets for sale!" Gaston sings out with a note of yearning in his voice now.

A few more of the guests, all of them female, buy a marmoset, leaving a single layer of them ranged across Gaston's shoulders, peeking out from behind his head.

Baila comes running up to them. "The big monkeys have all broken their chains—there's one!" She streaks after it, followed by several other children, all of them shrieking with delight.

Gaston consults his pocket watch. "We should go inside now."

They make their way back into Ali Baba's cave just on time to hear a gong sound and see a bare-chested, beautifully muscled Black man unlock the door of a great golden cage that takes up an entire corner of the room that is lit now by stage lights.

"That's Madame Poiret," Gaston tells Olga, indicating the slender woman lounging on silken pillows in the center of the cage. She leaps up when the door is unlocked, showing off her flowing harem pants and silver tunic, the bejeweled bangles on her arms and ankles, the gems on her fingers, toes, and ears—and a white and silver turban fixed with an outsized ruby and a white feather so fluffy and large that it looks as if she's going to take wing. After everyone has had a chance to admire her ensemble, she runs out of the cage, followed by a bevy of other pretty women meant to be the sultan's harem. The sultan—who is, of course, Monsieur Poiret in all his jeweled and turbaned glory—runs after them with surprising fleetness, brandishing a leather whip. The women run before him, screaming and laughing, all through the rooms of the house and into the garden before the sated guests, while he cracks his whip with a fearsome sound.

"It's all in fun," Gaston tells Olga when she clings to his leg. The memory of Jeannette's slap is still vivid for her.

Naomi, released from the costume room—gloriously costumed herself—stands before them, hands on her hips. "Well," she says. "Aren't we cozy!"

"Go with your friend, little one. Get some food. You've earned your wages tonight. And so have I!"

"Goodbye, Monsieur Gaston. Perhaps I'll see you again!" calls Olga as he and the remaining marmosets disappear into the crowd.

"Had fun, did you?" says Naomi. "And to think I was shut up in that smelly costume room all evening!"

Baila runs up to them, shouting, "The monkeys are all loose on the Champs-Élysées!" Her eyes are wide. "Didn't you save even one marmoset for me?"

Olga moves her scimitar out of the way and slings an arm over Baila's shoulder. "You know you wouldn't be allowed to keep it." All three of them know that Sonya might have been convinced, but their aunt wouldn't consent to having a pet monkey in their house. "You'd only have your heart broken again."

"They're so tiny—we could have kept it hidden from her!"

Olga has left a smudge of brown greasepaint on her sister's cheek. "Like that last kitten you brought home?"

Baila's eyes fill with tears, remembering the fate of the most recent small animal she'd tried to rescue. "I don't understand how certain people can be so heartless!"

"Let's get some food," says Naomi, linking arms with her sisters. "I don't know about you, but I'm famished!"

They walk along the banquet tables, heaping their plates with food—and find a sheltered place in the garden where they can watch and yet remain hidden.

"Have you seen Monsieur Cocteau?" asks Naomi, sucking on a chicken bone. "He's dressed, most fantastically, as a dancing girl. It's such a shame that Mama opted not to attend! What *is* that, Olga, in your hair? It looks like a little prune."

Olga pulls her headscarf off, then rakes her fingers through her curls, coming away with something small and sticky. She wrinkles her nose as she examines it—then throws it into the shrubbery. "Monkey shit," she says, wiping her hand on the grass that is moist now with the dew.

It's so irksome to be trapped in the body of an eleven-year-old. Olga comforts herself with the thought that in five years, if not sooner, she'll be able to break free and find her own path in the world. How glorious it will be to confront the world with all the agency and power adults enjoy—to embrace everything that seems right to her, and to reject everything she recognizes as wrong! She can't wait to leave the powerlessness of childhood behind her.

Paris

1911

Sonya's health has suffered since her illness. Her heart flutters inside her chest, followed by an inexplicable sense of dread, loss, and danger. She's been having nightmares, end-of-the-world nightmares, from which she wakens drenched in sweat. She's told no one.

She woke fearful, that morning of the premiere, that Baila might make a fool of herself on the stage—although she only told her daughters, and Jeannette, that she'd woken with a migraine, and couldn't possibly attend, despite the really good tickets Jeannette had managed to snag. It irks Sonya, in a way, that they had all been so understanding. She wishes someone had made her feel better, helped her get ready, and forced her to go.

How festive and happy they'd all looked, going out the door.

The handsome Regency clock on the shelf, a housewarming present from René Blum, seems to be ticking very loudly, now that she's alone. He'd sent a bouquet that afternoon—although whether it was meant for her or Jeannette wasn't entirely clear.

As much as Sonya longs to trust her twin in a way she's never trusted anyone else before, she's never stopped fearing that, deep down, Jeannette wants Baila to be *her* child—and will stop at nothing to make that dream come true.

༄

What Olga keeps thinking about, while she waits for the curtain to rise, is what might have happened during those nine minutes and twenty-one seconds that were lost when France abandoned the Paris Meridian in favor of Greenwich Mean Time.

Their family friend, Maître Blum, has been teaching Olga

about Judaism, journalism, and many other subjects. He has
told her that the theft of time is a crime like any other. Whenever she interrupts to ask a question or argue with something
he's said—or when Naomi expresses boredom or impatience
with their lessons—he tells them that one minute wasted is a
minute of learning lost—a precious minute of learning that can
never be regained.

What was lost then, Olga wonders, during those nine minutes and twenty-one seconds that were robbed from all of them
in 1910? The year of Tolstoy's death. The year of the Great
Flood of Paris, when Olga and her mother both so nearly died.
The year that brought Jeannette into their lives, folding her
into their family and, so often now, making Olga's life a misery.
How differently might everything have turned out, if she could
somehow regain that lost time?

If she could only go back to that day when the waters crest-
ed, with those vanished minutes in her possession—if she'd
known then what she knows now—perhaps she could have
changed the outcome.

Her thoughts are interrupted by the lavishly mustachioed,
frail-looking man sitting next to her, René Blum's writer friend,
whom he'd purposefully placed by her side. "Pardon me, Mademoiselle Olga," he says to her—and it's clear to her now that
he's been watching her face, waiting for her to notice him.

"Monsieur Proust?" she says, embarrassed at being observed
during such a private moment in such a public place.

He doesn't smile. "I was simply wondering what you were
thinking of just now."

Olga blinks at him then says, "I was thinking, monsieur,
about lost time."

"Indeed." He looks at her face again—then turns away when
the dissonant sounds of Maestro Monteux's orchestra begin—
the horns and flutes and strings all tuning, intensely private and
yet commanding sounds that make the audience go quiet.

The elaborately coiffed lady sitting in front of them turns
around with a chastening finger held up to her lips.

The houselights dim, leaving them all in darkness.

There's a solo drum roll then, the same sort they've heard at public celebrations of military might or at public demonstrations of an officer's shame.

Naomi reaches over and takes Olga's hand, squeezing hard. They're both terrified for Baila—and also proud of her, and a little bit jealous. Olga feels grateful that Naomi, at least, can understand and share these complicated feelings.

The black velvet curtain of the Théâtre du Châtelet, gleaming with jewels and mystery, rises to reveal a scene that's exotic and foreign, and yet stirs Olga with the emotions of memory.

The scene depicts, as described in the program for *Petrushka*, a Shrovetide Fair in Saint Petersburg in the 1830s. The set is a feast of bright colors and details that shout with the exuberance of a child's painting and a child's fears. Hucksters' booths and an ominous-looking Ferris wheel. Turrets and flags flying in the distance. Teeming balconies—and, stage left, a puppet theater hidden behind curtains of shimmering pale-blue taffeta.

The stage is bursting with a distinctly Russian and raucous early nineteenth-century crowd, farmers and soldiers and hawkers of treats and balloons, gypsies in their parti-colored, multi-layered silken skirts and scarves, and peasant women in their babushkas. Beautiful pink-cheeked Russian maidens, each with a thick honey-colored braid down her back, which levitates from beneath her kerchief as she's whirled around or lifted in the air by flirtatious suitors and soldiers. A frightening-looking man, his face and arms terribly scarred, lumbers on stage in the arms of a real—and huge—black bear as the crowd backs away with cries of fear but then soon forgets about the bear in the swirl of color, music, and joy.

The sisters scan the crowd in vain for Baila. But then she's suddenly there, one of a sequence of colorfully costumed children careening down a huge slide and then disappearing into the swarm of revelers.

Both Olga and Naomi know that if they were to find themselves on that stage, facing the audience, they would be rigid with self-consciousness and fear. But Baila, every time they catch a glimpse of her, looks at ease. She seems to be, indeed, in another world. A lost world that Olga never knew but nonetheless feels as if she remembers, somewhere deep inside her.

Booted, long-shirted Cossacks dance the *kazatsky*, crouching and throwing their heels out, jockeying their balance from one foot to the other—then leaping up with arms outstretched. Defying gravity, each man competes to outdo the others. Their wild dance is interrupted by a blast from the trumpet announcing that the real entertainment is about to begin. But then an organ grinder strolls onstage from the wings, alongside a beautiful dancing girl who plays a triangle while she does the sorts of things both Naomi and Olga have seen their aunt do when she's practicing ballet. It takes them both a moment to realize that this *is* their aunt.

Olga steals a look up and across Naomi in time to see Maître Blum's adoring gaze on Jeannette—and, for a moment, Olga can see her aunt through his eyes. She's utterly transformed from the person they've watched and heard every day since she moved in with them, sweating and swearing in front of the stove or screaming at them, whenever their mother isn't home (and sometimes when she is), to clean up their room.

A second dancing girl whirls onto the stage. This one is even more limber and graceful than Jeannette, twirling and leaping to the delicate, bell-like tones of what sounds like a music box or a toy piano.

All is chaos and revelry, with both Baila and Jeannette appearing here and disappearing again in the crowd till a spotlight shines on the puppet theater, and the shiny pale-blue silken curtains are parted by a tall magician clad in the same icy shade of blue, with silver-shadowed eyes and snowy white hair.

Three life-size puppets are revealed, hanging by their armpits as if crucified, several feet off the ground. There's a grinning black-skinned Moor in military garb, with large white sleeves sticking out of his braided tunic, loose white trousers decorated with embroidered stripes, and a wooden scimitar hanging by his side. The toes of his white shoes point sideways in opposite directions. In the compartment next to him hangs a gaudily pretty ballerina with painted lips and a vacant look in her eyes. She is hung so that she balances on the points of her turned-out toes. And finally there's a funny but sad-looking clown with one hand cocked by the side of his head and his booted feet looking as if they've become tangled in his strings.

Naomi whispers in Olga's ear, "That's Tamara Karsavina. I'll bet you didn't recognize her!"

"Of course I did!" she whispers back, even though she didn't, at first, recognize the ballerina. Naomi is infinitely better than Olga at noticing and remembering people's faces. But, anyway, she thinks with the usual flush of frustration and shame, the puppet dancers are so heavily caked in makeup that it's almost impossible to recognize them as even being real. She has inferred from the program that the clownish puppet with the sad face—the title role—is being danced by Vaslav Nijinsky.

But Olga would never have been able to tell if she hadn't known beforehand. He has seemed like a different person each time she's seen him onstage and, once briefly, backstage. And now, here he is, transformed again.

All three of the puppets' expressions are as unmoving as if they really were made of wood and paint and cloth instead of flesh. And yet, when the magician comes at each one of them, playing his little flute, their feet begin to twitch in keeping with their individual characters. With their lifeless heads lolled forward or cocked to one side, their limp arms and hands dangling, their feet and then their legs begin to dance, unable to resist the magician's silvery tones.

And then, to their horror, Naomi and Olga see Baila walking forward on the stage, as if in a trance—as if she, too, has been enchanted by the music, her head cocked and her eyes half-closed as she follows the flute's bewitching melody. The magician shoots a fierce look at her as, chastened, she hurries back into the crowd.

No one else on stage reveals that this was anything other

than part of the choreography. Both Naomi and Olga know there was no such solo moment assigned to their sister. Both of them burn with shame for her. Both steal a look at Monsieur Blum, who doesn't seem to have realized that anything has gone wrong.

The movements of Petrushka's legs and feet are extravagant and clumsy. The ballerina in her toe shoes dances in the air with vapid precision, while the Moor leaps and swaggers in two dimensions. All three of them seem to be alive only from the waist down. All three of them are at the mercy of their master.

This is the moment, Olga thinks, when the magic of theater takes over, blotting out every other reality. She wants to figure out a way to hold herself apart, so that she can come to analyze the phenomenon—when it works and when it doesn't. Why it works and why it doesn't. To become a connoisseur of this magic and the magicians who make it happen, to write about them and know that readers will hang on her every word. Perhaps to create that magic herself.

And yet it's impossible to hold herself aloof from the spell that's being woven on the stage. She forgets where she is, and who she is. She forgets that both Baila and her aunt are up there.

Olga's hearing and heart are commandeered by Igor Stravinsky's music, so unlike anything she's ever heard before, a fabric of sound composed of scintillating pieces of joy and pain melted together. As the ballet unfolds, her eyes and imagination are taken hostage by Petrushka's wild longing—his hopeless longing—to win the love of the empty-headed, faithless ballerina.

What fools people are when they're in love, Olga finds herself thinking at the end, blinking back tears.

Baila, there among the other extras hired for the production—hand in hand with all of them for the curtain call—is pushed forward by the children standing on either side of her. The audience breaks into laughter. Stumbling slightly, Baila looks as if she might cry. But then, with dignity—and, her sisters are forced to admit, with grace and charm—she curtseys, just as Jeannette has taught her to do.

They can see her changing, right there before their eyes, as the sound of applause sifts down on her like a shower of gold. They watch, amazed, as Baila takes two steps backward, with pointed toes, to assume her place in the line again.

The demi-soloists enter from the wings, each of them still dancing in character as they assemble in a second line just in front of the extras. Maître Blum is one of the first to rise to his feet, applauding hysterically. He shouts himself hoarse when Jeannette—along with the other dancing girl, the organ-grinder, and the man with the bear—takes her little bow.

PART IV

PARIS

1912

Sonya has sat up late at the kitchen table, which is the apartment's only dining table, awaiting her sister's return from the theater.

"It's all arranged," Jeannette announces as she walks in the door. Her feet are killing her, but she's happy, at least, that her nieces are already in bed. The last thing Jeannette wants is another argument with Olga. "A shop for you in the sixth arrondissement, in a pretty building on rue Saint Sulpice—with a ten-room apartment above. Space enough for some privacy and a proper practice room."

"You are completely mad," Sonya says. "How could I—how could *we*—ever afford such lodgings? And what kind of shop are you talking about?"

"Accessories. Those *chichis* you specialized in making for him. He's decided to set you up—as part of his empire, of course—in your own shop."

Jeannette, still wearing her sweaty dance togs under a raincoat, has brought home a still-warm bag of beignets. She's on a campaign to help Sonya gain back some of the weight she lost during her illness.

"Shouldn't you change out of those clothes, into something warmer?"

"Come on, Sonya! Act excited, please! Your own shop, close by the Boulevard Saint-Germain. Just a five-minute walk from the Luxembourg Gardens. And—he said you'd care about this—wonderful light."

"But it will be *his* shop, won't it? Am I to be on his payroll, once again? The entire idea is distasteful to me."

"You won't be an employee—he's assured me of as much. He's financing the project, and he'll take a cut of the profits. But, really, he's doing this because he has finally recognized the debt he owes us."

Sonya looks closely at her sister's face, which is so often different from day to day, depending on whether she's wearing makeup and how hard and long she's been working, and how much she drank the night before. Every day since returning from the brink of death, Sonya sees and understands something new about her twin. Most of what she previously imagined has fallen away, to be replaced by actual qualities—and faults—illuminated by Jeannette's words and behavior.

Jeannette has been treating Sonya like her own private miracle—she's like a proud mother who's just produced a newborn. For Sonya, Jeannette's doting attitude is a welcome change from her unequivocal hostility at the start. But being patronized in this way is also a little uncomfortable for her. She wishes she and her twin could simply find a place of balance between them, where each of them could feel powerful in her own right, while remaining aligned.

Sonya shakes her head. "How can you trust Poiret? How can *I* ever trust him? Do you think he'd go to such trouble and expense if he didn't imagine some advantage for himself? Perhaps he thinks we'll both make ourselves available to him. He'd like that, I'm sure."

"Aren't you the cynic. There's great selfishness in Paul Poiret. But there's also good in him—or maybe it's just guilt. He was shaken to the core by your near death and the destruction he realized he'd caused by keeping us apart. He wants to make amends."

"In my experience of him, he has wanted, above all else, to guard his place as the premier couturier of Paris—as well as to guard his profits."

"As to that," says Jeannette, "he no doubt sees you, and your skills, as just one more way to build his empire. He even has a new idea involving your eldest—and *her* skills."

"Naomi? Is he to set her up in a shop as well?"

"Don't be silly. It's something to do with working-class girls who are good at art. A workshop of some kind, all having to do with home décor or some such thing. You'll have to get him to explain it to you."

Sonya peeks into the greasy paper bag. "Um," she says, extracting a beignet and taking a bite. "There's still tea in the pot."

"I'll get it—don't get up."

"You're going to make me fat, Jeannette—and then no one will be able to guess we're twins."

"That's what I'm hoping!" Jeannette raises one of her penciled eyebrows in that way she has of expressing so much with the greatest economy of motion.

Sonya wants to keep her twin close to her—and also despairs of making it work. The way Jeannette treats the children has become increasingly intolerable. It's always and exclusively Baila, Baila, Baila. Baila's ballet lessons, Baila's musical education, Baila's bloody turnout. Whisking Baila off to concerts and rehearsals, leaving the rest of them at home. Baila is becoming a spoiled brat. Jeannette takes almost no interest at all in Naomi—and she really seems to hate Olga, for some unfathomable reason.

Jeannette had a stagehand from the Opera install a small ballet barre in her bedroom for Baila's lessons—at what price, Sonya continues to wonder, never daring to ask. Jeannette treats Baila like a piece of clay she hopes to squeeze, pinch, and prod until she becomes the kind of ballerina Jeannette herself never managed to be.

Naomi confided that she and Olga are in the habit of gauging their aunt's mood by the haste or care with which she's put on her makeup. *Watch out!* one or the other of them will whisper. *She has her witchy eyebrows on today!*

❧

It has been the great redemption of Naomi's life, getting this opportunity to sketch and paint six days a week at the light-filled atelier created expressly for the Martines inside the Poiret mansion at 107 faubourg Saint Honoré.

Monsieur Poiret has personally attended to every detail of this latest expansion of his fashion empire, which bears the name of his second-born child. He engaged a professional art teacher, the wife of the avant-garde painter, Paul Sérusier, to instruct his stable of twelve-year-old designers. He handpicked his girls by canvassing the local public schools and asking about any female students there who showed particular interest or talent in the visual arts. He specifically wanted girls from working-class families—girls who hadn't yet had conventional prejudices about beauty instilled in them by well-meaning parents or teachers. He wanted them old enough to acquire skills—but still young enough to imbue their designs with a child's freshness and delight in the wonders of the natural world.

It was to be expected that the Martines were beset and sometimes overwhelmed by all the changes and challenges faced by every child who has ever hovered at the edge of adolescence. And yet they thrived.

Paul has the satisfaction of seeing how well his investment is paying off, every time he goes upstairs and walks around the room, from easel to easel. Every day validates his conviction about the great untapped aesthetic resource to be found in the working classes.

After only a few short months, the girls have absorbed the rules and principles Madame Sérusier has pressed upon them. They've already become adept at mixing colors and using several different kinds of paint on a wide variety of surfaces, which they now know how to prepare. With few exceptions, swiftly punished, they respect the rules about caring for the expensive paints and brushes provided for them by Maison Poiret. Their fingers are stained and they wreck their clothes—but given who they are, this is not a great concern.

Naomi has become known among them as a well-mannered girl who works hard. She has tried to steer clear of the cliques as well as the overheated friendships that inevitably form among the Martines, many of whom are fairly scrappy girls.

With her own sisters' needs and complaints to deal with,

Naomi wants nothing more than to focus on the thrill of seeing her paintings transformed into objects of decorative art. It had been her own idea, after all, even though Monsieur Poiret never explicitly acknowledged that she was the one who'd planted the thought in his head, that sad day in the rain-sodden Bois de Boulogne.

The thrill of having such a job—and even getting a small daily wage for it, as well as lunch and delicious snacks in the late afternoon—has never worn off for Naomi. Such are the stresses and strains at home that she looks forward to going to work every day. Olga and their aunt are always at each other's throats when they're at home together, which isn't very often but is always unpleasant for everyone.

Monsieur Poiret takes pains to seem impartial. But it's clear that he has his favorites among the Martines—and that Naomi is one of them. She keeps wondering why Sonya doesn't seem particularly happy about this—and why her mother questions her so closely, from time to time, about how Monsieur Poiret comports himself around her.

Naomi, for her part, has no complaints.

After half a year, during one of Poiret's inspections of the workshop—in the late afternoon of a particularly harrowing day, when three of the girls had gotten into a fight that resulted in spilled paint, torn clothes, and pulled-out hair—Madame Sérusier confronts her boss with a demand. Fifteen girls, she announces, are too many for her to instruct and supervise all at once. Each of the Martines has her own talents as well as her own deficits of knowledge and craft, to say nothing of bad habits and the tendency shared by all girls of that age to push the limits of acceptable behavior. It's simply impossible for her, as a conscientious teacher, to nurture them adequately on her own. A second teacher was needed—another well-trained ped-agogue, like herself, who was also conversant with the best and brightest artists of Paris. She has a friend in mind, if Monsieur Poiret will be so kind as to heed her recommendation.

Monsieur Poiret listens politely to all she says. And then he kisses her hand—which makes everyone giggle, because Madame Sérusier is far from being either young or even remotely pretty. He tells her how delighted he's been with everything she's done for the Martines—and that he will have a solution for her the following afternoon.

Madame Sérusier is positively serene the next morning, confident that relief is at hand. She's unusually lavish in her praise—and gives the girls an extra-long break for their afternoon *goûter*, on the condition that they all clean up their workstations, and have their best work on display, on time for Monsieur Poiret's promised visit.

And then he appears before them. With ceremony, after a short speech praising Madame Sérusier's virtues, he presents her with a bottle of perfume, "as a souvenir of her time with the Martines." He has chosen for her *La Chemise de Rosine*, a fresh and innocent scent that comes with a nightgown in a gorgeous box the girls themselves had decorated with their designs.

Madame makes a valiant effort to hide her hurt and surprise when it becomes evident to her that Poiret is not only ignoring her recommendations, but has seen, as he puts it, the wisdom of allowing her to resign. There are some scattered, mean-spirited comments—but most of the girls, Naomi included, feel sorry for the teacher who has, after all, given them so much.

Poiret begins putting his new plans into effect even before Madame Sérusier has had time to clear her belongings out of the teacher's corner. He mentions that he's engaged a monitress to oversee the girls, at the same moment that a tough-looking eighteen-year-old Bretonne walks in. Everyone recognizes her as someone who's been working in the kitchen. She has brought a bit of knitting with her.

And so the girls are left largely on their own to create their designs. What teacher did these natural painters need, after all, apart from exposure to the glories of Nature and the occasional outing to one of the city's great repositories of art?

Poiret continues to take a keen interest in their daily production. Whenever it seems to him that their designs have become a bit dull, or they themselves are a bit cranky, he arranges a field trip for them. He himself often comes along to the museums, public gardens, and choice spots in the countryside he's chosen. They walk or travel by train, depending on the distance. Sometimes, for a smaller group—which is always keenly aware of the privilege—they travel in his Renault Torpedo, which his chauffeur keeps in a constant state of high luster.

What better way to fill the imaginations of these young artists with the glories of color and form than with visits to the aquarium or one of the hothouses of Paris, where the most exotic flowers bloom? The zoo is an unending source of inspiration and delight, with its many species of birds and sensuous felines—with their feathers and fur presenting so many possibilities for the artful repetition of patterns.

He finds inspiration in the girls' excitement—experiencing, side by side with them, the novelty of their observations in even the simplest places of Paris. The open markets, where many of the girls see vegetables and fruits they've never seen before. Where even the fish and shellfish are arranged by Parisian merchants in the most cunning patterns, contrived by generations of fishmongers to entice the eyes and appetite of passersby.

Often, on these outings, Poiret orders up some delicacy to be delivered to the employee kitchen in time for lunch. After his artisans have dined and rested, all of them retire to their canvases and sketchbooks with their heads as filled with color as a prism exposed to sunlight.

There's so much of beauty in the world, ripe for interpretation by the nimble fingers of these girls. The vision of an artichoke is reborn as a miracle of geometric design. The woodblock print of a poppy, with one hirsute stem blooming and others about to burst, serves as the print for curtains or cushions. Swallows in flight, starfish and coral, rocks and seashells can be stolen by the eyes out of their natural habitat and captured forever, to give joy and delight over and over again, imprinted on everyday objects, long after the living things are dead and gone.

The girls themselves are surprised by the beauty of their designs when they see them transferred to cloth or porcelain, right alongside the work of the grown-up artists befriended and championed by Monsieur Poiret—the handsome Raoul Dufy and Père Matisse, who is such a master of color. And their favorite, André Dunoyer de Segonzac, who will sometimes sit for hours in their workshop, entertaining them with his imitations of people they know, telling jokes and lending a general atmosphere of joy.

Monsieur Poiret sends half a dozen girls to Sèvres for a week to study the decoration of porcelain—and another group, including Naomi, to the workshop on Boulevard de Clichy to help Monsieur Dufy print fabrics based on their watercolors. The girls vie with each other for the bonuses paid when one of their designs is chosen by a wallpaper manufacturer brought to the atelier—or picked out by the buyer for an upholsterer or draper. Or chosen by Poiret himself for one of the evening cloaks to be worn by the richest and most beautiful women in the world.

Try as he might, he can't find a suitable establishment to weave the rugs he wants designed by the Martines. And so he buys some looms and brings in a Turk who teaches them how to make all different sorts of knots. The *haute laine* rugs they produce with their own hands are so beautiful and so luxurious that he organizes an exhibit of them at his Galerie Barbazanges. There's no keeping up with the orders that pour in.

The Martines paint chairs, tables, and even a piano designed by the young Pierre Fauconnet, who has devised completely novel ways to stain wood in colors that have never been seen on lumber before—an oxidizing bath of potassium bichromate to obtain a cherry color. Fuchsine for pink, and lead salts for gray. Following Monsieur Poiret's general instructions for the design, the Martines paint lavish screens, panels, and murals, which he showcases throughout his house, both in the public and private rooms. Using their finest Kolinsky sable round brushes, they decorate the eau de cologne bottles, diffusers, and packaging for the perfumes of Rosine.

Every day is exciting, filled with a sense of satisfaction in working well and hard and learning new things—all sorts of new things. Naomi learns how to wriggle out of the grasp of men who, pretending to greet her, grab at her bottom while kissing her cheeks. There's no remedy for the men who stare at the womanish chests of the girls who have jumped ahead of the others in the pace at which their bodies are changing. She has twice caught grown-up artists in romantic clinches with one of the older, tougher girls, who each time met her gaze with a brazen look of superiority. The monitress, with vague hints of disaster, ruin, and regret, has warned them all never to allow any man under their skirts, adding darkly that she should know. Naomi isn't altogether sure what this means.

When she gets her period, she has the other Martines to turn to for advice and instructions about what to do—and sighs with relief that she hasn't had to turn to her mother or Jeannette instead.

Mostly, Sonya hasn't seemed to notice that her eldest is growing up, but treats her with the same, slightly distant tenderness that has worked well enough in keeping all three of her children functioning from day to day, each one playing her role and fulfilling her duties. Naomi knows that Jeannette, as far as help or guidance goes, is completely useless.

ళ

Sonya spends nearly all her waking hours filling the flood of orders for the fashion accessories desired by women rich enough to possess one or more of Paul Poiret's dresses, coats, and gowns. The back room at her shop, as well as every available surface in Sonya's bedroom, overflows with wooden hat forms and Leghorn straw, aigrettes and plumes from the South American jungle, buckram and *mousseline de soie*, sparkly *pailettes* and silk rosettes, coq quills, Impeyan feathers, buckles, and beaver fur. None of her children will go into her room now because it makes them sneeze. Baila has a horror of the furry dead things. Finally, at Jeannette's urgent request, Sonya moves everything downstairs to the shop. She works there late into the

night, something she never would have been able to do before
she and Jeannette moved in together.

On one of these nights, Jeannette instructs her nieces to sit,
side by side at the kitchen table. "Here's the thing," she says after they're all hunkered down, with uniformly glum expressions
on their faces. "My indescribably stupid colleagues at the Opera
Ballet have voted to go on strike."

Olga's eyes grow wide behind her glasses. It pains her to do
so, but she swallows her antipathy. "To the barricades, *ma tante!*
I will march with you."

"Oh, don't make me vomit! I would sooner cut off my feet
than show up in a protest march with a gaggle of feminists and
lesbians."

Olga glares at her. Before she has time to formulate a come-
back, Naomi pipes up, "Does that mean your pay will stop?"

"Well, at least," says Jeannette, "someone seated here at this
table has a brain in her head—and is, I might add, contributing
to the cost of your feed." She turns her gaze on Olga. "Which
brings me to you, mademoiselle."

Crossing her arms, Olga mutters, "What have I done now?"

"It's not a matter of what you have done but what I want
you to do."

"Mama might have a say in it, whatever it is, when she gets
home."

"Ah, but she's not home, Olga, is she?"

Naomi puts a protective arm around her sister's shoulder
and whispers into her ear, "Don't react!"

Jeannette glares at both of them. How did she ever allow
Paul to convince her this was a good idea?

"Perhaps," says Olga, "you want me to put rouge on my lips
and walk the streets to help pay for your champagne!"

This brings sharp, angry tears into Jeannette's eyes. She rarely buys champagne! Standing taller, working hard to keep her
voice even, she manages to smile at Olga. "I only thought how
maybe you might want to try to go see someone at one of the
newspapers. There might be an interest—you never know—in

publishing one of your stories. Or essays. I don't know what you call them."

Olga's face turns the color of beetroot. "My stories! How or why do you even know about my stories?"

Jeannette shrugs. "If you weren't such a slob, I wouldn't be forever needing to put your things away."

"They're my things, not yours. How dare you read my notebooks?" She's crying now, which is rare for Olga. "How dare you?" she says in a much quieter voice, devoid of the pride and optimism that usually characterize everything Olga says. She feels, inside herself, a burning sense of shame. And then, wiping her eyes and taking a hard, deep breath through her nose, she says, "You're right, Auntie." Both Naomi and Baila look at her as if she's lost her mind.

"She's *not* right," murmurs Baila. "She shouldn't have spied on you."

"Of course she shouldn't have," says Olga. "But she's right that I should look for work—the sooner, the better. I'll start today."

"But you're in school," says Naomi, adding a little sulkily, "and you always win the top prizes."

Ignoring her sisters, Olga says to her aunt, "Really, I can't thank you enough for saying what you've said. I don't know what I was thinking."

Jeannette says nothing, but only looks hard at Olga, trying to penetrate whatever game the child is playing now. She has no doubt that Olga is hatching some plan that's bound to have unpleasant consequences. Half the time, she thinks she really would be better off if Olga ran away from home. She also knows that if the running away were ascribed to anything Jeannette did or said, there would be no forgiveness from Sonya—and Jeannette would be torn away not only from her sister but also from Baila, who is shaping up so well as a dancer and doing Jeannette so much credit as her teacher.

"Run along then, all of you—you've given me a headache again!"

It's a Sunday and everyone in the household is still asleep when Olga wakes, before dawn, to light the stove. With the stealth of an intruder, she puts on the warm clothes she set out the night before, after her mother had gone to bed and Jeannette had returned home from the theater, taken off her makeup, had a glass of something, and passed out in her room.

When the winter sun glazes the rooftops across the way in red, Olga opens the door as quietly as she can, slips into the cold hallway, and down the stairs to the street entrance, to rue Saint-Sulpice.

She pauses, for a moment, looking out from the doorway onto the street, remembering the floods of two years before, remembering how the streets of Paris were transformed into a network of waterways, carrying everything to the Seine—eventually, to the sea.

Olga has read many descriptions, in both poetry and prose, of the sea. If she'd been born a boy, she thinks, she would make her way down to Le Havre or Honfleur—or perhaps all the way south to Marseilles—and sign on as a cabin boy on some tall ship headed for places unknown. She would work by day, doing whatever chores cabin boys are assigned to do—and by night she'd write by candlelight below decks. If words ever failed her, she would climb up into the rigging to be closer to the stars, close enough to find whatever words she was searching for.

The parti-colored cobblestones are slick with morning dew, glazed with ice in the frigid air. If she were a boy instead of a girl, she would be set for a much longer journey than her zigzag walk along the rue de Babylone toward the banks of the Seine. Ah, she could, perhaps, find a tall ship on the river—or, at least, a barge that would take her northwest to the English Channel. There would be no limit then to the ships she could find—nor the destinations to which they could take her. She wonders how old one must be to get a job on that new British ship she's read so much about—the so-called Queen of the Ocean: the *Titanic*. If only Olga were taller, she might be able to lie successfully about her age and be part of its maiden voyage.

She knows that she will never grow tired of walking and dreaming along the pathways above the river, even though, this February morning, the wind is so brisk and the air so very cold. She walks faster, wishing there were a way to walk fast enough to sneak herself across that invisible border—away from all the petty and humiliating limits imposed on her, into the free and boundless territory of adulthood.

When she reaches the Avenue Anatole France, she sees more people than she expected to find at this hour. But, then, she's rarely abroad this early on a Sunday.

At first she thinks the people must be hurrying to church. But then she notices that most of the thirty or so men on the sidewalk are hauling cameras and other bulky tools of photography—and she realizes that they must be members of the press. There are some women, too, and there is an unusually large number of policemen. Everyone is well bundled up against the cold, all of them hurrying, like she, to reach the Champ du Mars before the bells of Paris strike eight o'clock.

Olga can see the daring Franz Reichelt in her mind's eye, as he was depicted, the day before, in *le Petit Journal* —his broad forehead and handsome face. His lavish handlebar mustache. The fiercely determined look in his eyes as he stretched out his arms to show off the wingspan of his *vêtement-de-parachute*— the garment he's invented to save the lives of aviators when something goes wrong mid-flight. *The flying tailor,* the newspaper called him.

Olga read his boast and studied his photograph. A dressmaker, like Monsieur Poiret, although at a far earlier stage of his career. Like her mother. Another aspiring immigrant tailor from Middle Europe—he, from Austria—trying to find success in Paris, to find a way to make his work stand out among all the other couturiers of the capital of fashion. Lured by the 10,000-franc prize being offered by the Aéro-Club de France for the fabrication and demonstration of a wearable parachute that works.

Olga had thought, from that first day when she'd read about

him, what a good match he'd be for Sonya. A brave man, like
Olga's late father. Clearly a forward-thinking man. Someone
Olga wouldn't at all mind calling *Papa*.

Reichelt has done several tests already, from lower heights
than the one he now proposes—in one case, breaking his leg.
Here, thinks Olga, is a man with the determination and perhaps
the desperation to risk his life, in public, to accomplish something extraordinary.

Would *she* risk her life to accomplish something extraordinary? She thinks about the wide world and all the opportunity
there might be, if she can only find it, for a girl with brains and
courage too.

An area beneath the Eiffel Tower has been roped off, so
that no one will be harmed by Reichelt when he touches down.
Police are patrolling the perimeter. Olga gets as close as she can,
finding places where she can slip through the gaps between the
woolen overcoats and curtained tripods of all those who have
come to observe and record.

She has an unobstructed view looking up—but is too short
to see anything straight in front of her. She hears Franz Reichelt's German-inflected voice, ringing out clear and confident—and sees only his cap as he waves it above his head. The
crowd cheers in response to whatever he's just said. Olga is able
to make out the words, *Vous allez voir!*—"You will see!"

That's what Olga would like to say to everyone who thinks
that girls should busy themselves with ribbons and ruffles—
and toe shoes! *You will see!* Her desire to achieve something great
in the world is all bollixed up with her desire for vindication in
a world that seems set up to thwart her.

Why shouldn't a girl aspire to heroism as great as that of any
man? Marie Curie, after all, was awarded a second Nobel Prize,
the year before. The time for women has finally arrived—and
yet there's no guidebook to follow and there are precious few
beacons to light the way. For thousands of years, women have
been disenfranchised, treated like chattel, and denied education,
opportunity, and even legal status, since the dawn of civilization.

It is the duty, Olga tells herself, of every girl to study the ways of courageous men and co-opt them. Perhaps for the first time since Eve bit into that apple, the female sex is poised to take its rightful place, not below but alongside the world's bravest and most accomplished men.

The cheers of the crowd are punctuated by impassioned pleas from a few bystanders, begging Monsieur Reichelt to reconsider his folly. And then he comes into view on the inner stairway of the great tower, very bulky but still handsome in his garment as he climbs, followed by two fellows who, unlike the intrepid tailor, walk haltingly, putting two feet on every step and looking down before progressing further. One of them is carrying what looks like a café table and the other is carrying a three-legged stool.

Higher and higher, step by step, the three of them climb, all the way to the first windblown platform, fifty-seven meters—over seventeen stories—above the ground.

When they reach the top, Reichelt waves his hat again—and, again, the crowd cheers, and Olga cheers along with them. He shakes hands with both his friends, ceremoniously, one after the other, after they've constructed the even higher platform of the stool placed upon the table. It looks like they're trying to talk him out of what he's about to do.

A policeman standing near Olga says, "It was supposed to be tested with a dummy. That's what the prefect said."

"It *will* be tested by a dummy," another policeman replies.

The photographers all have their cameras pointed upwards.

Dismissing the arguments of his friends, Reichelt steps first up onto the table and then up onto the stool at its center. The crowd lets out a collective gasp. The tailor pulls his cap down lower on his head, then waves again at the people below. All of them wave back at him.

And then he turns so that he's facing the river. He checks the apparatus of his parachute—a button here, a cord there—before raising himself to his full height, his head held tall. He's in profile for Olga. The upper edges of his garment are flapping in the wind. From his breast pocket, he takes out a little book—could it be a book of poetry? He tears a leaf from it and then drops the piece of paper and watches its course as the wind blows it gently, slowly, to the ground.

Now that it's clear that Reichelt intends to proceed, the crowd has grown so silent that the only sound Olga can hear is the wind from the river and, far beneath that, inside her, the beating of her heart.

Reichelt unfurls his brown silken wings and then closes them again when they flap in the wind, compromising his balance as he stands there. Then he lifts his cap in another salute.

What does he see, Olga wants to know, from where he's standing? What can Franz Reichelt see, as he's standing there—hesitating, so high above the Earth—that no one else can see? From such a height, can one see the future? Can one see, and finally understand, the past?

Without even being conscious that she was doing so, Olga began counting from the moment the tailor seemed poised to jump. She counts in rhythm to her own heartbeat.

It is as if both time and sound have stopped—as if cotton wool has been stuffed inside the world's ears. Olga hears her heartbeat, nothing more.

He balances. He waits. He looks all around at the world below him. Perhaps at the world beyond. Olga has counted to forty-five when, suddenly, with a slight lift of his chin, Franz Reichelt opens his wings in all their voluminous glory. Looking like a giant bat, the morning light shining through the fabric of his wings, he crouches then leaps off the stool, launching himself, just like he launched that page from his book, into the empty air.

Instantly, the entire garment folds up around him like the petals of a flower closing as darkness falls—and he falls. He doesn't float. He plummets like a stone.

Olga's mouth forms a scream but no sound comes out. Franz Reichelt's fall lasts for five miserly seconds before he strikes the ground with the full force of his manly frame, crushed in an instant. Clearly dead. As dead as the puppet dancers in *Petrushka* before they were brought to life by the magician.

But there is no magician who can bring Franz Reichelt to life again, bloodied, arms and legs akimbo in the crater formed by the impact of his fall. Olga turns from the sight of it, sobbing with a sorrow that she knows is much deeper than any feelings she might have conceived for this mad daredevil. Feelings as old as her own deepest sorrow.

She remembers, in some crazy, wordless reconstruction, a feeling that she knows is a memory of the murdered father she barely had a chance to know. She is sobbing, hitting her forehead with her fists, as distressed as if it were she herself who had caused Franz Reichelt to fail.

PART V

PARIS

1913

Once again, Jeannette assembles her nieces at the kitchen table in their new apartment, which—despite Paul's promises that all will be well—has been eating up most of their income. She stands at the sink, her arms folded. "My fiancé has informed me," she says, addressing Olga, "that the editor of *Le Matin* has divorced his Jewish wife and married his pregnant mistress, Sidonie-Gabrielle Colette. They are now in need of a mother's helper."

Baila says, "Aren't *you* about to be a Jewish wife, when you marry Mâitre Blum?"

"As rumor has it," Jeannette murmurs, glancing at the engagement ring René gave her more than a year ago now.

Olga beams. "Colette, the writer? How extraordinary that she has chosen to marry!"

"You are so naïve. He is a baron. And she is a music hall performer."

"'To receive happiness from someone,'" Olga quotes Colette from memory. "'Is it not to choose the sauce in which we want to be eaten?'"

"Well, the future baroness has chosen a very rich sauce."

"As well as a situation filled with opportunity," muses Olga. "I wonder if she'll write for the paper now. She could have her own column."

"And good luck with that, with a little vampire at her breast." Sighing, Jeannette stares out the window.

"Why is it," Baila asks faintly, "that she hates babies?"

"She hates herself," says Olga.

"Oh, you think you're so smart!" says Jeannette, turning to face them again.

Olga shrugs. "You've made yourself very popular with me just now—"

"As if I cared!"

"I'll go to the offices of *Le Matin* today—and apply for the job. I hope you'll convey my thanks—to your boyfriend." Olga ducks her head just on time to avoid the wet dishrag Jeannette throws at her. It hits the wall behind her head with a splat.

Naomi holds her face in her hands. "I'm so tired of this." Getting up from the table, she fixes her aunt in her gaze. "You won't make her leave school, I hope."

"I am sure Maître Blum wouldn't hear of it." Jeannette still hasn't figured out how to convince Sonya that Baila would be better off living with her and René, when he finally gets around to marrying her. "Olga, you are to tell the Baron de Jouvenel that you will only be available after school—and during evenings and weekends, of course. The more hours, the better, as far as I'm concerned. That is, if he and the baroness find you fit for the job."

ھ

Olga stands as straight and tall as possible. She's conscious of her short stature and how very little of her must be showing above the vast expanse of desk where the Baron du Jouvenal's secretary sits writing notes and ignoring her.

"*Pardonnez-moi, monsieur,*" she says for a second time, making an effort to speak in a lower, more commanding tone of voice.

Sighing, the secretary lays his pen and glasses down and then looks at Olga. He laughs sweetly, as one might laugh at the sight of a baby in a pram. "What can I do for you, little lady?" He uses *tu* with Olga, which she finds infuriating.

When she starts to speak, he cuts her short, lowering his head and winking. "Did your papa perhaps forget his lunch today? What's his name, *chérie*? You have very pretty curls, you know."

"I have an appointment with Madame Colette," she says, "for a job interview."

"Indeed." He puts on a different pair of glasses and looks

so closely at her that she wonders exactly what he's trying to discern. Olga doesn't smile. "Well then, mademoiselle, you'd better come with me."

She follows him through a large room filled with reporters, all of them men, banging away on their typewriters—then opens the door to a little office with Colette's name and her new title on the door.

"Another applicant for the job, madame."

Colette is far from what Olga expects, given Jeannette's characterization of her as a music hall dancer. Perched on a straight-backed chair behind her desk, she is dressed in what appears to be a man's suit, white waistcoat, and tie. Her pretty face—with her large, heavily made-up eyes, pointy chin, and mop of curly dark hair—gives her the look of a beautiful and rather dangerous cat. She's so lithe and lean that it seems impossible that she could have given birth only a short time ago.

She cocks her head at Olga, dismissing the secretary with a wave of her hand. "Oh, what a shame. Henri was to tell all the applicants that we've sent little Belle-Gazou away to live with her nurse in the countryside."

Olga wonders if it's common practice for women of a certain class to send their infants away to be raised by a stranger. She can't decide whether the idea seems imminently practical or rather ghastly. She's sure her own mother would never have done such a thing. She thinks the idea would probably appeal to Jeannette, if she were ever to give birth to a child. And it suddenly strikes her that, although both her mother and Jeannette are old, they're younger than Colette—and therefore not too old to have a baby. Could that be, she wonders, what Maître Blum has in mind? She wonders if Jeannette has thought of this!

"And, really," Colette continues in a pleasingly confiding voice, "do I look like someone meant to stay at home with a baby?"

"I don't know, madame. I think we're only used to seeing women in certain prescribed roles, rather than others."

"Come closer, please. Aren't you delicious!"

Olga steps closer. She hesitates, but only for a moment, before speaking. "It seems rather odd to me that the room out there is filled exclusively with men."

Colette smiles. It seems that Olga has said precisely the right thing. "It seems quite odd to me too. Maybe most women are too stupid to do what those men do."

"Surely you can't believe that, Madame Colette."

"Not in the slightest. But since being named the fiction editor of *Le Matin,* I haven't had a single story submitted by a female."

"And yet you've published several!"

"Pseudonyms. Do you like to write, my child?"

"I believe I am, by nature, a writer." Olga's eyes steal upward, toward the ceiling. She feels half afraid that the wrath of God will come down on her head for what she's dared to say—and in this place, to this person.

Colette raises a single eyebrow at her. "And do you have some stories to tell?"

Does she? Doesn't everyone? Olga remembers reading that exile is one of the best routes to becoming a writer. "I might," she says. "I was born in another land, speaking another language. My father was murdered by a mob. My mother—" She hesitates. "My mother is a woman of deep mystery."

Has she said too much? Has she spoken out of turn? Does she seem, as her aunt so frequently says, like an arrogant freak?

Pushing back her chair, Colette heaves a deep and contented sigh. "That all sounds quite promising." She's smiling at Olga. Her smile is—Olga can't think of another word for it—hypnotic. "Your French is certainly good—too good, perhaps."

She crooks her pretty finger at Olga, beckoning her closer. "We could give you a try. But we'll have to keep your name and age a secret. How old are you? Twelve?"

"Precisely, madame."

"Maybe we'll write some stories together, you and I. Would you like to kiss me?"

Much to Olga's relief, there's a sharp rap just then on the door. Henri du Jouvenal himself walks in. "Letty," he says.

Colette inclines her head at Olga. The editor glances at her, nods, then goes on with what he was about to say. "Bulgaria, Serbia, and Greece have declared war on the Empire!"

"Oh, how exciting! May I go, Henri?"

"Over my dead body, dear. I expect you to come up with some timely stories, though. Readers will be hungry to know more about everything Turkish—and everything about the Balkan League. I'm sending that chap Gustave Cirilli to Adrianople, Stéphane Lauzanne to Constantinople, Hubert Vallier to Bulgarian Army Headquarters, and Roger Mathieu to the Serbia side. Alphonse Cuinet will report on the Turkish army. Gabriel Bronnaire will leave tomorrow for Greece. And Zerbitz is heading to Montenegro."

"Oh, what fun for them! Shall we give them a going-away party tonight, Henri?"

৵

Suddenly the lights are on and Jeannette is awake—or, at least, her eyes are open.

They are all standing over her bed—Sonya, Naomi, Olga, and Baila. All in their nightclothes. Jeannette's heart is racing. Her breathing is ragged, as if she'd just been dancing.

"You were crying out," says Sonya, laying a hand on her sister's shoulder.

"We thought you were being murdered!" Baila says, her eyes wide.

And then Jeannette remembers—the final scene of *The Rite of Spring*, Nijinsky's new ballet for which she and the other dancers have been working so hard and so thanklessly. Punishing their bodies at every rehearsal, every rehearsal longer and longer now, as the date for the opening approaches. Being screamed at by Nijinsky and Stravinsky, whose quarrels are so loud, and sound so nasty, that the subject of their ballet—a ritual murder in Russia's prehistoric past—seems like it's about to take place right there in the rehearsal room.

Stravinsky bangs on the piano, counting out his crazy rhythms as Nijinsky, dripping sweat and rage, shouts at the composer that he must slow the music down. One doesn't need to speak Russian to understand what he's saying: it's simply impossible for his dancers to execute the choreography at those insanely fast tempi.

And then Nijinsky himself screams at them to stamp their feet harder, forcing them to jam their legs into the stage as they land, hurting their knees. He commands the Chosen Virgin to jump so high and come down so hard that there have already been several serious injuries. In demonstrating what he wants, he almost hit his head on the ceiling. None of them can jump as high as he can. They're running out of understudies. That's how Jeannette got her spot in the line of frenetically circling, stamping, expressionless dancers.

Her legs and feet are sore. Her hips hurt too. It's painful to turn over onto her side.

"What were you dreaming?" Sonya asks, sitting down on the edge of the bed.

When Jeannette blinks her eyes, the scene is vivid again, vivid and loud. She hears the staccato shrieks and percussive chords of the final ritual. "*Le Sacre du Printemps,*" she says. "I was the Chosen One, the Sacrificial Virgin." She closes her eyes and takes a deep breath. The Old Woman was reaching out to grab Jeannette away from the others. Away from everything that has ever made her feel safe.

Olga finds the very idea of her aunt as any kind of virgin to be rather amusing—but refrains from saying anything arch or from saying anything at all. Jeannette's skin looks as white as her linen sheets.

Jeanette pushes Sonya's hand away. "I'm fine. Go back to bed, all of you."

Baila sits down between her mother and Jeannette, leaning her sleepy head on Sonya's bosom. "It must have been very frightening, Auntie. Mama also has night terrors sometimes."

"You do?"

"Little ears," says Sonya.

Naomi and Olga share a look that says, *We'll get to the bottom of this.*

"Would you like me to stay with you until you fall asleep again?"

"Don't be ridiculous," says Jeannette. "I'm not a child."

"Auntie," says Olga, in what she hopes will be received as a kind tone of voice. "Do you think I might come with you to the theater, one of these days before the dress rehearsal? I promise not to get in the way."

Jeannette looks at Olga, noticing that she has a pimple on her chin. On the very verge of adulthood, is this child. She could, with her command of Russian, prove useful as a second set of ears, maybe giving Jeannette some insight into what both the composer and choreographer are saying during their shouting matches. "Maybe." She smiles at Olga, taking pleasure in what she's about to say. "Maybe if I tell them that we weren't able to find a babysitter for you."

Olga shrugs. "Whatever it takes," she says. From what she's heard, this ballet is going to be the most revolutionary cultural event of the season.

"We already have our tickets," Sonya reminds her, "and it's a good thing, too, because I've heard they've already sold out for the premiere. Isn't that right, Jeannette?"

"Please go to bed! I have a hard day in front of me."

As she tries to find sleep again, there in the dark, she can still hear Nijinsky's frantic voice, calling out the counts—and can see the Old Woman's hands reaching out to grab her. "No!" Jeannette says, with trembling voice, too quietly for anyone to hear.

❧

Everyone who is anyone is there for the opening of the Théâtre des Champs-Élysées and the debut of Diaghilev's new season. The princesses, duchesses, foreign royalty, and all the other *grandes dames* of Paris and beyond are sending out a dazzling reflection of the houselights from where they sit at the front row of the boxes. Their bejeweled tiaras, necklaces, bracelets, rings, and brooches glow like tropical flowers blooming in a dark jungle of black silk top hats. The ladies in their finery are flanked by mutton-chopped men in royal blue coats with fringed gold epaulettes trembling at their shoulders, their coats and waistcoats serving as a way to display the *croix d'honneurs*, embroidered emblems of aristocracy and ribbons of honor usually kept behind glass at their ancestral keeps.

In the ambulatory between the boxes, and in the cheap seats above, are all the black-coated, long-haired painters, poets, journalists, and musicians of the eighteenth arrondissement, all of them friends and champions of the impresario and his artistic collaborators.

Paul Poiret is wearing colors that harmonize with the theater's newly upholstered red velvet seats. He's sitting next to his fashion-plate wife Denise Boulet, for whom he's designed a special dress for the occasion—a dress he has named Théâtre des Champs-Élysées, an airy confection of ivory brocade and silk tulle, with a lampshade skirt. He is gratified to notice the many sets of opera glasses that are pointed in their direction.

Above and behind them, he's already noticed Sonya accompanied by all three of her children, all of them wearing very nice hats he's never seen before. They will, he imagines, soon be seen all over Paris.

Jeannette, he knows, will be on the stage. But he's not worried about anyone upsetting his wife. He has confidence in the twins' discretion, given that both of them, as well as Naomi now, have so many reasons to feel in his debt.

When he looks up and Naomi catches his eye, he gives her the tiniest salute with two fingers touched to his temple. Denise, who has had her opera glasses trained on a box across the theater, nudges him in the ribs. "There's Diaghilev!" she whispers. And then, shifting her gaze down to the first few rows, "Isn't that the composer? He's not much to look at, is he!"

"Ah, but he is a genius, my dear."

The houselights are extinguished, leaving them all in

darkness. Pierre Monteux strides out into the pit. Stepping up to his podium, he bows to acknowledge the packed theater and excited applause—then turns his back to the audience and raises his baton.

"Is that Nijinsky's sister, in the front row? Isn't she dancing?" Paul pats his wife's hand. "She's in the family way, my dear, just like you. Hush now."

Olga has brought a notebook with her. She's been scribbling in it ever since they arrived—and continues to do so, even in the dark.

The curtains part to reveal the set by Nicholas Roerich, a painter Olga has heard described as both a mystic and a scholar. How did he find his vision, she wants to know, of what the world must have looked like before there was writing—before there was art? When the baton comes down, the music starts with a lovely and strange solo, played on an instrument whose name Olga can't identify. Is it a bassoon? The sound is nasal, sweet, and plaintive. Full of yearning. It's joined by a horn—the type that hunters use. Olga has learned, from plays she's seen, to recognize this sound. There's a haunting melody played by flutes, ancient and evocative, echoed by the horn. But then the loveliness is trampled on by the sounds of low strings, massed together. The sounds make Olga think of an army—an army at war. It's a frightening and relentless sound. She can't understand how Colette could think of war as anything other than horrifying.

Snatches of that sweet melody rise up again from the flutes and the horns, only to be drowned out by that insistent, murderous rhythm of the cellos and basses. They pluck and bow in unison, punctuated by frenetic calls from the horns and trumpets. The shrieks of the piccolos make her think of gnomes rising up from the ground.

What rites of spring are these? Where is the birdsong, the sound of new beginnings and tender light? Where are the beautiful, ethereal ballerinas with their wings and graceful hands and cloudlike skirts of white tulle?

Something has begun to happen in the audience. A stirring and murmuring—and, yes, a distinct sound of hissing when the dancers first come on. All of them female, they are dressed in primitive-looking, unattractive costumes, with not a single bit of their beautiful bodies showing. They've been made as ugly as possible—and are made to move in ways that do nothing to show off their training as ballerinas.

The dancers look none too happy about their costumes. Olga knows that their blank expressions are part of the choreography. She heard Nijinsky shout at them at rehearsal, "Don't show me emotions! Don't make fearful faces! You are a plant, a clod of earth. A calf for the slaughter. Hold your fear inside your body!"

Two groups of red-clad dancers have entered in succession, walking in time to the lowest notes of the strings, which are being played in a strange syncopated rhythm. It takes Olga a moment to recognize Jeannette among the other dancers. Olga has never seen her look so plain. They circle, pounding the earth in rhythm to the ominous, threatening sounds that signal the worst things that can happen to a living person at the hands of a mob: violence, rape, murder. Facing outward, trembling, the dancers rise up on tip-toe, their arms held up to the sky. Then, dropping their left hands down by their sides with a percussive motion, they all jerk their heads to the right.

It's so different from anything that's ever been seen on the ballet stage before—and Stravinsky's music is different from anything anyone has ever heard. His score for *Petrushka* was wonderfully odd. But this music is willfully dissonant, ominous, and weird, an assault, in a way, on the ears. She writes this in her notebook: *A willful assault on the ears—a direct path to one's darkest emotions.* It is all, Olga thinks, absolutely fantastic. A revolution for the art world. A notion of spring that hearkens back to the ferocious time before civilization made the idea of human sacrifice abhorrent.

Are we so different now? she writes in her notebook.

Someone from the audience whistles—someone who really

knows how to whistle loudly. It's an impressive sound. Olga makes a mental note to learn, by whatever means it takes, to whistle like that. And yet it's horrible—she's never witnessed such disrespectful behavior in a theater before.

The ominous mood of the music is relentless. As those headache-inducing notes sound again and again on the basses and cellos, the dancers pull their elbows in at their waists and turn their feet inward. The movement is met with laughter from the audience.

"Call a doctor!" someone yells from the darkness, followed by more, and even more raucous, laughter.

One of the men standing in the ambulatory shouts out, "Show some respect, for God's sake, for the artists!"

As one, the dancers drop their heads to one side, their tilted faces propped on the backs of their hands.

"Call a dentist!" yells a booming male voice from one of the boxes.

Widespread laughter breaks out.

"Call two dentists!" another joker yells.

There are more ear-splitting whistles and even howls. More and more people, both men and women, are shouting insults so loudly that it's becoming hard to hear the music. The orchestra keeps playing though. Maestro Monteux seems impervious to the disruptions. With the courage of a soldier facing an on-slaught of enemy fire, he continues to jab at the air with the tip of his baton—and the dancers keep moving, although it's clear now that quite a few of them are close to tears.

Suddenly, the houselights come up, shocking the crowd into silence. In the flash of illumination, Olga sees Diaghilev him-self in the lighting booth. "I beg you," he shouts. "Allow the show to proceed!"

Someone near him calls out, "Listen first, you idiots! You can whistle later on!"

Shamed by the lights, the audience quiets down. But when it's dark again, there's more laughter and more shouting and whistling. A woman rises from the boxes, her tiara askew. "How

dare you!" she calls out in a quavering voice to one of the artist
types standing adjacent to her seat. Another long-haired man
says, "Shut your trap, you old bitch!"

Olga hears a slap—and, if she's not mistaken, she has just
seen two gentlemen exchanging cards. The theater is awash in
sounds of outrage and anguished calls for silence—and even
so, the dancers keep dancing their dance of death and the orchestra keeps playing.

A woman in the front rows gets up and looks behind her,
pointing her furled umbrella at a man who has just been sitting
there, watching the show. "Dirty Jew!" she yells, taking a swipe
at him. There's the sound then of fists hitting flesh, followed
by screams.

❧

When the flute melody is played at the start, Sonya's thoughts
wander off to memories of everything she loved about
Kishinev. Her brother Lev carrying her on his shoulders, pretending to be a horse, when she was a tiny girl, while he was still
living at home. Walking hand in hand with her mother through
the open market in the square, surrounded by the sights and
smells of the countryside's bounty—the vegetables with the
dirt still clinging to their roots. The fragrant baskets of berries
and apricots. The fresh-baked bread and the bundles of herbs.
The feeling of falling asleep with her head cradled against the
pillowy softness of her mother's bosom, arms wrapped around
her, her mother's heartbeat in her ears.

But when the flutes are drowned out by the low strings of the
basses and cellos, sounding the same relentless, monotone notes
over and over again, her thoughts take a darker turn. She recognizes those sounds. They are the sounds of hatred and fear. The
sounds of a mob that's hungry for flesh. For someone to blame.

It goes on and on like this. She sees Jeannette on the stage—
but it's as if she's looking at her across a chasm. As if her sister
has once again been lost to her. Her own breathing is shallow
and rapid. Her heart is racing and her hands feel numb.

When someone shouts out, "Dirty Jew!" it's altogether

unclear to Sonya whether the shouting has come from the present or the past. Shouts and screams are erupting from all over the theater. Her chest starts hurting, just below her heart—a sharp pain that makes it hard to breathe.

In the aural frenzy that follows, Sonya's mind spills over with images of the pogrom as she has seen it again and again in countless nightmares. The anti-Semitic mob with their crowbars and cudgels. Asher, unarmed, but standing his ground in front of their shop. She hears the sickening sound of iron crashing into his flesh. She hears his bones breaking and sees his face bloodied and bruised again, as she saw it there, in the makeshift morgue. The flesh of his face swollen, his arms akimbo. His eyes—his dead eyes—still open.

The pogrom is suddenly as vivid to her as if she and the children hadn't been hidden safely away in the attic of the church while her husband was murdered and their home destroyed.

She only realizes that her face is wet when Baila shakes her as if waking her from a dream. But she hasn't been sleeping. "Mama!" Is it Baila's voice, or is it her own voice, crying out?

Sonya closes her eyes, trying to collect herself—but she winces every time she hears another shout, another slap, another insult. It's harder and harder to breathe. She feels like she's dying. She doesn't dare to look at Jeannette on that stage, in that circle of red-clad, trembling girls, each one of them hoping not to be chosen as the one who will be murdered for the tribe, murdered so that spring will come again with its bounty.

"Don't choose my sister—not her!" she whispers, her eyes still closed, carried across the chasm of time to that moment so long ago—when hands reached down and plucked Zaneta out of the crib, and Sonya was left there alone and abandoned. A tiny child desperately crying, but no one heard her. No one came to comfort her.

"Mama!" cries Baila.

"We've got to get her out of here," Naomi says.

All around them, people are shouting and tearing at each other's clothes. Women's hats are torn off their heads and men's beards are being pulled, even as the dancers keep dancing and the orchestra keeps playing. Monteux never once turns his head to look behind him but continues to wield his baton with his right hand, while with his left he turns the pages of the score. Nijinsky is visible in the wings, standing on a chair, shouting out his eccentric counts in Russian, "Fifteen! Sixteen! Seventeen!"

"Good God," Naomi says. "This isn't going to be easy."

PARIS

1913

Olga breaks the silence. "Do you remember our father?" she asks Naomi.

The three sisters sit together in an antechamber at the mayor's office, dressed in their wedding clothes, waiting for Mâitre Blum's secretary to come collect them.

Naomi shakes her head. "Not really. I remember that he could always make me smile, even when I was sad. I remember being on a train once, with you and Mama. Papa couldn't come with us. He made my dolly talk."

"Is that all? Can't you remember anything else?"

Naomi tries harder—and even wonders if she's making this up, just to please Olga. "He wore glasses," she says slowly, "like you. He loved reading."

"But his face? What did he look like, Noni? You're such a genius with faces."

Naomi sighs. "When I try to see his face, all I see is the portrait."

They've spent a lot of time, together and separately, looking at the framed sepia wedding portrait of their mother and father, a photo their uncle Daniel had given to them. It is the only photo of their father they have ever seen.

"I can't remember anything before Saint Petersburg," says Olga with a sigh. "When we saw *Petrushka*, I felt like I was remembering Kishinev—but it was my mind, I think, playing tricks on me."

Naomi looks into Olga's eyes but only sees a small reflection of herself in her sister's glasses. "Mama says that, of all of us, you're most like him."

Baila sees an opportunity to contribute something to this conversation. "Our aunt says there's no way of knowing if he *was* my father."

"She didn't!" says Naomi, at the same moment that Olga says, "That bitch!"

Naomi takes Baila by the shoulders and waits till Baila meets her gaze. "Get this straight, Babochka. Asher Danilov was father to all three of us."

Baila, who hates her sisters' nickname for her, pushes Naomi away. "What does it matter, who my father was? I never had a father for one single day of my life. I'm glad our aunt is marrying Maître Blum! I wish Mama would get married."

"I think it's important," says Olga in her most maddeningly grown-up voice, "to help each other remember. To keep whatever memories we have alive."

"Our lives are ahead of us," says Baila. "What good is there in trying to remember what's gone now?"

"How can you say that?" Naomi asks, just as she wonders why she and Olga are both so sentimental about a past they hardly even remember. Certainly, this nostalgia must be due to their mother's influence, really, always going on and on about Kishinev and all its sights and smells and stories about their little home behind the shop with its ceramic stove and steaming samovar. About the antics of their uncle Lev, a person they've never met—who has entered the realm of myth for them, along with the grandparents and other relatives they never knew, and the father she can barely remember. Maybe, she speculates, this persistent preoccupation with the past is keeping their mother from getting on with her life.

"Those who cannot remember the past are condemned to repeat it," says Olga.

Baila, who struggles in school, often rails at God for having given Olga all the brains. "Did you just make that up?"

"I wish! It was written by an American named George Santayana."

Naomi is accustomed to the scholarly nuggets her sister

brings home from the library and introduces into their conversation whenever possible. She has found occasion to repeat some of the better lines, when the opportunity arose, in front of someone she wished to impress.

A rap at the door announces Maître Blum's secretary, who pokes his head inside. "All ready, are you?"

"We're ready, Eugène," says Baila, reflexively—unthinkingly—making her eyes shine and looking even prettier than she had a moment ago.

Eugène sits on a chair across from them. "Aren't you excited about the wedding—and the honeymoon? My goodness, Mademoiselle Baila, *you* must surely be excited to be going on the tour!"

Baila is excited but also filled with dread that she's bound to disappoint her aunt, no matter how hard she works at her ballet lessons. What are the chances of rising to the top of the heap, after all? Her aunt had worked at being a dancer as if nothing else mattered to her—and still never managed to progress beyond demi-soloist, and that only two or three times in her entire career. And now her knees are nearly shot, and she'd be ready to throw herself off a rooftop if she hadn't finally gotten Maître Blum to make good on his promise to marry her.

Olga sighs, thinking about how unfair it is, once again, that Baila is to get a treat that will be wasted on her. What will she even notice about South America? What an opportunity it would be, aboard the *Avon*, to observe at close hand—and write about—the inner workings of Europe's most innovative dance company. "This is a marriage of convenience for everyone involved, wouldn't you say?"

"You're very cynical for one so young," says Eugène, who gets a soft, nostalgic look in his eyes. "Your aunt was, and still is, a beautiful dancer."

"Ask her sometime if she's pleased with her career—or well content that it's nearly over!"

"Over?" says Eugène. "How can you say it's nearly over when she's just been hired to go on tour with Diaghilev's company?"

Olga suspects that Jeannette is only getting to go on the tour because the Ballets Russes is strapped for funds. Mâitre Blum will pay for their passage aboard the *Avon*, and Baila's too. It wouldn't have taken a good deal of persuasion to convince Baron de Gunzburg, who's in charge of the tour, to hire Jeannette as a supernumerary dancer for *Swan Lake* and *Schéhérazade*. It was just too good a bargain to pass on, getting a competent dancer who would pay her own way.

"It will be an unparalleled opportunity for me, taking classes with the company," says Baila, parroting her aunt's words—and assuming what her sisters have come to regard as her ballerina pose, head held high and slightly to one side, shoulders squared.

Olga sighs again, thinking about how Baila will be seeing all the wonders of the world—and how little detail she's bound to convey in her letters, no matter how many promises Olga extracts from her.

They hear raised voices from the other side of the door—angry voices. Eugène tries to smile reassuringly—but clearly something is wrong. And then Mâitre Blum and their mother burst in.

"Well," says Sonya, pinning a lock of hair back in place. "It seems we're to skip the wedding and go straight to the party."

Blum appeals directly to Olga. "You'll understand, I'm sure! I've found a publisher for Proust—and must see the whole thing through for him. I can't possibly take two months off now."

"Aren't you marrying our aunt?" says Baila.

All eyes are on him—but Sonya answers, in a voice dripping with irony. "Destiny has called upon Mâitre Blum to devote all his energy and skills now to the service of high art."

"But isn't Auntie disappointed?" asks Naomi.

"She's piping mad," Sonya answers.

"But she'll get over it," says Blum, "when she realizes the importance of getting this book out into the world."

All of them, in concert, roll their eyes.

"Please hear me out! I care about all of you—and I care

deeply about Jeannette. Olga, you know what I'm saying, don't you?"

"I think I do, René. Marcel Proust is, if I understand you correctly, a true artist. His work has come from that otherworldly, timeless place where all true art comes from. And, as is the case for so many timeless and true works of art, the world into which it has emerged may not be ready or even capable of appreciating its value. And so you see it as your—" She pauses, searching for the right words. "As your sacred duty to shepherd his novel out into the light."

Blum has the look of a proud and happy teacher. "Precisely, Olga! I couldn't have said it better myself."

"But what about the South American tour," says Baila, "and my classes with the Ballets Russes?"

"I'm giving my ticket to your mother. The three of you will have a very wonderful time—and we'll have a big celebration when you return!"

"And what's to become of Olga and me, while they're gone?" says Naomi.

"Why, you'll carry on as before," says Sonya. "You have your work with the Martines. And, Olga—you'll have the unprecedented opportunity to hone your craft at the side of some of the most brilliant journalists in Paris today. Who will carefully and respectfully look after you." The look she shoots at Blum is so menacing that he visibly cringes.

"Absolutely," he says to Olga with what appears to be sincere enthusiasm. "Between Colette and my colleagues at *Gil Blas*, you will have the chance to develop your prodigious gifts to their fullest potential."

Aboard the RMS *Avon*

1913

Baila can tell which of the passengers are part of the Ballets Russes and which are not, even though she has yet to be introduced to every member of the company. The dancers move effortlessly on deck, even when the *Avon* is rolling and pitching. Other passengers are thrown from side to side or lurch forward, grabbing on to any handholds that present themselves, whether architectural or human. Even those dancers who are seasick—and a lot of them are—make their way gracefully to the railings where, green of face, they vomit. If they're smart or lucky, they've chosen the ship's downwind side.

Both Jeannette and Sonya are ill for the first week, which allows Baila to roam freely and make friends everywhere. She becomes a favorite of the *grandes dames* traveling in first class with their dogs—or, if the ladies are sensitive to the ship's motion, Baila befriends their servants, who are even snobbier than their employers. Her favorite people on the voyage are the dogs, with their guileless love and utter sincerity.

When the dancers practice on deck, Baila is allowed to stand at the back and practice with them, always being careful to stay out of the way. There are certain sequences that she isn't able to execute. But there are other maneuvers, such as the fouetté, which plague many ballerinas but come easily to Baila. She doesn't know why. Once, after class, she makes Nijinsky laugh by executing ten fouettés in quick succession: a double pirouette, then one shapely leg extended to the front, whipped to the side à la seconde, and pulled back into passé for another pirouette. Again and again, on demi-pointe, a grin on her face and her eyes trained forward.

After that, the dancers allow her (but not Jeannette or Sonya) to sit at their table in the second-class dining room. The only other outsider is a pretty blond Hungarian, Mademoiselle Romola, traveling in first class. Always beautifully and expensively dressed, she appears every time Nijinsky chooses to sit among them. She is not well liked by the dancers, with the exception of Nijinsky, who becomes nervous and excited in her presence.

Mademoiselle Romola—who speaks Hungarian and French but no Russian—enlists Baila to translate for her when she wants to talk to Nijinsky. Romola speaks in French, gazing at the dancer with her large, anxious eyes, while Baila renders whatever she's said, as best she can, into Russian.

They don't, as far as Baila can tell, say anything of much consequence. But as a consequence of the service she renders, Baila becomes a great favorite of Nijinsky. Unlike so many of the other men on board, who look at her as if she were a pudding they want to devour, Nijinsky seems to love her with the guileless love of the shipboard dogs.

&

Dear Olga,

Before I tell you anything else, I must tell you about the dogs. There are eight of them I've met and befriended so far. You won't believe this, but there's also an absolutely gorgeous cheetah, although his owner is in first class and doesn't seem to want to have anything to do with the dancers.

I'm greeted with joy now by two King Charles spaniels who are as alike as twins, a sweet and ridiculously shy Havanese, a shih tzu who tries to bite everyone else who comes within range, a Maltese who wears a diamond collar that any girl would feel lucky to have for her dowry, an adorably ugly French bulldog, an elegant Italian greyhound, and a thirteen-year-old Boston terrier who seems to think he was my doting grandfather in a past life.

I know you're probably fuming at the moment, thinking, "That stupid Baila! Why can't she describe any of the things I care about?"

And so I will. You see, I've heard your voice, my angry sister, halfway across the Atlantic Ocean. Actually, I have no idea if we're halfway, or how far we've come. There's been no way to tell where we are, from the moment we lost sight of land.

Last night a sailor told me, before I ran away from him, that there are ways to calculate one's position at sea by looking at the stars and consulting special instruments, if one knows how to read them. How I wish you could see the stars from the middle of the ocean, on a cloudless night! We've had only two of them so far—but I will never forget the sight as long as I live.

I had no idea there were so many stars in the sky. Or that the sky, at night, looks like a great inverted bowl, studded with jewels. Or that, finding oneself beneath such a sky, it can seem that everything one knows, and everything one is, has shrunken to the size of a lentil. We are so small, Olga! Even the greatest among us is so small.

I hadn't a clue about how many cunning arrangements the stars, as they're revealed out here, form against the perfect black velvet of the sky. Wherever you look, if you look long enough, you'll see one of them leaping so quickly from its perch up there that, if you blink, you wonder if you only dreamed you saw it. And then you look at another place in the sky for a long enough time, and another star does the most graceful grand jeté you can possibly imagine.

The constellations are all completely different, here in the Southern Hemisphere. The sailor told me the names of several of them before he put his hand right down my knickers. Instead of the kiss he asked for, I gave him a kick in the shins and ran as fast as I could—and you know I'm fast—all the way to our stateroom. I don't even know some of the words he was shouting at me, but I can guess that they weren't very nice.

Now that I've spent hours under the night sky, out at sea, I know that we misuse the word "star" to speak of one performer who shines more brightly than all others. The stars, when the city sky is peeled away, are a living fabric of bright, shining, pulsating points of light, as chockablock and indistinguishable as dancers in the corps de ballet. Like the corps, they work together to form a picture—or the kind of picture you, Noni, and I make when we play "connect the dots."

But the sorts of performers that we have been used to calling "stars"—dancers such as Karsavina or Nijinsky—should be called something else instead, "a sun" or "a moon," maybe. Such people are able to express what they are—and how special they are—with the simplest movements, without any words at all.

When Nijinsky takes his class on deck in the mornings—sometimes by himself and sometimes with others—it's impossible not to see in a glance that he embodies everything that is ballet. He is the sun that shines in the eyes of all the dancers and many of the passengers aboard this ship. And at night he is our moon.

ॐ

The child is the only one who knows the content of their conversation, which, in the end, Nijinsky is able to complete without Baila's aid. "Would you like—?" he says to Romola, her white frock with its layers of lace and pearls glowing in the moonlight. Nijinsky has only to take her right hand and pinch the ring-finger between his middle finger and thumb as he steadies her with his other hand at her waist, all the while searching the depths of her blue eyes for an answer.

Baila, at this point, has put her hand over her mouth, cognizant of the intimacy and importance of this grown-up moment she's witnessing at the railing, while the phosphorescent sea sluices by them, far below. Romola blurts out "*Oui!*" in the same instant that Baila begins to say, in Russian, "Yes, she is accepting you." But there is no need, as Nijinsky, his eyes shining, has clearly understood her on his own.

Romola, from behind Nijinsky's back, signals Baila to get lost.

OFF THE COAST OF BUENOS AIRES

1913

Nijinsky is sure he's dying. Yes, it is his little wife who is suffering so terribly from the ship's motion in her delicate condition, with his baby starting to grow inside her. He and she are both sure—the ship's doctor is sure. She's throwing up all the time now, whereas, on the previous part of the journey—the worst part, crossing the Atlantic—she'd been fine. Now her face is green and the smell of any meat or fish makes her flee.

The ship's doctor only laughed when Nijinsky told him that he was also ill.

What can it be that's growing inside him, making his stomach strain against the waistband of his silk tights—making him examine what comes out of his body into the toilet? Every day, he expects to see blood.

There is no one he can trust to help him find the truth—and help him to get well. He lies awake at night, worrying that it's from the things Diaghilev did to him, all those years, when it would have been an act of folly and ingratitude to refuse Sergei the satisfaction of his lust. Or was it love? Sergei always said how much he loved his Nijinsky. *A god of the dance*, he said, repeating what they wrote in the papers about him.

He finds the child standing by the railing on a night he can't sleep. Both of them stand there, in companionable silence, looking down at the phosphorescence of the sea as the *Avon* slices through the water like a silver knife cutting into a blancmange made of moonlight.

What would his child be like? Surely he will have a son! Or will Romola give birth to a little girl, like this one?

"Baila," he says to her, kneeling down to speak to her eye to eye. "I want to consult a doctor—a real doctor, a fine doctor—when we stop again in Buenos Aires. But I must find one who speaks Russian or Polish. Will you help me?"

Baila puts her hand on his shoulder. "Of course, Gospodin Nijinsky!" She shivers suddenly, although it isn't cold. "I won't be allowed to go ashore without my mother or my aunt."

"Does either of them speak Spanish?"

"I don't think so."

"Never mind. Let it be your mother then. I don't want any of the dancers to find out." He sighs, standing again, turning away from the sea toward the ship, with its rabbit warren of staterooms and dining rooms, ballrooms, passageways and bars, all of them teeming with people who can't be trusted. Any one of them who might be a spy for Sergei.

❧

The first pharmacy they come to not only has a pharmacist who can speak several languages but is also able to recommend a doctor—a famous doctor—who speaks Russian. Vaslav Nijinsky is already a celebrity in Buenos Aires. The pharmacist is able to get him an appointment that very morning.

Baila and Sonya wait in the doctor's reception room while Nijinsky is brought inside by the nurse. After ten minutes or so, looking much relieved, he walks out with the doctor beside him, a kindly hand on the dancer's back.

"I am not dying!" he says to Baila and Sonya. "There is even a name for the symptoms afflicting me—symptoms that afflict, it seems, many new fathers-to-be."

"Couvade syndrome," the doctor says. He puts his hand on Baila's head. Then he looks at Nijinsky with a smile. "Not your daughter, surely." And then he notices Sonya, who is staring at the nameplate displayed on another door.

All the color has drained from her face.

"Are you quite well, madame?"

Sonya is holding her hand to her heart and breathing rapidly. "A moment, please."

Etched into the brass plate is the name *Jascha Gittelman, MD.*
When she's able to speak again, Sonya asks, "Is your colleague here today—behind that door?"

"Dr. Gittelman is on leave. Do you know him? Perhaps you know that his wife very recently passed away."

Sonya shakes her head. The others are all staring at her.

"Do you know him, Mama?" asks Baila.

Sonya had never told her children about her first love—and why would she have ever done so?

Baila has come up close to her, nestling in the crook of Sonya's shoulder.

"Jascha and I grew up together, in Kishinev—years before I met your father, darling."

The other doctor has cocked his head at her. "You aren't the famous Sonya, are you?"

"I'm certainly not famous."

Nijinsky speaks up then, still buoyant with good spirits. "Come, my friends," he says. "If we don't get back to the boat soon, it may leave without us."

"It won't leave without you, Gospodin Nijinsky!" says Baila.

The doctor gets a glass of water for Sonya and says to her softly, "Now is not precisely the right time, of course. But later—soon—I'll tell him I saw you. I know he won't forgive me if I fail to find out where you live and how you can be reached."

She's shivering. The famous Sonya! Famous in what way? Famously unsuitable? Famously not good enough for Jascha? But if he'd spoken of her in such terms, surely his colleague would never have let on that he'd heard of her.

The doctor gives her a card printed with the name and address of their practice.

"Are you ready?" says Nijinsky, not unkindly.

Baila takes her mother's hand. "Let's go back now, Mama. Aunt Jeannette will think we've run away."

&

Jeannette and Sonya, practiced sailors now, stand at the railing, looking west at the last of South America's silhouette against the twilit sky. Neither speaks until the land has disappeared.

"I'm wondering," says Jeannette, "whether I shouldn't have just stayed there—and started over again."

"But René is waiting for you—"

"René! I don't think René really wants to marry me." The wind drops—and the sigh of the ship's wake is suddenly louder.

"I think René wanted to marry *you*."

Sonya has felt guilty for the pleasure she herself has had in this thought. "René was once in love with me. But in you he found something he could never have found in me—a Jewish wife he could bring home to his mother—"

Jeannette snorts. "A Jewish wife! You must be joking, Sonya!"

"—and a dancing girl he could bring home to his bed."

"Why are you so intent on marrying me off when you yourself are so determined to stay single?"

"I am a widow with children."

"Your children are nearly grown." Jeannette narrows her eyes at her sister. "What is it that *you* want, Sonya?"

"The biggest thing I longed for was finding you."

"And was finding me everything you hoped for?"

Sonya notices that she and Jeannette are looking less and less alike. "Yes—and no." She turns her face away, toward Argentina's shore—at least she thinks the shore is there, somewhere, through the darkness. "There's still that place inside me that feels so—bereft. That feels so alone."

It surprises Jeannette, how hurt this makes her feel. "Do you ever wish you had gone to Argentina, when your boyfriend invited you?"

"I would never have found you then."

"You haven't answered my question."

Sonya sighs, feeling a sense of oneness with the sea sliced open momentarily by the movement of the ship—and closing up again, all its darkness and all its secrets locked away. "Yes," she says. "I have a deep sense of regret, and it pains me—because I would never have had Naomi, Olga, and Baila then."

"You would have had other children—Jascha's children."

"It wasn't meant to be."

Jeannette is wondering if she shouldn't just keep her mouth shut. She knows that if she were Sonya, she would resent the hell out of it later, if she were kept in the dark by her twin about something so important to her. "René told me something, supposedly in confidence—but I really think you should know about it."

"What?"

"You know that letter you once showed me, the one in Russian—the one you've kept, all these years?"

"Jascha's letter."

"There were others. Your brother Daniel—he was only *your* brother then—urged your mother to destroy them before they ever reached you."

Sonya closes her eyes against the sudden dizziness she feels. She's at her mother's bedside again, her mother's labored words in her ears. Had she been about to confess that too?

Gently, Jeannette puts her hand over Sonya's on the railing. "He was worried—both of them were worried—about you leaving Russia. About never seeing you again. And I suppose they were simply worried about you. They thought of Argentina as some kind of wilderness. And your mother—"

"Our mother."

"—our mother. Really, *your* mother, because she never knew me. Your mother loved you more than any of her other children."

"That's so patently untrue! She loved Daniel best. She put us in an orphanage!"

"In the coinage of children," says Jeannette, "boys are made of a more precious metal than girls. If girls are silver, then boys are gold."

"Olga would have something to say about that."

Sonya's heart is doing flip-flops inside her chest. What had Jascha written in those letters she had never been allowed to see? Had he loved her, as she loved him? Had there been a proposal of marriage?

Had Jascha married someone else, just as Sonya had married someone else, because marriage was necessary and his first love—his great love—had disappeared?

Jeannette asks quietly, "Would you have made a different decision, if you had known?"

"I don't know." Inside, Sonya is saying the word for *yes* in Russian, over and over again.

And yet she can't bear to think about Naomi, Olga, or Baila never having come into the world. Does the essence of who we are exist somewhere outside the world—and find a way in, by whatever means it can, if it must? Aren't all of us, thinks Sonya, so much more than something made of, and by, our parents?

Jeannette can tell that Sonya is lying and doesn't care. She's learned that there's precious little they can hide from one another. "If Paul had never met you," she says, "I wonder whether he wouldn't have grown tired of me sooner."

"Paul never grew tired of you. I'm quite sure of that. And whatever feelings he had for me were based on my resemblance to you."

"It's a kind of curse being a twin, isn't it?"

"Or a kind of blessing."

"Do you ever wonder," says Jeannette, "what our lives would have been like if we'd grown up together—in Russia or in France?"

"I used to think about it a lot. But now, I think we'd forever have been trying to prove how different we were, one from the other, and competing for everyone's love. But I would have loved having you as an ally, as a friend."

"And you have that now."

"I have that. And still—"

"And still there is that empty place inside us—inside us all."

"Maybe all of us long for that place," says Sonya, tipping her head back to look at the sky, "that timeless place, before life begins and after it ends, where all of us are starlight."

"Instead of trapped inside these bodies," says Jeannette.

Baila comes running up to them. "I've been looking everywhere for you!"

"We were looking at the stars," says Sonya.

"Did you know," asks Baila, inserting herself between her mother and her aunt, "that the constellations are different here than they are in the northern hemisphere?"

"The only constellation I ever learned to recognize," says Jeannette, "was Gemini—the twins. Paul Poiret pointed it out to me."

Sonya says, with faux naivete, "I wonder why."

"It isn't here then." Baila's voice is filled with a sort of triumph she rarely gets to feel. "The twins don't exist anywhere in this sky!" She looks up at her mother and aunt, and adds, almost as if speaking to herself, "I wish Noni and Olga could be here now."

"It won't be long now," says Sonya, "until we're all together again." She looks up just in time to see a falling star—but too late to point it out to the others. "I wonder what 1914 will bring. The world has a way of changing so quickly."

PART VI

PARIS

1914

Olga surges along with the crowd at the Place de la Concorde, eye-level with the soldiers' epaulettes, clutching her notepad and pencil. Where to start? How can she find the lede for her story, surrounded by so many chaotic and yet heartbreaking details?

Women are desperately kissing their sweethearts and husbands goodbye. *Cocottes* turned patriots are handing out bacon sandwiches and red roses at booths set up by the Red Cross. Children, their innocent faces filled with hope and belief, are waving tri-color flags.

What will happen to the fathers and husbands? What will happen to Paris? Even now, the German army is surging through Belgium toward France. All the able-bodied men are leaving the capital. Nearly every single one of them has answered the call to mobilize. Only women, children, and men too old to help will be left in Paris, undefended, on their own.

Some of the soldiers look quite dazed. But others look exuberant, so proud in their new uniforms, oblivious to the implications of the mobilization. Have they thought about what this means for them—what it means for all of Europe? How the government has failed them in choosing war above diplomacy? How they are the playthings now of national pride?

The words of the socialist leader Jean Jaurès, that great and humanistic opponent of war, keep echoing in Olga's head. How clearly and truthfully his words rang out when he spoke to the crowd, asking them to envision a world where the resources used to prepare for war were instead used to make a better life for all humankind.

Olga is still reeling from the news she heard this morning, at the offices of *Le Matin*. Jean Jaurès has been murdered, shot in the back by a French nationalist, through the window of the Café du Croissant, where he was meeting with his fellow socialists, tireless in their efforts to expose the French president's secret alliance with Russia and his morally bankrupt rationale for going to war.

Could Jean Jaurès, if he had lived, have stopped this madness? Why do all these people look so excited and happy? Don't they see, as Olga can see, the months and perhaps even years of suffering that lie ahead, the young men who will murder and be murdered, the mutilated bodies, the grief that always follows in the wake of war?

Olga is shoved up against the backpack of a Zouave in billowing red trousers. His face breaks into a smile when he looks down at her. "Gaston!" she cries.

"Marmosets," he croons softly. "Beautiful marmosets!" Olga's eyes fill with tears. "You mustn't cry, little one."

"But, Gaston, it's too horrible—war! And you in those bright red trousers. They might as well paint you with a bull's eye."

"Ah, but I am proud to serve with the Zouaves! And I am proud to serve France."

Olga takes off her glasses and wipes her eyes. "It's the sickness of imperialism, don't you see?" She gestures at the crowd. "What if all this money and all these resources were spent instead on useful things—to increase the well-being of people, to build decent houses for workers, to grow more food so that no one must go hungry? War is wrong!"

Gaston kneels down in front of her, as he did that other time, so long ago now. He takes a handkerchief out of his pocket and dabs at her eyes. And then he hugs her.

It's a long hug. Olga is sobbing now. She hates herself for being so emotional. She's here to write a story for *Le Matin*. Even the Baron de Jouvenel has gone off to fight the Germans, leaving a skeleton crew to publish the paper. Colette is being so stupid about it. Colette thinks the war is a big adventure.

Gaston holds her at arm's length. "I must go now—I'll lose my battalion," he says. "Here, keep this." He gives her the handkerchief.

"No," she cries, "you'll need it!"

"I insist. Keep it as a souvenir of me—of our friendship." Olga looks into Gaston's lovely, long-lashed eyes. What fun they'd had that night, at Paul Poiret's famous party! How all of that seems so long ago and like something from another world, a world that seemed as if it would last forever—but now it's gone.

She'd wished ardently for time to pass, so that she could escape her childhood and everything that seemed so oppressive then. And yet she wishes now that she could have it back again. "I'm fourteen now, Gaston. I have never been kissed—and there is a war."

He seems to consider this. And then he bends down and kisses her, chastely, on the lips. "There now. You've been kissed. And there will be many more kisses for you, Olga." He stands up straight again, looking ahead of them through the crowd, finally spotting another Zouave. Over his shoulder, as he strides away, he calls, "You've become a beauty, you know."

PART VII

PARIS

1915

I can't decide what to take with me," says Naomi, standing before her little suitcase, half-full now.

"But, Noni, do you have to leave?" Olga is at the stove in René's abandoned kitchen, trying to remember whether it's chicken stock or water she's supposed to use for the lentil stew—and wondering, if it's stock, what the possibilities are for finding some, or finding a chicken, with so many shops shuttered, their shelves empty.

"I can make a difference in Normandy!" Naomi calls from the other room.

Why is it, Olga wonders, that Poiret's plans, no matter how altruistic they sound, always involve some benefit to his fashion empire? Besides this initiative for the Martines—having them set up workshops to teach new skills to wounded soldiers—he was also trying to press his design for a new and better uniform on the French high command. Naomi, though, only thinks good of him. He is, Olga knows, almost like a father to her.

When they sit down to eat their last supper together, Naomi asks Olga for the hundredth time whether she won't come to Normandy too.

"Someone has to stay here and report the truth," says Olga. "Every day, a messenger comes to tell us what we can and can't report on."

"Will you stay until the war is over?"

Olga shakes her head. "I don't know. I suppose I'll stay as long as the newspaper allows me to write for them. And then, who can say?"

"Mama is desperate for you, for both of us, to come to Argentina."

"And I miss her desperately," says Olga.

They'd decided, together, to encourage their mother to pursue her old dream of love and happiness. But both were a little skeptical about the circumstances—a new country, a new language, another woman's children, and a man Sonya hadn't known since he was seventeen. They wrote to her, as promised, every day. But, between the two of them, they thought of their mother's absence as a kind of vacation she was taking from her real life. Both of them thought she deserved it—and hoped it would renew both her strength and her sense of joy.

They eat for a while in silence while Olga thinks about what a wonderful thing it is to have a sister with whom one feels close and safe and loved.

"Do you think it's true," Naomi says, "about Mama and Monsieur Poiret?"

"Even if it is true, I don't see why our aunt would feel compelled to tell Baila. Why should she ever have to know such a thing, especially since Mama thought it best—if it *is* true—to keep it to herself?"

They'd had a letter from Baila the day before, posted from New York City. Both she and Jeannette were dancing with the company now, which was such a ragtag version of what it had been before, in the glory days, before Diaghilev fired Nijinsky.

No one had ever expected that the war would still be raging—or that it would have spread so far, on so many fronts. Or that so many men, on both sides, would have lost their lives and limbs and sight. Or that Paris would have been brought so low.

The next morning, at the Gare Saint Lazare, Naomi puts her suitcase on the train—and then jumps down to the platform to embrace her sister one last time.

"I'll write to you every day. The war will surely be over before the end of the year," she says, "and then we'll all go back to our lives—and everything will be as it was again."

Olga is terrified that nothing will ever be as it was again. She looks at Naomi's face in a way she never has before, noticing and cataloging every detail of her eyes, her nose, her pretty lips, her lovely skin, and the delicacy of her underlying bones. How is it that she never really looked before? She clings hard to her sister's hands, long-fingered, like their mother's.

"You look so much like Mama, Noni! I feel her presence, with us here today."

"I always feel her presence," says Naomi, "like a bright, warm light."

PART VIII

BUENOS AIRES

1929

The moment explodes with buttery yellow light: the sea! Waves are breaking gently on the shore—and sinking, hissing as they recede.

Sonya can smell salt spray, and hear and see the gulls, swirling and calling above her, bright white against the tender blue sky.

And there is Jascha, walking beside her, barefoot, his trousers rolled up to just below his knees. He's holding her hand. His still-abundant hair is the color of pewter now. His face is the same face, though a little heavier. He has a mustache. It suits him. Jascha's grandchildren, so dear to her, are cavorting on the sand ahead of them.

And yet the pain of all she's lost never goes away.

Everything disappears—everything we love and everything we long for. What remains is something Sonya has a hard time putting into words. It has to do, she now knows, with holding her loved ones close, even if they're far away. Even if they're no longer alive.

The light is so bright that everything she sees is ringed in gold.

GLOSSARY

anti-Dreyfusard
> For over a decade, from 1894 to 1906, France was bitterly divided over the case of a French artillery officer of Jewish descent, Alfred Dreyfus, falsely accused of espionage. The famous "Dreyfus affair" divided France into pro-republican, anticlerical *Dreyfusards* and pro-Army, mostly Catholic, anti-Semitic *anti-Dreyfusards*.

arabesque allongé
> Pose in which one leg is extended behind the body, forming a right angle with the back, while the dancer's supporting leg is straight and both arms are fully extended.

balletomane
> a ballet enthusiast who attends as many performances as possible

cocotte
> a slang term in French for a less-than-respectable woman; a tart or a trollop

femme de ménage
> cleaning lady

Gospodin
> In Russian, a term of address for a man

le goûter
> The equivalent of "high tea" but with sweet food only, such as bread and chocolate—a 4:30 tradition for children in France, where families usually don't sit down for supper until late in the evening

haute laine
> deep pile (wool)

jambon beurre
  a ham and cheese sandwich on a buttered baguette

l'eau mineral
  mineral water

Mâitre
  In French, designates that the person being addressed or referred to is a lawyer

"Monsieur, s'il vous plaît!"
  "Sir, if you please!"

"Enchanté!"
  French for "A pleasure to make your acquaintance!"—literally, "Enchanted!"

en plein air
  out of doors, in the fresh air; outside

entrechat quatre
  a spectacular jump in ballet, beginning in fifth position, during which the dancer rapidly crosses and re-crosses her straight legs at the lower calf while suspended midair

Époisses
  a pungent soft-paste cows-milk cheese made in the Côte-d'Or region of France

Ja estoy estudiando
  In Spanish, "I'm already studying."

le Tout-Paris
  everyone, most especially everyone who matters, in Paris

mayn klug froy
  In Yiddish, "my clever wife"

origine du monde
  "L'Origine du monde" ("The Origin of the World"), painted in 1866 in oil on canvas by the French artist Gustave Courbet, depicts a close-up view of a woman's genitals.

ma puce
  In French, "my flea" (an endearment)

"parade"
>   The term commonly used for the in-house launch of the
>   new season's fashion line at a *maison de couture*: the prome-
>   nade of models wearing the season's designs

en pointe
>   dancing in toe shoes, which requires putting the entire weight
>   of the body on the tips of the ballerina's toes

petite amie
>   (romantic) girlfriend

midinettes
>   the girls or women who work in Parisian clothing stores

podstakannik
>   in Russian, a decorative metal holder with a handle, which
>   encases a drinking glass for hot tea

rat or *rats*
>   the same literal meaning in French as in English, used as a
>   slang term for the lowest ranks of company dancers

regisseur
>   in classical ballet, a title for the person who restages or re-
>   hearses a ballet company and/or manages the rehearsals

Saison Russe
>   Russian Season: refers to the year 1909 in Paris, when Sergei
>   Diaghilev's nascent ballet company staged their first perfor-
>   mances

ACKNOWLEDGMENTS

This novel took a very long time to be born, and benefited from the encouragement of many readers, starting with Linda Asher at the *New Yorker*, who read it in its earliest incarnation as my pre-first novel, which I wrote as a twenty-one-year-old in an isolated hilltop cottage (lent to me by Louisa Putnam) in West County Cork, Ireland.

Decades later, after my first two novels had been published, I returned to the material, inspired in part by the magnificent first-edition books about the Ballets Russes in the private library of Dr. Adela Spindler Roatcap of the Fromm Institute at the University of San Francisco. Professor Roatcap, who had sought me out as a speaker, was as generous with her expertise as she was with her books.

The archivists of the Jerome Robbins Dance Division of the New York Public Library let me pore over rare photographs that provided a key to understanding the young Nijinsky in his earliest days with Diaghilev and see through the glamour to the vulnerability, unbounded ambition, and courage of all those artists who came together to create the Ballets Russes.

My dear friend, the late Marcus Grant, read several drafts of *What Disappears*. His comments were always both perspicacious and helpful. I shall always feel a debt of gratitude, both for his literary acumen and his mordant sense of humor.

When my novel had already entered the production pipeline at Regal House, Gavin Larsen's newly published memoir, *Being a Ballerina: The Power and Perfection of a Dancing Life*—and Gavin herself—provided validation for the truths I endeavored to find. In the case of one particular step in the ballet vocabulary I'd described inaccurately, she broke the movement down for me and provided new language to help me get it right.

Pianist and conductor Allan Dameron lent his invaluable

insider's knowledge for the chapter describing the debut of *The Rite of Spring* under the baton of Maestro Pierre Monteux.

Many of my friends gave me encouragement as well as the benefit of their experience. Laura Schulkind's tender poem about her mother, "Her Porcelain Skin," informed my description of Sonya's deathbed vigil. *What Disappears* is the second novel for which I owe a debt of appreciation to the marvelous San Francisco Symphony violinist and native Russian speaker, Polina Sedukh. Arline Wyler has been, through the years, a generous and gracious reader of both published and unpublished works of mine—and uncomplainingly read several drafts of this novel. Liz and Jeff Stonehill will always occupy that special place in my heart reserved for friends who are also canny and insightful readers.

My dedication of this novel to Grace Cavalieri, Poet Laureate of Maryland and a champion such as I've never had before, will, I hope, trumpet my sense of gratitude.

Regal House Publishing was a small independent press when I signed a contract with them in 2020. Thanks to the boundless energy, vision, and enthusiasm of the entire crew there, but especially the founding editor Jaynie Royal and her delightful colleague Pam Van Dyk, the house has grown up to become a thriving literary community in a shrinking landscape of commercial literary publishers.

Finally, I wish to thank my husband Wayne Roden for making it possible for me, these past twelve years, to abandon myself to my writing.